Praise for *Fun and Games*:

'*Fun and Games* is blisteringly tender, while being sharp in its observations on class, love and coming of age'
RTÉ

'*Fun and Games* is a charming, funny and sensitive novel about the fleeting moments in a teenage boy's life'
NICOLE FLATTERY, author of *Nothing Special*

'Bighearted and boisterous, bursting with life and humour … a gorgeous, aching whirligig of a novel'
COLIN WALSH, author of *Kala*

'A completely candid and totally believable tale of late adolescence, with all of its tiny tragedies and tiny triumphs. Heartbreaking and raucous and filled with love, *Fun and Games* is a joy unconfined'
AIDAN COTTRELL-BOYCE, author of *The End of Nightwork*

'[An] unflinching look at teenage masculinity. The good and the bad of young men, the vulnerability but also the cruelty. He's an excellent writer line by line, very lyrical … It's a very subtle, powerful novel'
FERDIA LENNON, author of *Glorious Exploits*, in the *Irish Independent*

'*Fun and Games* portrays young adulthood in Ireland with amazing, excruciating accuracy. McHugh writes with exceptional honesty, nuance and humour. His powers of observation make this study of masculinity universal and brilliantly brutal'

CAOILINN HUGHES, author of *The Alternatives*

'It's a beautiful, sad and funny novel. I loved it! John Patrick McHugh possesses the rare ability to write elegantly without losing any of the raw emotion. *Fun and Games* takes the reader deep inside the confused heart and head of a teenage boy'

DANIELLE McLAUGHLIN, author of *The Art of Falling*

'I loved *Fun and Games*, which is as sharp-witted as it is warm-hearted. I was pulled along by the zippy, telegraphic descriptions, with their big veerings between comic and desperately poignant ... I was right in John's head the whole way along'

TIM MACGABHANN, author of *How to be Nowhere*

'I absolutely loved *Fun and Games*; a book so true to life, and to adolescence in Ireland at that moment in time. A rare and tender insight into the fragile but complex emotional lives of young men ... John Patrick's novel is deeply funny and moving, and is rich with empathy'

REBECCA IVORY, author of *Free Therapy*

FUN
AND
GAMES

ALSO BY JOHN PATRICK McHUGH

Pure Gold

FUN AND GAMES

JOHN PATRICK McHUGH

4th ESTATE • London

4th Estate
An imprint of HarperCollins*Publishers*
1 London Bridge Street
London SE1 9GF

www.4thestate.co.uk

HarperCollins*Publishers*
Macken House, 39/40 Mayor Street Upper
Dublin 1, D01 C9W8, Ireland

First published in Great Britain in 2025 by 4th Estate

2

A catalogue record for this book is
available from the British Library

ISBN 978-0-00-851734-2 (hardback)
ISBN 978-0-00-851735-9 (trade paperback)

Set in Stempel Garamond LT Std
Printed and bound in the UK using 100%
renewable electricity at CPI Group (UK) Ltd

For Ciara

Tuesday, 30th June 2009

He looked up. She was lying on her back, her elbows set to rigid angles with her hands laced together at her chest as if she were dead. Her expression was inscrutable, seemingly content to read the patch of sky and drowsy cloud overhead, but maybe slightly dead-looking, too. Her grey hoodie was bunched above her waist, where dappled sunlight fell like freckles against her stomach, where he could make out teeny white wires rimming her belly button. They were in a secluded tract of woods. His jumper was fanned out beneath her, and he had managed to tug down her jeans with only a small plea for assistance. His finger was burrowing inside her. They were kissing and then they were doing this. He was the horniest, he was seventeen.

In and out and now he sought to extend his middle finger as well.

'No,' she said with a distinct tsk, a flinch of shoulder, and he said, 'Cool, cool,' without understanding.

He continued with the one, in and out.

It was undoubtedly nice for him, this probing, and he reasoned it must be for her too because she rocked her hips

1

a little, because she was allowing him to do it in the first place, but could he be a hundred per cent certain about her enjoyment? It was easy to do something wrong and he had just blundered with the middle finger hadn't he and was this actually tedious and unpleasant for her? The thought of fucking this up. The misery of her telling other people about him ruining this intimate moment and those people knowing he was a gigantic weirdo loser creep. But, also, the wonderful thought of being inside her: control, puppetry. It was nice for him, for sure.

She was nineteen.

You could describe her as prettyish, or at least you couldn't automatically say she was a dirt: she was sufficiently good-looking for everyone else, he reckoned. He liked her enough, he liked talking to her, and she didn't pretend she wasn't wise to the photo of his mother's breasts that had floated around the Island, which was, bizarrely, a relief, but he mostly liked what was before him now. He liked it to the point that it hurt. The sheer appreciation was painful. It burned inside his cock. And what was suddenly burning now too was his wrist. This motion was starting to inflame whatever rubbery material it was that controlled this action, and he thought it best to change tactics, alter the movement and ease this scorching tension and yet continue her – hopeful – buzz, but as he began to jig his finger up and down, she told him, 'Hold on.' She clasped his wrist and slowly brought it in and out of her once more.

She did like it.

Exhilaration.

A victory.

It felt as if his entire body was trembling, as nerves before a match, but his arm was steady as they moved his finger in and out of her and when she eventually removed her grip, he kept this tempo, not hurrying, no, disciplined, in and out. He wanted to memorise everything. Her thighs. Her messy pubes: the colour of peat. The whitened pressure points denoting her hips and other strange bones. How her mouth momentarily scrunched to a small o before grimacing as her hands screwed up the strings of her hoodie, like you would a straw when bored. The intensity of this feeling: untoppable, unbeatable, enormous, and it was as if he were plunging from a height as he did this to her. 'God,' she said, and a stifling hand to her mouth. 'Oh god.' It was glorious, gold, until his wrist began to prickle anew, tingling discomfort, then a stiffening, then a hard and fast locking and he had to withdraw his finger with a gasped, 'Aahh.'

She peered down at him, alarmed. Her hand dropped to cover herself.

'My arm's gone dead,' he explained, and clenched his fist as a demonstration. He added, 'Shit.' He pushed himself up with his elbow – cautious not to spoil the right hand – and then, kneeling, felt ice on his neck and glanced over his shoulder.

But no one was there.

Only the same beige and browns as earlier, the pools of shiny green above and below with faint spotlights breaking through. He could hear birds talking amongst themselves, somewhere. His own breathing and her more precise breathing behind him. And then a clean, high shout, followed by another, which must have arrived from the GAA pitch on the other side of the woods.

He rotated the wrist, flopped the hand forward and back. 'Sorry,' he said. 'I'm really sorry about that.'

Fully on his feet, he tucked his cock into the band of his trackies and walked a step or two from her. He gripped the aching wrist, pressed a thumb into the firm white string below the palm, muttered grievances loud enough for her to hear and comprehend his anguish and frustration, and then lifted the finger to his nose.

The smell of gone-off milk, a musky odour. Oh.

'My wrist is so gammy,' he complained, and then repeated, 'I'm sorry.'

And once more she didn't reply, and turning to check that she was alive and merely upset and pissy, he saw she was still panned out with her hand shielding her private self like she was in a wall for a free kick. Utterly motionless apart from the tip of her tongue carefully rolling over her top lip. 'It's alright,' she said then and sighed emphatically. She sat forward, pulled up her knickers and started to shrug on her jeans and he turned around again.

As a kid he used to prowl the entirety of these woods in search of suitable branches to become his swords. Older, he had choked down a goon of cider while braced against a toppled trunk, a shoddy fire dwindling before him and his buds. Older still, he had shifted his first and, so far, only girlfriend, Seóna Fahy, here last October: a relationship that had lasted for three and a half months and which was presently a filthy purple bruise in his mind because she was fixed to the mouth of somebody else and wouldn't you know: he had discovered he loved her to death.

It was his idea to use the woods, he had suggested it this morning. He thought of it as secret, and doubly so on a Tuesday. She had smirked at him while they rearranged the restaurant for dinner in the hotel – flapping out white sheets to drape over the tables – but she had also shown up.

From behind him, she now spoke, 'That was nice, thank you.'

He swung round. 'Yeah, no. Class.'

She half smiled and passed him his jumper and he hung it over his shoulder.

Should he compliment her and her performance? Or broach the issue of his own bit and the evidence of his pants staying on and not to be pushy but how he hasn't, you know, oozed himself yet? Or should he just stare at her?

'Well,' she said finally. 'We head?'

They began hiking back towards the trail. She was walking ahead of him with her arms crossed. 'So,' he said, 'you're on tomorrow morning?'

She nodded. 'Split shift.'

'Killer,' he said with a drawl, and silence then until they neared the designated oak tree, and he stopped decisively.

But she didn't, so he had to call her name. He had to say, 'Watch this tree?'

She turned and said, 'What about it?' and why did that startle him? She had eyes that reminded him of wet roof slates, blue-grey-green that unnameable combination, and a beauty spot on her cheek and these sad, bushy eyebrows that were dark brown.

From his pocket he retrieved his set of keys – home house, the backdoor for Gaga's aka Dad's current house, his school locker, a key speckled with Man United crests which unlocked nothing. 'I actually thought of something funny with the tree.' He gestured the keys at the trunk, then shook them for further effect. 'We could mark it as our spot,' he said and produced a noise that could be construed as breezy laughter. 'I don't know, we could mark it. Our spot, like.' Her face was blank, unmoved, and he made that throaty noise like laughter again. This was premeditated, this, he believed, would seal something metaphysical and airy for her and allow him to bask in the understanding of future dividends. That there would be another next time. And still this is how he pitched it despite rehearsals in the bathroom mirror. He didn't wait for an answer, but strode towards the tree, reddening. He no longer required the locker key, so that was the one he fitted between his index finger and thumb.

He began to carve into the bark.

The sun on his neck, the heat softened somewhat by the foliage. His tongue soon protruding through his lips, and he could feel her watching.

She said, 'What're you doing, show us?'

A caustic tone in her voice, like she was the one better, superior, and not a full-time hotel worker, and this needled him.

Instead of laughing along with her, joining in the fun, he said, irritated all of a sudden, 'Hold on, will you.'

'You're so precious,' she said. 'Jesus.'

It was a far more arduous process than he had expected, and it took much longer – one single letter necessitated three or five cuts before the groove was readable – and it looked far, far uglier than he had envisioned: worse even than the ratty initials scrawled with compasses on the desks in school. The increasingly indisputable knowledge that this was a huge mistake, a bad and stupid idea, and with that echoed the horror of her telling others. Their judgement. Their voices whispering to one another about him at that evil volume which you could hear but not quite understand.

He was no longer sure what this act was meant to demonstrate. What had he been thinking?

He decided to be finished. He heard himself say, 'All done.'

He let the key fall to his side. Flecks of bark were sprinkled on his runners. She stepped nearer him, and he noted three scrutinising indentations in the middle of her brow: three subtraction signs. He noted especially how she grasped his upper arm as he tilted aside to provide her with a better view to see the tree trunk.

JOHN

4

AM

His name, and a decent fraction of hers as it was truly strenuous work, and a four which he meant as an obvious gag, further verification for her to think upon him as a funny yet intelligent individual. But she didn't laugh robustly at this ironic four, nor did she giggle at the entire enterprise itself, which had a fair whack of irony stirred into it, because how was she to know that it was a joke as she didn't really know him?

She stared at it.

Then Amber said, 'Does *Am* really mean what I think it means, John?'

Some hours later and with his boots on his lap, John Masterson sat in the front of his father's car and said, 'Let's go.' John was wearing starchy green socks with three white bands, a zip-up imprinted with the Island crest – a ball and a Viking ship with the red bridge in the background – and dainty white shorts that he was obliged to constantly tug down lower. The boots were Adidas World Cups. They were new. He reckoned their black leather finish would be less conspicuous than his silver and blue Total 90s.

The car beeped a goodbye – John cringed, pictured his mother's expression in the living room – and then eased itself through the estate, out onto the main road.

His dad's name was Peter. He possessed a beaky nose, the fatherly paunch and behind his steel-framed glasses, fluorescent blue eyes which John had inherited. Lately, John had noticed how deeply etched were the rings below these blue eyes and noticed, too, the growing number of waxy liver spots dotting the back of his father's hand, like a leak had sprung somewhere under the flesh. These were observations John didn't wish to have, as to reflect upon his dad caused John to feel lonely, adrift or actually worse: it made John feel bereft, regretful, half orphaned, even though his dad was unequivocally alive and arguably well.

It was no good to spot the frailty of a parent and it was additionally no good to think of your father as a massive waning loser.

Three weeks ago, his dad had packed up and out of the home house because John's mam, Yvonne, had been texting someone else and had sent this someone a snap of her breasts. It had unfolded like this: on a night out, John's only sibling, Kay, was ordering a drink at the bar when a phone was waved in her face. The phone displayed a photo. The photo was wretched, heavily pixilated as if constructed via individual grains of coloured sand, and the glare from the flash in the mirror morphed everything in the top portion to a single sparkling star. It only became a body when Kay identified the nipples. Then Kay realised it was a pair of breasts shelved atop a forearm. Puzzlement, and the phone was slanted closer and Kay recognised the composition of the room and the panelled armchair jammed in the corner and the bed practically up against the mirror and.

War the same night: John was woken by voices from the kitchen below, slammed doors and a drunken Kay sobbing on the stairs. For a while, John had lain in bed listening to all this until he realised his hands were trembling, and then he got up, shambled downstairs.

Throughout the neverending next day, a Sunday, John's mobile phone flared an eerie green and vibrated madly. Word of the photo had spread across the Island. Friends texted unhappy-looking smilies. A stream of prank calls. Unknown numbers wrote to him, inelegantly.

'your mothers tits'

'(.) (.)'

'Tit boy'

'Hahahah shit one 4 you'

'darting 1 out over ur mam riht now'

In the evening, his magnanimous friend Tony Dineen had rung the landline, and in lieu of a greeting, went, mournfully, 'Did you see, yeah?' By this stage, John had of course. He had studied his mother's tits. Much like any milfy duo obtained from the internet – fingertip nipples, blue veins etched like lightning bolts – but devastatingly his mother's. John hated her, and the whole Masterson family, and for a time everyone alive. John had concluded that life was stuff that happened without your consent, your control

– or if you did have control, it was tenuous at best because he hadn't sent that photo and yet his life had been upended by it. Life careened into you and there was nothing you could do about it and so what was the point? Life, he wrote in a notebook, was pointless! He wrote: I hate my family and I hate my life!

This was in the middle of May, about two and a half weeks before the pivotal Leaving Cert exams and the culmination of the previous two years of study. John stopped attending school for the remainder of term. How could he trudge down those linoleum corridors as if nothing untoward? How could he meet the gurning, pimply faces of the boys he so admired when they had come as close as could be realistically expected to the purest schoolyard aspiration of all: riding a dear friend's mother?

Now Mam wasn't talking to Dad or supposedly the person she had been texting, and Dad wanted to talk to Mam and bandage whatever had fractured in their relationship, and Kay wasn't talking to Mam because she had ruined Kay's wedding that wasn't on till August, and John didn't want to talk to the lot of them.

Ascending the hill after Lavelle's Restaurant, Peter said with grave emphasis, 'First training with the seniors.'

John nodded.

'Well able for them,' Peter said. 'They will be strong, physically. You expect that, but.' Peter raised a finger. 'You've the skill. And the speed. They won't be able to live with your speed. You'll show them.'

'You're my son, after all,' Peter continued, smiling at the road. Along the embankment either side, the blemished cotton of sheep and their black faces rearing up at this passing vehicle. To the distant right, the sea was just about visible, a twinkling grey line. The training pitch was inland, newly opened with an Astro at the rear: the old pitch by the Sound now reserved exclusively for match days. 'Aren't you, John?' his father added, and he sounded genuinely curious.

Instead of replying, John rotated his entire torso to stare out the window.

He had been asked to tog out for the seniors right before the Leaving Cert – the Monday ahead of the Wednesday's commencing English paper – but his mother had informed the management he'd be waiting till the exams were over. 'I don't think you need any more distractions,' Yvonne had said.

John was a half-back, a defender. He was a persistent runner, clever at standing a forward up and not gifting cheap frees, and his kicking was mostly accurate. Okay, problems with catching a ball above his head, specifically with regard to the mechanics of jumping, but John was a good to decent player. Not gifted, but good. So he wasn't altogether shocked by the call-up – three others from his age bracket had also been solicited and John knew that the Island senior team were middling at best and consistently losing heads to Dublin, Galway and shores beyond – however, he was surprised that he wasn't exactly excited by the thought of being on the senior panel. When John was fourteen, when his harboured dreams of playing professionally for Man United were revealed to be crushingly unrealistic – the first big life disappointment as he compared his date of birth with the date of birth of those currently signing for professional soccer clubs in England – he had started to imagine playing senior football for Mayo. That had been his ambition, if asked. But only ever in the sense of the glory associated with such an accomplishment.

The triumph.

He'd imagine himself staggering off the pitch in that green and red jersey, fist raised in recognition for a stand that wobbled in celebration. The roar of 'Up Mayo' ubiquitous. Surrounding. Sustained.

It was never for the actual sixty-minute game itself.

John was shitting it for training tonight: as soon as he had cycled home from the woods and effortlessly ejected the viscous build-up in his dick, an ejection that was steaming almost, he had begun to feel nauseous. A sloshing within his stomach. Hands twitchy as if home too early from a night out. Face down on his bed, he listened to his **PUMPED** playlist on his Creative Zen MP3 player – a playlist consisting of the sprightlier tunes of the guitar bands he could publicly like – and tried to still himself.

He knew Tony would be there, and Rooney and Studzy. They were his age, his best buds. He had texted all three: 'Training tonight yeah ?'

He knew the manager – the tall, wiry Anthony Barrett – was sound, or seemed sound in the scant interactions they'd had.

The car swung right.

A chalky cloud rose as it pulled into a space behind the goals. Five or six figures were out kicking a ball. Cones were laid in patterns on the pitch alongside a pile of bibs. John slipped on the boots but didn't tie them – he'd wait in case he needed to pass a conceivable minute in solitude – and he clicked open the door, announcing over his shoulder, 'Thanks for the lift.'

With a grunt, Peter reached and touched a hand to John's back. 'You're well able, son.'

'Thanks, Dad.' John produced an impression of a smile. He had one foot free from the car, floating in arcs before the gravel.

'Your mother is collecting, correct?' The hand was still tentatively parked on the middle of John's back, but his father's seatbelt was cutting across his chest as he leaned over the handbrake to establish this contact: it had to be uncomfortable. Even in the sweetest gestures, his father was a hopeless embarrassment. John nodded and Peter said, 'I'll see you Thursday. Same time.' His father winked. 'Same place.'

John thanked him again and climbed out of the car. The clack of stud on gravel. The warm odour of cut grass in the air. His father slumped back to the driver's side, wrestled with the belt so that it wasn't lodged against his arm. 'My man,' Peter said then, and John gave his father a thumbs up and firmly shut the door.

The men on the pitch were unknown to John – well, he was familiar with them but only by surname and reputation – so by the sandy path laid between car park and grass, he knelt and tied his boots. One of the kickers was Daithí Joyce. DJ. He was the centre-forward. In the past, DJ had been asked to train with Mayo, but, reportedly, he was a dire boozehound. Finished, John untied his laces and began this task anew until someone toed him up the arse.

It was Tony Dineen. 'Ho ho. Well, Tits.'

The other two lads behind him chuckled. Punchy greetings were exchanged, and John labelled Rooney a shaper for his white boots – 'We're playing with men, bud' – and the brayed response from the others settled John somewhat.

Rooney's name was Patrick, but he so hated the idea of it being condensed to the derisive Paddy that in the first year of secondary school he christened himself Rooney after the famous Wayne. He answered only to that, stubbornly X-ed out Patrick and scrawled his name as Rooney O'Riordan on registers, subject choice forms, tests. Ridiculous until he kept it up and it was accepted, almost thought of as courageous. Rooney was slender, puffy lips as if allergic to life, terrible skin, with longer hair that he was growing out: Rooney was set up to be a joke except he excelled at every sport he tried his foot and hand at. Him and his girlfriend

Karen had been going out since second year. Karen's parents allowed Rooney to stay over at the weekend and Rooney informed the boys about this without pride, or graphic detail, and more like it was a chore. This struck the boys as strange. Rooney now said, good-naturedly, for John to go fuck himself.

'You're a training virgin, Tits,' Studzy said to John, and then Studzy groaned like sex. More laughter. A feeling of security within John – his father nude and protecting him from the wicked shadows as he peed late at night, that same feeling – and an unconscious grin breaking across his face, and then the peep of a whistle.

A lap around the pitch. The pace set by the bulky midfielder Seamus Fallon and the team's captain: a man named Mac. Mac had a crew cut and a small, hardened face like a conker. He was in his late thirties. Old. Ancient. And as the team stretched in a circle by the sideline, Antony Barrett went through what they would be at tonight. Handling. Pace. Aggression was mentioned four times. 'It's about consistency. What we will be doing here this evening, we will be doing again throughout the summer. It will become second nature to you.' Barrett spoke with his hands behind his back and a foot trapping a ball with ISLAND written on it in red marker. 'You hear me, lads? You won't even get to think, you'll do it.'

Scratching his chin alongside Barrett was Ultan – John didn't know if the man had a surname, didn't know if he owned a pair of jeans or any other garment apart from this

two-piece club tracksuit. Ultan was a husky man in his
fifties or sixties who John had seen on the sideline at every
game growing up. He devoted so much of his existence to
the club that you couldn't think of him as a real living
person but only as an institution: a statue that was often
vandalised. Ultan had texted on the worst Sunday of John's
life: 'Dear John . Ultan here . The club can provide support
if required . ULTAN .'

Inappropriate, weird, not a text John would in a million
days reply to, but generous all the same.

'The league is nothing now,' Barrett went on. 'We forget
it. We've moved on.' Heads nodded and John was nodding,
too. 'We are building for Championship. So utter focus on
that, right?' Murmured agreement and Barrett tapped his
earlobe and there was the agreement repeated, more
pronounced. John was currently latched onto the shoulder
of a man whose Spain jersey from the 2002 World Cup was
smeared with VapoRub. This man's biceps were hills, and
he had a lined face that was cubist: *The Weeping Woman*,
image of that, honestly. They both held their ankles,
avoided eye contact.

'Good,' Barrett said. 'And it's fantastic to see all the
young fellas with us tonight. They're part of the panel now.
And I'm telling you, I won't be afraid of playing them
either.' Barrett clapped then and John and Spain Jersey
unclasped from one another. 'Let's get going.'

A handpassing drill to start. A four-cone parameter and
you criss-cross with ball in hand and if you meet someone,

so be it, contact, physicality, before passing it to the next person. The first couple of times, John went through clean – striding nicely with a demonstration of his speed because they could not handle his speed – but the third time he encountered a body – this bruiser named Tom Cafferkey, a stocky defender with lashes as if mascaraed – and in the freshly crosshatched zone, Cafferkey tensed, awaited John, and the two collided, shoulder against shoulder.

Like clattering into a wall.

The air squished from John's lungs.

The jolt sideways of his upper body and the world swayed, swayed in the other direction.

But John managed to stay on his feet – teetering momentarily, yes, but steadying, righting his stance. Stumbling on, he then completely skewed his handpass, the ball skimming off his wrist rather than his fist. A frustrated bark from the next in the line as John waddled to the back of the queue. There, he gripped the end of his zip-up and leaned forward, huffing.

'Are you alright, young man?' a voice asked.

The fella in front of John turned and slapped him on the shoulder with a smirk. It was Spain Jersey.

'Sound,' John answered eventually. 'I'm sound. Yeah.'

The remainder of the training was relatively tame, what John was accustomed to, and it ended with backs versus forwards and midfielders.

Idling on the periphery with the other boys – the loose change of the drill – John watched the first four runs. Two of them petered out in the corner, another ended due to a brilliant flick of hand by the defender – the captain, Mac – and the last attempt was a sharp sequence of handpasses between DJ and the corner-forward Oisín Hanley before Hanley pinged it over.

After that, Studzy was subbed in and during the next run, made three diagonal bursts across the square without a sniff of a pass being whacked into him. Studzy was nippy if lithe. He was good. The next time, the ball did arrive into Studzy and he swivelled, shot, but it dropped short, yet Barrett cheered as if Studzy had scored a point.

Tony was called to be one of the midfielders, and he hit a neat one-two with DJ before tapping it between the posts. Tony was lanky with a cowlick and was the most natural footballer out of the boys in terms of size and shape. The only thing he lacked was aggression: too nice, too cautious.

Then John's name was yelled, and Cafferkey was jogging in his direction and John was a corner-back. The man he was marking was named Eoghan Moloney. He was broad with flurries of highlighter blond in his mullet. He worked in the offie in Sweeney's Supermarket – had refused the boys on occasion. From what John had witnessed so far, he was an accurate kicker but immobile. So John pressed up on Moloney straight away.

The ball was walloped onto the opposite side of the pitch.

Moloney feinted to sprint forward, and John didn't buy it.

John's right hand was clenching and unclenching, and his eyes alternated between Moloney's grizzled neck and where the ball was presently hanging.

Eventually possession was recycled to DJ, who blazed it wide and then glared at the ground as if it had kicked the ball.

The management praised the defence. John had barely shifted a couple of feet and yet he felt exhausted, breathing through his mouth, and then suddenly the next ball was arrowed into his side of the pitch and Moloney collected, and John was behind him. Moloney went to immediately swing with his left foot, but John provided no viable gap for the shot, and Moloney faltered, was forced to bounce in fear of too many steps and John was on top of him. Touching, grubbing, feeling. They were on the edge of the thirteen-metre line. The turf sliced up by dragged stud. Shouts, shouting and once more, Moloney attempted to kick, but John was closer, both arms out, no opportunity to shoot, and Moloney bounced the ball, and John shrieked, 'Two hops. Two hops. Two—'

The whistle.

Barrett declared a free-out. 'Well done, defender.'

'Are you serious, Anthony? He was grabbing hold of me,' Moloney shouted while pulling out his shirt to demonstrate the grabbing. 'Anthony. Seriously?'

John felt good, he felt alive.

Hanley replaced Studzy and right away Hanley demanded the ball and skipped far too easily by Spain Jersey and smashed it into the net. It was the first goal of the session. Lumbering to his feet in the sandy rut encompassing the goal, the keeper berated Spain Jersey, who roared right back. Then the ball was clipped in towards John's corner again.

Moloney burst forward and John slipped.

Moloney thumped the ball over the bar.

John punched the turf.

'Where were you that time, young buck?' Moloney muttered to John as they backed once more into their corner. John was surprised at this remark, maybe frightened. John stayed silent, seemingly in concentration for the next play, but, truthfully, John did not reply because he hadn't learned how to reply up here yet.

At home, John showered, investigated the crusted spots around his lips and nose by inclining his chin at the steamed bathroom mirror, and then investigated, more generally, his large bumpy head, his unsatisfactory hair, his body that was so mockable.

John was not fat, but he was not skinny.

Now he pivoted and held his breath till his tummy frowned.

He considered, then hatefully reviewed himself.

Back in his room, he snagged his phone from the charger. The chrome lamp burned white on his desk, where his study stuff was still piled high: exam papers, A4 notepads, a sketch book. John nibbled at his thumbnail and perhaps it was because he was so wrecked after training that he didn't have to dare himself tonight before texting her.

'Hey :) xxx that was good today'

He waited on the edge of his bed for a minute. Two. He texted Studzy: 'What u make of training?'

Another minute and he spat a sliver of nail onto the carpet.

Then he went downstairs.

His mother was leaning over the kitchen counter and directing smoke out the unlatched top window. She was in a shabby pink dressing gown that revealed normal clothes – a maroon jumper, cream cropped trousers – and the non-cigarette hand was tucked inside the dressing gown. The blatant smoking was new. In the past, it had been undertaken with mediocre secrecy. John would find the butts wedged in the grikes of the patio or in the potted plants. He would see his father sulk and flex the newspaper over and over. 'Bedtime soon,' Yvonne announced as John stuck his head into the press.

It could have been a question or a statement, and he didn't reply regardless. Yvonne talked to herself: narrated her day, her actions and to-do. Of course, John also talked to himself, but in confirmed solitude, whereas his mother's speaking was flamboyant. He used to find it comforting. An affirming noise that hummed downstairs when he paused his video game, or when he opened the door after school and heard her airy reporting from the kitchen.

John took out a bowl, decided on cornflakes.

He placed the phone on the table, screen down.

'Are you tired, superstar?' she asked, and he nodded.

'My poor tired superstar,' she said, and the swoosh of drawn cigarette. In a less theatrical voice, she said briskly, 'What're you doing Thursday?'

'Working in the morning. I don't know.' A message rumbled through. It was, disappointingly, Studzy. A spoonful of cornflakes and then John amended, 'I have training in the evening, actually.'

'You'll come me with to the exhibition in the afternoon, so,' his mother said. 'That's fantastic. All sorted.'

He swung round, elbow on the back of the chair. 'What exhibition?'

'Don't be so cross, John,' Yvonne said. 'It's Maud's exhibition.' Her cigarette was practically buckling under the spent ash and now she tapped it against the edge of the sink. 'You like Maud, don't you?'

'No I fuckin don't,' he muttered, and she said she heard that.

Maud was Dutch and gay and an artist – importance in that order. She was part of a collective that had shacked up on the Island decades back. Yvonne had started painting three, four years ago, and that's how she befriended the collective: their art lessons held in the community hall down the Sound, every Saturday from ten to six. His mother was a decent painter, but her preferred themes were properly demented. Elves peeping mischievously through wildflowers. Elves fishing. Elves gardening before a mushroom with a billowing chimney. Indeed, stacked somewhere in the attic were four portraits Yvonne had completed of the Masterson family: pointed ears, the button ends of each of their elongated noses daubed with red, but apart from these embellishments, they were pretty alright, John thought. Lifelike. For a time, they hung on the stairs – the portraits rising in line with seniority, so John was beaming toothily at the bottom – and then his father had invited someone over from work and suddenly they weren't.

'You're booked in.' A last savoured exhale and the cigarette was twisted and crushed down in the sink. Yvonne swiped at the remaining smoke, saying, 'It will be fun. The Dutch ladies are fun. And your sister said she'll pop along.' She stood beside him, scratched the back of his neck, and John looked up at her, trying not to seem surprised. 'Accompanied by her wonderful husband-to-be.' She smiled at him, then rolled her eyes. 'Mr Kilbane.'

John ground his molars and then said, 'Right, fine. I'll go with you.' In a meaner voice, he added, 'But I've training at seven, so I want to be home early.'

'My darling boy, the superstar,' she declared.

He ignored her, dug with his spoon.

'My darling, darling boy,' she said, and he told her to stop, but couldn't not smile. 'Bed soon, okay?' Yvonne said then, and he rose his cheek to meet her lips.

While slurping down the end of the cereal, John bravely texted a row of xs to Amber, and she replied almost instantaneously: 'Ahhh didn't see this'

Then: 'Yeah it was x I have work tomorrow fml'

Then Amber wrote, 'Sorry ! how was training?'

John was gladdened by this, she should ask such a question, she should be curious, and he replied, 'Good yeah xxx Intense'

The age difference between him and Amber Goold had seemed freakish at first but freakish on Amber's side only. For John, the whole thing was a mysterious adventure, a useful opportunity. He had informed the boys vaguely about her – that she worked with him in the hotel and her name and her age and yeah, tap – to respectful nods, to praise of him being a sneaky cunt. Older hence easier, softer: John knew these factors were darkly presumed by the other boys because he himself presumed them, but John made sure to leave them unsaid that day.

When Amber replied saying, 'Well done', John wrote that he'd made a nice tackle, and she texted, 'Well done' once again. And when John composed a text saying, 'Landline ?', his phone had just received, 'OK !!! BED x' so there came another text a moment later, which read: 'Too late! Nightnight'

John waited a suave eight minutes before pausing *Final Fantasy X* – he was replaying it for the sixth time because it was summer and life was periodically, if not primarily dull – and replying, 'Goodnight'

Then he remembered Studzy's text. The boys started to message each other about who was good at training and, importantly, who was shite – Studzy said Ewan Gormon was rubbish and John discovered this was the man in the Spain jersey – and then John sent: 'You think u can make the team?'

Studzy replied: 'Maybe .. Yea. U have a good chance 2 bud'

Was this the exact response John was hoping for? Had he been angling for this assurance from the start? It cheered him immensely anyway. Buoyed him so that he was compelled to pace his room. John should start for the seniors and what an accomplishment that would be and what might everyone think.

At ten to eleven, inspired by his new-found greatness, John thought to write to Amber once more and his text read: 'We should meet up again xxx'

Imperfect, but the best he could do.

Thursday, 2nd July

The Island Head was located at the very tip of Keel: a two-storey three-star hotel with fifty rooms, a function hall furnished with a stage and a dancefloor, and a restaurant that accommodated both a leisurely breakfast buffet and an evening-time fine-dining experience. The foyer was floored in chequered tile and through the double doors on the right was the bar, and to the left was the restaurant. Past reception was a carpeted hallway – a chevron pattern of grey and another sort of grey – leading to bedrooms, and a staircase leading up to more bedrooms, and three bounding steps down this hallway, before the stainless-steel handle for the gents' toilet – indicated by an emblem of a man doffing his top hat to a urinal – there was an unmarked door with a small glass hole, which John now pushed and entered.

He was in slacks, Vans that he'd soon swap for slip-on dress shoes, a black buttoned waistcoat over his father's baggy white shirt, a red tie, and a clipped name tag which said DAVE, as that was who John had replaced and why bother substituting, the goateed general manager Ethan had argued, as you'll only be here for the summer, yes? John was a waiter, which meant seven a.m. starts and evening shifts that dragged till after ten. It wasn't a job John had undertaken for the money: it was a job for something to do for the next two months.

Eight names were rostered for the restaurant, and of those, three were seasonal workers like John. The other five were saddos whose career was this hotel.

Amber was one of these saddos and for his first day, John had shadowed her. That was how they'd started. John had the hunch she might fancy him – in how Amber looked at him with her face tilted as if water stuck in her ear and how she laughed erratically around him and that was all really but enough for a tingle at the rear of his brain which seemed proof of something – and so John manufactured a private gag about how pricey mobile phone credit was against the freeness of the landline, about how everybody should just talk on the landline rather than this costly texting business. A private gag which had ballooned into John locking the door of the living room and keying her number into the house phone and actually talking to her for fifteen minutes. They had kissed soon after: bodies soured by five hours of work, they had nonetheless pressed together against the whitewashed wall of the house she shared with her father. It was her idea and her mouth tasted of nicotine and gum. His hands slid down her waist and hips and her arse was a pillow to grab, to grapple with, a plump pillow genuinely, and it begged to be squeezed, which caused Amber to retrieve her tongue abruptly, so she could shake her head, laugh without looking directly at him.

That had been about a week ago.

This morning Amber was supervisor as it was Martina's day off. She had greeted John casually and said for him to look after the carvery and this was where he presently stood, the harsh golden light taped inside the vented roof causing his right eye to squint. He was flanked by Samantha Moyles and Hughie Denton. The upward waft of fat and grease and pulsating heat, and he could feel this odour cling to his clothing and squash itself down inside his pores. Samantha handed John a plate with brown sausages and a hash brown, and it was his task now to interpret a series of stabbed index fingers and add a slop of beans or a scoop of mushrooms. Eight a.m. and it was manic as they had a thirty-strong tour group in. These tours were the hotel's bread and money during the summer season.

By half eight the group had cleared off. The five on duty wiped and reset and began the wait for the regular hotel guests to descend.

At ten to nine, Amber allowed John and a Polish fella named Zibby out for a smoke.

Hunched on a crate, Zibby rolled his little fag, and it reminded John of paper planes in primary school, the dainty crimping and grave concentration, and they sat in silence until Zibby asked John if he thought the hotel was a shithole yet?

John looked up at a grinning Zibby, and said he did, yeah.

They both laughed and then silence fell between them again, but nicer.

Zibby had two kids: an impossibility to John similar to flapping his arms and flying, the notion that absurd. Zibby seemed at most six years older, but he had two kids: John had seen them in a small blue car, seen the taciturn if not altogether grouchy Zibby stretching out his arms like a zombie as he tromped towards this vehicle to their ringing amusement.

Warm jizz and what it could potentially beget. It was one of the two big terrors around the act of sex – the other biggie involving being plain useless at it. The first time he and Seóna had completed it fully, John was certain that he had got Seóna pregnant. And not subsequently, but during: with each thrust and wiggle, Seóna grew more and more pregnant in John's mind, her belly bloating and filling, and so by the end of the six minutes, it felt as if their baby was born and sucking on its thumb and, freakishly, watching its own conception. His life was decided, it was irreversible, and John didn't even know what kind of music Seóna liked, or whether she was lying most of the time when they spoke like he was.

The next day John had confided in Studzy, who understood women and sex as he had kissed the most girls since he was thirteen. Studzy congratulated John on the news, added, 'Finally got there, bud,' before reverting to John's original concern and enquiring: 'So, you didn't wear a johnny? That's a shocking move.'

No, John had. It was an EXTRA SAFE number. Seóna had stolen it from her sister's top drawer.

'And did you?' Studzy asked. 'You know. In her?' He gestured with a loosely closed fist – up and down, quickly.

The indelicate sign language of boys, and John understood.

He solemnly shook his head. 'No. I finished into the sink in her ensuite.' With gravitas, John then said, 'Seóna watched me, though.'

'Right, right.' Studzy clucked his tongue. 'What you worried about again?'

Seóna was only sore afterwards. Her voice rose when John pressed about the pill and her hopping on a bus to Newport – he had prudently looked up return times – and her voice went especially high when he compromised and requested that she merely text a secret code – he suggested the poetic '…' – the second the blood kind of dribbles down there or whatever, you know. Gushes. 'Do you ever listen to yourself, John?' was one of the irate questions Seóna had thrown at him that afternoon, but surely the problem was more that John listened to himself too much?

When John and Zibby came back in, Amber instructed Zibby, Hughie and Samantha to look after the remaining guests while they – she and John and a thrill as John clocked this subtle coupling – would sort the laundry for tonight.

Amber held the door for the laundry room, and John squeezed by with the trundling wheelie bin but was conscious to brush into her slightly. There were six washing machines atop each other, and a length of wooden shelves containing stacks of white. It was intoxicatingly warm, this unpleasant trapped heat. Amber stretched and yawned, revealing a peek of skin above her pants. She wore dark eyeshadow and black nail varnish. She was a head shorter than him. Hairbands were wound around her left wrist – the little metal squares catching the light now and again – and she had a tattoo of a cluster of stars below this wrist: four stars. John blurted: 'What you at after work?'

'I'm on again this evening.' She smiled at him. 'But I suppose I'm doing nothing until then.'

'Ah right,' he said. 'I have training later. And I'm heading to an art thing with my mam before that.'

She let out this nasal laugh that didn't sound sincere. 'Why did you ask me, so?'

John said he wasn't sure, and that was the truth. He hadn't forgotten his own plans or anything, but he had wondered about what Amber was at today. They began to chuck the stained sheets and cloths from the wheelie bin into a bigger basket. Then John said: 'We could go cinema next time? Beforehand.'

She slanted her face at him, the three lines on her brow. 'Oh, could we?'

'Yeah,' he said, and his voice was small. Something had been miscued and he wasn't sure what.

Amber said, 'I'm so glad to know that, John.'

Then she laughed hard. The real thing this time. 'Look. Let's just keep that stuff outside work, alright?' He agreed, began to apologise and she stopped him with a raised hand: 'We'll see what happens. Okay?'

'Yeah. Cool. Sound.' He thought about it and still for some reason said, 'Sorry.'

Amber told John to gather twenty-five fresh sheets. She moved down the back of the laundry room, where there was a queue of luggage carts and no visible security camera. She brought her phone to her ear. As slowly as possible, John collected and piled this load atop the wheelie bin and tried to make out what Amber was saying, who she was talking to. He caught pieces of words and conversational white noise but not enough to draw any conclusions. He was jealous but the jealousy only stemmed from curiosity: if he knew who it was on the phone he wouldn't care. Even if it was another lad. Another lad she was kissing or fucking or whatever. He didn't like Amber beyond the recognition that he could do stuff with her. The same was true for her, he figured.

Yet he did feel wounded.

Like he had fingered her two days ago, basically seen her naked, and she acted now as if he was a pest.

What he knew about Amber's broader life was nothing much: she worked here, she smoked weed and could get him some – frightening – and from what he'd gleaned from overheard conversations in the hotel, hyperbolic in tone and content, she seemed to only hang out with others from the hotel. Realistically, John probably didn't want work to know about them either, if there even was a *them* to consider. She wasn't that great. And this was her life, he supposed, the scope of it, and let her enshroud it if she wanted. He didn't remotely care, now that he thought about it. Why should he? His opinion: she was probably a mosher at school – the tattoos a hint, the black-ringed eyes another – and had not many friends and this was the breadth of her life: a hotel job, mooching around with co-workers, the Island. She may be wiser than him at certain arts due to age, experience, but that was it. He was no doubt smarter overall and bonus points: he wasn't going to be chained here forever. John started to feel much better once he placed himself above Amber. It was a handy way to dispel gloom, but John could only do it when he believed it to be a hundred per cent true. Otherwise, it was as effective as telling yourself grass was red and that Seóna actually loved you despite the texts stating the opposite.

Amber caught his eye then and said to the phone, 'Hold on.'

Amber spoke to John, 'Can you go make a start on setting the top?' She waved a hand. 'I'll be up in a couple of minutes.'

They didn't interact for the rest of the shift but when he was slipping back into his Vans, Amber told him in a sing-song voice to try and enjoy work without her tomorrow. She was behind him, so John had to glance over his shoulder as he retorted, 'I'll do my best, like.'

She was in a rain jacket and he didn't think she'd wait for him, but she did: a handbag with a strap like chainmail held in her hand, she waited while disdainfully eyeing the rota pinned to the kitchen door. They walked out together, and John tried to slyly scan for his mother's parked car. The sky was low and the clouds were bruised with an ominous underbelly, but there was warmth somewhere behind them. 'I can't wait to get out of here,' Amber announced with a sigh.

'Really?' John said. 'I didn't think it was that busy this morning?'

'No.' She rolled her eyes but smiled. 'I mean the whole place. The Island. Didn't I tell you I'm heading to South America?' He shook his head. 'Well. Surprise. I'm heading to South America.' She retrieved a box of cigarettes from her outer jacket pocket, her car keys jingled in the other hand. 'Going in September. We'll backpack for a while, you know, do the sights, and there's these surfing parties in Brazil that are meant to be class. Then I'll probably teach somewhere. In a small school, or something.'

'Sham,' he said.

'I can't wait. Honestly.' She wasn't looking at John, but straight ahead to the distant curve of Keel beach and the consecutive lines of gleaming silver beyond it. A car beeped annoyingly then, and John knew it was his mother. Amber said, 'Is that her? She's pretty.' Amber looked at him. 'I can understand why someone wanted to see her tits.'

'Get away,' he hissed, marching across the car park.

She was laughing behind him.

In the car, his mother asked who was that young lady he was talking to, and John answered accurately: 'Just a person I work with.'

The exhibition was held in the Beeswax Café down the Sound. Not in a backroom with lush white walls, or in a luminous conservatory, but in a café that was teeming with lunchtime customers. John and his mam had completed a stop-start lap, gawking studiously over heads at canvases covered in what Yvonne described as very, very abstract art. The painting they were staring at presently showed intersecting blobs of greens and blues with a humped collage of cars salvaged from old advertisements at its bottom. The title was *Exploitation of Self*.

'This is crap,' John muttered, and Yvonne countered that it wasn't crap, but challenging. 'It's art that provokes you. And that's Maud's thing.' Hands linked behind her back, Yvonne leaned closer towards the canvas. Black-framed glasses rested at the top of her head and she had tied a silk scarf around her neck before leaving the house, and John figured this was her arty outfit. 'I think this one is about the environment. Pollution? Anyway' – she straightened up – 'you can't simply dismiss something because you personally don't get it, John. That's not how the world works.'

'Well. What do you get from this one?'

After a moment, she said, 'A slight headache.' She smiled at him. 'But don't you say that to Maud.'

Maud and the other Dutch ladies were out the front, perched around two tables shoved together, smoking merrily. His mother had cheered when she'd clocked them from the car park, and they'd stood up one by one to hug her. Maud had called John's name, and he'd waved from afar. The outdoor patio was also where his sister, Kay, and her fiancé, Denis Kilbane, had decamped upon arrival. Kay had said that they might skip the exhibition after all.

'Your paintings are better than these,' John said. It wasn't totally true, but it also didn't feel like a massive stretch either. 'At least they make sense. Your elves. They're clearly doing stuff. Or it's their garden?'

Yvonne let out something like a laugh. They shuffled on to the next painting. This one was a splattering of primary colours with no discernible pattern. The title was *Pre-History*. 'I like this one, now,' his mother said. 'The colours. Hard to do that. You'd think it'd be grand, but it's not.'

'I'm serious,' John said. 'Why don't you put on a show?'

With a sidelong glance, Yvonne told him, 'You think I need more attention around this place?'

John stuck his hands into his pockets, slouched.

He didn't really mind his mother's tits, aside from how he and the Island had seen them or heard about them. In theory, it didn't offend John – it was icky and gross, yeah, course, but only because he had beheld the photo. If it had been more like her painting, undertaken quietly and stored thereafter in the attic to steadily accumulate dust, then so what? If photographing her boobs had induced a flood of happiness, then, you know, class? But it had spread over the Island and so it was horrifying, degrading for him, and disgusting by her. The fact that it hadn't been for his dad's attention was mortifying, too. Yvonne had sat John down one evening to discuss it, explain the situation while stressing its unexplainable complexity – at one stage she bluntly brought up innate sexual urges as if John didn't rationalise most life decisions according to the likelihood of a grope or a touch, as if John hadn't done an unholy amount of weird shit due to rousing blood below the belt – and afterwards they had hugged for a long time and, to his ear, Yvonne had whimpered and finally asked if John still loved his stupid old mammy.

'My art is not ready anyway,' Yvonne said then. 'One day, maybe. I don't know. But.' Her voice trailed off and then she clicked her fingers, pointed at him. 'You need to start back on those driving lessons. I'm not escorting you to that hotel every day.'

'How can I do any lessons?' he said with an tut. Now a deepened voice: 'Aren't I practically working twenty-four hours like you wanted?'

She ignored his tone. 'Your father should be teaching you. Ask him.'

John slouched a little more.

Yvonne continued, louder, 'Right. Let's go check on the two philistines.' John recognised a quiver of apprehension in these words. A nervousness that you'd only deduce if you loved the speaker, knew the speaker too well. He followed his mother out.

Denis stood to peck Yvonne on either cheek, and then shook John's hand. Kay remained seated, watching out at the road as John and Yvonne manoeuvred themselves onto the picnic bench.

Kay was eight years older than John and John felt her birthday was somewhere in March. She was generous when she wanted to be, had studied business and French in college, and she used to have a bump nose but it was now suspiciously straight. John and Kay talked when in the same room, otherwise they didn't.

'How was it?' Kay said. She was wearing aviator sunglasses.

'Brilliant,' Yvonne replied. She had taken off her nice scarf and it rested on her lap like a pet snake. 'Lot to take in, but very good. Stimulating, I have to say.'

'And what did you think?' Kay turned to John, who glanced at his mother before concurring: 'Yeah, brilliant stuff.' His sister made a hmm sound. 'I'm happy out here.' Kay angled her face for a non-existent sun. 'You dragged me along to her last one, Mam. That was enough for me.'

'In the hall in Castlebar?' Yvonne asked, surprised. 'Was that Maud's show?'

John began to fidget with a sugar packet as Yvonne answered herself, 'No, I think that might have been some-one else, Kay?'

It was Denis who broke the silence: 'You'll be glad to hear, Yvonne, that I got the upstairs loo working. So we have the two in the house now. And a functioning shower.' Denis jutted his chin. '*Finally*, says you.' Denis was a plumber by trade. Dark-haired. Stubble with silver pinpricks and silver too along his temples. Fierce handsome, according to everybody. John had been introduced to him on four separate occasions and each time got the impression of a guy who never questioned but lived on whatever fortune was sent his way, or whatever fortune he wrenched in his direction. A man who burned his rubbish and also firmly believed the guards were too soft on petty criminals. That was not to say Denis wasn't sound: he was. But he was oblivious, John thought, and aware of his obliviousness, and yet content to carry on living obliviously. 'You must come up for a visit,' Denis said to Yvonne. 'Changed a lot since you last saw it. No longer a building site.'

To Kay, Denis said now, 'Mustn't she visit us?'

His sister's fingers drummed the table before she said, 'Yes. Mam, you're welcome up.'

This made Yvonne smile. 'Oh, I'd love that. Thank you. I'd go up any evening that suited you both?'

Kay nodded and then said sharply, 'Have you got a dress yet?'

Kay had fled the Island as soon as she could. Dublin and then over to London, where she'd encountered Denis on the tube one morning last May – he'd been travelling to a site with a schoolbag snug between his boots, she was heading for a high, glassy office. She was the one who'd recognised him. Denis was ten years her senior. Kay had known him forever as the oldest wayward brother of a schoolfriend. The two of them had been back on the Island since Christmas: Denis owned a sizable portion of land near Keel, where a house was almost built. They had been engaged for all that time. The way Kay talked about the wedding was how John had once spoken about Santa: an even mixture of magical wonder and petrifying disquiet in case the incorrect presents were stashed beneath the tree. The ceremony was to be held in the church by the Sound. The reception was booked for The Island's Head.

The engagement hadn't been met with unanimous joy at home. Everyone had assumed there had to be a baby, but there wasn't one. Then the age difference was a concern. Plus, the brevity of the relationship itself: six months, eek. And there had been deception on Kay's part about the nature of the relationship and as a result the old schoolfriend was no longer her friend but was still, obviously, Denis's sister.

But the tit photo and its turmoil and the separation – though neither parent labelled it as such even as they started to live in separate buildings – had warped the entire nuptial situation, twisted the circumstances until the wedding was now viewed as the only good thing on the shimmering horizon.

The coda after the longest, shittest summer.

Yvonne answered that no, she hadn't quite found the right dress, but she was searching. Actively. Kay shook her head. 'It is less than two months away, Mam.' Kay sighed. 'Where have you been looking?' The two of them began to discuss shops in Castlebar, in Westport, then a roll call of websites, and Kay mentioned hats and that became the pressing issue. Throughout their talk, the date of August the fifteenth recurred like a threat.

Denis winked at John. 'How's the football?'

John answered and Denis said halfway through this answer, 'Good man yourself.'

'I mean, Mam,' Kay was saying, impatiently, 'you kind of have to get a move on. You do realise how close it is?'

Yvonne was explaining how she was trying her best, but it was an altogether stressful period in her life and there were other priorities and John was still playing with the sugar sachet and now he tore it open by mistake. At this, John announced to the table he was heading to the toilet.

John waved at Maud once more as he hurried inside the café.

He felt duty-bound to wave to Maud because she had been a frequent tutor to his art class during the Leaving Cert. She had covered the practical stuff: clay sculpture, lino prints, drawing. During her last masterclass, as they had sketched and shaded a composition of a banana, a sock and a tungsten screw, Maud had leaned over John and commented that his artistic future could be stupendous if he stayed at it. She had met his eye and repeated this.

Stupendous. For a moment, John was aglow, maybe he wasn't bang average despite the contrary visible evidence, maybe he was an artist, gifted, special, a road opened before him, and then he saw that Maud was orbiting the entire class and expressing a similar version of this positivity to each head – he caught a snippet of his neighbour being informed she had colossal potential if she nailed herself to the mast. Studzy was the only one who didn't receive any enthusiastic forecast. Studzy, Maud had declared in a stiff monotone the same afternoon, was a rascal.

He sat on the toilet seat, staring at the tiles, his phone, hating everybody, and upon his return to the table, his mam and sister had reverted to more genial wedding chatter. It was about last-minute RSVPs and how deeply ignorant certain second cousins were, and Yvonne was consoling her daughter, 'That's just the way those people are, Kay. You can't fix 'em.' Kay still wore the sunglasses, but she now held a ratty tissue paper. No one enquired about his fifteen-minute absence. With a wiggling index finger, Denis gestured for John to shrug in closer and John obeyed. The odour of Denis's aftershave – piney, a grove of fir trees – and then Denis abruptly craned his neck over his right shoulder.

John looked at where Denis's neck seemed to be indicating: the two tables of Dutch women.

Confused, John turned back to Denis, who smirked. 'They're all lesbians.'

John agreed. 'They are lesbians, alright.'

* * *

The thing was John didn't have a future. He had a next day, obviously, and one after that. And certain dates were lodged firmly in his brain, like for work and its fickle schedule and senior training and the drinking with the boys Saturday and the league match in less than two weeks. These dates were evidently important to him: his mind flashing red, as in danger, as in watch out, when he recalled while shooting people on the PlayStation that he was on an eight to four shift next Wednesday even when he hadn't really forgotten this information and it was late Friday night. Additionally, there were the obligations: the sister's wedding the biggest, but also the evenings he had to visit his dad. But a future, whatever unfathomable mistiness that entailed, didn't seem like a phenomenon for him. It wasn't because John believed a future timeline a pointless thought bubble – unimaginable thanks to warmongering, decaying climate – nor did it stem from any morbid inclination – though John had waded through a spell of reading up online about ropes and nooses when he was sixteen, but surely everyone had done that and he couldn't recall what had sparked this suicidal obsession so it meant nothing, essentially – rather the whole notion of some vast future felt removed from John's own life. Incompatible. The wrong shape, like the plug sockets in Spain.

He had studied hard for the Leaving Cert. He had wanted to do well in it, but that didn't correlate to him wanting something special on the back of it. On the CAO form for his college application, he had scribbled the ciphers of various Bachelor of Arts degrees with the order scaling from most points required to least points required rather than most desired to least desired, and it had felt quite arbitrary to John. Actually, no, completing the CAO form had filled John with a profound sense of nostalgia. It was like picking French in lieu of German in first year. The same as ticking Art, History and Accounting for the senior cycle when in fourth year. The courses were all for NUIG in Galway.

The scenario of John not being enrolled in college had never played out in his mind. That he would not be in Galway and in a lecture hall, collegeing, once the second week of September commenced was an absurdity akin to fathering that voyeuristic baby with Seóna. It wasn't an option. He was aware some of the other lads agonised over this prospect – Studzy was notably silent when they discussed where they were all heading next as if one giant family and Tony, the swot, was going for medicine in Trinity and had confided in John that he might have to repeat the Leaving, the entire wearying year, if he didn't acquire the perfect six hundred points, or thereabouts, necessary for medicine, Trinity – but John felt he didn't have to worry about this at all. It wasn't even a vague, watery concern to him.

Not in a cocky way.

It just.

It just wasn't an option for him not to be in college.

He couldn't explain it beyond that, and he had tried to explain it better to Amber, who had queried about his plans post-summer one sluggish morning. In response to his muddled explanation, Amber had commented with a funny tut, 'Isn't it well for some.'

Basically: John would do something. And then he would do something after that. Like work as a teacher, or in some office, or he didn't know what yet, and now the Dire Straits were singing about a mean old town as the car bounced into the gravelled lot by the training pitch. The car nosed forward before curling backward, reversing into a spot between two hatchbacks, and so John remarked, 'You're not staying?'

It was blustery outside. The sky gone manky.

'No,' Peter said. 'Unfortunately, I have something on tonight.'

The car stopped with a sigh but the Dire Straits still sang. John decided to tie his boots inside the car this time.

Peter went on, 'You'll be fine. As I said, you didn't look out of place the last evening. Though, there was something.' By the change in his father's tone – a staticky inflation, like a child preparing to say 'happy birthday' – John knew some hilarious provocation was incoming. 'There was a bit of a slip at the end, wasn't there? How about that? The little slip. At the end there.'

'The new boots' fault.' John groaned underneath the glove compartment. 'And that Eoghan Moloney is no good either. He's useless.'

Peter laughed, kept laughing to himself.

His father had stuck around the last night for longer than John had assumed. Pretty much the entire session if he had witnessed John's dumbass slip, and yet his father had managed not to be parked up when Yvonne had arrived to collect, and that was classic orderly cowardly Dad.

Boots tied, John rose in the seat and unclicked his belt. 'Studzy did well, I thought. The last day.'

Peter agreed. 'Enda's a fine little player. They have big hopes for him, I'd say. Oh.' His dad faced him. 'Driving lessons.' A pause and Peter squinted. 'Next Monday. Will that suit your busy schedule?' John said yeah, fine, and his father smiled thinly at him. 'Looking forward to it.' The engine was back on: a gargled sound and now it was noisily ticking. The headlights blew a powdery path in front of the vehicle, two strokes of chalk, and the rain started to fall through this. Door open, John grimaced and asked quietly, 'Do you think I could make the team, Dad? Like, start?'

'Why wouldn't you?' Peter answered. 'You're well able.'

John nodded and felt happier.

The floodlights were on this evening and under their illumination the grass was greener, the sidelines whiter, and shadows fell in lacy fours rather than singles. John stretched out his left hamstring as Studzy recounted a story from work about a customer tripping over a cereal box display in the petrol station, which then became a report into how Studzy's supervisor was a braindead handicap idiot who knew nothing. Both boys wore gloves – the black O'Neills with the cream-coloured padding – and Studzy had on a red beanie sewn with the Liverpool bird. In intervals, John declared: 'Jesus', 'gas', 'fuck'. It was only John and Studzy:

no Tony or Rooney yet. It was quarter to seven. The rain was building and resembled flurries of unsticking snow when caught in the glare of the floodlights. The guy in the dated Spain jersey was in the same jersey tonight: he stood talking to another man a foot or two from the boys. Studzy's socks were pulled to a fingertip below the face of his knees and John thought this looked tome, John wished he had done the same with his own socks but now knew he never could. A ball flew past them and was kicked back the way it came. At last, Studzy's story came to an end as he summarised with an air of finality that yeah, the supervisor was just a dumb fucker, and so John stated in agreement that yeah, Studzy's supervisor sounded like a dumb fucker, alright. Studzy nodded and hoisted both arms above his head, one hand clasping the other, and asked quite quickly, 'How's things with that bird in work? You still texting her?'

Surprised, John said uneasily, 'Yeah, I am.' John awaited a barbed comment – a question like that from Studzy shouldn't be authentic, there had to be some pit John couldn't foresee and was about to plunge into – but when no such comment immediately materialised John was forced to elaborate: 'I met her Tuesday, actually. So, you know. Going good.'

'Oh yeah?' Studzy said.

'Yeah, for the second time. It was the second time meeting up.' Studzy didn't interrupt but nodded his head thoughtfully, and John continued, 'Nothing much, but. I got a bit of box.' John sniffed and sniffed once more. 'And then a blowie too, like.'

'Fuck,' Studzy said, and it was astonishing to John as well. It was a bold lie. It was a strange lie. But Studzy looked impressed so perhaps it was an ingenious ploy on John's part: because who knew Amber and who could discredit?

John could sense himself climbing the ranks in Studzy's eyes. A blowie was the difference between one point and three. 'Where?' Studzy asked and John told him some of the truth: the woods but not the pinpoint location, or the correct time of day. In his heart, John could thus argue he had protected Amber and the sanctity of them. John could feel less bad and once you begin to feel less bad, you basically have washed the error and fault away.

'That's between us,' John said then and Studzy was still nodding his head. 'Course, bud.' Studzy moved closer. 'That's unreal, though, Tits.'

John agreed: it was unreal. Hands out in front, John's upper body assumed the position of a wheelbarrow as he put one foot atop the other's heel. A clench in his calf and he held this pose for ten.

'She's loose, like,' Studzy said. Studzy had stopped stretching completely. 'I'm jealous here.' There was something enigmatic in Studzy's face when John peeked up: he appeared to be inspecting the Velcro strap of his gloves, confirming that they were secure maybe, but it wasn't convincing, it seemed phoney, a performance, and again an inkling that a trap loomed somewhere. And Studzy's voice, normally harsh, sounded more sombre, subdued, and if another familiar head was beside them now, John would have pointed this out, mocked Studzy's gentled tone and cadence, ridiculed Studzy's sincerity because that's what it was, John realised.

Sincerity.

At the root, Studzy was likely a good person, as John believed all people at root were good, but John had witnessed Studzy being a bad person more often than not. Bad as in frenzied, domineering messing that could be termed bullying, particularly if you considered the profile of the victims – the lowest ranked, the younger and fragile – bad as in being cheeky and obtrusive to teachers, bad as in starting drinking earlier than John had done, bad as in regularly hilarious before an enraptured audience but an audience that was due to shrink considerably come September. It was in this context that the sincerity was disorientating to John.

Why was Studzy being sincere about Amber?

'Really good by you,' Studzy admitted. 'I need to up my game.'

'Yeah,' John said and then he said, 'How d'you mean?'

Studzy's brows were low and almost touching – he could be angry or concentrating, John couldn't tell. 'Like, I've been texting a few, here and there,' Studzy said, and he looked down at John, 'but nothing's giving. I'm getting spits this summer. It's embarrassing. Honestly. Embarrassing.' Studzy sucked his teeth for a moment.

'Though I was thinking, right. Wild one, but. We could share your bird, maybe?'

John didn't reply, didn't know how to reply, and Studzy said to him, 'No malice.'

Studzy looked away again, and spoke, 'Like, you're not into her or anything, are you, Tits? You said it was only a tap before. A soft tap. And she's loose, isn't she? No malice, just an idea.'

John could barely get the words out: 'I don't know, man.'

There was a bright shout: Tony and Rooney were approaching. John was grateful to see them. John was relieved, in fact. Ultan was walking behind the boys with a case of plastic water bottles that rattled with each step forward. Those inside the flat-roofed dressing room were being ushered out. Training was about to begin, and John could tell himself that what was said a moment earlier had been a misunderstanding. A joke that didn't land.

After, the boys congregated around Studzy's Peugeot 206. No one speaking, all four contemplative. Collecting their thoughts from the exhausted crackle in their brains: that was what it felt like for John anyway, a toning-down of a thrumming racket and his own voice resurfacing. Around them, cars reversed and growled in first gear and the flinging of gravel as if from invisible hands. Rain, still falling. It was probably cold out, but John didn't feel it. His body coursed with adrenaline and he felt only a twitchiness. A desire to touch and grab. His mother was parked up already, and he had implied by a succession of finger motions and dour pouting that she should stall a couple of minutes so that the boys could have this important discussion.

Studzy was in the driver's seat with the door wide open. There was a pink towel underneath him, and the rectangle interior light cast a jaundiced tint to his pale face. They were here to coordinate Saturday: to figure what heads were around and the girls who might join and the venue for the drinking. It was a sticky situation as some of the boys had turned eighteen while others hadn't, and so were, technically speaking, cheating everyone else out of better fun in nightclubs. John and Tony were in this latter group of swindlers, and it was Tony who spoke now: 'I definitely have the free gaff. The rents are heading off. So there's an option for Saturday.'

Rooney shrugged. 'I'm game for that.' Rooney was eighteen, as was Studzy.

Studzy muttered, 'Sound, sound.' He was gazing out the front of the car as if driving.

John asked who was about? A list of names from Tony and five of them were girls, which was reduced promptly to four as Rooney corrected that Karen was away and Studzy interrupted, 'When you eighteen again, Tone?'

Tony answered, 'In a week. The tenth.'

'Right,' Studzy said. 'Right. Nice one.'

Rooney was picking at the grass wedged between the blades on his boots – right foot first and onto left – and

John faked an interest in this tidying until Studzy said what John knew he was going to say: 'What about you, Tits? You're in September, aren't you?'

John said he was, yeah. The fourth of September and Studzy's knuckles began to tap the wheel. 'Look. No offence, but I'm sick of house parties,' Studzy said. 'We need to be clubbing this summer, like. We're not a bunch of fuckin losers.' He sat back in the seat and his hands went behind his head like an approximation of calm and relaxed and not severely irritated. 'Both times I was in Clowns with the brother were outrageous. The tunes, man. And there were these poles that you could, like, dance around. And then the second time, they had these foam guns. You got shot with foam when you came inside. Honestly, it's just better, lads. And I beg you. The birds.' Studzy met their eyes one by one. 'The birds in there. I genuinely beg.'

John understood that what Studzy said now was a thousand per cent true. Nightclubs were superior. Nightclubs were where they ought to be this summer. It was undoubtedly true despite John not having wandered inside a nightclub in his life, it was true despite John having only been refused gruffly from Clowns in Castlebar after their graduation ceremony in May and witnessing, in the proceeding scrimmage, only a tantalising glimpse of what might lurk inside: stairs lit up by silvery discs in the floor, and music, and tanned legs beneath skirts that were universally short, legs that seemed as if they might stain your fingertips if you so touched them, legs that soon disappeared up the stairs with the littlest clicks so that John caught a final forlorn peek of a glitzy high heel and a sticker unpeeled from its sole as he was being shoved away and warned for the last time, by the surly bouncer, to piss off from around there.

Rooney went, 'It's not John's fault he isn't eighteen.'

Studzy looked up at Rooney. 'Yeah, I know. I'm not having a go at him.'

Studzy looked at John. 'I'm not having a go at you, Tits.'

'It sounded like you were,' Rooney said. His longish hair was matted and black from the wet. On his chin there was a cluster of pimples and Rooney currently itched at this area with four curled fingers.

'Well, I wasn't,' Studzy replied tersely. 'So I don't know what your deal is.'

Rooney and Studzy had never got on: palpable tension when left with only the two of them, furtive remarks about the other, the most inane squabbles that lingered and soured lunches and FIFA tournaments and entire nights out. It was simple geography that strung Rooney and Studzy together. The Island was small. The number of heads you could knock about with were smaller still. What were they meant to do?

To Tony, Studzy now appealed, 'I'm only saying we need to suss an ID for Tits. That's it. We can't wait till September to go clubbing. You'll all be gone off then, like.'

Studzy said to John, 'Isn't that not fair enough?'

'No, I get you,' John said, and why wouldn't his head stop nodding? 'It makes sense to me. I agree.' Nod, nod, nod. 'I need a fake ID.' Nod nod nod. 'And I have been asking around for a lend of one. There's a lad I know in the hotel who's the image of me' – who this was wasn't clear to John as he was saying it, and only now, as he allowed a silence to enhance his point, did John think who this could be: Hughie Denton – 'And I asked him, actually. He said he'd get back to me by next week. Fingers crossed.' This was another peculiar lie but – John could immediately intuit – a tranquilising one.

Hughie had sandy hair, freckles everywhere, but he was twenty and John did kind of know him.

'That's us sorted so,' Tony announced, and the boys were muttering agreement, positivity, and then all at once everyone was calling out a form of goodbye and John was splashing towards his mother who had the car's full beams on, so he was forced to shield his eyes from its blinding glare.

At home and Amber had texted: 'Heya x'

What to say back, how to reply, and eventually John wrote to her – 'Well xxx Wat u at?' – and Amber texted back right away – 'watching friendzzz x What u doing?' – though he only saw this text after his shower and so Amber had also sent a follow-up message.

The follow up read: 'Hulloooo?????' Johnnnn??'

Downstairs, the TV. Voices, but muffled as if speaking through a cloth.

It was after half nine.

He was towelled and dripping and evaluating his next reply – John had provisionally written, 'Which ep of friends? Joey is a legend… How you DOIN? Haha xxx' – when Amber broke order for the second time by texting: 'landline? x'

John responded immediately: 'Two mins xxx'

He eased down the stairs and shouted into the living room that he was taking the hands-free phone. 'Tony,' John explained without being asked to explain, 'wants to chat about something. I don't know what. But, yeah. I need the phone.' Yvonne turned her head from the TV. 'You want my permission for that, is it?'

'No. I'm just telling you.' He stood in the hallway. Yvonne had her shoes off and her feet tucked up under her and John now spoke as if offended: 'I'm trying to be a thoughtful son. That's all, Mammy.'

'Wow. Thank you.'

She turned back to the TV. 'My thoughtful son. Amn't I a lucky duck?'

John collected the hands-free from her – their – bedroom before striding into the kitchen. He shut the doors and sat at the table. He took a deep breath. He practised saying a couple of words aloud to make sure his voice sounded alright: low but not croaky. Then he tested whether he could pull off certain slick phrases and expressions. E.g.,

'You wanted to talk to me, kid?', 'Well, smell', 'What you been going at?'

He texted Amber: 'Ready'

Then he wrote: 'You call tho'

The phone rang at most ten seconds later.

'Why are you so paranoid about ringing me?' It was Amber's voice. Unfazed. 'You know it was you who started this. Land*line*, land*line*. And now I have to be the one to ring you.'

He smiled into the receiver. 'I'm not paranoid, like. Just making you work for it.' A spike of laughter at that – you couldn't predict which joke would land safely and which would crash in a fiery ball – and John smiled some more. It was nice to hear her voice and nicer to hear her laugh. She said his name but kind of wistfully, and, emboldened, John went, 'You up to much this evening, kid?'

'I have been up to loads and loads,' she said. 'But I can't tell you, kid. Top secret, kid.' Now he laughed into the phone involuntarily. She sipped something – he heard a distinct slurp. 'But I can tell you what Samantha did this afternoon?'

'Go on,' John said, suddenly eager.

Her story was about a mix-up in the formatting of the tables for an incoming tour. The middle section was not meant to be used, or only half of the middle was meant to be used – it was confusing to John over the phone so he could imagine why it was confusing in person – but Samantha had set the whole middle of the restaurant. Ethan had got involved, Ethan had been a dick, and in the end,

Amber had had to stay behind for forty-five minutes fixing it. The story didn't mean anything beyond the phone call, it didn't have a punchline, and still John would have liked for it to go on and on.

'So,' Amber said, 'Samantha is either a thicko or she wants to get me fired. Or maybe both.'

'That's bad form, like,' John said, and Amber agreed with a throaty sound, and so he added, 'I hate Samantha. She's really annoying. So, I empathise.'

Amber smiled at this – John could hear it, and so he pictured it and it was lovely to picture with the phone perhaps trapped between her shoulder and ear – and she said, 'I don't believe you, John. But thanks. Anyway. You had training?'

John told Amber all about it. The numbers attending, the drills and how he fared in each, and then he described the team's new counterattacking tactics and felt it was paramount he explained how defending changed once a third man midfielder was introduced and he was hearing himself by this stage as if on a radio phone-in – a caller obsessed and simultaneously furious at their own obsession – and it sounded nerdy, dull. It was an error to have embarked on such a tangent.

'Yeah, no,' John said in blunt conclusion, 'that was training. Sorry to go on. It's not that interesting. I don't know why I went on. Sorry.'

'No,' she replied. 'It sounded fun, I guess?' In the darkened glaze of the kitchen window John saw himself: arched forward with a hand roving through his still-wet hair, the phone almost in his mouth, a gruesome and stupid and unskilled boy. He craned his neck until the reflected head was decapitated by the window's frame.

Amber said, 'Do you think you'll start for the next game or whatever?'

He looked from the window to the cabinets, then to his left hand, which was itching the table. 'Probably not, no. But there hasn't been any proper matches played since I started up with them. So. I can't say for sure.' He lifted the left hand to bite at a thumbnail that was already bitten so his mouth mostly chomped at nubby skin. 'I only joined up with the team so I suppose I probably shouldn't be starting. By rights. You have to understand that, Amber? I'm not expected to start by any account. It's senior, like.'

'I understand, John.' She laughed and then she said, clearly amused, clearly riling him, 'Touchy, aren't we? About your little team.'

'I'm not touchy at all, actually,' he said, which was a very touchy reply. 'You don't have a clue about football, so I'm trying to inform you.'

'Inform?' she said.

'Yeah.'

Laughter but not near to the receiver. Trailing away from the receiver.

'Why you laughing?'

'No reason,' she said. 'No reason at all.'

He didn't respond. Bits of skin in his mouth and they tasted of nothing, like how communion tasted of nothing.

She said, 'You're very funny, John. Do you know that?'

After a moment he said, 'Okay.'

The noise of her in a fit of laughing at this too – unhinged, like a hysterical joke at the back of class that you are not privy to – and Amber said something more but while still laughing so it was hard to grasp and John shut his eyes and said, 'What are you on about, Amber?'

'I said.' Still the trickle of amusement in her voice. 'Have I really annoyed you?'

'I'm not annoyed,' he said.

'Aw. I'm sorry,' she said, and John stressed again that he wasn't annoyed. Silence and John could hear a rustling from her end and someone chirping that could have been a TV or radio rather than a person. He thought she lived alone, or as in alone with her father, but he didn't know for definite, and it was possible Amber had siblings, even housemates, even a dog – he had no notion though he was fairly positive there was no mother. He had never asked plainly about this, but Amber had never referenced a mother. Under her breath, Amber now sang: 'Gas, gas,' and John said, all of a sudden, 'Actually, Amber. Do you know Enda McNamara?'

There was a thump from her end, a door closing maybe. 'I don't think so. Why? Who's that?'

'He's my friend. You must know him? He's from around here.' John felt he spoke casually. 'Studzy is his nickname.

You might have heard of him as Studzy rather than Enda. Everyone knows Studzy, like.' No response and John considered and said, 'He has an older brother who's around your age, I think? Steven is the brother's name. Steven McNamara.' John waited a second and then he asked, 'Do you know him?'

'I do,' she answered flatly. 'Steven is a prick.' Real venom when she said this. 'Why are you asking me about this guy, John? He's your friend. I don't care.'

'I was just asking if you knew him. No malice. And yeah, Studzy's brother is a dick, I agree, but Studzy's not like that at all. Studzy's a good guy.' John said, quicker, 'There's no malice.'

Amber broke in: 'But why are you asking me about him?'

There was a sizzling. Or no, a sound like a pool cue being chalked. Then a click. A drawn-out breath that was noticeably strangled as it went along and was Amber weeping in that near-silent, distraught way girls weep as if their faces are crumbling? John cleared his throat. 'Honestly, Studzy's not like the brother, Amber. You'd like Studzy if you—'

Amber said, 'Hi?'

'What?' John was puzzled, raised his voice a pitch. 'Can you hear me?'

The phone replied cheerfully, 'I can hear you.'

'Hello,' the phone said again, and John snapped, 'Mam. Get off.'

'John, it's quarter past ten and I need the—'

'Get off now, Mam.'

'—phone.'

Amber was giggling.

Yvonne said knowingly, 'That doesn't sound like Tony.'

John said, 'I'm serious.'

Yvonne went on, 'Well, I'm serious too. You can call your girlfriend back tomorrow.'

'Mam. I swear.'

Amber said, 'It's lovely to meet you, Mrs Masterson.'

'Amber. Stop.' John found he was on his feet.

'Amber, is it?' Yvonne said and said it again as if testing it out. 'He never told me a bit—'

Amber laughing her head off.

John spoke: 'Amber. Hang up.'

'—about you,' Yvonne said. 'Are you from around here?'

'Amber,' John said and his hand sweeping through his hair.

'I am,' Amber replied. 'Do you want me to visit you sometime?'

'Amber,' John said close to a shout. 'Hang up. Please.'

'You'd be more than welco—'

'Alright, alright.' Amber was still laughing. The pronounced click of a receiver being set down. A single beep, the line was disconnected.

'That's a shame,' Yvonne said after a moment.

John said, 'Why did you do that?'

John shook his head. 'For fucksake.'

He stormed out of the kitchen and still talked into the hands-free despite his mother being down the hall: 'I can't believe you did that to me.'

'Oh, will you relax,' she said. 'Now give that phone into me—'

He wanted to hurl the hands-free at the wall or fling it into the gorse bush across the road or grind his heel into the phone until it was blocky silicon chips and split-ended wires and tiny screws. John wanted to do all this as he let the hands-free fall onto the unoccupied armchair in the living room – careful not to accord Yvonne even a scornful glance – and raced up the stairs. He slammed his bedroom door and for a minute straight began to stamp on a specific spot in his room: where there was a depression in the carpet, and periodically a yelp from a wonky plank. The injustice and the trampling upon his human rights and imagine if he invaded his mother's private conversations and imagine and how could she do that? He was angry, seething. Breathing through his nose. Bitch. He said aloud, 'Fuckin bitch.' Both of them were pathetic. Both his mam and dad. They were intent on ruining his life after ruining their own. But it will be his pleasure to turn his back on them come September. To leave them here alone to wallow, die. They deserved each other because they were pathetic fuckin rude bastards.

He went and stamped on the depressed spot again.

Once, four times.

She shouted up and he opened the door an inch to snarl down his central, trouncing argument: 'Imagine if I done that to you, Mam? If you were on the phone and I picked it up.'

He heard his own hot and desperate and snotty voice, and a part of him cringed, which naturally defused his furore somewhat. It was no good to hear yourself talk, worser still to hear yourself sob or rage.

Coldly, his mother said, 'John. I'm warning you.'

He shut the door and flopped onto the bed and then got up and unlatched the window. He felt the air like a damp cloth against his face, listened to the night's indifferent stillness, and into it he asked, 'Why are they always out to get me?'

The stillness continued.

A neighbour's upstairs light switched on and off.

The hedges at the back of the garden stirred.

The smell of incoming rain: metallic, coiny, but also dug-up earth like soil beneath your fingernails. John went to touch his pocket and only realised then that the familiar weight was absent. Realised he had left his mobile on the kitchen table.

Into the nightgloom, John now said: 'Fuck.'

He tiptoed down the stairs and through the hall and she was in the kitchen: of course she was. 'Your girlfriend seemed very nice,' she said to him, and he reddened, hastened his steps after seizing the phone from the table. Over his shoulder came: 'Goodnight, my thoughtful son.'

At a terrible angle as if the screen might spit in his face, John eventually looked at his phone.

There were five messages. All from the same contact: Amber Work.

'hahahaha'

'hahahahahahahah'

'Dying here. Love ur mam so much!!!'

'hahahah. Don't be mad it was gas'

'hahahaaaaaaaaaaaaaa still can't believe that happened'

Another message from the same contact arrived while John was perusing these messages once more and smiling widely.

The sixth message read: 'don't be mad at me xxx'

Saturday, 4th July

He was up at quarter to nine and scraped crust from beneath his eyelids and was now wheeling his bike from the shed. He was cycling this morning since training, the practice match, was happening on the old pitch by the Sound, just over the road, practically next door, so no point drive. The sun pouring down and he leaned the bike against the wall by the front, rechecked his gearbag: he had packed a towel, yes, and there were the boots, good. The air tasted ripe, imbued with this clean newness, and it evoked in John a memory: ripping open a packaged Action Man doll and undressing the tiny clothes to sniff at the nude-coloured unblemished plastic. The sun was to his right: a white circle with oily feathers. Dew on green things, sparkling. Everything alive this morning. Then John was pedalling.

At the church.

And there was the bulk of Sweeney's Supermarket and presently the bridge seemed to wobble as John tilted forward to pump his legs for no reason other than that he could pedal faster. Now he was speeding by Alice's Bar and Restaurant and up the last incline – two extra pumps and his momentum carried him thereafter – and a glimpse of the tin roof of the stand and there was the pitch. A profusion of white daisies amid the grass and chalked lines and the strong smell of pollen and petrol and he was ahead of his own elongated shadow and excited. The spools of his wheels swishing. The purr of his tyres. He lifted his right arm to signal right turn despite there being no one behind him. John was excited to play ball.

The practice match was twelve on twelve rather than the normal fifteen. Bibs against non-bibs with rolling subs. Barrett picked the teams and once everyone was roughly in position, Barrett pitched the ball out to the lefthand side and the game had begun.

In a bib that stank of curdled sweat, a bib that clung a little too snugly to his tits, John started as a corner-back marking Oisín Hanley.

Hanley scored the first point of the game after a nifty one-two with the midfielder Raymond Cooney with no real chance for John to intervene.

Hanley scored the second point of the game after John dived in following a handpass that dropped short. It was a split-second decision. John had banked on his upper-body strength and the ponderous nature of the pass – the ball fumbling along the turf rather than zipping – but to his surprise and dismay, Hanley easily palmed him off with a stiffened arm, flicking the ball upwards with his left foot before popping it over the bar with minimal fuss.

Barrett roared, 'Up it, Masterson. Will you up it, for god's sake.'

After ten minutes, John was switched to his preferred half-back role.

John did well there, he felt. Or at least better.

He was subbed off for the last five minutes of the first half.

Barrett gave him a brief pat on the back and Ultan produced a water bottle from his tracksuit pocket as if it was contraband. John unscrewed the lid – germs – and sipped and sought to quell his breathing, reduce its volume and frequency. The perceptible effect of strain and effort and he did not want this measured unfavourably by Barrett. With his wrist, John wiped at his forehead and the snaking droplets of sweat. Around him, the noise of feet pattering and half-completed yelps for a pass. The inflection of delirious, hostile argument though there were no arguments. The compact clatter of bodies meeting, bodies skirting by one another. Everyone on the pitch moving in some way. By the railings on the opposite side, long yellow weeds trembled and there was his father, Peter, watching with his arms crossed: a covert salute from John and it was returned.

At half time, Barrett encouraged fluids. He clapped in recognition for the desire and hunger. The score was irrelevant, Barrett stressed, and yet John knew that the bibs were losing by four points. 'There is one league match remaining,' Barrett said, 'and then we're staring into Championship. Right down the barrel.'

Players nodded, hands on hips.

Players shook out thighs, hamstrings and the visible quiver of muscle like contours on a map.

Barrett looked at a different row of bowed heads. 'A sweltering day like today, it will be standing to us for Championship, lads.'

After a couple of minutes spectating the second half, John was absurdly brought back on as a forward. 'Give it a lash,' was the extent of the instruction Barrett imparted. John was marked by Spain Jersey – a fat vein throbbing on Spain Jersey's temple like a worm – and John was blank about how to play a game that he had routinely played since he was eight years old.

The ball was caught up around the midfield and John started to jog towards this action and was howled at by Ultan to stay inside. So John sprinted vigorously towards the goals, waving his arms, and the ball wasn't punted in despite four separate runs, with Spain Jersey hissing a length behind him in each instance.

The bibs relinquished the ball – a fist from Tony as Raymond Cooney sought to solo by him – and the non-bibs were on the attack and the ball was being fed into DJ.

Non-bibs scored.

Scored again from a mix-up in the subsequent kick-out.

Another score.

Then as John was manoeuvring between the sideline and the square – John figured this was what was known as lively attacking movement – the ball was thumped his way. A frivolous hit and hope. Over the heads of the half-forwards. High and climbing. In the July sun, the ball was rimmed violently, then blurred to a mauve colour, then hoary, and then it was that familiar white once more, like a button had been done on a blue shirt. It landed around the twenty metre line, bouncing nicely before hitting a divot and flying up and a dust cloud after it.

John was immediately galloping towards the ball.

Spain Jersey was slow reacting.

Spain Jersey wasn't any way tight or near as John leaped and grasped the ball and still John shimmied as if Spain Jersey was tight, near. He was half turned towards the goals, the ball clasped in both hands. Straight away a voice cried for a pass – from the corner of his eye, John saw it was Eoghan Moloney with a single arm raised – but the posts stood clean and tall and appetising in front of John. Where he stood was a favourable angle for a right footer. No wind to negotiate. Spain Jersey miles off still. And not much precision required for the shot: distance was the sole concern and even that wasn't a concern as long as John kicked through. Imagine: a point scored when John wasn't a forward and how that might drastically improve his odds of starting Championship? Imagine. John's feet were already making teeny adjustments for a strike that he had yet to consciously determine to take on. Moloney was still calling for the pass, more desperate, more like a bark than words. Spain Jersey bearing down. The sun on John's neck, and sweat like small bitty plasters all over his skin. Only now was the decision formally settled in John's mind: I will take on this shot to fuck. His left foot planted. Not quite slow motion but everything marginally slower. Concentration centred on the ball and the kicking thereof. No wind. Easy-peasy angle. The ball slipping through his palms almost like he didn't want to let it slip. A glance up: the final check of the posts. Then his right leg becoming bent. His head craned forward and over a ball that was slipping free. All this happening. A lever shifted in his brain and the body undertook everything by itself. The ball freely floating in the air and his right leg in full swing. The distance: not far. The angle: very doable. His boot's connection meaty, on the laces, but perhaps the contact was not totally sweet: no tingly vibration afterwards along his foot like electricity. But the distance was not far, the angle more than doable.

John's foot above his hip, above his own tits, toes presently in line with his chin.

Spain Jersey lunging to block the kick, but out of performance rather than expectation.

A flare of pure white in his right eye as the ball travelled through air and blue.

The trajectory of the ball swerving slightly, wrongly.

John was on a single leg, hopping. Then he was on his two feet again and retreating from where he'd taken the shot, short backwards steps.

A grimace on his face.

A clench of teeth as the ball arrowed to the right of the post and wide.

Well, well wide.

He waited by Meagher's Garage, hunched on the kerb with a foot shaking up and down but not quite tapping the tarmac. By the edge of the forecourt sagged a lone palm tree. Five minutes now waiting for Studzy, and John checked his phone.

No missed calls and there was no text from Amber either. John had messaged Amber first yesterday so he knew he shouldn't do so again today. John was adamant, in fact. There were distinct rules and John was vaguely aware of some of them.

He put the phone away.

A yellow reg zoomed by and John thought, passively: English wanker.

It was still hot but not as unbearably so as this morning. Milder. A breeze like somebody breathing close behind you in a queue. John had an olive bomber jacket bundled under his arm. He was in white Lacoste runners with frustratingly dirtied laces. John's facial expression was set to pensive and displeased – lips apart, left cheek angled towards left shoulder – because Studzy had alerted John that he was collecting Audrey Irwin and Orlagh Landey and this face was, in John's own opinion, his most appealing face. John didn't desire to shift these two girls or anything – John considered them first and foremost his friends – but he also wouldn't want to rule the prospect out totally and so initial facial impressions were key.

First impressions was also why, when the Peugeot eventually pulled up – driver's window down, a loud fisted honk even though John was already lumbering to his feet – John sashayed towards it with lopsided steps and eyes scanning either side of him, as if there might lurk some would-be assailant. For this, in John's own opinion, was his most appealing gait.

'Well,' John exclaimed through the window, and once sat inside, spoke to the back of the car, 'Well well well.'

Studzy didn't respond verbally but shot John a Hawaiian thumbs up. The Ronaldinho trademark.

Orlagh said, 'Hey, John.'

Audrey nodded while clicking on her phone. Then looked up but said nothing.

Orlagh was a ginger and today her hair was lank, but likely on purpose – straightened or whatever. Acne pitted her chin and she often covered this chin when in photos by placing a finger-gun across it, and she had a pretty smile, albeit with too much gum and too-tiny teeth, so kind of like a piranha when she opened her mouth despite it being, all in all, a really pretty smile. Orlagh was unanimously declared the soundest girl by the boys. Chatting to Orlagh was the same as chatting to one of the lads: they all agreed and respected Orlagh enormously for this.

Audrey was shortish and sallow with these disconcerting green eyes that she adorned with thick, arrow-ended mascara. Her mother was from somewhere not Ireland. She had a pin in her nostril, a new ring through the middle of her nose, and was the first girl in John's year to have her belly button pierced and was suspended for not covering it up during PE. Audrey was the best at art in the school, the only one who was talented beyond being competent at straight lines and tracing: Audrey's stippled drawing of a hand holding a pencil for the Leaving Cert practical was, as John said at the time, unbelievable and so like a real physical hand. Art was what Audrey was doing next: a college in London, a course then a degree, and John envied her steadfast assurance in this future.

John's mother knew Audrey, for Audrey had tagged along to the art classes in the Sound since she was thirteen. 'A smart cookie' was how Yvonne described her. Then also: 'a tough cookie'.

Both girls were dressed for out out. Audrey was in a lace shirt and these ballet pumps with little knots. A cardigan was folded on Orlagh's lap, and she wore a dotted sleeveless top with a neckline that revealed the chalky V of her boobs. Between the girls' legs was a pair of plastic bags that were weighed down by alcohol. Studzy had gone offie.

The car glided to the edge of the forecourt before the ticking sound and it swung out.

John squirmed in his seat. 'Orlagh.' A performative tut, then: 'I thought you said you weren't coming today.'

'Yeah, well. I wasn't going to,' Orlagh said. She was peering out the window. Sunlight fell on the crack between her boobs, whitening it further, and John instructed himself to look up. 'I'm opening at nine tomorrow,' Orlagh went on, 'but. Fuck it. We mightn't get another chance to trash Tony Dineen's house.' Easy laughter at this and Studzy said he was planning to take a huge dump upstairs in Tony's – 'clog the toilet, like' – which made John cough and laugh and the girls groan as they couldn't openly giggle at such crudeness.

Ahead, the road was sizzling, a heat haze atop it like a rainbow liquefied and spilled. 'I was thinking actually,' John said, and he looked across at Studzy. 'Do you reckon Tony will pop his, fuckin, cherry before heading to college?'

Audrey made a snorty sound.

Studzy was laughing.

'That's so mean, John,' Orlagh said, and shook her head, but John felt confident the gag had landed and so he said, 'I'm only messing.'

Studzy glanced in the rearview mirror. 'You'd nearly have a go on Tony yourself, Orlagh?' John giggling now as Studzy took over proceedings. 'It'd be very nice by you. Lad needs the confidence boost.'

'You guys are gross,' Orlagh said and faced out the window, but smiling.

'If you are so concerned,' Audrey said, and she leaned forward between the front seats, 'why don't you ride him, Enda?'

Hard laughter at this. Studzy muttered, muttered something else, and then went, 'I might so, Audrey. Thanks for the idea.'

'Fuckin Tony,' John said, which meant nothing and yet successfully enhanced the giddy atmosphere.

John had kissed Orlagh at a disco years ago. His first ever kiss. Nearly fifteen and terrified and Orlagh had braces at the time and John had learned from a newspaper's advice column how to appropriately smooch, that a tongue was supposed to mimic a delicate butterfly when thrust inside someone else's gob, and so in the course of their three-minute shift – his hands hovering above the rhinestone belt wound around Orlagh's denim skirt – John regularly brushed against Orlagh's dental wires as he spun his tongue round and round, like a delicate butterfly. Nothing amorous had ever happened between John and Audrey: he might have queried a shift at the same disco, but you pretty much asked the wall to shift you at that disco.

Studzy had shifted Orlagh on numerous occasions – most recently at Christmas, and there had been some texting afterwards which went nowhere beyond a fruitless drive in this car, Studzy had disclosed this particular non-event to the boys with his head in his hands, and John hadn't been sure if Studzy was fooling around or not. And Studzy had completed the full deed with Audrey while bushing last summer: John recalled them climbing a gate together and everyone squawking as these two figures blended into the blue darkness and then everyone forgetting about them until someone sought to borrow tobacco from Audrey.

These weren't boasts, or the root of present awkwardness and sensitivity: no, they were simple facts.

John could list what every girl in his year had given out and to who.

John could recite what exactly each of the lads had done and hadn't done and additionally – if pressed, if given a minute to work it out – where and when it had occurred and if the girl was nice or a dirt.

Sex was a league table. Active. Ever fluctuating. The context for victories being revised as you aged and what was attainable changed: from texting and kissing with tongues to the ladder steps of fingering and handjobs and blowjobs to the current supremacy of feeking, fucking, riding.

It was embarrassing to be languishing in the bottom half of this table. Mortifying. For example, to not have had your crotch squeezed even briefly by a hand with painted fingernails at this stage meant you were hopeless, a pathetic ugly disgrace. To be at the bottom was to be riddled with self-disgust and self-doubt and, most of all, hate. However, this hate wasn't directed towards the girls – why would they go near you, realistically? – nor was it charged at the bucks towering above, rather it was that you hated how desperately you yearned to be those boys and to be with those girls: you'd swap places in an instant, you'd trade in your life for theirs with no questions or regrets or sorrow. You'd take being a general grade A thicko like the terrifying Aaron English over being untouched by girls. How sad was that? How fucked? But the oddest thing was – John now understood – it was equally troubling to be orbiting the top. From this lofty vantage, you anguished over being superseded, over an accomplishment being toppled, over the triumph of a stuck-in finger becoming mouldy and dried up and all of a sudden redundant. The dread of sliding to the bottom was nearly as bad as the reality of stewing down there.

Nearly.

Prior to Seóna, John hadn't been the butt of jokes or anything remotely traumatic like that. Yet still John felt a clench in his chest during huddled exchanges about the ins and outs of girls. This cold chain tightening around his heart and lungs as accomplishments were detailed gorily. A fear would seize him that at any moment he could become the joke, he could be strung up for being a pitiful virgin, for his unfucking and unfeltness, for kissing nobody special in the time since those randy discos had become something for the kiddies they no longer were. No matter that there were other docile boys in and around the group that had undertaken substantially less than John: before Seóna, John had fingered a fresh called Hazel Canning at the disco and secured a handjob outside the pants from Hazel in return, or at least Hazel had scrubbed her open palm against his fly for twenty hot seconds. And never mind that John was good at sports so was shielded from attacks to a greater extent than those who didn't seem capable of fathoming the circumference of a ball – protection that Tony wielded to this day – it made no difference to John's brain. Logic and rationality offered spits: the terror wouldn't evaporate. John would be called out sooner rather than later. John would be shown as abnormal.

But then Seóna had flaked a pen at John's head one drab Tuesday, and her best friend Louise Conway said to John a week later that Seóna mightn't complain if he texted her one evening – you know that, right? – and slowly, surely, John's disquiet began to drain.

So, yes, John loved Seóna to death, yes, he still pined for her, but John also loved what she had granted him abstractly. She was a method to confirm he was better than most.

Tony's house was out in Polranny. Up a zigzagging road, halfway up a brown and craggy mountain basically, and there it was: a two-storey gaff with a cattle grid. The house was painted yellow with brown windowsills. A Mayo flag fluttered in the middle of a crescent of mulch in the front garden. Studzy parked around the rear of the house and Rooney, sitting in a white deckchair by the backdoor, indicated where Studzy should throw the car while collaring Guinness, Tony's golden retriever.

Rooney was in a buttoned cardigan with luminous yellow lining and the grey loafers from the rack aside the till in Topman. His legs were crossed at the ankles and his cheeks were blotchy, which was attributable to the cans beneath his chair and the green bottle in his hand. John dropped one of the plastic bags beside Rooney and another atop a free deckchair and only now did John seek to actively investigate their contents: a box of Bulmers, three cans of Karpackie, and an eight-pack of Dutch Gold. It was too much drink but was precisely what they required. Rooney greeted Audrey and Orlagh and they brightly asked after Karen before they headed inside. Tony had not invited Seóna today – loyalty – though John had heard Seóna was in Spain with her family so wasn't around anyway.

Rooney passed John a bottle of beer and John sat beside him.

They clinked bottles and Rooney seemed about to say something but didn't. Tinny music coming through the unlatched kitchen window: John only caught it now. It was Rooney's sort of music, grungy, heavier than the stuff John secretly liked, and John could foresee it being changed shortly by one of the girls, or Studzy: which might prove prickly.

John took a sip of the beer, and it tasted the same as every other beer: licked carpet.

It was coming up to five o'clock.

Over the next hour boys began to show up and each entrance provoked greater excitement amongst those already in attendance: like a gearstick shoved to faster numbers. At half six, the rest of the girls landed all at once: five of them clambering out of a jeep. Among this lot – who hobbled confidently by the boys and into the house without pause – was Louise Conway, Seóna's bestie. John spotted her and glared at his phone as she strode past.

There was awkwardness and frostiness between him and Louise Conway because it was awkward and frosty between him and Seóna.

By seven, everyone Tony had invited had arrived plus a handful of stragglers he hadn't, and by half seven, those inside were mingling with those outside in small squawking clusters. The music had long been switched to rap and YouTube remixes. The smell of aftershave and cigarettes and strawberries from the girls and their glossed lips, but also the warmth and earthiness of fresh dog shit because someone had trod in poo but hadn't confessed and instead dragged it clean in sections on the ridged ends of the patio. John was still sitting beside Rooney, and across from them now was Audrey, who was fashioning a rollie. Rooney was telling them – well, telling Audrey – about his plans for September. Rooney wanted Galway, but he mostly wanted to be off the Island. John was half listening. He had heard all this before. Rooney despised the Island. Rooney believed anyone who stayed around was a loser plain and easy, and probably also had worms in their brains. Every few moments, Audrey would glance up from her fiddly handiwork and nod at Rooney to signify attentiveness and only then would John spy the white filter in the corner of her mouth. Rooney said, 'I think. Like. Galway is a buzz. You get me?' Behind John, a cohort of boys were earnestly ranking their top three movies ever: *The Dark Knight*, *Shawshank Redemption*, *Gladiator*, and then whines for the inclusion of *Scarface*. A thought struck John: how would they rate Amber? Would she be that much lower than Seóna? Rooney was saying, 'And Karen can visit all the time.' John drained the bitter ends of his can and he was admittedly a tad buzzed by this stage, the world shifting and sliding ever so slightly like a hand beneath a sheet, and Amber had still not texted him and John was wondering who he might go talk to next when Audrey said, 'What about you, John?'

A beat and John said, 'What?'

Audrey grinned. 'Where you going next?'

'Do you mean for college?' John asked and Audrey lifted her eyebrows at him to signal yeah clearly, and John said, faster, 'Galway. I applied for college there. So. Hopefully Galway.'

Audrey's attention had returned to her thumb and index finger shaping the thin paper and bitty strands of tobacco, so like razored pubes on bathroom tile, and she brought this paper to her lips now and sealed it shut. There was a yellow pouch on her lap. An orange lighter.

John tugged his T-shirt from his stomach, and then added, 'Galway's meant to be fun. That's what everyone says.'

'That's legitimately what they say about Galway, man.' Rooney yawned and then tipped his can vertically to his gob.

The rollie was lit and to Audrey's mouth, indulged, smouldering, and then caught between two fingers away from her mouth. Audrey lifted herself up from the seat and pocketed the lighter and then crossed her legs. 'What will you study there?' She grinned again. 'In *Galway*.'

'Oh, like, general arts,' John said, and this didn't seem to satisfy her. 'So, I suppose I'll probably study English and History. Philosophy maybe? I'm not fully sure yet. But, yeah.'

'Will you be able to study art?' Audrey asked.

Was this genuine interest or was Audrey mocking him or was she merely trying to steer clear of Rooney, who had a habit of being intense when drunk and liable to weep over a dead cousin he never mentioned otherwise? John couldn't tell and so he thought it prudent to joke. John thought it safer. 'Nah, sure what would I be doing with art? I'm no Picasso.' He looked aside at Rooney. 'I'm almost as crap as Studzy.' John laughed, but Audrey didn't.

Audrey exhaled smoke and her wrist dropped limp when the rollie was not in use. 'Do you not like art history, even? Cause you're good at it. Your essays are amazing. You know they are.'

'No, I like that part of it alright, the writing about stuff and context, but what can you do with it? You know, afterwards. Is there such a thing as an art historian?' A nervous chuckle from John's mouth and Audrey answered, 'Yeah. There is such a thing as an art historian.'

'I know,' John said, and he grimaced. 'I know but. It's kind of an impossible career, isn't it? Improbable, like.' He looked for support from Rooney, or at least a distraction, but Rooney was picking through his phone with a scowl.

'You should probably go somewhere where you can do art history,' Audrey said then. 'If you like it.' She shrugged at him, and John shrugged back. 'Or at least that's what I think.' She leaned forward to put the end of her rollie into a cider can. 'It's your life.'

That same nervous chuckle from John's mouth: a bicycle tyre being manually pumped, it sounded kind of like that. 'Yeah. I don't know,' John said finally, and Audrey said nothing but played with the flap of her yellow pouch of tobacco. John said once more, 'I don't know, Audrey. I haven't thought about it.'

Then someone was shouting. Someone shouting at them, seemingly.

John checked over his shoulder, a relief to do so.

It was Orlagh Landey. Unsteady across the patio. Her hair was different though John couldn't pinpoint how exactly other than it was different. 'Audrey,' she called as she crouched behind Audrey's chair and hugged her neck. 'I've been looking for you.'

Then Orlagh let go of Audrey and shot up straight. 'Can we go inside? I'm freezing.'

Audrey said sure, and Orlagh looked at John, blinked as if she didn't recognise him, and then cried his name like a song.

John was on surer footing here, and he replied, 'You're on it, kid.'

Orlagh brought a finger to her lips, laughing.

Rooney glanced up from his phone. 'Who's on it?'

Audrey dusted her lap, stood and answered, 'You.' She linked arms with Orlagh and started to head for the back-door and then Audrey turned around and her face was all pitying, aslant, and John's stomach dropped before Audrey had even asked the question: 'How's your mam?'

'Good, yeah, she's fine,' John said, and he drank from his empty can. 'She's grand.' Audrey seemed to expect more, or at least her expression remained solemn, and John said to this expression, 'It's fucked up, I don't know.'

Audrey nodded once. 'I can imagine.'

'I don't think you can, actually,' John snapped, and he was surprised.

After a moment, Audrey said, 'Well, tell her I was asking for her. Your mam and those Dutch headcases were always nice to me.' John nodded and he watched them both waddle inside with a queasy feeling of regret in his stomach. But why? He pitched the empty can into the flowerbed to his left. A line of blood orange sprawled itself across the underside of the sky. Snippets of conversations swirled around, mostly unintelligible but then sometimes not, like a phone suddenly finding reception. John was still thinking sadly about his mother's tits when Rooney leaned over and asked in a woozy, inflated voice: 'You want to be some big fancy art historian, is it?' John pretended to punch Rooney for a time.

The night deepened.

Everybody migrated to the sitting room: the girls cram-ming onto the couches with cushions on their laps, the boys roosting in corners. Empty cans and mixers cluttered the coffee table and the TV was playing music videos that didn't align with the music that was playing aloud. John was perched on an arm of a couch, his phone out.

Still nothing.

Nothing from Amber.

The sudden dreadful thought that maybe her liking of him wasn't as concrete as John assumed. Maybe it was porous and beaten, like the majority of concrete John had seen in his life. Maybe he was a tool for her bit, and it wasn't the other way around at all. What if he was puppet?

He rose from the couch and the entire room rose up with him.

Amy Winehouse was singing about rehab and John was beside Studzy, who handed him a fresh can. Pictures being taken by small cameras with wrist straps: Louise Conway and Niamh Regan posing peacefully nearby. Everywhere better jokes being told. Orlagh was on the couch supping water while Audrey clasped her hand. John checked his phone, checked it again a second later. The class graduation song was put on – 'Chasing Cars' by Snow Patrol – and sped forward to the final gigantic chorus and Studzy gestured for Louise and Niamh to come closer and all of them arm in arm, singing at each other.

The song finished and Brendan Hare switched to Oasis, but Tony told Brendan to knock the whole thing off – Tony with an armful of empties as he requested this – and an argument erupting because Brendan increased the volume instead.

John watched this unfold and only now did he relinquish his arm from around Studzy and Louise Conway. Studzy was talking to Niamh Regan, trailing after Niamh Regan, and it was suddenly just John and Louise standing in a doorway. The chalky scent that John associated with chalk and girls done up glitzily for a night out. She was sipping from a mug with a striped straw. Girls and how can they stomach acidic spirits and their chemical pong and John asking Louise this very question because it was all he had in his head: 'How can you stomach that vodka?'

Louise looked up at him with the straw between her lips.

'It's rank,' John continued. 'The smell is enough for me. I'm gone at the smell.'

Louise smiled but coyly, and indentations on the straw from her teeth, like stapler marks. 'Genuinely,' John said, 'how do you drink that crap?' and still Louise did not say anything, and did John sincerely expect her to answer how she drinks her drink? John needed to change tack. Or could he walk away? Did he even want to talk to Louise? Then John said, 'How's Seóna getting on?'

'She's great, yeah,' Louise said. 'On holidays at the moment.'

'Oh, that's class. Holidays.' John nodded and nodded and then said rapidly, 'I'm guessing Seóna probably hasn't been talking about me lately?'

Louise ran her finger around the rim of the mug and that caused the straw to twirl and there was an unexpected and terrifying lilt to her voice when she said, 'Not lately, no, John. You haven't been the topic of conversation for a while, to be honest.'

'Yeah, sound. I was thinking that myself,' John said, and his brow was furrowed. 'By the way, I know Seóna has this new fella and that's fine by me. You can tell her that. You can quote me. John Masterson said he doesn't mind about you and your new lad.' Why this last bit felt essential to add, he wasn't entirely sure.

'I don't think Seóna is hiding that she is with Craig,' Louise said, with her head to one side. 'Do you want to get back with her or something, John?'

'No,' he sneered. 'Obviously not.'

'That's funny,' Louise said, and this fleeting smile. 'Because you do remember you broke up with Seóna, don't you? For no reason.' She picked up her straw and it dripped at one end. 'You do remember that, don't you, John?'

'I do actually, yeah,' he said. 'I just meant it's fine by me. That's all. I'm trying to be nice.'

Laughter from Louise at the mention of nice.

John clenched his jaw and peered over Louise's head for the boys, for Studzy. The living room was emptying out, and then Louise asked, 'Where're you all going later?'

John turned to Louise. 'What you mean?'

Dimples appeared and then disappeared, and Louise said, 'I mean, what nightclub?'

'Nightclub?' John repeated, and the word tasted cold.

Louise didn't seem to hear him. 'Some of the girls don't want to go to Clowns. But that's where all the lads are going, isn't it?'

John managed to answer that yeah, broadly speaking, Clowns is where they will probably head to. He looked around. It was about ten, maybe half ten, maybe even later. Bodies in the kitchen gazing into the white of the fridge. The front door was open and noise from out there. Niamh Regan was glaring over, wearing a blazer with army-man shoulders. Louise was speaking still, and John faced her again and asked, 'What'd you say?'

Louise eyed him carefully. 'I said do you think the taxis are ordered? Because it's getting late.' His mouth was unusable, suddenly. There was a hollowness in his body, and every normal function was inoperable apart from rage, apart from this overwhelming anger. An anger that was amplified by the booze, clearly, but nonetheless completely reasonable as this was naked betrayal. They knew John didn't have an ID and still they'd planned this out and everyone was in on it, everyone laughing at him, and Louise said, 'I can ring my dad? He'll give some of us a lift.'

John stupefied, staring at her and then also Niamh Regan, who was presently handing Louise a coat.

'Should I call him?' Louise asked and both girls looking at him with expectation.

'John?' Louise said and John replied, 'Do whatever the fuck,' as he bounded for the front door.

There were groups loitering here and there on the driveway. The bitty crunch of heels as girls stepped side to side to stay warm. Only a handful of the boys wore anything over their polos, their lumberjack shirts. Breathing through his nose, John didn't search for Tony, didn't yell for the host – the idea never crossed his mind to berate Tony, to scream at Tony – rather he looked for Studzy: he called Studzy's name, called it again.

And there Studzy was, staring back at John.

He was beside the Mayo flag with Frank Kiely, Brendan Hare and sort of Rooney, who was crouched with his head lolling between his thighs. John marched towards them, exquisite vindication hastening his steps. 'Clubbing?' John squeaked, incredulous. 'Why didn't you tell me?'

Studzy glanced at the others. 'I thought you knew.'

'How could I?' John's voice went higher before it settled to the mumbled static of the betrayed. 'It was meant to be a house party. That's what we talked about. House party. And now I'm finding out you're all leaving for town?' John spread his arms and spoke over Studzy: 'What I am supposed to do? I don't have an ID.'

'Bud.' Studzy gave himself two chins. 'Relax. We'll get you in.'

'No,' John said, and he was compelled to spread his arms wide again. 'You knew, man. And you didn't tell me. That's not right.'

Frank Kiely said to John, 'What's the problem?'

John responded, 'It's not right.'

'Don't be blaming me.' Studzy was suddenly the one indignant. Nostrils flared. 'Tony wanted to go clubbing. The girls all wanted to go.' Studzy gestured to a group of girls, gestured at the Mayo flag. 'You want everyone to do what you want, is that it? Get your own way?' Frank Kiely put a hand on Studzy's chest and Studzy asked Frank Kiely, 'What's his problem, like?'

Diplomatically, Frank Kiely said, 'Lads.'

'That's not it at all, Studzy,' John said and Studzy said, 'What is it so? Tell us.'

'Just. You knew,' John said, and he repeated this for effect, or maybe time, 'You knew.' It was hard to forge a coherent argument when drunk, it was hard to fully recall the intricacies as to why John was so in the correct. His anger was being dwarfed by the open spectacle of this quarrel and the many eyes, and mortifyingly, John's voice cracked as he finally said, 'We're meant to be best friends.'

'Ah, bud.' Studzy looked at John and then Frank, then Brendan, then even the oblivious Rooney.

'Forget it,' John said, and he stamped off dramatically but there was essentially nowhere to dramatically stamp off to – the front lawn was hairy and his Lacoste would be ruined and he couldn't retreat inside as Louise lurked there and he couldn't swing around and march for the back without losing a fair chunk of his current moral authority – and so John ended up a mere foot away from Studzy, his back to the boys. He heard someone ask what's the matter with John: a girl's musical voice and that made the question ten times worse. The clouds above were pewter and smudged between two such clouds was the fattened moon and from it, the dirt road and fields beyond the gate acquired a ghostly hue.

He exhaled and watched his breath crystalise then glimmer. He rubbed his nose, spat. He wished he hadn't drank tonight, or even come over here for this party that was now pre-drinks, or became friends with those bucks in primary school, and Studzy was a prick and a bad friend and John owed him nothing, owed him no one, and why was life not fun and easy and where was John doing life wrong because he did try his best? Eventually Frank Kiely approached, and he petted John's shoulder and after a while, Frank said, 'No malice. But you had a nightmare there.'

John declined to argue against this statement and Frank said, 'We'll get you into Clowns. I know how.'

Soon headlights were progressing up the winding road – cones of light vanishing and reappearing and vanishing – and then the first taxi rattled over the cattle grid with the second tailing directly after. Eight-seaters, both. Hazard lights began to turn the gravel into rubies. Tony was locking the front door, and through the sitting-room window, Guinness was visible with her paws up. Frank Kiely explained the process to John for sneaking into the club – it involved licking a stamp on someone's hand, or licking someone's hand and then stamping, and attaching yourself to a flock of girls, and then you were inside – and in return, John said nothing, nothing at all.

John watched the girls pile into the taxi, and then the boys, and some of the boys had to scramble out again as alcohol was forbidden.

Frank said to John, 'We go?' and John, shaking his head, began to trudge towards the gate.

Aghast, Frank said, 'John, man.'

Someone else yelled at John – Tony, it was Tony – 'Where you off to, Tits?'

John swiped at this question: once, twice. Then John whimpered aloud, 'Home.'

He was aware he was ruining his own night but what else could he possibly do?

Well.

John could explain himself, detail more calmly his point of view and why it was a betrayal and eke out an apology – because everyone apologised to the sulking head as it was less hassle that way – and then hop into a taxi and risk Frank's ploy re stamps and licking?

Yes, John supposed he could do that, but his heart wouldn't allow him to. His pride was a magnet he couldn't pull himself from. The high road: that was his destination.

Tony called his name once more, then his actual name, and John shouted back, 'I have no ID, Tony. In case you forgot.'

Tony said, 'Sure, I don't either?'

'Tits. We can get in together.' Tony again and a beep from one of the taxis.

John was on the dirt road and walking quickly down it. Almost at a trot due to the steep gradient, which aggrieved John: he wished to appear composed, the tragic figure who ambled. It would take him close to an hour to get home – this repercussion had been present in his mind when he'd made his choice, but the benign reality of it was only truly exposed to him now. The wistful sound of a stream hidden behind gorse and briars and whatever else. The lights from Tony's gaff dwindling in the corner of his left eye. To himself, John said, 'Dickheads. All of them.'

He hadn't thought about her in a while but now he did. Amber.

No texts still and he shouldn't be the one to text because he had texted last.

A beep and John stood in knee-high grass and a taxi wended by before stopping completely. A door shunted aside and Studzy was leaning out of it. 'Tits,' Studzy said with a grin. 'Get in the taxi. It's our last summer, bud. Come on.'

Here was the final chance of redemption, of salvaging the night, and with a sudden shyness, John said, 'No, man.'

'John.' Studzy sighed. 'You positive?'

Incoherently and quite confusingly, John answered with the same husky, 'No, man,' but Studzy seemed to understand him, or at least he seemed to intuit from John's defiant expression and stance that John meant the grammatic opposite. Studzy sighed again with more exasperation: 'Suit yourself.' The door was wrenched shut with a screech and a pronounced click. The taxi drove on and the second one bumbled after it. Only when the former's tail lights disappeared behind a bend did John begin to walk again.

A dog barked when John finally reached the end of the dirt road and crossed onto tarmac. Ahead was overhung with trees. Lush blue leaves. He was two-eighths of the way home, he told himself, and then he reminded himself he was a disgrace.

'You're a loser,' John said to himself. 'A loser. Why do you do this, like? You've no friends, you've no girlfriend, you're no good at football. You're a loser, man.'

He couldn't text Amber, of course, yes, the rules were the rules, but he did proceed to ring her a fair few times – ungentlemanly conduct perhaps, but present desperation outweighed this concern – and John heard nine consecutive beeps on the first two calls before a blankness, a sonic void, and then upon subsequent dials, it went straight to a robotic voicemail – no explanatory note that this was Amber Goold, just a number disclosed in an irregular mechanical cadence – and when John was cutting up by the electrical substation towards the main road to the Island – he reckoned this was at least three-eighths of the way home so half, so practically home – Amber did in fact text him first: 'I'm outtttt talk 2morrorw xxx'

In the middle of the road, he stared at these xs, pressing a button to rouse the phone when the screen dimmed. They were all he had now in a way, these three xs. These three kisses. And if you ignored that he had rang Amber a half-

95

dozen times, then the xs were particularly potent as he hadn't sent any persuasive kisses in her direction nor deposited a lovelorn voice message – though tempted, though leaving five or six seconds of dead air – and yet Amber had thought to send him these three xs. She was thinking of him. Missing him. Pining for him, even. 'You've done well there now, pal,' John cooed to himself. 'She does like you. And you know, it's soft. Fair play there now, bud. It's yours, like. She's soft enough. She's loose.' It was in this blissful stupor that John noticed silver light bleeding over his runners and he abruptly stepped off the road and nearly dropped the phone.

A car was coming.

He squinted up the road and there were no fluorescent headlights, and behind him the same: only tarmac lit up silverly with metallic shrubs to the left and right and the edges of fields all metal and tin, too. It was then John remembered the moon.

It was almost twelve. Midnight. They'd be in the club by now, if they had got in.

He gazed up at the widest sky with his phone clutched to his chest.

You know, John had forgotten about the moon.

Tuesday, 7th July

He was on a shitty split. For the a.m., he was rostered with Samantha, Hughie and Martina and, thankfully, it wasn't too hectic: a busload of Germans was due to check in that afternoon, so the hotel was underbooked. Twenty rooms and the majority were older, greying couples – down early, practically apologetic they couldn't wash the plate for you – and then three or four families with little people and high-chairs had to be hastily assembled. By eleven, the radio was switched from classical to pop music and the waitstaff sat for breakfast in the back of the restaurant. John talked to Hughie about soccer, summer transfers and then about a favour regarding a spare ID, and while scrutinising the rota with a highlighter, Martina talked across and said John would be looking after the group this evening, but Martina didn't mention with who and whether with Amber, and the general manager Ethan wandered in then but didn't sit down, and everyone grew uncomfortable, quiet.

At half past eleven, Martina told John he could head home and before exiting, John located from beneath the bundle of coats and jumpers the gilt-edged hardback that had 'DAYS OFF' writ in Tipp-Ex on its front. He flicked to the weekend of the eighteenth and nineteenth of July and relief when he saw there was only one request: Samantha sought Sunday off for a birthday and she had even doodled a cake.

In the Saturday the eighteenth column, John scribbled: JOHN MASTERSON. DAY OFF. REASON = CHAMPIONSHIP.

The date had been confirmed via an impersonal group text from Ultan yesterday afternoon: the Island was officially drawn at home against Louisburgh in the first round of the knockout Championship. Throw-in was two o'clock. The text concluded with: 'Preparation started ASAP . ULTAN .'

John was missing tonight's training. No huge deal, only one session, and yet the certainty of Championship shadowed everything now: one loss and it was over, the season and the summer too, kind of.

The season was suddenly finite.

It was all or spits from here on in.

He waited outside the hotel entrance and inserted earphones and selected one of the eight songs his phone could hold and in the fifteen minutes before his mother pulled up, John reread his inbox.

Reconciliation with the boys had happened fairly seamlessly: he had awoken Sunday morning to a text from Studzy – 'Actually Love you' – and three missed calls from Tony. Rooney had texted at midday: 'Don't remember a thing'. Then sent a follow-up: 'Were you in taxi home with me ??? Lost wallet'. Then Rooney had phoned. John hadn't replied to the other two boys till the afternoon – he thought they should fret some more – and John had ended up apologising profusely himself once Tony and Studzy had expressed a smidge of guilt. Eventually, all four boys had gone for a cruise to McDonald's in Castlebar as if nothing untoward had occurred, as if John had simply been out the night before as well.

Amber meanwhile had messaged the once on the Sunday. It dinged at nine at night and it read: 'dead :(:(:('

John had received it in Studzy's car with a McFlurry melting between his knees, and while hiding the screen, had replied that he was dying too – 'haha' – though he wasn't at all, and he asked: 'How was your night tho? xxx'

Amber hadn't answered till the Monday and even that wasn't a direct answer to his texted question: 'Work tomorrow?'

After five minutes, John had replied: 'Yeah xx You?'

'Yeah! See u then'

This message seemed off to John, and he hadn't known how to respond to it. Should he play it cool and not reply and remember the famed mantra: treat them awful and mean and cruel to keep them keen? Or should John maybe ask her a new invigorating question, or daringly repeat his original question about her night out, which Amber had possibly, hopefully, maybe just not seen?

In the end, John had sent Amber a single creepy stalker smiley – ':)' – and regret immediately boiled in his stomach.

Presently, as the car passed through the Glon, his mother announced she had to make a pit stop at Sweeney's, and John took out his earphones to hear this and then had to take them out again to hear the follow-up question. He shook his head, suddenly aggrieved. 'I'm not going in with you, Mam.' A scowl dragging down his face. 'I'm in my uniform.'

His mother said, 'Who'd be looking at you?' and John plugged back in his earphones and ignored her loudly. It was overcast. Sunlight through the leaden clouds, hazy pricks of it. Smoke from chimneys, feathery, and how you could smudge a pencil line with your thumb to achieve that effect on paper. Then there was bog and more bog with a trailer abandoned every so often that broke this flatness.

In the car park, they eased into a space beside a tall heap of timber – Sweeney's Hardware Store was appropriately adjacent to Sweeney's Supermarket – and while Yvonne was rummaging excessively for bags in the boot, John undid his belt and muttered lowly to himself, 'Fucksake.'

'Fine. I'll go in with you,' he said, stepping from the car, and Yvonne smiled at him. 'Language, John.'

They manoeuvred along the cramped aisles – it was more than a pit stop, this was apparent as soon as Yvonne started groping the bread – and the trolley let out a whine when the front wheels turned over the vinyl flooring. Midwest Radio played, two DJs were chatting cheerfully about death. Yvonne pondered aloud dinner choices: she was at her art class on Saturday so maybe a shepherd's pie on the Friday and John could zap leftovers in the microwave? John said, 'I'll eat whatever. I don't care.' In general, it was no longer utterly ruinous to be spotted with your aul one, but John still didn't wish to be seen with her and especially when stinking of fat and grease, especially when tired and hair unstyled and resuming work in less than six hours, especially after what his mother had become. Turning from vegetables and fruits and onto teas and coffees. Condiments. Bags of sugar like dumpy hotel pillows. Finally, they came to a complete halt before the glass doors containing yoghurts and Yvonne said, 'I was chatting to your sister last night.'

Eyes on the line of yoghurts, John said, 'Okay? Good stuff.'

'We were talking about the wedding. Well. What else do we talk about, says you.' His mother did a tut thing as it was a gag, and though it warranted a sympathetic chuckle at least, John didn't react. 'Your sister is getting all worked up over numbers, who's coming, who's not, and that man is no help, as you can imagine.' She stopped herself and then added wearily, 'I don't know sometimes.'

John nodded. 'Right.' There was a dim blue LED light glued vertically to the inside of the door. The hum of refrigeration and its wispy artificial cold that felt medical. He thought to say, Nice you are chatting though, you and Kay. He thought to say, I'm happy you are talking normally again. Yvonne reached across for a pack of yoghurts with a layer of raspberry at the bottom like pooled blood and John remarked, 'That one's disgusting.'

His mother paused. 'It's not for you, is it? I might like it.'

'It's rank,' John said. 'I'm only telling you.' A scowl on his face once more.

His mother placed the yoghurt in the trolley, continued, 'Anyway. Your sister is going nutty over numbers, and she mentioned if you had a plus one. For the afters, or whatever' – He could feel his mother peek at him, this sudden heat, and then it was gone – 'And before you get excited, I didn't say a word. She just asked. I said I wasn't sure.'

His mother grabbed three rice cups and then a fourth as there was a deal: four for three. 'She can come if you'd like, John. Your girlfriend—'

John interrupted: 'I don't have a girlfriend.'

'Oh, alright. Your friend.' She rolled her eyes. 'You can bring your friend to the afters. Or we can make room at the ceremony, if you want.' Now Yvonne picked up an eight-pack of Actimel – not the strawberry kind because that was the flavour his dad preferred and nobody else – and the glass door was shut. 'Your sister wouldn't mind, I'm sure.'

They moved down the aisle into an open space: the butcher, the fishmonger and their shared horseshoe counter.

Onto the lane of cereals.

Past the length of freezers.

Then through shelves of crisp packets and fizzy drinks and John could not hold it in any longer: 'I'm not bringing anyone to the wedding. I don't know where you and Kay are getting this from. That I want to, or something?' He wagged his head as if further words were stuck on the roof of his mouth. 'You don't have a clue. Either of ye. You're both clueless about me and my life. I don't even get why you brought that up, Mam? Like, what's your deal like?'

'Lower your voice,' Yvonne warned, and she looked right at him. 'You know, I have been around for a lot longer than you have.'

'I do know that. Actually.' This said with a hard edge, and he didn't want to meet her gaze anymore. Sprite, Club Orange, the many types of Coke: he stared at these and felt his tongue probe at his molars.

'Girlfriends. Boyfriends. Do you think that makes a blind bit of difference to me?'

'Right.'

'I only want there to be honesty between us, John. That's all.' She turned back to the shelves, picked up a bottle of 7UP and put it in the trolley. 'You are not my little boy anymore. There will be college soon. Moving out. Decisions to be made and I won't be there holding your hand. So, some maturity wouldn't go astray.'

She said, 'You hear me?' and John said, 'What about you?'

There was a long pause before she responded, 'What about me?'

'Are you bringing a plus one to your daughter's wedding?'

'John.' She pronounced his name slowly. 'Don't be a bully.' Her voice was flat. 'You are acting like a bully right now, so stop.'

'What? What's the problem?' John said, and he didn't mean for it to sound so sarcastic, but it did. 'I'm only asking, that's all. Same as you. Are you bringing a plus one to the wedding or not?'

They did not speak for the rest of the shop.

Outside, feeling guilt slosh in his gut, feeling bad about her and her life and the state of it, John was the one who broke the deadlock by asking if she needed a hand with the trolley. 'I can push it to the car,' he said, and gestured towards the car. Without even a glance in his direction, Yvonne answered, 'I can manage on my own, thank you.'

The trolley jangled against the car park's divots.

Wind brought a newspaper forward in a loop and then put it back down again.

By the ATM, a posse of scraggly thirteen-year-old boys lolled, mountain bikes sprawled at their feet, the spokes gently twizzling and the flicker and glint of metal. Four of them. First years: no, sorry, wrong. Second years now. There was theatrical sniggering from this lot as John and Yvonne approached the car and John found himself biting his cheek till this intense shock of pain. The boot was opened, and wordlessly they started to load up.

Back home and in his room, John stripped from his uniform to boxers and then decided to put on a T-shirt and after some rudimentary stretching, proceeded to undertake the 'Thirty-Minute Complete Ultimate Home Workout' he had printed from online for twelve minutes before clambering into bed. The alarm was set on his phone for five on the dot. The sheets were crisp and new, and he felt worse. He felt evil.

He tossed from one side of the bed to the other, kicked a leg out from under the quilt.

He thought of work tonight and surely it won't be busy aside from the group and he'd snatch a moment with her, surely?

The talk with Hughie had been productive this morning. Hughie had assured John he'd check if he had a spare ID. Hughie had said, 'You know I have blond hair though?'

John felt the pre-rumble of a fart, the effervescent build-up in his stomach, and into a cupped hand, he let it rip and then sniffed. Noxious, with an oniony afterbirth. Like cheese and onion crisps smushed by a grassy runner.

John could hear his mother downstairs: she was in the kitchen because the distinct rasp of the corner press.

Then the clunky sound of the backdoor being grappled with and eventually unlocked.

He opened his eyes and wondered about his mam and dad, his family, and what they meant to him, and the answer arrived quick and easy: a house, this house. The only house he had lived in, the only house he knew by heart – the spots behind cupboards where builders had left pencil lines, an ability to intuit which step on the stairway was being stepped on when he heard a certain rickety strain – and that was family to John. Family was them all living under this slated roof even though Kay hadn't lived here for years, and his dad no longer did, and soon John would be vacating it, too. But still. The home house was the home house. Family was inescapable, like chain, like fetter, like *is that your house there?*

A good memory from here: snow had fallen thick one January evening and in the morning it had stuck. From his bedroom window, John gaped out at a dazzling bank of white that seemed to almost move. It must have been a Sunday. He was six or seven, and it exceeded Santa and presents in spectacle, excitement: snow. As a family, they had examined the garden, then the estate, then beyond. A reciprocated awe at the snow. They pointed at it. They said look at the shed because it was covered by snow. Look at the mountain. His sister flaked a snowball at him but in a friendly, sisterly way. His father recited other significant blizzards and his mam's breath was like she was smoking when she wasn't at all. Toots from meandering cars. In the fields, the sheep disappeared and then reappeared. The feeling of being home sick from school and watching *Oprah*. Another snowball had hit him in the back of the head and his sister was promptly advised to stop by his mother. They had returned home with cheeks as if skinned on tarmac and by the evening time, the snow was slush and through John's bedroom window, the back garden looked waterlogged. Unplayable.

A bad memory from here: the titchy silence when arguments were ongoing, when they weren't talking directly to one another but around, and how that stilted everything else: a shard of glass embedded in a tyre and the slowest puncture, it was like that. How balanced an evening had to become. Each word and sentence said, carefully. The feeling of frost even though both were smiley, talkative to him. How he wanted them to joke. How he wanted them to hug, touch. How he picked and prised and bit nail from his fingers until the prickly sensation of sloughed flesh was too much and his mouth sizzled. How this memory wasn't individual but numerous. Multiple.

Were you allowed to hate your family – individually, collectively – and yet still yearn for them to be bound together?

Or was it a selfish, childish wish?

He awoke five minutes before his alarm and lay in the groggy aftermath of a two-hour nap. The sensation that his limbs were immobile and maybe even hacked off. His mouth vile with sleep like he had glugged vinegar. He considered the ceiling, the wheeling dust motes, he considered the desk beside his bed where he had studied and studied and what for, really? It was as if he had not slept at all. Then the alarm beeped, and John grudgingly rose, re-dressed for work. He washed his face in the sink, then examined the blackheads on his nose – stippled and similar to a strawberry's teeny teardrop seeds – and the dried-up spots around his lip that were currently like orange rind to touch. Sometimes when encountering a mirror, John discovered he hated his face very much. His personality and body were a constant source of anxiety: the anxiety related to his face, however, was periodic, like full moon, like bank holiday.

Yvonne was in the living room. A cup was on her lap, and the remote control was pressed to her temple. John held the doorframe, and asked with a preceding cough, 'Is there any food, Mam?' Neutrally, she said there was a curry inside on a plate and John thanked her, and as a result of the jumbling nature of a tempered argument he felt obliged to confirm: 'Can I still get a lift off you to work?'

She looked from the television. 'Sure.'

On the drive over, it started to drizzle and then properly rain. Darker browns. The road blackening. His mother had changed: she wore a khaki pleated skirt to about her ankles, flats with a buckle. Lipstick, too. He was dropped by the hotel entrance and while he was shoving open the door, Yvonne said, 'You'll find someone else to ferry you home later, won't you? I'm heading out.'

Dots of rain on his Vans and onto the moulded plastic of the door. 'Yeah. Fine,' he said.

'Get onto your father.' She yanked down the visor – he heard that. 'Or even your sister.'

'Yeah, sound.' John could see where the tour bus had parked and he noticed a certain other car. A zero-zero MO spruce-green Citroën: a bumped fender, a missing alloy. A car his father would merrily describe as a hunk of junk. John was still grasping the handle of the door and he said, 'I'm sorry, Mam.'

'I know you are,' Yvonne said.

Amber was slicing a lemon when he bumbled into the pantry. A pint glass of MiWadi – the blackcurrant kind and tinkling with too much ice – was beside her, plus a pack of cigarettes: a small red and white box. Her hair was up in a bun with one of those claw yokes like you use to remove a staple and it revealed the tattoo of a small bird on the base of her neck. John was in the middle of retrieving his right arm from his jacket and said in a shrill and flustered voice: 'Oh, hey.'

Amber's head shook. 'I knew it was you. You're like an elephant. Do you know that?'

John laughed to himself and hung up the jacket, then found his loafers. 'Nice to see you too.' He went to lean against the wall between the pantry and the restaurant. The tang of citrus. Her wrists were deftly moving once again and the occasional squelch from the lemon. He said after a moment, 'You were hungover there, at the weekend?'

She let out a grunt. 'Don't remind me, please.'

'Yeah, no. Same. To be honest, don't remind me either.' He had slipped one loafer on and now the other. 'Saturday was a heavy dose for me. I popped it hard, like.'

Amber produced the agreeing up-and-down sound. She was onto a new lemon. The sliced hunks were on a saucer, wet and shiny.

'So, what are you doing tonight?' he asked. 'On top, is it?'

The fourteen tables that comprised the top section of the restaurant was where those who weren't part of a tour group were served. John had not yet been entrusted with looking after the top, which was fair enough: he wasn't able to carry four plates at a time and he wasn't altogether proficient at small talk, never mind the requirement to uncork a bottle of wine without fuss, without sheltering behind the partition and extracting it with teamwork via someone holding the bottle as you gritted your teeth and heaved the corkscrew back like a tug of war and John had been given out to a good bit for that particular incident. Amber could do all this, though. He had watched her up there pretty much every evening he himself had worked – showing teeth sweetly over her shoulder as she breezed from a table, this fake altered voice along with this fake altered laugh, and the ease with which she balanced and dished out plates and how it was so difficult to do this in tandem and yet she made it appear easy-peasy. Amber was good up there, but then again: it was her job, so she should be.

Amber swivelled her head now to catch his eye, and she was pretty: why was he inevitably surprised by the fact of her prettiness? 'I don't know yet, John.' A tight cryptic smile – friendly or unfriendly, he could not decipher – and then back to the cutting.

'I'm on the tour, anyway. Martina told me this morning.' He smoothed the wrinkles on his tie with his thumb, stalled in anticipation of her asking about the morning – was it busy, how many rooms – as that was what normally happened when you yourself hadn't been on a previous shift, but Amber didn't say anything, didn't pass comment. She had finished chopping, and he watched her wipe the knife with a tea towel. 'Who else is working tonight, d'you know?' John said, and he stepped to the rota pinned onto the kitchen door. 'It's myself. Yourself. Martina and Zibby. And Hughie.' John lifted the sheet closer, fixed his eyes on it as if truly investigating, as if only discovering this info now. 'I'm thinking cause Hughie is in, you could join me with the group? Teamo Supremo might be back in business' – he had used this moniker before and usually it generated a teasing roll of eyes at least, but nothing today – 'and Hughie can look after the top.'

Amber hunched down and from beneath the steel counter, gathered eight water jugs: four in each fist because she was a pro. 'I'm not the boss, am I?' Amber said as she placed the jugs by the sink, and John replied, 'You should be, though. You're miles better than Martina.'

'And I was wondering,' John began. 'I was looking at your car outside and—'

She stopped him by saying his name followed by: 'Would you do something?' She was in profile to him: he could see the beauty spot on her cheek and acne around it like paint grit on a canvas and the delicious run of her body. Into each jug, a lemon slice had been deposited, and with the back of her hand, she tested the water. 'Go fill up the ice, okay?'

When he returned with bucket and ice, Martina was detailing what was to happen tonight. A pile of printed menus in Martina's hand, and her finger riffled through them like playing cards. Candles had been lit on the tables, flickering, and the lights were dimmed. John spooned three or four ice cubes into each jug, a clunk and rattle, and heard that Amber was on top, the boys were looking after the tour.

It was five to six.

The Germans were fussy about sauces for the main courses, but apart from that, it was a typical tour affair and now and then he'd cast a glance towards the top section to see Amber – a pen newly sideways in her bun – skirting about a table, or feeding a glass some wine, or laughing fraudulently.

By eight, the Germans had relocated to the bar and the clean-up had begun and by half past, Zibby and Hughie were gone, and Martina was presently heading home, too: they were all working in the morning.

Alone, John set the middle section for breakfast and then he made a cautious start on the top section. Amber nodded at him once as she hurried towards the kitchen, but that was the sole acknowledgement he existed until around twenty past nine when she asked him to retrieve an order from the bar – her handwriting bubbly, each tail of a letter resembling a defeated balloon – and John carried the drinks to the precipice of the top section before Amber snatched them, declaring him a lifesaver.

By the pantry, John watched a group of six request dessert menus. They were the only table remaining.

Through the windows, he could see that night had fallen. The steady patter of rain on glass.

At ten, the group of six finally rose to leave. Loose ringing laughter. Amber lugged back the door with a sweeping gesture and more hearty laughter, and then John ventured forward with a tray twirling in his hands.

'I thought they'd be here all night,' John now said. 'The fuckers.'

'Ah, no,' Amber said, 'they were nice people.' She jiggled the door handle once to confirm secure. In the scrolled mirror hung behind the cash register, he saw her face, and when she ducked down to lock the lower half of the door, he saw that part of her, too. With a lift of shoulders, she added, 'Americans.'

'I should have known,' he said and laughed. 'Yanks. Yankie Doodles, like.'

No equalling laughter and he followed her sheepishly into the top section. From their table, she toppled coins into the hollow of her palm and then Amber said to him, 'Will you get this sorted and I'll do laundry?'

Once finished, John sat by the pantry and waited for her. Elbows on the table and phone aglow. The lights were off bar a fly-light high up in a corner. The sickly sting of industrial cleaning products from the kitchen. He had missed a call from his dad, and had rebuffed him earlier with a text – 'Working can't talk' – and now John messaged his dad again: 'Can I get a lift home?' John was wearing his jacket, his Vans. He moved his jaw slowly, side to side. There was something off with Amber, and he didn't know what it could be except that she was bored of him and his needy voice and shoddy texts, except that romance was fickle and just look at his parents, except that she was probably with Studzy now and John couldn't complain because he never said it was not sound whether Studzy had a go with his tap or not.

John's phone vibrated: 'OK'

He heard the squeak of the wheelie bin and then someone not her in the kitchen talking. A deep voice. The night porter? Ethan? The slap and peeling of shoes against the mopped tiled floor, and then she was behind him in the restaurant, asking, 'Why are you sitting in the dark, weirdo?'

John stood up immediately. 'I wasn't.'

Smirking, Amber grabbed her hoodie, her handbag. Her phone was out, she read something and then her thumb pounded the phone. 'So,' she said, pocketing the mobile. 'You were staring at my car earlier? Is there something new wrong with it?'

'What?' he said, and she smiled so a pressure lightened. 'No. I wasn't staring. I was just wondering if I could steal a lift. That was all.'

She cocked her head to one side. 'Do you still want one?'

Knotted around her rearview mirror was a green and red woollen band. The sort you wound around your head at a game for the glory of Mayo. John punted it with his middle finger and tsked. She looked over and then went back to scanning left and right. 'My dad's, not mine,' she said. 'I was thinking of you though, when he put it there.' The indicator was still ticking even though she had pulled out, was on the road with a waspish rev.

He liked her saying that, mentioning him, and he wanted to tell her so – that's nice to hear, that's lovely to know – but couldn't.

It was his first time in her car. It was dingy. Untidy. Clothes spilled all over the back. A plastic bottle, somewhere underneath the seats. But it smelt pleasant: like cut flowers, like candles, like her.

'Your dad is a Mayo die-hard,' John said. 'The green and red.'

'Of course he is,' Amber said, but absently.

John continued on, half laughing, half singing: 'The green and red of Mayo, like.'

They were winding down from the hotel and then the car noticeably slowed by Curran's Butchers. His father had texted, 'Outside', and John now responded without any guilt: 'Got lift. Thx.' On the left side, John's side: the glass bank, the clothes depository, streetlamps with long gaps in between. On her side: the caravan park with the playground and Keel beach and you could smell the sea even through the window. Amber asked, 'What's the quickest way to yours?'

'You can go through the Glon, I suppose,' he said delicately. 'That's the quickest way, factually, you know.' He was thinking of the Sea Road and a layby up there: from the moment he had found himself in her car he'd been picturing it. An unfrequented spot at night, where he and the boys often passed an hour in Studzy's car, chatting or playing serious games like rating girls out of ten including decimal points. It was gravelled, with two battered picnic tables. Once, someone had commented it was the ideal place to bring a bird – seclusion, darkness – and John had made a note of that. 'Though there's also going by the Sea Road. You take a left up here' – he pointed, though it was still ages down the road – 'and it circles back around by the Sound.' John did a voice: 'Personally, I'd head in that direction. More scenic.'

'Yeah?' This made her smile but not at him. She held the wheel with both hands and in the technically correct positions and John never did that despite his dad's scolding. 'But it's not the quickest way, is it, John?'

'No, it's not,' he admitted and tried to seem blasé, but it was like a burning coal in his chest: the fact he had roved this far forward and the want. 'But it's the livelier way, Amber.'

John courageously added, 'And what's the rush?'

A sidelong glance from her. 'Fine. We will go that way, so.'

The car motored on, picked up speed. They were on the outskirts of Keel – houses on top of each other like head-stones – and now past it and almost to the Glon. He was thinking of the spot and his cock was already kind of hard – purely from the thought of the possibilities, what could happen and what had happened before – and he willed himself to say now what he'd wanted to say earlier: 'You know what you said there about the Mayo band? That it reminded you of me?' She said, 'Yes,' and John swallowed, continued, 'Well.' His voice quivered and then, steely and low: 'I like being on your mind.'

They swung left for the Sea Road, uphill, and her car gave out.

The surrounding land darker than the night sky.

She said, 'Thank you for saying that.'

Silence ensued until they were close to the layby and then John shifted forward: 'Why don't we stall here for a bit?'

No response from her, no subtle difference in her body position – he allowed himself a moment to peek over. Only the changing noise of the tyres as they crunched over gravel confirmed she had heard him.

The interior light flicked to life, and his fists were clenched without his noticing. A small square reflection of them in the windscreen amid runnels of rain. Like a framed photograph on a fireplace: in terms of shape and size, sort of.

Finally she said, 'Well, we're here.'

He turned to her and spoke in the sultriest of whispers, 'Hey,' and she said in a monotone and with a lopsided grin, 'Hi, John.' She was looking right at him and that was a lot to take in, actually.

Her eyes were darkened with mascara, gothy, but the rest of her face was unmakeupped: freckles the colour of brown sugar smudged on her nose, and a lone red spot flowering on her chin – for a second, the crazed urge to remark upon this spot, *you have a spot* – and her lips, bare and scarred. The engine was off and the rain drumming atop the roof filled the car. Each breath smaller and smaller, thinner and thinner from his mouth. He thought: make the move, perform audaciously, yank the string.

'Hey,' John said again, and she laughed this time, and his chest thumping and she leaned forward and so did he.

They kissed and kept kissing.

Her tongue had tobacco on it, tasted of this, and it was over and then under his own, clumsily, playfully.

The rustle of his jacket as his other arm rose, held more of her, and her lips closing and no tongue, all of a sudden, as she pulled away from him and he was startled as if rocked from a deep sleep and dreams. She tipped her head back and kind of shivered. With an index finger, she scratched the corner of her mouth and told him, 'We need to talk, I think.'

'Now?' His upper body was tilted over the clutch, the gearstick. His hand still held hers and presently she shook it free but not unkindly: gentle with a firm press of thumb into his palm before her hand was hers once more.

'Yeah. Now,' Amber said. 'I want things to be clear with us, John. I don't want there to be any confusion. Or, like, for someone to get hurt.'

John nodded at this but didn't really comprehend because all he could think of was the kissing and recommencing that ASAP.

'I like you, John, but I don't think things should get too serious. Or complicated. In work, and like. In *life*.' The last part said as a joke, and she turned to him. 'This is nice, and fun, and that's enough. You're free, I'm free. It's easy.' Her fingers made a motion like playing the piano: index, middle, ring and pinky all moving down and back up but not at the same time.

'Yeah, no,' John answered. 'I get you. I didn't think it was more than that. I wouldn't want more than that. This is loads, Amber.'

She was facing forward once more but frowning. 'Alright. That's good, so.'

'I get you. You are going travelling, aren't you? I have college.' He thought and then said, 'We have an agreement.'

'Agreement?' she repeated in a high voice, and he couldn't tease out if it was sarcastic or not. He wished she would look at him.

'Yeah, like, have fun or whatever when we want to? It's casual. As you said, this is fun. So, we have fun together this summer. Casually.'

She said after a moment, 'You are very young.'

'I'm not really,' he replied. 'Like, what? You're two years older than me?' She eyed him and he said, 'And I'm on the senior panel, don't forget. I'm a senior footballer. So, you know, respect.'

A shake of head but he could discern a grin. 'I'm glad we're on the same page, so.'

'Yeah, absolutely,' John said and kept talking, 'I'm sorry about ringing you the last night if that bothered you. I was mouldy and I didn't mean anything bad by it. I wasn't trying to get anything. If you thought that I was ringing for that? I wasn't, honestly. I only wanted to talk. But I'm sorry.' He could see her front teeth gnaw at her bottom lip and he wondered should he shut up? Should he apologise some more? Should he place a hand on her knee and squeeze it and ask her to kiss him? It was not often John got what he desired – or so it seemed to him, anyway – and now he felt like it was siphoning through his hands: this, her.

'I didn't mind you phoning,' she said then. 'It's not that. I don't know' – she raised her hand and then it dropped to her lap – 'I think limits could be good for us both. That we know where we are and where we aren't. Otherwise.' And she didn't finish this sentence.

'For sure,' John said, and he was utterly confused. 'Limits are good. I love limits.' He was looking at his hands now: he addressed the next part to his hands. 'I like you too, by the way. You said it first there, and I do too. Whatever about the agreement. I like you, Amber.'

In response to this, air from her nose – a short puff of it like aerosol, like air freshener – and her mouth moved as if it were chewing and then she reached across to him. No tongue and then tongue, lots of. Her left hand around his collar and his face slanted and John bent towards the slope of her neck – open-mouthed, an unconscious decision to slobber at her neckskin and bones – and strands of her hair in his mouth, and she produced a low sound – reminiscent of the fingering and the sound she'd produced in their woods – and presently John returned to her lips because he was summoned there by her hand. Their noses colliding and then not when they reshaped. Eyes closed. Squelching and spit and wet sounds like teeth being sucked. His hand on her back and the shape of her bra through the top and his fingers squishing down against it. To force it open? He wasn't positive himself. As if in response, her left hand slid from his neck and along his chest and stomach – stormclouds and hair perking up on your neck, this feeling entirely now – and it found and then played his cock like a joystick.

He broke from the kiss, from her mouth, so as to comment: 'Fuck.'

She looked at him and her eyes were mischievous, misbehaving, and he gazed down to see her hand hold it through the slacks and another gasped, 'Fuck,' and then her lips atop his again.

She jigged his cock up and down – a pinching sensation, but pleasurable, but achingly nice – and they kept kissing, mouths wider, and then he heard the tear of his fly, and her busy hand searching through shirt and cotton boxer, and he helped her. The chill of bare arse on cushion, and she held his cock proper, began to sweep it up and down. He opened his eyes to catch a glimpse of this action: the swelt lilac head, glossy as if usable to glue and paste, as if dappled with sugar, and her fingernails painted black and it was beautiful to see her grasp and work his cock: honest to god, it was the same as Bernini and the subtle dents of muscle from marble. He closed his eyes again and blindly groped for a boob and her hand moving quicker and the slight clop of his balls against the underside of her clenched hand and her asking whether he liked that and John unsure if Amber was refer-ring to the clopping bally sounds or the wanking in general and his breathless reply regardless, 'Yeahyeah,' and their tongues tussling once more and then not for John was groaning.

In an instant, she lowered her head and into her mouth he squirted.

A tingling throughout his body, this pulsation in his groin and balls and the tip of his cock.

He saw the paleness of her scalp – heightened by the glare of the interior light – and watched how her skull bobbed momentarily, like a buoy.

A deep breath from him, and another, and her head rose with a grin.

His cock was wilting: pinker and pinker and like a curv-ing index finger.

She kicked open her door and spat him onto the dirt and rock. The sound of the sea audible, immense, as if they were descending into it. 'I guess it's home time,' Amber said then, closing the door.

Thursday, 9th July

By the deli in Sweeney's, and Rooney was saying to the fella behind the glass counter, 'White, yeah. The spicy chicken. Cheese and mayonnaise. That's it. Thanks. No. Don't cut it. And a portion of wedges, too. Thanks.'

John was next.

Tony was already queuing to pay – he had scooped cold pasta and some fleshy salad into a plastic container for which both John and Rooney had labelled him a wanker – and John received his own roll now and joined him. 'What you get?' Tony asked without turning around.

Their bikes were strung up outside. The three of them as Studzy was working in the petrol station. A balmy afternoon. They were in shorts and T-shirts – John's T-shirt had a Transformer on it and had cost forty-five euro from online and he had to have it because retro, because different – and Tony had a Mayo training top tied around his waist. John wore dainty white ankle socks: the other two did not.

Straight away, John had reported to them about the encounter in the car and how far he had travelled: a mild lie in his admission of a thorough blowjob but not as much as previously as it had been inside her gob for a moment so

124

actually not a lie at all in the grand scheme. Both boys shook their heads in honouring disbelief. Rooney commented, 'The horny bitch,' in an appreciative way. But afterwards John didn't feel totally victorious. He wished he had waited: it would have been better to have rubbed it in Studzy's face, too.

The three boys perched by the pier to eat their lunch: on a stone wall and looking out across at choppy water. A funky, pissy smell: from the sea, the slimed lobster pots. The high-pitched clink of a boat moored along the wall. They ate and wiped their mouths with the backs of their hands. Only when their lunches were gathered up and balled did they talk beyond half-sentences and gestures, and it was Rooney who said to John: 'Did you show your folks the house yet, Tits?' – Rooney swallowed something, fisted his chest, and went on – 'Cause I need to have an answer for my uncle by next week.'

John's feet were rocking back and forth. 'Yeah, I showed it to Mam yesterday. She liked it.'

'And?' Rooney said, and he offered the box of wedges to John, then Tony.

'I have to check it with my dad as well,' John said, with a note of pique. 'He came home late last night and I was in bed, like.'

Tony looked at John but said nothing.

Another fistful of wedges before Rooney said, 'Let me know by next week. Latest. I have to fill it before the uncle will agree to rent it to me. Either in or out, bud.'

The house was in Galway, in a place called Newcastle. A semi-detached with four bedrooms and two bathrooms and a single pink bathtub slash shower. The college was a fifteen-minute walk from its front door. 'It seems good to me,' Yvonne had said while fiddling with the pointer on the computer screen for no discernible reason, and in response, John had parroted a similar agreement while secretly longing for her to declare the house filthy, a pigsty, unsuitable and not worth the admittedly meagre rent.

'I sent it on to you, didn't I, Tone?' Rooney asked.

'You did.' Tony nudged his shoulder against John's: the sea was sideways for a moment. 'Looking forward to bunking with Tits when I visit.' John grinned and Tony asked Rooney who else had he lined up to move in?

'I said it to Brendan Hare, the last day,' Rooney said, and a clucking sound from his tongue. 'That'll hopefully be the third bed sorted. But the fourth is tricky. There's a couple of candidates but most of them are gurnicks.' Rooney showed his teeth. 'Like, even Hare is a dope.'

Laughing, they started to list other known gurnicks, and then Rooney glared at his phone suspiciously, went silent, and so John questioned Tony about Dublin and Trinity and where would he live up there?

'It's a bit different.' Tony sniffed. 'They have halls up there and you get sorted once your place is confirmed and stuff. Into a hall. Which is a type of room. Not bunkbeds anyway, I don't think.'

'Not too bad so,' John said, 'you're more or less organised.'

'Yeah, man. It's a class system.' Tony nodded. 'Genuinely.'

'How you feeling about it all now?' John said.

'About what?' Tony said and John replied, 'Dublin, medicine. You know, about getting enough points?'

'Nervous, I suppose,' Tony said and his hand on his neck. 'It is almost six hundred points needed, you know? The max. It's not easy.' Tony glanced at John. 'But nothing I can do about it now, is there?'

John waited, and waited, and then said, 'You'll get in. No bother to you.'

It was a sore subject for Tony, and John knew that. The idea of his friends failing didn't warm John or anything psychotic like that, but, conversely, the idea of them succeeding made him feel a tad sick. Basic grubby envy: but actually worse than envy because John didn't want to attain medicine at Trinity, didn't wish to see Tony not secure admission, John merely wanted to see a pal falter momentarily before rising, gallantly.

Tony smiled at John and said, 'Appreciate that, bud,' and then Rooney spoke in a moany voice: 'Boys. Karen is actually here. Is that sound?'

The boys said it was grand, and soon they saw her threading down the pier's walkway, arms folded as she watched her step. Karen: tawny hair with a fringe set to her eyebrows like a curtain tassel, and long-limbed, and another fact was that she didn't drink. John had never seen Karen in makeup – no sparkly eyelids or varnished lips, not even a small tin of lip balm daubed at delicately – and now to John that made Karen seem sophisticated when it used to make him think she was very odd and perhaps ill. She'd been in their secondary school – hence meeting Rooney – but had switched to Sacred Heart in Westport after the Junior Cert.

Rooney had explained this school transfer succinctly: Karen's parents were out-and-out snobs.

Now Karen lumped herself atop Rooney – on mostly his right thigh and her arms wound around a neck cratered with nasty crimson pimples and Rooney's own hand tucked itself into her arse pocket like a taunt – and it seemed a mightily uncomfortable position for both, perilous even considering the lapping water below, but they didn't readjust.

Immediately, the tone and vocabulary of the conversation changed, and Tony asked Karen how her summer was getting on?

Karen answered that it was good, and Rooney eagerly elaborated for her: Karen was working in her mam's office, she was playing loads of hockey, she'd been in Paris with her mam and sisters for a weekend two weekends ago, she was having a buzz.

John said, 'Sounds class, Karen,' and she nodded at him while Rooney summarised Karen's last hockey match for the group – it had been for Connacht, the under-eighteens, and Karen scored twice and hockey is a class sport to watch live. 'You wouldn't think it,' Rooney said. On this final point, John concurred, despite never having watched hockey in his life. 'It's a savage sport,' John said. 'Fierce skilful, like.'

'The wrists,' John added and rotated his own.

'You guys eat?' Karen asked then, and Rooney proceeded to detail what everyone had eaten.

It went on like this for a while.

And when John felt sufficient time had elapsed – so that Karen wouldn't suspect it was because of her presence, so that Rooney couldn't ask the next night he was drunk, 'Do you hate my girlfriend, man?' – John hopped from the wall. 'I better head,' John said, and he caught Tony's eye. 'Get ready for training.' John patted his pocket to confirm the essentials – wallet, house key, phone – as Tony announced that he might go home now too, actually.

Rooney removed his hand from the arse pocket to proffer a fist and while bumping it, John went, 'See you soon, Karen.'

And instead of a twinkling goodbye, Karen asked, 'Did Rooney say to you about the house, John?'

Rooney said, 'I did, yeah.'

Karen squinted at John. 'Will you take it, d'you think? It's nice. And really reasonable rent.' She swung back to Rooney. 'You told him about the rent, didn't you?'

Rooney nodded with theatrically widened eyes.

'I probably will,' John said. 'I just have to check with my dad first.' She didn't look away and John continued with one hand suddenly on his hip, 'But yeah, probably take it. More than likely.'

Karen made a hmm sound as if John had disclosed something worrying, or plain wrong, and then she turned her face once more to Rooney. 'That's three rooms, isn't it? John, you and Brendan. You only need one more. That's doable, isn't it?'

Rooney said, 'Yeah, no. It is, babe.'

'Did you ask anyone else?' she said. 'Because your uncle said it was urgent.'

'Not yet.' Rooney grimaced, and Karen complained he wasn't taking it seriously.

'Do you guys know anyone?' Karen asked John and Tony, who both shrugged. She made that hmm sound again and went, 'What about the other friend? Enda.'

'Studzy?' Rooney scoffed. 'No.'

Tony laughed awkwardly, and John felt compelled to say, 'Well, Studzy did apply for Galway.' John hesitated. Was this a joke, was he being earnest? 'You could ask him, to be fair?'

'No, he didn't,' Rooney said.

'Studzy did, yeah,' John said. 'Science, or some shit like that. He told me.' John glanced at Tony, who looked blankly back at him. 'I think it was marine science. Fish? But yeah. He applied.'

'Interesting,' Karen said, and Rooney said, 'It's not interesting.' Rooney eyed John. 'As if Studzy's going to college. Let's be real, bud.'

Once more this rushed feeling of duty in John's stomach like a finger thrust down his throat and he heard his own voice say, 'He could, easily. Like. He applied. You don't know that he won't go.' John chuckled. 'Results aren't out, are they? Are you psychic or something, Rooney?' This meant as humour but it sounded pugnacious. 'You can tell the future now, is it?'

Rooney muttered and John went, 'I'm just saying, Rooney.'

Karen seemed wholly confused: gaze flitting back and forth between Rooney and the two other boys.

'No malice,' Tony said then with palms showed tactfully to all sides. 'I love Studzy. But come on, John. That lad's not getting into college.' Tony repeated, 'No malice.'

Rooney said to Tony, 'Thank you. A bit of sense.'

'Neither of you know that for sure, though?' John said and his frustration apparent in arms that spread wide and wider. 'You're both guessing.' It was a surprise to John: why was he so insistent on this issue and did John believe what he was saying? Because John believed Studzy was as thick as the wall and the truth had been apparent in the tests throughout the years and when Studzy had mentioned the science course to John and his hope about maybe scraping together the points, John had felt only pity as if Studzy was a one-eyed dog who yearned for a home, as if Studzy didn't know who he was and where he was situated in the world. John now said, 'The least you could do is ask him, Rooney.

If you are that desperate for people. That's all I'm saying. You should ask him.'

'Will you stop?' Rooney said and he was shaking his head. 'I'm not living with that prick. Fuck off, John.'

'Okay,' Karen said after a moment. 'Enda is officially ruled out of moving in.' It was a statement spoken in a funny monotone, deadpan, but only Tony laughed and even that was forced, a chesty cough with tethering after-effects. John and Rooney were silent and looking everywhere but at each other.

'What was that about?' Tony asked as they unlocked their bikes from the railing by Sweeney's.

'Nothing,' John said and then, 'But just I don't like that attitude on Rooney. That Studzy couldn't possibly get in.'

John said, 'And I don't like Karen, to be honest. Shite personality. And hockey? Really.'

John said, 'And I don't like this idea that you have to go to college or you're a dumbass. That you're useless if you don't leave and go to college,' and Tony interjected here: 'But no one said that, Tits?'

By now Tony had his bike freed and led it away from John's own. A tattered plastic bag was snug over Rooney's saddle. Tony went, 'You know those two don't get on? They clash. Like, Studzy was a dick to Rooney in school, in fairness. At times, it was real bad.' John finally manipulated the code on his lock correctly – ZERO ZERO ZERO

ONE. He began to wind up the cable and Tony was saying, 'Look, Studzy's not getting into college. He knows that himself. There's no point in you spoiling that house over Studzy.'

John said nothing to this, didn't acknowledge it, and he waited till Tony was at the bottom of the ramp before snatching the plastic bag from Rooney's saddle.

At the bridge, they separated: Tony blew left and John idly circled and then propelled right. As he pedalled past the pier, John glanced and could just about see the two and they were no longer sitting atop one another. Then grey walls and a window and John looked ahead once more.

College is not the be-all, end-all: his father had said this once to John. It was imparted to presumably soothe a stressed and panicky son: it was the time of the mock exams, when all of a sudden Higher Maths became squiggles and the mere thought of mathematical functions and lettered equations initiated such dread in him that his skin began to dry and eczema formed on his wrist like blistered paint and this same dreadful affliction had only since flared up during that time in May and it had not involved maths then. But even in that dire moment, when John had greatly appreciated this lowering of expectation, John had understood that his father fully anticipated him getting into college: as of course John did, too.

Peter was saying it to make John feel better, to allow John to perform better. He wasn't saying it as truth, as his real conviction and belief.

His father had also said there were different paths laid out for everybody: his father had often said, 'Different strokes for different folks.'

Studzy was different to John and would go on to do different things. It was as simple as that.

But did different mean lesser?

Yes. To John, it did, yes.

He didn't like that he felt this: it was vaguely immoral, but it was truth. John sensed it was common knowledge. Everyone thought this. To not get into college meant you had failed: actually, it meant you could go no further. It meant you were shackled: rightly or wrongly. Here.

John had his eyes locked on the first cone and his hand out and readied. His team were already a length or so behind the others and this distance growing, becoming more and more insurmountable.

Four teams and four cones to tap and race back from.

Simple, and the first team to complete the full sequence were the winners: but it only mattered who was last.

The other teams were about to slap in the next runners and the fella from John's team only now scampering back towards them, on the straight home: Seamus Fallon, brawny and giant, but stiff, struggling to bend and touch the cones and twice being called out by Barrett for not touching the cone and having to turn, redo, losing valuable seconds and John felt he could see those seconds being lost: like sand in the wind, sparkling as it whizzes away. It ached John to see this lost time because he wanted to win. John always wanted to win.

For the first chunk of training, it was to be conditioning. There was to be no ball work. The justification: Barrett said the team needed to be at its fittest for the new defensive system to excel. Barrett spoke: 'You will have to suffer. There's no hiding it.'

Finally, Seamus Fallon flapped at John's outstretched hand and John pelted forward, fingers bunched together, feeling fast and nimble and strong. Accelerating, quicker and quicker after each footfall. Maybe six seconds to reach the first cone and he hunched to touch it and then immediately zipped diagonally across to palm the next cone and only two more remaining and he spun and bounded to his right before veering to the cone closest to the starting position. The surrounding noise abstracted, a hissy babble as if underwater. He started for home, an arid sensation in his throat, like dust in his mouth, and his gait was less steady in terms of direction, in terms of coherent efficiency. John was wobbly as he eventually clapped the next man raring to go.

Hands atop his head, John tottered to the rear of the line.

Now was the opportunity to rest, regain composure, and the air was gusting from John's mouth without control and the concern that his calf muscles might just split apart, like a petrol station chicken wing and its easily splayed lilac skin. Unspecified and imprecise encouragement abounded from Barrett.

Follow it up.

Drive on to hell.

It was a chilly evening, enough to make you shudder and huff, but no longer after a round of sprints: the thickened heat from the bodies behind or in front of you like an electric blanket.

From John's team, Spain Jersey tripped after lunging to touch the second-last cone. He was on a knee and more seconds were being squandered. Studzy was next and a loud groan from him.

Barrett shouted, 'Push through.'

The other teams were practically finished as Studzy gamely set out for the first cone and once Studzy returned, Barrett instructed John's team to get on the ground.

The forfeit for losing was thirty push-ups and during the last five, John's elbows were squealing at him, his biceps twitching with agony.

As soon as they completed the push-ups, the next drill began.

A circle was called at the end of training. Vapor rising from the players, coiling skyward, and John was next to Mac and Tony. 'The team for Sunday,' Barrett began and everybody a little more on their toes. Barrett advanced into the centre of the circle and a clipboard was in his hand with a dangling pen. 'It's the final league game and obviously, we are all aware Championship is around the door. So, look. There will be lads rested.' Eye contact for all, or at least the impression Barrett was confronting you, singularly. 'But I want you to think of it as an opportunity. To show myself and Ultan that you deserve to start for Championship. Because' – Barrett lifted up both hands at this point and the lone sheet affixed to the clipboard had a formation of names on it in blue pen, but it was unreadable to John even as he squinted – 'my brain is not made up. There are positions to be won. Understood?'

'We'll begin so,' Barrett said, and the clipboard was read out.

Rooney was starting as corner-back and John was scanning for his reaction when his own name was called out as right half-back: a flick within John and brimming nerves, worry, and then thoughts of glory, winning, and John felt a bump on his arm from Tony.

Tony himself was in midfield alongside Seamus Fallon, and Studzy was named as corner-forward in a two-man full-forward line.

'Right. That's it,' Barrett concluded and there was muted applause. And it was when the panel was beginning to meander towards the car park and dressing room, towards home, that Spain Jersey erupted: 'What the fuck, Anthony?' His eyes were wide, and his mouth agape. 'I'm not getting a game?'

'I'll talk to you in a second, alright, Ewan?' Barrett said after a moment, and some were still walking on, but others now stalling, ambling, intrigued, and John was one of them.

'No,' Spain Jersey snapped. 'Let's have it out. I don't care if they hear. I'll say it front of any man.' Spain Jersey's hands were clenching and unclenching. 'I have been togging out for this club for sixteen years and this is how you treat me? Not even a run in a nothing game. I mean. Sixteen fuckin years I have been at this.' His voice was rising, and Ultan presently seeking to calm the situation, Ultan was cooing, 'Ewan, we'll take it handy, will we?' and Spain Jersey spoke over him, finger pointed at Barrett, 'That's not decency, Anthony. Where's the gratitude? I played alongside you. I have been down here, night after night.' The finger jabbing forward and back, punctuating his fury: a baton, kind of. 'How much of my life have I given to this club, and this is how I'm treated? Like shit.'

Tony pulled a face, and John mouthed, What the fuck.

'Like shit on a shoe,' Spain Jersey said and his voice squeaky as a dog toy.

Barrett said, 'Time catches up with us all, Ewan. I don't know what to tell you. It's nothing personal.'

Mac was actively ushering along those watching. A firm hand on John's shoulder, then firmer, and reluctantly John began to move, but then another outburst from Spain Jersey. The gratitude line again plus the shit-on-shoe add-on and John watched Spain Jersey take a decisive step towards Barrett and John was positive Spain Jersey was about to swing, but instead there was a final, 'Fuck you, Anthony.' They were all soon overtaken by Spain Jersey: a furious swagger, and no one chased after him as he marched towards the car park.

A group text dinged an hour later: 'Abusive behaviour will not be tolerated by management . No person is bigger than team . As of now Ewan Gormon is no longer a member of the Island senior football panel . See you at 2 pm Sunday @ SWINFORD . ULTAN .'

Studzy rang John. 'You see the text? Sham alive.'

John laughed. 'That was bonkers.'

'Ewan is a nutjob. Proper,' Studzy said. 'What was he hoping for? I thought he was about to deck Barrett.'

'Yeah, no, same,' John said, then a delay and John went, 'but I do kind of feel bad for him, in a way.' Studzy asked what the fuck John was on about and John explained, 'Sixteen years playing for the club and that's your end? It's scabby enough. At the very least, you have to admit it wasn't handled great? He should have been told beforehand, or something. I don't know. But, like, it's brutal.'

'Ewan is fuckin useless, Tits,' Studzy said. 'He's been stinking up training all season. Barrett was being sound letting him tag along till now. He should have been booted ages ago.' A jaunty whistle through the receiver and John had to laugh. 'Get the memo, like,' Studzy continued, 'sling your hook. You're shite, man. Shite.' And John had to laugh at this, too.

Rooney texted about it – 'WTF', and John replied, 'Insane' – and Tony rang and expressed a similar sentiment to John: 'He was hard done by,' Tony said, 'but the reaction. Can't excuse that, can you, Tits? I don't think you can anyway?' When over the landline John told Amber about the mental aul fella axed from the panel, he had adopted a comedic, flippant register despite still feeling altogether queasy about the situation. 'He was screaming his head off. But get the memo. You know? Sling the hook, like.' John whistled, waited for Amber to laugh, giggle, and instead the phone asked, 'All that over a football match? My god. That's depressing.'

'Oh, it is, yeah,' John said, and he was caught off guard. 'No, I was a bit shocked myself, now that you say it. I thought it was stupid and, you know, kind of sad? I felt sad for the guy, really.'

Then John said, quicker, 'Anyway, sorry. How was work?'

Sunday, 12th July

'Easy on the clutch,' his dad said through gritted teeth, and twenty seconds later, his dad once more but louder and open-mouthed: 'The clutch, John. The clutch. Will you ease off it.' The car was revving hard – metal scraping metal, an unhealthy and potentially explosive noise – and John's left foot was seeking to decompress cautiously yet decisively from the pedal and such concentration it was like a head-ache, and John brought the foot back a little more and the car shot forward all of a sudden – totally out of John's control, as if the vehicle had a will of its own – and then the car bucked to a standstill before conking out: the glowing dashboard blank and the multiple red arrows flopping to the left forlornly. Peter pinched the bridge of his nose. 'Are you even listening to me? You can't just lift your foot all at once. You have to ease off the clutch.'

'It doesn't help the shouting, you know?' John shot back and he cursed under his breath and Peter warned him and John went on, 'What you're saying doesn't make sense?' John's knuckles were bone on the wheel, and he was hunched forward with a rounded back. 'Like, you are tell-ing me to ease off? But then you're telling me press down on the other yoke? The accelerator. And the biting point. I don't know what that is.' He glared across at his father. 'What is a biting point?'

They were in a business park off the Glon. John's gear-bag was in the backseat. It was ten in the morning and at this stage, John had been in the driver's seat for fifteen minutes, but it felt like an hour. Two hours, genuinely. Into his mouth, a finger, and he bit some nail and then spoke: 'You're not making any sense, Dad.'

Peter said, 'It's not rocket science. Ease off the clutch and press down the accelerator.' He exhaled loudly. 'John.' In a gentler voice, Peter said, 'You can do it.'

John turned the key. The razored snarl of the engine and then it hummed more agreeably. He pressed down the clutch and then the accelerator and a spluttery roar, but nothing happened.

Horror.

Fear.

Had John broken the whole thing?

Air through Peter's nose and he said, somewhat calmly, 'You're still in neutral.'

'I know that,' John lied. 'Give me a second. I'm checking my mirrors.' Again, foot on the clutch and he heaved the stick to one and then touched the accelerator: harder and harder and the pedal was vibrating against his sole.

The car rolled itself forward.

'That's it,' his father said, and the car said with a degree of hostility, 'Rumrum.'

Tentatively John raised his left foot – not fully off the clutch but at least three-quarters of the way, he estimated – and still the car was crawling, and John's tongue was sticking out as he turned the wheel, smoothly, ever so smooth, and he was doing it.

He was driving.

The engine was still moody, growling, and his father reminded him about the clutch. 'Ease off it now.'

John obeyed and lifted the foot off and the car jerked and his right foot reacted in panic and jammed on the accelerator and then it was too fast – the car was moving way too fast – and his left foot retracted and the wheel juddered in his hands.

John lurched forward and back: both bodies lurched forward and back.

The car conked once again.

'Jesus Christ, John,' Peter shouted. 'You're not listening to me. Will you listen for god's sake?'

John's arms were folded, and he looked straight ahead. 'I'm not driving with you anymore.' His mouth pinched tight. 'I don't care. No. Not doing it ever again.'

'Put up the handbrake and get out of the car,' Peter said, and John was saying, 'I'm never doing this again. I'm never driving with you. No. No way.'

They didn't talk until Peter's phone rang as they approached the town of Mulranny. The phone was mounted to the grill, and the car slowed as his father answered it – 'Hello, hello. Kay. One second' – and Peter failed to hit the button for loudspeaker – Kay's voice tiny and repeating, 'Are you there?' – and eventually John leaned over and did it for him. 'Thank you, son,' Peter said, and John did not reply.

Kay was phoning about whether Peter wanted to call out for a Chinese later and then about whether Peter wanted to collect a table she had ordered from Sweeney's before the Chinese because Denis was away. 'If you don't mind, Dad,' Kay said, sweetly.

John gazed out at water and patches of sand and the mountains across the bay. He thought that his sister was a spoilt brat and far more spoilt than John, who actually wasn't spoilt at all and perhaps was neglected. His father tilted unnecessarily towards the phone when he replied, and this intensely bothered John – why couldn't Peter compute the self-explanatory implication of a loudspeaker system? – and so John looked at his phone.

Amber's last text read: 'Hope u win today kk x'

He had replied: 'kkkk xxx'

It was a new joke between them and John had planned a joke for later if the Island were victorious: 'Won game 4 you kkkkkkk xxx'

Through Mulranny and the father–daughter conversation was finally beginning to wane, and Peter said, 'By the way, your brother is here beside me.'

Kay said, 'Oh. Tell him I said hi.'

With a big smile, Peter said, 'You can tell him yourself. You're on the speaker.'

'Oh, right,' Kay said. 'Hi, John.'

'Hello, sister.'

'Let me tell you, Kay. He has an important match today, for the senior football team.' Peter winked at John. 'Against the mighty Swinford. We're on the way there as we speak.'

Every one of these statements uttered like a bullet point, each of these statements irritating to John.

Kay said, 'Well done.'

'Thanks,' John said, and Kay said, 'Did you tell him about the dinner, Dad?'

'I did,' Peter replied.

'What dinner?' John said.

'On the first of August, we have a dinner with Denis's family,' said Peter to John, and Kay said, 'So you didn't tell him, Dad?'

'I'm telling him now,' Peter said, and he winked again at John. 'And it's in the Mulranny House Hotel.'

Then Peter asked the phone, 'It is in Mulranny, isn't it?'

Kay sighed yes and said that Denis's whole family would be present which included the sister and the stress of it, honestly. Laughing, Peter said it would be fine and Kay let out a sceptical hmm before announcing she had to go. A flurry of goodbyes, the phone clicked off. They were soon passing Niven's Restaurant, and by then John had arranged the words to ask, 'Will Mam be at that?'

'At what?' Peter said. 'The dinner?'

He looked at his father's face for a hint. 'Yeah.'

'Of course she will.'

'Sound.' John returned to looking out at hedges. Then marshy fields the colour of copper coins, swathes of uneven land. 'I just wanted to make sure.'

'Things are tricky, John,' his dad said. 'Between your mother and me.'

'I've noticed.'

Peter looked over. 'It's not easy for you, I know.'

'Yeah.' Sheep. A long slender driveway to a bungalow.

'Sometimes, people see two paths,' his father said. 'Separate paths when there used to be one. And sometimes they don't reconverge as much as you want them to. The paths. You try your best and through no fault of either person, it just doesn't become one path.'

'Does that make sense?' his father asked, clearly unsure himself, and John hesitated and then said, 'I don't want you to break up. Divorce. Or whatever.' John shook his head. 'I don't want that.'

His father nodded. 'Neither do I.' A laboured breath, ponderous, and it was a sound John didn't like to hear. 'You have to bunch up the sleeves sometimes, son. You have to get on with it. The punches that life throws at you. You take them. And you have to respect the punches.' One hand was lifted from the wheel. 'You have to respect the punches, John, even if they hurt. You've got to.'

'Was it just over the photo?' John said and he blinked rapidly. More fields and houses, flying by. To abandon this topic would feel good, it would be a release, it would be an understandable swerve, and yet John committed to it: 'Like everything between you. Your fights. And you living over there in Gaga's. Was it to do with her sending the photo and nothing else?'

'The photo. Yeah. That certainly didn't help things, I suppose,' his father answered. 'But no.' He sighed but not aggrieved, not angry. 'People drift apart, John. People change. You can't control people. I have tried to figure out why this happened, as I'm sure your mother has, too. And I'm not certain there is an exact why. It's, you know, how many spots does a zebra have? There is no correct answer to that. The zebra has loads of spots. And life, unfortunately, has loads of spots, too.' A sound of rustling and John wouldn't look over. An estate made up of red brick. A petrol station with an ice-cream cone out front. 'We still love you and your sister. We're still a family. And we still love each other, myself and your mother. But maybe differently.'

His father said, 'Here.'

A tissue and John took it. He hadn't known until then he was crying. His nose scrunched up. His mouth gasping. But it was lower-level crying, John told himself. It was unremarkable, uncowardly. It was no big deal.

'I'm sorry to bring this up, John. Today of all days.' A scoffed laugh from his father. 'My main man is starting for the seniors. It's a happy occasion.'

'It's fine,' John said. 'It's grand. I'm not even really crying.' He dabbed his eyes with the tissue some more. He cried some more. 'I know you're not,' Peter told him. 'But if you were, that's alright, too.'

The first half was tight. Tit for tit in terms of scores. John marked a guy who was around his own age – perhaps a year or two older with a slit cut through an eyebrow and a plaster covering something on his ear. He scored a nice point early on – a dummy that sent John to block a shot that suddenly wasn't there – but apart from that one instance, John believed he was a hundred per cent marking him out of it. By the close of the half, John had even begun to gallop beyond his man, combining neatly with midfield, and during more or less the last bit of action of the first half, John had retrieved a wayward lob before jinking past the forty-five and clipping the ball through for Studzy to slot over with aplomb. This put the Island one up and claps from the sidelines. 'Well done, Masterson,' someone yelled, and John pretended he did not hear this. He kept his facial expression set to determined, to severely focused as he jogged back, spitting only once and even that awfully cinematic, he felt.

At the peep for half time, bodies immediately trotted towards the dressing room and John was intercepted by Peter. His father congratulated him, reassured him, but mostly suggested where John could improve. 'Take your man on more,' his dad said in a hushed tone, and John bent his ear closer. 'Look at me, John. You're well able.'

When pitch gave way to gravel, Peter slipped off with a squeeze of John's upper arm and a final whispered, 'My man.'

The dressing room was a cramped oblong. Affixed to the wall were slatted benches: a clatter as they were heaved down unceremoniously. The sole window was behind John's head and it let in a shaft of silky golden light.

Quiet and still except for the omnipresent tippy-tap of stud against cement floor.

No stink of sweat and body odour – surprisingly – but rather grass and shovelled muck and the antiseptic smog of Deep Heat.

Barrett didn't impart much stirring wisdom nor contribute any tactical deviation to account for the wind the Island were facing in the second half. Barrett basically said everyone was doing fine and dandy. His voice was uninflected. A direct quote: 'Keep her ticking.'

The first gathering since Thursday but no mention of Spain Jersey. No inquest. No churlish jokes. It was like Spain Jersey had never existed. A blank in memory already.

Barrett then clapped. 'We right?'

About ten minutes gone in the second half, and John's fella was subbed off and in his place a man. He was up to about John's ear in height. A sturdy if altogether gaunt frame. He must have been about thirty, this new guy. Older, even. Thirty-three: imagine. They shook hands and as they retreated into their positions on the pitch, the old guy introduced his shoulder to John's – an abrupt bang, not painful but startling and then it was painful – and now the old guy screamed for a pass, thrusting from John and breaking left.

But when the ball arrived, it was John who was out in front to fetch it. It was John who was able to hurtle forward – managing a cheeky solo, evading a paw – before slicing a pass at a juicy angle for Tony to chase and gather. The old man was nowhere near.

Walking backwards, panting, John thought: I'm going to clean this old fucker.

Soon after, the Island went two points up: a free kick from Eoghan Moloney, kicked off the ground and glancing the crossbar with a satisfying ping as it travelled over.

And then there were five minutes remaining and Swinford were resorting to hopeful punts into the full-forward line in search of the goal that might snatch the game for them.

One such Hail Mary kick bounced near the penalty spot, and it was scramble thereafter, a Swinford player tumbled followed by an Island jersey, the keeper Robert Coleman darted from his goal line and added to the confusion, and Rooney emerged from this scrum clutching the ball.

Roaring his name, Rooney fisted the ball to John, who spun and skipped by the old man: a hasty step as if John was heading infield and then twirling one-eighty and John's pace taking him further away.

A hop of the ball, and John glanced up.

The wide-open pitch before him: resplendent in the sun.

The back of his jersey puffing out behind him.

Players scattered and gaps where there had been none earlier. Faces, turning his way and arms raised.

But no clearest bestest option for a pass, John felt.

Then a solo, and John figured he should lump it in long – aim for the general area where the full-forwards might be – when Seamus Fallon shouted. He was only a spit from John, his two large hands out from his chest as if the ball was already in flight to him. 'To me,' Fallon commanded. 'Masterson. Me.'

John thought, safety first, John thought, two points in it and depleting time and maintain possession, John thought, Jesus Christ Fallon is frightening, and he went to handpass it to Fallon, but found he could not.

All of a sudden, his left hand would not budge. Couldn't move. A phantom force halted it. Freaked, John looked down to see his forearm being clenched to his hip by an alien hand: scraggly with moss on the knuckles. On John's blind side, his left side, the old man had pinned John's arm. It was a foul. It was a blatant foul. It was an easy decision for the referee, but still John tossed the ball as if to strike with his left fist so as to prove beyond all reasonable doubt that he was being obstructed – because you can't hinder some-one striking the ball, because there has to be an attempt to play the actual ball – and lo: there was a sharp toot.

But the referee was pointing in the wrong direction.

The referee signalled towards the Island's goal.

The referee had blown for a free-in.

John couldn't believe it. Head in hands and mouth open with shock. Outrage. 'No way.' His voice pitched high and higher as he asked, sincerely, 'Ref, what the actual fuck?' The lunacy of such a call. The ridiculousness. It was a joke. It had to be. 'You're joking me, ref,' John spluttered. 'He fouled me.'

Was the referee blind?

It was the only explanation for such a call and so John was forced to pose this delicate, sensitive question: 'Ref, are you legally blind, like?'

It could be construed as an insult, as abuse, yes, and so John received the subsequent yellow card with grace, but it was an objective and fair question because honestly how could anyone see that as a free-in unless blind or having misplaced one's glasses? 'Ref,' John asked now, 'where are your glasses?'

The ball was under Fallon's arm and presently a scuffle as a Swinford player sought to seize it and in response Fallon brought the ball pettily above his own head. Jostling and Rooney got involved and John didn't notice the specifics beyond it being a mass of bodies, grabbing and pulling each other: all John was concerned about was the referee and correcting this sickening miscarriage of justice. 'Ref,' John was saying, 'ref.'

Another whistle and Fallon released the ball.

John said, 'Ref.'

'If you don't shut it,' the referee warned John with a wagging finger, and still John pleaded, 'But I was the one being fouled.'

'That's it,' the referee said and indicated for the free to be brought in closer.

Fallon told John to leave it, to get back into position, and where was John's man in all of this mayhem, this ruckus and noise? His absence only struck John now as significant: Where had that old fucker got to?

John looked and looked over his shoulder and couldn't see him and then he did.

The old man had drifted into the space vacated by Rooney, by John. He was alone, near the white lines of the square, practically one-on-one with the keeper, and he was beckoning for the pass. Immediately, John sprinted – arms pumping and tongue between teeth – and the ball being kicked over his head.

A shadow and then an object.

With an unnecessary leap, an overcompensation, the old man caught the ball and turned and was into the box and John was gaining on him, fractionally, because John was fast, because no one could handle his speed. A small chance of blocking, of successfully smashing free the ball, which was increasing as the old man dawdled, struggled to sort out his feet – he was no good, John was better than him – and the old man soloed the ball and by now John was truly gaining on him: stopping a certain goal and how that might be perceived in the watchful eyes of the management. The goalie Coleman was edging out, wide and imposing. John was within an arm's width, he could stroke the old man's neck if he so desired, and time falling fast and lethargically, a temporal imbalance induced by John's overbearing alarm, so that when the old guy's leg swung back and connected with John's calf it was both instantaneous – the dramatic collapse of the old man, the cry from his lips as if gunned down by sniper – and incredibly slow – the ball slipping unhurriedly from the old man's grasp and the puff of sandy dirt as John hit the ground too and how the ball spun on a white line before spinning gently onto grass – and then all at once time shook itself to normal and with it, the realisation that John had fucked up.

In that moment, if John could maim himself, offer up a hunk of his own meat and bone in exchange for the penalty being revoked, he would. He would without reluctance, without any scruples. Voices thundered above John. Hostile. Explosive. He was content to let everything unfold without his involvement, he wanted to be bypassed, he yearned to leak into the earth like bubbling piss, and only when the old man stepped over him with a brusque untangling of legs did John himself rise. On his feet, John looked at the referee, the red card being held up, and did not argue. Others were protesting, of course. Rooney was trying to convince the referee the foul had occurred outside the box, Rooney was indicating a rut in the ground. A yellow was being shown to Seamus Fallon and a Swinford player for tussling. Tony was on his haunches, observing all this at a safe distance while grinding his fist into his palm, and when John limped by, Tony did not acknowledge him.

From the sideline, John watched the keeper jump to the right and the ball fly to the left.

The ripple of the net and the rambunctious celebrations after: John watched this too, despite his face being screwed up.

The match ended one goal and thirteen to Swinford against fifteen points for the Island.

The Island had lost by a single point. A single score. The team had lost because of John.

With total sincerity, John flung a water bottle at the dressing-room wall. Then he booted his gearbag, once, twice, then another kick before dropping to the bench with his head between his knees. He was stunned by his own badness. The magnitude of his error. He replayed the challenge, and it wasn't even a proper challenge to begin with, was it? Rather it was plain stupidity on John's part. What was he good for if not this sport, what had he going for him in life if not this game and being good at it? This was his thing: being on the team, being better and on the team. Around John, the zip of bags being opened or closed, and then the hiss of the showers. They all hated him now, the team correctly blamed him for the loss, and he wondered was he the de facto Spain Jersey? The joke of the panel. Soon John could feel the heat from the showers misting the air.

A weak pat on the crown of his head and John peeked up.

It was from Ultan, and he was already onto the next person. Proffering condolences.

The door was ajar and a polite applause from the opposing dressing room and then Barrett reappeared.

Men were exiting the showers. Bodies puffy from the scald. Footsteps suddenly atop the cement floor. He watched Coleman wrench a towel back and forth between his legs – the crosshatched path between testicles and ass – while talking to Seamus Fallon, casually. Hooped hair on Coleman's shoulders: grotesque. There was also hair in patches on his upper back, like an old-timey map where forests would be marked via a row of chevrons. Other naked men wandered into view. Droplets clinging to grizzly pubic hair like cobwebs after a downpour. Chests with no pudgy tits. Tattoos John had never seen.

He returned his gaze to the floor.

He had seen plenty of men naked in his life – his father, the cocks in pornos with the purple heads, Studzy once at a sleepover and it resembled a rope before becoming a hilarious propeller – but never so many, so comfortably.

John could never be naked like that and there was scorn for his own personal prudishness, too.

'Fuck it,' a scratchy voice said, and it belonged to Studzy. Topless but still in the white flashy shorts and he slumped down beside John. At nothing, but with severe gravity, Studzy gestured. 'What can you do, like?'

Studzy's abs were protruding through his stomach: durable as if hammered from marble. John had always thought of Studzy as scrawny, a runt, but that wasn't factual anymore. He was built.

Toned.

A mini-tank: if John sought to put him down while still ostensibly complimenting.

Studzy looked at John. 'Honestly. It's over. Forget about it, Tits.'

His father mentioned stopping at Supermac's and John declined with a rueful shake of the head and brought his face nearer to the window, and at home, John refused his mother's suggestion of a meal out someplace, or a burger and chips from Hurley's, or she could throw on an oven pizza: this being the final proposal John heard as he marched up the stairs. He did not want food. He did not deserve food. He ought to grieve with hunger pangs. The boys were heading out – Studzy had belled – but he would not join them. He didn't deserve to join them. It was only correct and noble for him to suffer. Yet after his shower – a torrent of boiling water as he sought to strip his body raw – and a further ten-minute spell of stoic reflection, John plodded back downstairs and asked his mam could she put on that pizza, actually.

Curtains drawn, he ate braced against the bedframe. He was knackered by now. The various muscles packed like gum along his legs were all individually tender, and in particular his lower left calf – the clumsy instrument of his ineptitude – was cramping up and was increasingly painful and he had swaddled a towel and ice pack around it to no remedy.

His phone lay face down beside him.

It had vibrated a couple of times and now it did so again. Her last text had read: 'How did it go? kk x'

This one read: 'Hope ur ok?'

He didn't want to speak to anyone, he didn't want to hear from anybody except her – a truth abruptly revealed. A memory of a film or a music video and this pretty flower budding, blooming in fast-forward speed: the revelation was like that to John. He wanted to talk to Amber. He needed to. What else did he have this summer but her? He replied with a simple and informative, 'Hey xx I'm fine', and he started typing the next message as soon that one slipped into its blockily animated envelope. John had to admit he didn't have a clue what he was hoping to say and even when the message was securely in the outbox and gone, it was surreal that it had been texted by him. It was free of stagey aloofness, free of jokes and kks, and almost scrubbed clean of amorous implications. A genuine plea to someone John had assumed he'd never be totally genuine with: 'Can we go cinema some time? We can still be free and have agreement but Id like to go somewhere with you xxx'

Wednesday, 15th July

The kick to his lower left calf had formed into a splotchy bruise: a dreary yellow like water that had seeped through plaster wall and wallpaper. An excuse and a reasonable one. On the phone, Barrett had ordered John to rest up, to ice it hourly, and be ready for Saturday. Championship. Ultan had texted that they had rescheduled training to accommodate niggles like his and was he sure he could not train. Then Ultan had forwarded on a physio's number and a note for John to get it sorted today. Instead, John was in her car and travelling to Castlebar and its seven-screen cinema.

The drive hadn't been as uncomfortable as John had feared because they talked exclusively about the hotel for its duration. This blissfully undemanding work chatter only started to wane while Amber circled the cinema in search of a suitable parking spot. It was then that John found his hand grasping the window crank and his thumbnail digging into the fingertip of the opposing index, it was then the prospect and potentially irreconcilable failure of the evening loomed before him. Because this evening was not a benevolent hook-up: a naughty activity that by its definition contained no requirement to talk unessentially nor open up and share. This evening was romance, a romantic construction, and the strict, stately rules that were thus invoked. It was a date.

They had an hour to kill before the movie at half seven – they had decided on the new *Harry Potter* flick, though John had skipped the previous one. The sun was blurring through the cloud like in desperate need of a coaster, and for only the second time that summer, John was in jeans.

In a technical sense, it was probably John's first ever date. Despite his profound relationship with Seóna, they had never really gone places or did things just the pair of them: more they hung around other friends together and had only been alone when free house or room or alley presented itself as an exciting opportunity.

To John, a date meant you couldn't presume upon a shift or box at the close. Rather a date established that you had to toil and impress for your bit – frankly you had to be impressive in a manner John worried he was incapable of. In dating – from what John learned from TV shows, from Rooney and snippets from older boys – there were extra, subtle rules, but the benefits were deeper, more nourishing. Rooney had once drunkenly described Karen as a star he used to navigate his life and though everyone had howled at him, at this girly metaphor, had eventually brought it up sober to Rooney's staunch silence, the idea had always stuck with John as a powerful and unlonely one. Indeed, when John had been boyfriendgirlfriend with Seóna he had felt a degree of protection beyond even the sex league table, and had sort of grasped at what Rooney had drunkenly disclosed: it was like an extra coat, this feeling, and suddenly John could wander out into a wild snowy storm – not literally – and be sure he'd return, or at the very least that someone might chase after him if he did not.

Now John and Amber began to walk. Nearby was a go-kart track, a bowling alley with laser tag, and John had no notion what any of the other businesses around here did. Seemingly no predetermined route other than exiting the car park until Amber said, 'Could we get a coffee? I'm wrecked after this morning.' She was in skinny pants that didn't seem to have the robust texture of denim and this shawl-like scarf about her neck: black and white in a gingham style. Her fingernails were cherry red and not her usual black, and her hair was down with a side fringe.

John said great idea, even though he did not drink coffee.

Heading along the main road and no flowing conversation and so John thought to say aloud one of the few things he knew intimately about Amber that he could say aloud without being a creep: 'How's South America looking? Your holidays.'

'It's not a holiday,' Amber said with a cryptic laugh. The planning and logistics were more or less finalised, she explained, though she hadn't booked her actual flight yet. Her friend had backed out of a certain date due to a family reunion but by October, latest, she would be saying goodbye to this place and heya to Mexico.

'Unreal,' John said.

Then John asked, 'Oh, but what happened to South America?'

On the road, a line of cars, their fumes faint like a watermark over the exhaust. John didn't know the outskirts of Castlebar, where they were presently, where they were heading, but she must.

'We're still going there.' Amber shrugged. 'We just changed our mind and are now starting out in Mexico. Stay there for a bit and then travel down along the coast.' At every pause or beat in her speech, John commented automatically: Jealous. 'Plus, it's off season in Mexico when we arrive, so everything will be cheaper, if you get me? Save some money.'

'Makes total sense,' John said. 'Jealous.'

The road had begun to narrow, and they were standing at a pedestrian light: Amber thumbed it.

'There'd be tome museums over there, I say,' John said. 'Real fascinating stuff.' For clarity, he added, 'Aztecs, you know? Madness with the sacrifices.'

'Yeah, totally,' Amber said. 'We're going to do all that stuff. Ruins. Art museums. Everything.'

'One of my mam's favourite artists is Mexican, actually,' John said. 'Yeah, what's her name?' – he pretended to forget and stroked his chin for a second, another – 'Frida. Frida Kahlo. You might know her? The unibrow?' Amber smiled as if John had declared aloud his most favourite colour in the entire universe and then John went, 'My mam loves her, anyways. Her favourite artist by a mile. Actually, no. The guy who painted the mountains is her favourite. Henry. And she probably loves some fuckin fantasy dickhead, too. She's into all that stupid shit. But the Frida one is definitely in her top five, for sure.'

Amber murmured a bright sound to show she was listening, and the light flashed to a green man.

They crossed the road.

On the other side, Amber said, 'Not to be funny, John. But do you not get on with your mam?'

'What?' John said.

'No. Of course I get on with her,' John said.

'It's just I've noticed you give out about your dad at work. Little comments about him. Mostly funny stuff he does. Nothing major, or anything.' Amber's voice more slow, delicate as she proceeded along. 'But you never mention your mother in that kind of way? Even though she's the one who collects you after work. It seemed strange to me that you don't really talk about her.'

Terraced houses had begun to appear. From a plum-coloured hedge, John tore a handful of leaves and then let them fall.

Amber said, 'Am I being harsh?'

'What am I meant to say? It's complicated. And you know why it is.' John looked at Amber directly for the first time since leaving the car – a brief sideways look and maybe a look that could be classified as a derisive glare – and then his eyes set back to the path. 'Both my parents are fuck-

ups, like.' A big breath. 'I don't hate my mam, though.'
Amber said something – he heard the very beginning of a
sentence – and John spoke over her: 'But my mam has done
stuff that has affected me in a horrible way. My life and
school and, I suppose, relationships and that.' All of a
sudden, John stopped in his tracks. 'Honestly, what am I
meant to say here, Amber? Never mind taking photos of
herself naked and sending them to people. Or like hurting
my dad. Causing him to move out and making it awkward
for me and my sister. But all she does is paint elves.
Compulsively. I'm not going to talk about that, am I? I
don't hate her, like.' John shook his head. 'I love her, obviously. But.'

After a moment, Amber said, 'Your dad moved out?'

'Yeah,' John said. 'He's been gone for almost a month
now. It's shit.'

'Sorry,' Amber said and another moment and then she
went, 'She paints elves?'

'Yeah. Elves. With the ears.'

'I suppose elves are regal enough, aren't they?' She was
facing him, and he was grimacing down at nowhere. 'In the
movies, they are.'

'Yeah, but Noddy and them? They're not regal.'

She laughed drily at that.

They kept walking. The town centre had to be close.

'I'm not trying to make you sad, John.'

'I'm not sad,' he replied. 'I feel sad for my mam, actually.
The photo. It was bad form. Whoever sent it on, there was

malice. And by the way, I don't know who she sent it to, so don't ask me, alright?' His left hand flapped at air and returned to his pocket. 'I don't have a clue and I don't care, personally. What difference does it make, if like, you knew? For example. What would change?'

John answered his own rhetorical question: 'Literally nothing. If you knew who it was, it would still mean nothing.'

Amber didn't say anything, she did not react. Two of them walking steadily along. John felt words billowing up within his stomach: distinct feelings he had never talked about and she was allowing them to ferment and swell. Bunsen burner and the many millions of bubbles in the beaker above it: sort of. How you could type anything in online and then delete search history afterwards: sort of like that, too. Amber granted this. His ease in talking to her because in two months, three, she would be removed from his life, naturally, so he could fill her in on more and more and more without repercussions or lingering shadows.

'I think,' John began.

'I think sometimes,' John began again, 'that she wants to be someone else. My mam. That she doesn't like her life. Dissatisfied or whatever. I know for a fact that she'd love to be one of them Dutch hippies from the Sound. The freedom they have. Not because she told me or anything, but I just a hundred per cent know. I can see it how she talks about them. Maybe she's depressed? If that's what you're thinking. It's possible. Yeah, to be honest it is possible.'

Both hands were in the front pockets of his jeans and he removed them abruptly. 'But she can't fully commit to any change. That's the problem. Maybe she can't because of me and my sister and raising us. Or maybe because of my dad. The way her life works, or how it turned out. Where she is now, all isolated, you know? And that's sad. If she is unhappy or whatever. Or feels stuck. That is sad.' He thought then said, 'Like, I wouldn't want to be alone on the Island, wanting to be someone else.'

'None of that is your fault, John,' she told him, and he said, 'I know it isn't. That's not what I'm saying.'

Finally the main street. She indicated a café called THUNDER ROAD and they walked wordlessly towards it. A chime from the bell above the door as it was pushed and his voice tremulous as he asked, 'Can we stop talking about her?'

Without turning around, Amber said, 'Yeah. No problem.'

Takeaway cup in hand, she steered the conversation on the walk back. A snaking queue inside the lobby and John stood behind her, investigating the blue carpet riddled with colourful fireworks. At the counter, they each purchased their own ticket despite John remembering he should buy hers.

Screen two and they were in the middle row. His popcorn was plump and spilling between his thighs: they had each got their own respective bags – hers a small with a bottle of water, John's a large with a large fizzy Club Orange – as

John couldn't deal with not having enough popcorn regardless of romance, rules.

It was about twenty to eight. Or even quarter to at this stage. He imagined the men gearing up for training. He pictured Ultan and Barrett at the pitch already: filling water bottles from the tap at the side of the dressing room and discussing who was excellent and who was average and who was poor.

There was a clammy guilt for not being at the session tonight: John felt it atop his skin all day and it was like when he'd call his mother a bad word, the guilt of the action lasting longer than whatever punishment was doled out in the immediate. By team code, John should be there. In the past, other injured or muscle-tweaked parties had stood at the side of the pitch, spectated through rain or sun. It was what you did as a member of the panel. It was expected.

John thought of his boys – how would they fare tonight, who'd do best and who'd gain an unfair advantage – but then his attention was drawn by a movement beside him: her hand delving into her zip-up pocket and returning with a case.

A brown leather case with a buttoned clasp that was currently being unbuttoned.

Glasses.

A solidly black pair with thick lenses that John would label geeky, nerdy: or at least say these descriptors into Studzy's ear, who might bellow them. They were not designer anyway: not dainty like his mother's with a label gilded on the hinge. A pair, John figured, you might pick from a spinning rack in a bookshop. Inexpensive. Cheap.

The things John did not know about Amber – these frumpy spectacles, who exactly was the friend joining her on the big trip that was definitely happening, the mole on her upper forearm that he only noticed today when she hiked up her sleeve – and yet the dastardly things John did know and could vividly recount – the colour of her pubes, the flavour of her tongue, and how it was to jig a finger inside of her and draw an unfettered blast of air from her lips.

'You wear glasses?' Genuine shock shooting John's voice way up, and Amber groaned. 'It's only for screens I need them. And even then, I don't really need them.' Amber asked John not to laugh, and the urge to do so only flowered in him at this very mention and he did try his best not to chuckle.

'Stop,' she said but exaggerated. A nice jokey tone. 'Will you grow up?'

Snorting, John replied, 'What's up doc, like?'

A pop culture reference that did not sit entirely right in the context – Bugs Bunny did not himself wear glasses and John could not remember if Bugs ever uniquely addressed critters who wore glasses – but they laughed together, nonetheless. Loudly, happily.

The film started and then it went on and on as films are supposed to do. At a certain point, the story lost John – he could no longer pretend wands were anything other than incredibly lame – yet he stuck with it nobly until he reached the end of his popcorn bag – the salt prickling the chewed skin around his fingernails and confirming only inedible nuggets of corn remained – and then he started to rearrange his focus somewhat. He continued to face the screen, sure, and his eyes were mostly following what was happening up there with a studious expression, but every atom and tingling cell of his being was fixed on the hand that lay on the nearest armrest: the fingers coiled towards her body and so not an outright invitation. John was utterly still, but he felt like he was shaking, convulsing, and in his mouth, he could not summon saliva nor articulate to Amber his simple request – because she wouldn't deny him such a minuscule demand as to solicit a firm feel of her hand, probably? – and when he instructed himself to behave normally – i.e. cease feeling like you're shaking when you're not, i.e. relax and pick up her hand as you might pick up a book from a bedside table – this only engendered in him the feeling of being increasingly abnormal and in the forbidden.

To reach for a hand: a simple gesture but apparently impossible. He had done so much with Amber, possessed such sublime tactile knowledge, and yet this froze John completely.

Now and again, the screen would flash, a switch of setting or some pretty spell cast, and the hand would be preserved in a different light.

He thought: stop being an innocent boy.

With Seóna, John had held her hand tightly climbing the stairs for their first time and apart from that occasion very rarely and actually maybe only when drunk and bumbling to a secluded zone: the reason being that this same fear froze him then, too. It was not exclusive to Amber. Even with Seóna he'd worried what others might think, despite knowing what the majority thought about Seóna – before they had gone out, Seóna had been appraised and ninety per cent of the boys had expressed some urge to feek her – but still the dread of what others thought and how it entombed him. It was such a huge statement – to hold someone's hand when in public, to display them and you as a package with a bow. What if others thought it wrong, what if others thought Amber tarnished and dirty? What if others thought you were committing a mistake?

He wasn't ashamed of Amber. Or he was, yes, but it had to do with himself too: John was ashamed of himself as much as her.

But John wanted to do this: hold her hand.

He issued himself an ultimatum.

He would count to ten and then grab her hand or else.

He would count to twenty and then grab the hand or else.

At the count of forty, he seized her right hand, and she didn't wrench it away. Nor seem surprised or put out. He was grasping it lengthways, and in response to his contact, she merely adjusted her hand, flipped it so that their fingers

– hers long and elegant as if piano player and not full-time waitress – were now laced together. He looked across and down and then back up to the screen. The heat of their hands and something smaller than sweat beginning to fur between the interlocked digits. It wasn't a comfortable union, the entwined hands, but it was something else. After a moment, John found himself pressing his fingertips into her dimpled knuckles – it was a reflex, this light pressure, a natural reaction from his extremity like how he sometimes shifted a ball between his right and left foot during soccer as if his feet were controlled by a skilful other and not uncoordinated John – and she glanced at him, smiled, and the movie mirrored in her glasses and also there in her glasses was his all too familiar bulk, and John thought, we're on a romantic date, John thought, not an appropriate instinct as on a romantic date, and then John fell towards her, mouth open.

Her subsequent bray was resonant and prompted harsh shushes from above and below. Tutting, too. 'The movie, John,' Amber whispered, and she bit her lower lip.

Still sort of laughing, she asked, 'Can you not wait?'

The answer to this was no.

John could never wait for anything he desperately wanted.

What lifeless sicko could?

She didn't extract her hand from his, but simply returned her attention to the screen, and once his dizzying dickhead had elapsed after a period of inner reflection, so did John.

They watched the rest of the movie like this, a giddy feeling coursing through him: a high like a cold sugary drink.

And as soon as the sconce lights snapped on at the rolling of credits, their hands broke apart: John felt suddenly bashful about such a wholesome connection, and she must have too, as there was no resistance or a clear one-sided tug to untwine. He nodded at her, tried to smile, and she muttered something – that was fun, that was good, John wasn't positive what '*that*' was exactly and whether it referred to the act of handholding or the movie itself – and then Amber fussed with her scarf thing, gathered something at her feet: a tortured water bottle. The screen began to empty out and they stood, retrieving their phones as they waited.

Inside her car, and after a bout of reversing when all was silent except for the rasp of gearstick being wrenched forward and back, they were moving. The radio was on, and they were talking over it about the film. Amber loved it, John pretended he did. It was nice, the atmosphere in the car: it was safe. Coming up to a roundabout and passing by McDonald's and headlights coming towards them and then zooming by. Discussing the town of Castlebar at large now, and John had something else to say.

The arrow for Newport.

On a bit and the smaller arrow for the Island.

She was in the middle of detailing a particular pub she loved the most when John finally got it out: 'Here, Amber.

Not to like, put a downer on things, but I wanted to say.' He looked forward: they were on a regional road with soil banked high on either side. 'I appreciate you asking me about Mam earlier. It's hard for me to talk about for obvious reasons. But it helped that you're a good listener. It made a huge difference. Like. Thanks, and.'

He waited a moment, needed to take a breath, and it wasn't done for dramatics.

John said, 'I trust my friends a lot, you know. But I can't talk about any of this with them. Or, like, I don't want to?' He fiddled with his seatbelt. 'I told none of them about Dad leaving the house, but I could tell you. You make it easy, and I really appreciate that. You're kind, Amber.' A feeling then like he'd overfilled a glass with water, and it might spill everywhere, so John said, 'Plus, my sister has a wedding to organise so I can't talk with her about it either. So, yeah. Thanks.'

Amber said, 'Don't be too sweet, John.'

He grinned at this. 'Truth. You're the sweet one, not me.'

Amber looked across and John said, 'You are.'

It wasn't immediate when she next spoke. John was feeling sort of drowsy due to the radio, due to the long road ahead with no streetlamps, and then with a jump, he heard: 'I'm glad you trust me, John. I get it with parents. How complicated it can be.' She went on then, but in a different tone: light-hearted, as if executing a huge gag for a baying crowd. 'From my own personal experience, of course.'

'Yeah,' John said, and then he said, 'What do you mean?'

'No one said it to you in work?'

John shook his head and then answered no.

'I thought they would have. They're a gossipy bunch.' She ran her finger around her scarf as if to loosen it. 'It's not a big thing. I wasn't hiding it or anything.' Two hands on the wheel once more. Ten and two. 'My mother lives outside Castlebar. In this assisted care unit. After I was born, and probably before I was born in all honesty, she began to suffer with really terrible paranoia. People being after her. Talking about her. A kind of schizophrenia, basically. It progressed, got a lot, lot worse. There was an incident with a collection of knives.' The same light-hearted tone as earlier as she said this bit. 'We minded her. We did the best we could. Or my dad did. But it got too much, and she lives there now.'

'Jesus,' John said. 'I didn't know that at all.'

'Yeah, well,' she said. 'It's been years at this stage. What, like? Maybe five or six years? More?'

'Jesus.' John again.

'We go and visit her and stuff. Obviously.' Amber laughed though it wasn't her normal laugh. It was a short, raggedy laugh. 'She doesn't have a clue who we are sometimes, but we visit her' – John said, 'Jesus, man' – 'for holidays. Christmas. Every second or third weekend we drive down. Her brothers, too, my uncles, they visit. Both live nearby. They are good to her.' He couldn't make out Amber's face, whether distressed or stoic. Occasionally a bar of light from oncoming traffic and that was the extent of illumination, so he couldn't read her. 'She isn't neglected, that's for sure. And it's a nice place. My dad and mam are not officially divorced, but he has had a girlfriend in the past. It was serious enough.' That short laugh once more. 'I'm not sure why I'm telling you all that? You don't need to know that much.'

'Jesus.'

'Yeah,' Amber said, 'it's been years now. It's not that traumatic, or anything. But, you know, when I visit her and she's lucid, she worries about people being after me. It's, yeah.' A pause, and then: 'It's upsetting. But what can you do?'

'Jesus, though,' John said. 'I'm sorry.'

She glanced over. 'Thanks, but don't be. It's fine, I'm fine.'

Five minutes later and John's mouth burst open with: 'Fuck. I'm really, really sorry, Amber. You and your poor dad. And your mam, too. Jesus. I'm so sorry.'

She laughed and a moment later, reached and pinched his thigh.

They didn't discuss it further, and they didn't really talk further on the drive home in any meaningful sense, and though it should be awkward, John should panic over the loud quiet between them like he had earlier, it somehow wasn't like that now. Why was that and what was changed? Soon they were coming up to the bend for his estate and Amber asked, 'Will I drop you out here again?'

'Actually,' John said and cleared his throat. 'It might be easier if you drove into the estate. There's a place to turn round the back. Good bit of space to turn.'

She smirked – there were streetlamps now, that tangerine hue, and he could see her – and Amber said, 'Alright.'

The ticking of the indicator.

There was his house – the outside light left on – and the neighbour's and they were through to the end of the estate where a detached house stood but no one lived in: using its drive, she reversed and with a bump parked up on the kerb.

They kissed for a time and there was no need for some beckoning gambit: they just started automatically, as natural as booting a ball as it plodded towards you. It was thrilling: to feel her tongue and taste her unique spittle – salty from the popcorn and no ash because she hadn't smoked today – and to open his eyes to see hers shut. Thrilling: all of it. John felt special, he felt infallible.

And then her hands were on his chest: not pushing but sufficient force to warrant his head to retract a fraction. 'I better go,' she said. 'I'm in early tomorrow.'

'Sound,' John said and moved his head all the way back. 'Yeah, no. Completely sound.' He unbelted and said, 'Right,' and opened the door, causing the interior light to switch on and he said, 'Cool, right,' and still he did not exit the vehicle. Without turning around, he asked, 'Will I see you soon? Or, do you want to do something like this again?

Or even, like, just do the arrangement stuff together soon, maybe?'

A painful pause before she answered, 'I suppose I might see you Saturday.'

'You mean Friday?' John looked over. 'I'm not working Saturday? I have Championship.'

'I know,' she said, 'that's where I might see you.'

'At the match?' he said, and frowning, Amber nodded as if he indeed was the most innocent boy.

A beat and he grinned. 'You want to see me in action, is it?'

'My dad asked me along, actually. But you can tell yourself that, if it helps.'

'I will,' he said, still grinning. 'Extra motivation.' Very pleased with himself, John stepped from the car, shot the windscreen a thumbs up before walking on and in his mind, he was considering, weighing up odds, and then he was retreating towards the car: his knuckle rapping on the driver's window and into it he presently said, 'I just wanted to say thanks for today. It was class, I thought. I thought it was unreal. Genuinely.'

Amber said his name and then, 'You're awful sappy tonight.'

He laughed hard and said for her to leave so. Seeya. KK, like. 'Why you still hanging around?'

He watched the car edge away – no goodbye beep, she knew better than to do that – and he exhaled and there was a catch in it.

He repeated the last joke to himself – why you still hanging *around* – and sniggered. That one landed, he reflected. That one was Heathrow Airport and not Luton.

The things John did not know about Amber: her crazy schizo mother, that he liked her a good bit.

Friday, 17th July

He was on the eight to four. Long, laborious. An acute ache in the hole. A shift where you were supposed to undertake a scouring deep clean in the restaurant while also being available to help in the bar when it picked up. A shift where you never ever knocked off early. What especially pricked about this shift today was that John had to grovel for the privilege to work it: last night he'd had to text and plead and agree to additionally cover Samantha's split next week so Samantha would swap with him today and cover his six to ten. An awful trade, a scandalous one-sided trade, and all because there was an impromptu team meeting called at half five in the clubhouse and John was obliged to attend.

At least the morning had flown, though even this consolation was dirtied with the knowledge that it had sped by because it was busy and thus more clean-up for later, and presently John was filling up a bucket with hot water that was becoming sudsy. His phone rumbled and it said it was nearly two o'clock and that he had a message.

Amber wasn't on this morning. She was rostered for the evening slot, and so he would miss her. She'd been out last night – she had replied 'Drinking kkkk' and much later to another couple of three texts from John, 'Home x w' – and she had yet to text him back today.

Insanely jealous and worried? No, no. Not at all. No.

John was merely curious about whether it was an excellent night or not.

The text wasn't from Amber but Rooney: 'PARTY HOUSE is ready for operations', and in his customary bathroom cubicle with his feet against the door, John sent back, 'Unreal! Who u get?'

John had agreed to take the room in the house in Galway.

Despite his legitimately troubled conscience, John couldn't not take such a good and soft deal.

Rooney replied, 'Timmy Crotty. U wouldn't know him. But v sound', and John reckoned a reply wasn't necessary to this message.

The top of the restaurant was glistening, white sparks appearing on the floorboards from where the overhead spotlights hit, and now John started running the mop over the pantry floor – beginning at the back where the glass-washer and filter coffee machine were perched and scooting steadily down. About halfway through, John heard the kitchen door swing, and he glanced up as Hughie Denton entered.

'Well, boss,' John said, and Hughie replied croakily, 'Story.'

Hughie grasped a tie from somewhere in the pile of clothing beneath the coats before sitting up on the counter. John continued to diligently mop. Hughie looped the silky red tie around his neck, measured both lengths and decided which was to be the shorter end – it was a narrow, compact area, and John saw this without wanting to see – but Hughie did not commence the tying of the tie. Rather Hughie yawned and said to John, 'You're working.'

Hughie now worked in the bar. Upon being informed of this sort of promotion, Hughie had found John behind the carvery and stuck his middle fingers in John's face before commenting, 'Unlucky.'

John answered that he was working, yeah, and Hughie asked, 'Ethan's here?' John nodded, and Hughie said, 'Wanker,' and John nodded at this, too. Hughie jumped from the counter and with his pinky, hooked a coffee cup from a tray and declared to John, 'You're going to be pissed now in a second,' and then Hughie proceeded to tiptoe onto the freshly wet half of floor – John blurted, 'You dickhead' – and giggling, Hughie spewed black soupy coffee into the cup – a metallic scalding smell, ribbons of steam – before scurrying past John and clattering out the backdoor: to smoke, as when John trudged out to tip the wash bucket five minutes later, that was what he found Hughie doing: smoking with a foot resting atop a plastic crate.

The whoosh of scummy water down drain and Hughie remarked, 'I needed that coffee, in fairness.'

'Dickhead,' John said again.

John sat himself on the crate opposite Hughie. They were abreast of the hefty industrial bins and their reek: organic and mushy and nearly pocketable. 'Fuckin,' Hughie began, and John looked up at him, 'were you out last night?'

John shook his head. Then answered, 'Championship tomorrow.'

'Shite, yeah,' Hughie said. 'I might go to that.' As if consulting his stunted fag, Hughie added, 'Yeah, I might.'

John nodded and started to think about what to do next, the blunt itinerary of the eight to four and which small box remained unticked, when Hughie said, 'I met your bird last night.'

'Who's my bird?' An immediate reply and John's expression had soured.

A crooked rakish smile on Hughie's face: irritating, smug. With a check over his shoulder, Hughie answered, 'Miss Goold. Amber. She was in Alice's for a bit there.'

'Amber's not my bird, Hughie,' John said, and he tried to seem utterly perplexed by the innate foundation of such a theory: me with a girl, insanity. 'Don't know where you're getting that from?' John let out a gaspy laugh. The same amused simper on Hughie's face and John argued with it further, 'We get on. Amber's good craic in work and that. But, she's not my bird.'

'Oh, right,' Hughie said eventually. 'You two are always going off talking together though?'

'Yeah. Well.' John squirmed, looked at his clumpy loafers. 'She's sound. Like I said. We get on.'

'You're gone all red, kid,' Hughie said, and it was true, John had – he could feel it tentatively on his cheek, like a leg brushed against a glowing oven – but John snapped, 'I'm not, man.' Hughie was laughing for a time and then he squatted down to slot the butt of his fag between the grates of the drain.

John cracked his middle finger, then index.

She didn't want work to know, and maybe John didn't either.

'Do you think she's hot?' Hughie was back before John.

'Who, Amber?' John exhaled performatively as if stumped, as if Higher Maths paper two and skinny triangles stuffed with capital letters. 'She's grand, I suppose. But she's not my type.'

'Why's that?'

'I don't know. The hair or something. Her hair. Just not my type of hair.' Then John accused with a pointed finger, 'Do you think she's hot or something, Hughie? Is that it?'

'Fair question,' Hughie said, and he started to ponder the sky. Professional deliberation and John wished it was an effortless answer. A straight verdict of good or dirt. John sought to crack his ring finger but no sound, only a bony wiggle, and Hughie then said, 'She's not *ugly*, that's for sure. Definitely not rotten. And I heard—'

Hughie stopped himself. 'Are you sure now there's nothing between you two?'

John said of course not, no, and Hughie raised his chin and repeated, 'Are you sure?'

'Honestly,' John said. 'We're just buds.'

'Right. Okay,' Hughie continued, 'I only heard she's a bit of a bike.' John lifted his brows to convey he didn't remotely care but was nonetheless very interested, and Hughie went on, 'I heard stories about her from staff parties. Nights out and that. It seems she rode a few heads from here. The hotel. Supposedly, a fair few like. That's what Rodney in the bar said to me. She's very, very bad for it. And you have to consider that, too, when rating her.' His voice receding, Hughie said, 'I don't care personally too much, but you do have to factor that in—'

The bang of the backdoor interrupted.

They both turned around instantly, guiltily: Ethan, and his hand was dithering over the inner pocket of his blazer. 'What're you two doing out here? John. Kitchen, now.'

Both spluttered apologies – or John said sorry whereas Hughie offered an excuse about checking empties for the bar – and they both stomped inside as Ethan glowered and held the door with an outstretched arm. The kitchen was frenetic, and into John's ear, Hughie presently whispered, 'I hear he's one of the culprits with Amber,' and John's mind blank for a second – waking from a nap and where am I and what is real? That cloudy sensation – before John could say, 'Actually?' But too late. Hughie had overtaken John and was trotting through the unmarked door for the hallway, his elbows hoisted as he fixed his tie. The pant of an oven, plates being prised from underneath other plates, and the head chef shouted at John: 'Table seven, will you get a move on, young fella.'

It stuck in John's head, of course. It was unremitting. This knowledge, or was it accurately gossip and what was the split between the two if John believed it truly and deeply and others might as well? A pale white ulcer in your mouth and how you couldn't not nudge it with the nub of your tongue and inflect the brightest pain repeatedly: like that. Amber had texted – 'Can't believe I have to work. SHOOT ME kk xx' – and John had left it unanswered.

After his shift, John had the guts of an hour to kill so he undertook a circle of Keel – conscious to end up near the caravan park, the beach – and during this ramble, his mind was aflame with images of her with others and not him. Being grubbed and spun and passed about like a tatty parcel. John not knowing and everyone else knowing. He was grieving, and mostly for her because she had dulled it. Amber had spoiled it for herself, actually. She had contaminated them. It was not that John expected purity, but, also, he didn't want this: he didn't deserve this. And what would the boys say? She was dirty. She was nasty, a bike, loose, but wasn't this why he had been sniffing around in the first place, wasn't it exactly why John had gracefully extended himself towards her?

Because older and softer in granting access.

Because she might allow him to do stuff.

Because points and victories.

Didn't I want this? he asked himself. Shouldn't I be glad and giddy?

She was a tap and what had changed for him in that regard?

His phone beeped and his father flashed his headlights obnoxiously as John walked towards the caravan park, the gearbag digging into his shoulder.

John answered, 'It was normal, I guess. The mood. Everyone seemed fine.' Another earnest question John was sure he had already basically answered. It was difficult to ward off exasperation, restrain his tongue, it was proving difficult to keep spiky hostility beneath the surface of his voice. His father, as per, made it difficult. 'They didn't name the team, or anything. Just went over Louisburgh a bit' – a tut from John's mouth here as if sucking a sweet – 'and who were their good players and that.' John didn't look across the room. In his father's presence, these one-on-one inter-actions, John's neck always seemed to droop towards his chest, and he wondered was this same posture utilised in every father–son standoff throughout the globe. You love your mother, you get on with your father: this seemed to be the way of things. 'And then the new tracksuits were handed out.' John gesticulated at the table. 'That was it.'

'Yes,' his father remarked softly, 'the tracksuits.' Peter picked the tracksuit back up off the table. It was still in its wrapping, and it crackled as Peter lifted it closer to scruti-nise the collar before complimenting the workmanship with a frown. 'No,' his dad said, 'it's very good quality.'

The tracksuit was navy with an emerald green streak along the length of the arms and legs. The Island crest was stitched over the heart and to the right of the crotch. The tracksuit felt coarse to touch, the zip was stiff, the trousers emitted this swishing noise when in motion, but they were undeniable proof of a team.

Everybody the one and the same.

Like a school uniform in that, better or worse, once donned this was where you now belonged and here were your pals and rivals.

'And tell me this.' Peter leaned back against the cooker, folded his arms. 'Did Barrett say anything to you, personally?' His father elaborated, 'Vis-à-vis, you playing tomorrow?'

They were in the kitchen of John's grandparents' bungalow. The metal-framed window was opened a notch, causing the lace curtain to flutter, and through it was visible a wall of bulky fir trees – shelter from the gale, the original purpose, and now overgrown with their fallen needles springy underfoot. On the cool lumpy walls: a portrait of a sexy Jesus and multiple photos of relatives with colour dots in their eyes. John's sole grainy memory of his grandmother was contained in this kitchen, in the exact position in fact where his father slouched his body: his nana stood over the cooker and the splatter of oil and he was peering up at her on someone's knee and that was it.

'No, he didn't,' John said. 'I told you this already, Dad. It was general enough.' John grimaced. 'It was a waste of time, honestly.'

This wasn't a leave-me-alone fib. It had been a total waste of time for John. He had been unable to concentrate during the half-hour meeting. It was bluster to his ears. White noise. She had cracked his concentration, too.

'And did Mac give a speech? As captain.'

'Dad.' John sighed. 'Why do you need to know that?'

'What? I'm only interested.' His father's voice was pitched to jolly as if a jaunty wind-up, but John knew how readily inoffensive switched to bratty offence with this man. A flick and Peter was affronted, he was in a sulk. As well as the eyes, John had probably inherited a smidge of this temperament from his father.

John sighed again and said no, Mac did not say anything, and his father replied, 'That's all I wanted to know, John.'

John had buckets of memories of his gaga because Gaga had died only two years back. Large hands with neat and clean fingernails. A wheezy laugh. The slowest eater, so that it was understood not to wait for Gaga before starting on dessert, and it was such a feature of Sunday that John hadn't realised it was bizarre etiquette until Tony had asked about it after a sleepover. Also: the memory of Gaga dead in this house.

'Will we go watch something, Dad?' John asked now, and he met the blue eyes that were completely intent on him. 'Sure, son.' His father bowed his head and made a perfunctory sweep of arms. 'You lead the way.'

In his entire life, John had only seen his father cry on two occasions. One of them was the night, or technically early morn, of the tit photo fiasco – Peter against the kitchen wall and weeping quietly, hideously, and John's heart thumping as he saw this, and his mother sitting perfectly still on the step outside the backdoor, strenuously pinching the skin beneath her chin as if seeking to peel off her face before turning over her shoulder, blinking up at John and then beckoning him to come closer and John did not move – and the other was on the afternoon of Gaga's funeral. At the top of the church, his father had read out a self-penned elegy and even though it was a bit nuts – it depicted scenes of already deceased family members preparing for Gaga's arrival into heaven, which was then revealed, in the final rhyming couplet, to be the very bungalow John and his father currently stepped through (*'And look beyond the green field, lo/He's heading happily for that whitewashed bungalow'*) – it was also strangely stirring. Beautiful in the way a kid's crayon scrawl and scribble might be termed beautiful. John had felt pride flourishing within him and when his father had sidled back into the pew – after a last pat of the shiny coffin, crying at this stage – John had reached across for his father's paw and Yvonne had put her hand on top of this enjoined pair and then Kay – mascara running, twigs of lightning – placed hers atop her mother's so that, for a brief moment, the Masterson family were like a crew of action heroes readied to transform into their colourful costumes and doubtlessly, heroically, save the day.

It was a moment John still sometimes thought about.

The point he booted over last minute to seal an unexpected win for the school against St Gerald's of Castlebar in front of a crowd of everyone important to him – girls in his school, the boys on the team – and how John recalled that kick sometimes and felt radiant, literally, as if a screwed-in bulb: the same as that.

The living room was dominated by an art deco fireplace and the stove within it. Atop the mantelpiece was a crystal vase with wildflowers the colour of rust shavings and John wondered who had dropped them over. The stacked courtroom thrillers, the two jackets laid over the couch: these were his father's scant personal effects. Everything else was fundamentally the same as when Gaga had been laid out in this room.

Four terrestrial channels available and so they watched a subtitled documentary on TG4 about the Burren and its limestone and then there was a circle of fiddle players playing intermittently as the presenter watched on. His father sat in the armchair with fingers steepled atop his belly and during the ad break, John took out his phone and looked at it for something to occupy time other than talk – Amber's message still loomed unreplied-to in his inbox so instead John thumbed through the numerous functions in the settings menu – and then he returned the phone to his pocket once the documentary resumed. It was an hour long and when it was over, his father switched wordlessly to *Father Ted* on RTÉ TWO and when its credits rolled, John reckoned half nine was a reasonable hour for bed.

'Oh, alright,' his father said, and hitched his trouser legs as if to stand, but did not. 'I thought we might watch the movie tonight. It's *Predator*. The aliens. You still like them, don't you?'

John ignored this last part and went, 'With the game tomorrow, Dad, I need to get proper rest.'

'I won't keep you so.' His father sat forward, his expression solemn all of a sudden, the same formal stiffness he had worn to announce Gaga's death – a knock on John's bedroom door and John intuiting from the figuration of Peter's face alone that it was about death – and of course his father had something heavy to say when John was about to leave, of course, and so John chose to pre-empt him and gestured at the vase. 'Did Kay drop those over to you?'

His father strained, looked. 'No, actually.' Then Peter said, 'Would you believe her Denis did.'

John snorted as if he did not believe, said, 'Really?' and his father nodded without laughing.

'That's weird,' John said.

'Well, no. It isn't. He's up visiting here the odd time,' his dad said. 'I want to tackle those trees out the back, and he's going to lend a hand. So, not that strange.'

'Fair play,' John said. 'I didn't—'

'I think he has been told to check on me.' His dad beamed at this, glanced at the ceiling frivolously.

'Right,' John said. The flowers in the vase were called montbretia: John remembered his father telling him this. Why did flowers have such ugly and ill-fitting names. His father continued, 'Kay's orders, I bet. Making sure I'm alive. Someone has to, I suppose.' The last part a joke and exclaimed rapidly like a joke, but still awkwardness as John forced a laugh. John should just stand up from the couch and exit the room. He had already mentioned bedtime so he should disregard all this without guilt and stand and march off and don't engage. He didn't need to. September approaching and he'd be gone and he didn't need this.

The movie had started. A spaceship, a helicopter. John glared at it and spoke as if to the television: 'That's nice of Denis, to visit you. And great about the trees. They are pretty tall.'

His father replied, 'A daycent man. Denis. A very daycent man.' Another attempt at lightness: the incorrect and likely offensive pronunciation of the word being the punchline: but once more, John wasn't sure what was a joke and what was rather a sincere appeal.

'I don't really know Denis,' John said and still he watched the screen: big juicy boys had appeared.

'He's a nice fella. Easy-going,' Peter said, and John nodded at this and was still nodding when his father went, 'I know your mother isn't too sure of him. But he looks after your sister and that's the main thing.' A pause and his father in a lower volume: 'Your mother can be a critical woman sometimes. She means well but.'

'I think Mam just feels it's rushed or something,' John said. 'The wedding, like.' John's voice was uneven but not hysterical or close to such levels. 'They haven't been together for that long.' John looked at his father briefly. 'Less than a year, isn't it? I suppose that's her concern.'

'Maybe it is quick,' his dad said. 'But what difference does that make if they're happy?'

'Yeah, no,' John said. 'I get that. That's true and I'm pleased for Kay.' John was on his feet finally. No more of this. Bed. Then John said, 'But, you know Mam worries they're rushing into something bad. That they don't know each other that well. I don't think she's being harsh for no reason. Or what you said. Critical.' His hands out in front of him as if holding a stack of firewood. 'She's looking out for Kay.'

'They mightn't be compatible. That's true. But who knows?' His dad was stuttering to his feet now, too. 'You have to live and let live.'

'I just don't think Mam's being harsh for no reason. That's all I'm saying.'

'I wasn't trying to imply that.'

'The age, that was another thing. The age difference. Which is factually true, Dad.'

A short silence.

'Who am I to judge, son?' his father said. He was smiling but it appeared pained, sore, now that John did not turn away from it. 'And who is she to judge? Look at us.'

'Right, yeah,' John said. 'I'm not having a go at you, Dad. I'm not trying to pick a team or anything.'

'There are no teams to pick,' his father said simply and this, it struck John, was blatantly true. What had his father done wrong other than be a loser and why did John resent him more than he resented his mother when his father hadn't been unfaithful? Was it because watching his parents interact often felt like icy water dripped onto John's neck and at least his mother in some respect was brave if hopelessly technologically illiterate, if idiotic and selfish? The almighty question: what do you truly owe your parents? Money, okay. Fair: pukes of money. But aside from the financial, what else? What further could be expected from you as a son? John had once asked his father who his best friend was. They were in the car, heading someplace. It was a nothing question, posed without motive beyond something to say. Peter had replied after some audible deliberation: 'You, probably. I'd say you're my best friend.' It was the saddest thing John had ever heard, and he could not explain why.

Now John said, 'I'm working loads these days, Dad. And the training then. That's why I'm not always around.'

'I know.'

'It's not personal. And with the house, with Mam and lifts, it's sometimes. You know, inconvenient to get over here. I'm not ignoring you on purpose.'

'I know that, son.'

'And, look,' John said, 'could we try the driving again? I do want to learn.'

His father's face brightened. 'How about in the morning, we'll head out in the car? We'll take it slow and steady this time. How about that?'

John smiled. 'That be good.'

'We'll take it shaken not stirred,' his father added with a wink. From any other person, any other mouth, you'd surely suspect there was a possibility of a lewd innuendo here or that you had missed some bawdy reference, but John knew better. Knew his father better. It was neither dirty nor profound. It was thoughtless. And yet John still found himself sniggering at this dumb line and that was all his dad was after. The extent of a father's wanting: a laugh from his son.

In the spare room, John attempted to read the paperback he had been reading for the past month – he knew to pack it because no PlayStation here, no computer – but he kept checking his phone after every other sentence. The phone lay on the floor, charging, and each time he flipped over to reach for it, John thought: why did she have to do all that and why had she wrecked it and was she with someone else right now? A while went by, and John got through seven whole pages and then tossed the book aside.

His father was still up. He could hear him bumbling about the sitting room.

No need for an alarm for tomorrow, no anxiety about oversleeping monstrously: his father would pound on the door early in the morning, John knew his dad would do this without asking him to.

In the cold bed, John then proceeded to have a very sad wank. Mental snapshots of Amber were a no go, and reverting to Seóna increased his loneliness, so he ended up replaying in his mind favoured porno scenes and when these didn't suffice, he fell upon the bewitching image of the Maja: dark-haired and lounging on a bed of white, naked. It was an image he had succumbed to before: many times before, truthfully. John had first encountered her during Leaving Cert in a paint-mottled book entitled *Essential Goya*, his teacher contrasting the nude version of this painting with the clothed one. Note the frankness in her expression, the teacher had said, and Christ almighty John did note it.

An erection from a painting: creepy, not something to brag about nor dwell upon, and still John had delayed leaving the class, lagging behind others to smuggle the book out in his schoolbag.

That evening, he'd laid the book flat on his desk and gazed down. Her eyes were brown, but the brown of sun-scorched tree bark. They were alluring, sultry eyes. The old poems he was forced to read for English: the antiqued substance of those in her eyes, yes. You couldn't use a word like hot, feek, decent with her: it had to be exquisite, divine. That word too: erotic. Not sexy, not horny, but *erotic*. She was smirking up at him, as if he should be the one embarrassed. It reminded John of being questioned by a ruck of girls about whether he had kissed anybody yet when he was thirteen. The tethering, the lowered eyes and exchanged glances. How he had lied elaborately about holidays and this girl named Kate – who didn't have a phone, as her parents were strict about electronics and not poor or anything – but they had shifted, loads, John and this Kate. That same charged feeling was captured by some Spaniard years and years and years ago. The feeling of power slipping from your hand, but kind of pleasing as it does.

She had pubes, the Maja, a tuft of smoky black hair like a terrier's docked tail. Her skin was pale as a china cup and almost blending with the pillows and the sheet.

She was beautiful, it was beautiful. He was captivated.

It had felt scholarly to wank over the painting. It had felt intellectual. He had experienced a greater appreciation of the work, of the artist, a deeper understanding, or was it an understanding of something he had previously not even noticed. It was the first time John had witnessed the scope of art. Genuinely. It was like discovering a key to a door you hadn't been aware was locked: there was a click and nothing much changed, but you could enter this new spacious room.

Afterwards John cleaned himself, yanked up the cover, and he stared at the ceiling and wondered for a time about the match tomorrow: about the prospect of his potential admission or omission from the team, about whether Rooney or Studzy or Tony would get a run. On his side now, one hand tucked beneath the pillow, his mind buzzy with anticipation and dread in competing amounts, John started to roll towards sleep.

Saturday, 18th July

They were inspecting the pitch – John, Studzy, Tony, Rooney. Hour and a half before the game and everyone else seemed to be undertaking an intimate review of the white lines and freshly shorn grass so the boys figured they should as well. First gawking down at the lined square beginning at the goalposts and then surveying the larger box that encased this square and admiring, too, the chest-high flags denoting where the sidelines were situated along the vast body of the pitch – the flags chequered, small green and white squares and flapping wildly – and then stomping a heel at random to test whether the ground was squishy or firm and presently Studzy crouched to pinch free a clump of grass and, above his head, he let this clump fall with a dramatically splayed hand. The grass hairs dropped then fluttered, blew onwards. The boys watched with sullen curiosity. Studzy declared, 'It's windy today,' and Rooney bent to snatch some grass to double-check this meteorological fact and then Rooney stood tall and concurred with Studzy's assessment: 'Yeah. It's windy enough, alright.'

At an hour and ten before throw-in, the Louisburgh bus swung through the gates.

A huff followed by a long drawn-out hiss as the bus heaved to a stop aside the stand.

One by one, they disembarked. Men and boys.

Louisburgh's tracksuits were pitch black with a gold band around the bicep part. Aside from that: identical haircuts, similar faces. A mirror seen across the room when drunk and momentarily freaked by the ghost of you. At their arrival, Barrett ordered everyone inside and as John marched towards the dressing room, he felt someone shadow him.

It was Ultan and Ultan said in a whisper, 'Are things better with you, young man?'

For a second, John didn't have a notion what Ultan was saying, what Ultan could be implying, for a second John genuinely believed Ultan might have heard about Amber and her humiliating past, and then Ultan repeated himself and his eyes swivelled downward and John understood: 'Oh, yeah. The calf is a hundred per cent.'

'Good stuff,' Ultan said, and Ultan made a small fist and raised it, and was this a clue specifically for John?

Was he starting and essential to the team now that his injury was confirmed to be healed?

These thoughts were ringing through his head as John filed into the dressing room marked HOME. Barrett clicked his fingers and told them to get dressed. Barrett wore a weathered baseball cap. John wrenched off his runners rather than simply unlacing them, then rummaged inside his gearbag. There was a wiggling in

John's stomach: some*thing* wiggling. He thought: I'm starting maybe and can I do this and am I good enough. He was between Tony and Studzy. Studzy was topless and tying the dangling laces on his shorts and Tony was widening a sock before a prone foot with a whorl of russet hair on each toe. John shrugged on his jersey – an away Celtic one – and then the Island tracksuit over this because that's what everyone else was wearing. Boots being tied atop the bench and the clatter as one boot replaced the other. Ultan was assisting Seamus Fallon in strapping his right thigh. The winding of skin-coloured cloth. Rooney sat with his eyes closed. In the centre of the room was a massage table – this luxurious scarlet leather that was wizened around the edges and John had never seen it used for massage, only as a shelf for nets, footballs – and Barrett now slammed a palm hard against it. 'Let's get going.'

Out for the warm-up – jogging first then dynamic stretching then normal stretching and then two sprints with Barrett calling out, 'Intensity,' as if Intensity was a dog who was purposely ignoring him – and then ten minutes of ball work before the team hurried back into the dressing room with chests stuck out. The crowd was noticeably larger upon this second exit. John's family would be attending, and she was coming to watch him, too.

Upon the team's return, jerseys had been laid out on the massage table: numbers side face up, one to fifteen. A change in the atmosphere. Nerves in the jittering leg. The paled faces. Barrett was telling everyone to settle down, settle. Ultan locked the door with a distinct click and braced his body sideways against it as a further obstruction. John saw the number seven jersey, his jersey, and a cold pressure in his chest like a lump of ice and he looked away. 'Listen up,' Barrett said. 'It's concentration time.' With a gunned finger, Barrett pointed at his head and seemingly shot himself. 'It's time to listen.'

A fiery spiel beginning with preparation being done and dusted. 'We've worked and worked on our system, haven't we?' Barrett said, and it was a question that wasn't a question. An exaggerated clarification followed that today was Championship football. Championship. 'We lose and that's it. One and done. One. And. Done.' A lull as Barrett let this consequence linger and John glanced up – heads in hands, boots tapping – before Barrett asked the room if they were ready for war today?

An actual question in this instance – because Barrett added a spiky, 'Well?' while cupping his ear – and there was a decisive roar in response.

'That's what I want to hear,' Barrett said. He cleared his throat and retrieved the baseball cap from his head and then packed it back down to where it had been, saying, 'The team is as follows.' At this, Ultan stepped forward and clutched the keeper's jersey. 'In goals,' Barrett said, 'Robert Coleman,' and the jersey was flung in Coleman's direction. The lump of ice had melted within John. All of a sudden, there was an empty space in his chest, an expansive gap, and that was somehow worse.

'Right corner-back,' Barrett said, 'is Tom Cafferkey.'

John peeped over at Rooney as this was Rooney's position, and John saw his friend's mouth tighten: two lips becoming a single furrowed line.

'Full-back,' Barrett continued, 'and captain is Mac. Left corner-back is—'

John hadn't expected to start. This morning he hadn't woken up thinking: I'm definitely playing. It was only that Ultan had muddled the situation somewhat. It was only that in his heart John had foreseen himself as starting. John reminded himself that by rights and laws and mistakes for penalties he shouldn't be in the fifteen and yet as Barrett moved through the half-back line to the two midfielders without a clipped mention of Masterson, John felt shocked. As if he had missed a step on a stairway: the subsequent totter and heavy fall onto tailbone. He leaned forward and his hands fidgeted with the ends of his shorts. Shocked. Stunned. Perturbed.

Barrett said, 'Right half-forward, we have—'

John's breathing was shallow and hot. The shock had dissolved into devastation.

This was his thing, wasn't it?

He had never not started, never not been in the team.

The sole consolation John could find was that at least Rooney and – as Barrett currently named DJ as centre-forward with no acknowledgement of Dineen – Tony were not starting: at least John had their disappointment to blot at some of his own dejection. At least John could soothe himself with a swiftly built mythology that they had all been deemed too young to start senior. It had nought to do with the boys' respective ability. It was age. An element outside John's control and responsibility. A girl's rejection and how you could label her a snobby bitch afterwards, how you could state you never wanted to get with her in the first place: it was like that. This was some comfort until Barrett announced that Hanley was in the two-man full-forward line along with young – Barrett used that damning word – Studzy.

Now devastation was replaced by betrayal.

John was dimly aware that much more was being said by Barrett – specific instruction, reminders of who was supposed to track a certain Louisburgh player – and then a jersey was thrown unceremoniously his way. The number twenty-four.

It was a hideous number.

It was a humiliating number.

The entire team was on their feet and John slotted into a huddle with an animated Barrett at its centre: Barrett prompting gruff responses, saying words like Discipline, Game Plan and, rapidly, Aggression Aggression Aggression. It was impossible to listen to Barrett without feeling sick. It was impossible not to feel bitter and that an unjust decision had been reached. And as the team readied to leave the dressing room for the final time – greedy slurps of water, surnames echoing in the small room – it was difficult not to wish dirty luck on Studzy today. It was difficult not to want Studzy to snap something important while out there. It was hard to grin at Studzy and flick his earlobe a couple of times in a congratulatory manner. But John did manage to do this in the end. With a marginal squeak in his voice, John managed to say, 'Buzzin for you, Studz.'

Massive cheers as the team emerged.

The stand was crammed, and other spectators were slumped against the railing, their hands together as if in prayer. Mac led the starting fifteen onto the pitch, a ball tucked under his arm, while the substitutes took a hard right behind the goals and began their trek towards the dugout. Head down, John carried the bottles of water and was grossly offended to have been asked to do so. Rooney held the first-aid kit, and he was ambling beside John, but neither was speaking. Tony was well ahead of both.

Louisburgh were out on the pitch: taking potshots at their keeper or cutting long raking passes across the field.

The referee signalled for the captains.

Rooney and John settled into the dugout beside Tony, who grumbled now from behind tented fingers, 'Fuckin bullshit.' Shaking his head, Tony went on as if countering an argument: 'We should be out there. That's what I'm saying. Like Tom Cafferkey? Eoghan Moloney?' At each name he flashed John and Rooney a maddened look and meekly, Tony then said, 'And I should be in midfield.' Rooney labelled the whole situation a plate of shite, and John stretched out his legs and crossed them at the ankle, allowing his back to slouch disdainfully down in his seat:

his uncomfortable posture a medium to suggest his own unhappiness. Ultan spoke into the dugout: 'Stay warm, lads. At a second's notice, you could be required.'

John thought: if I was needed, I'd be playing.

John thought: if I was any good, I'd be playing right now.

Rooney leaned over and whispered, 'Here, I'm glad we squashed all that by the way.' When John didn't reply, didn't even face him, Rooney explained himself in a lower register, 'About the house and Studzy. I felt bad, Tits. I didn't mean to upset you.'

'Sound,' John said. 'It's done.'

Then John went, 'I wasn't upset though.'

On the pitch, shouting. Names being yelled from the stand. Anticipation tasteable: salty and dry, like a burnt crinkled chip. A shoulder meeting another. Faces, already sheeny. The pitch split evenly between green and white, black and gold. The same handful of statements and commands being roared out nasally from the stand, from the sideline, from the other team.

It was an even first half. The Island went ahead early through a couple of handy frees from DJ – one of which Studzy had done unfortunately well to win, drawing a foul after a deft jink. But Louisburgh grew into it and about twenty minutes gone, Louisburgh should have scored a goal – spilled possession and Coleman the keeper spread himself and parried – and John dearly wished Louisburgh had scored that goal. And when the Island subsequently surged up the other end, a five-on-four counterattack, and Louisburgh defence eventually cleared it after a poor decision from Hanley to chop back onto his right foot, John felt relieved.

Glad.

Maybe even happy.

In every individual duel – a footrace for a pass, a goal kick lofted into the centre of the park – John found he craved for the Louisburgh player to gather the ball, to gain the advantage over whatever Island player was involved. Of course John didn't exactly celebrate and whoop when Louisburgh scored a point or won a fifty-fifty or efficiently shepherded Moloney till he overcarried or anything like that. John wasn't directly pleased for them, no, but rather he was pleased that someone from the Island had messed up. John didn't want Louisburgh to win, and he did want the Island to currently lose: these did not feel like contradictory points of view. It didn't seem treasonous. Rather it felt like what a sub should feel: smouldering hatred for the teammates out there huffing about instead of them.

With five minutes remaining of the first half, the game was level – six points apiece – and then Louisburgh went ahead after a gift of a free from the referee. Then Louisburgh scored another point and another after that and they were three up and how did that happen? Suddenly the Island looked ragged. Panicked. John had been there before: a goal scored against you when comfortable and flick, everything was moving too quickly and the whole entire team couldn't control a simple pass, and it was like being strapped into the pendulum ride at the Hurdy Gurdies: the whirl and spin and the disorientation. Prowling the sideline, Barrett was ballistic: he was frantically gesturing at space, he was barking for composure. The ball was lumped forward with no direction, and it came right back at the Island and a moan from the stand. Rooney lifted his eyebrows and John knew what this signified: major changes at half time, surely. Surely. A cynical foul from Fallon in midfield, a yellow brandished. From the free kick, Tom Cafferkey misjudged the flight of the ball and was caught floundering underneath it and another easy point for Louisburgh tapped over. The Island were four points behind. Players talking darkly to themselves, players throwing up their arms. The whistle for half time, when it arrived after the next goal kick, was a relief.

A smattering of polite applause as they trudged towards the dressing room and his dad was waiting there. Peter wordlessly clenched John's arm, offered a small sorrowful smile, and then stepped off. John was glad it was the only face he recognised.

Mac punched the dressing-room door upon entry. Mac was saying, 'Woeful, fuckin woeful. What are we doing?' A bottle skidded across the floor. Another clattered against the wall. DJ was saying for Mac to chill the fuck out and two of them in each other's face – their knuckles a stark white and it happened so spontaneously that it almost seemed fake, a strange hollow prank – until Ultan's arms were between them, shushing both.

Smeared grass stains on shorts. Sweat on the smalls of backs.

The sniffy sounds of winter and flu and doctors' visits.

Studzy's face was scarlet and his lower lip pasty as if rolled with glue. Tony reached over and patted Studzy's thigh and Studzy was unresponsive. Dazed.

Barrett appeared and he slammed the door, then had to conventionally close it before booting the massage table. 'What was that?' Barrett asked, and John felt himself shrink. The massage table received another whack and one of the legs wobbled. Barrett asked again, 'What was that? Can anyone explain that half of football to me?' No one spoke, no one dared respond. 'Louisburgh have arrived for a battle and we haven't put it up to them. I can't believe what I'm after seeing. Honestly. Aggression, wasn't that the word I used?'

John wasn't the only body squirming, shirking: all around men cowering, avoiding eye contact.

'We can lose because another team's better. You can lose properly. That's life. But to lose a game because we're being bossed around. Because they're hungrier. It's not acceptable.' A snotty sound expelled from his nose, and Barrett went, quicker, 'Or is it acceptable to this team?'

Mac was the one to reply, to look up guiltily, and pierce the silence: 'No, it isn't, Anthony.'

'That's right,' Barrett shouted, and the massage table was kicked once more. 'It fuckin well isn't acceptable.'

A tremendous amount of screaming thereafter from Barrett with F words acting as punctuation.

The fury surrounded like vapour, like boiling shower and the bathroom smog.

John could feel it atop his skin, beading there.

'The only fella who comes out of that half with a shred of dignity is the youngest member of the team.' Barrett paused. 'Fair play to Studzy. He's the only one who wasn't afraid out there. The only one who showed some balls.'

The rage was recast into disappointed looks as Barrett began to circle the room – lapping the massage table, basically – and set forth his tactical adjustments for the second half. There was to be one sub. Though, Barrett swore, he could have produced the curly finger for the whole pack of them. Rooney was on for Tom Cafferkey at corner-back, a straight swap, and John chewed his thumbnail at this announcement.

Tony whispered to Rooney, 'Well done, bud,' and John discovered he couldn't mumble anything kind or supportive on this occasion.

'Up,' Barrett instructed, and everyone rose obediently. Barrett said he expected to see a completely new team in the second half with a totally new, fuckin, attitude. The game was there for the taking, Barrett promised. So grab it. Why not? Why wouldn't you? 'Go do your parish and your family proud,' Barrett said, and his eyes were wide. It wasn't a melodramatic statement. Excessive, out of proportion: no. 'That's who you're playing for today. Not me, not, fuckin, Ultan.' He gestured at himself, prodding the middle of his chest, then a little sadly pointed at Ultan. 'But your family, your community, your loved ones. That's who you're representing. Go out there now and show them some respect.' It did not feel OTT or extreme or outrageous: what Barrett said felt truthful.

And the Island were a different beast in the second half. It was apparent right from the restart: Seamus Fallon laid out his man with a thunderous shoulder and zipped a hand-pass to DJ, who drifted a kick towards Hanley and Hanley dispatched it over the bar.

A huge roar from the stand.

Then from the kick-out, Louisburgh knocked it short and the possession was tipped leisurely about their back line until their corner-back tramped past the forty-five and then, all at once, the Island swarmed, harried, and under this pressure, the ball was punted forward to nowhere especially.

The drum as the ball hit turf and chalked line, bounced and bounced up.

A scattering of painted grass floated after this initial impact like spent matchsticks.

The ball stopped a yard, two yards, before the sideline.

The dugout stooped forward to see, to watch.

Rooney and his man were racing towards it, and Rooney was first. He grasped the ball to his chest and the slightest contact from the man in pursuit – a nothing bump – and Rooney hurled himself to the ground. The ref blew for a free-out. John muttered, 'Soft call,' and Tony looked at him.

'Comeon to fuck,' Rooney cried to no one, to everyone, and both arms raised triumphantly above his head. A ludicrous pose, comical and embarrassing, and John wished he was the one performing it now.

Momentum was with the Island.

It was a three-point game and then there was only a single point in it.

Another substitute for the Island: but neither Tony nor John beckoned over for instruction.

The match was soon level. A stoppage as Louisburgh were making three subs at the one time. They were the team panicking: handling errors, misjudged passes, and one fella literally bashing his forehead with the heel of his hand after conceding a foul.

Finally, the Island took the lead – a lovely score by Raymond Cooney after intercepting a handpass – and there were four minutes to go.

There was an opportunity for another point squandered by Hanley and then Louisburgh went up the other end and should have levelled the game: a miscue by their centre-forward when he had been slapping them over all day long.

Still Louisburgh were galvanised by this missed chance and the Island shook. Spooked. One fuck-up, a single slip, and Louisburgh could claw it back.

Tony was brought on for the fatigued Hanley. John lifted out a hand and Tony slapped it before he sprinted onto the pitch, shouting and pointing.

A foul given away by Rooney – he was spun near the halfway line, and in response he grabbed a hunk of his fella's jersey – and there was some wrestling afterwards.

A great catch by Mac from the free-in and Louisburgh were beseeching the referee for another free – John wasn't sure why, what had provoked such shrieks – and the referee crossing his arms into an X in a sign of get-on-with-it.

The ball advanced. There was a sequence of handpasses and then a long swerving kick from Tony that was more than likely a thoughtless, impatient hump forward and it was pursued gamely by Studzy, who managed to keep it in play with a wicked soccer backheel. A surprised coo from the stand. The muscular sound of attention being drawn, backs straightened. Options abounded for Studzy: he could thump it backwards for a supporting runner or take the shot on himself or meander into the corner and purchase his foul and help time trickle by, and Studzy undertook the hardest option: curling his foot, Studzy lofted the ball towards the figure of DJ loping into the square.

The ball floated.

The Louisburgh keeper charged out, and DJ jumped with an outstretched fist and the ball plopped over the keeper and into the net.

A goal.

Howls. Jubilation.

DJ was wheeling away, gesturing with one finger to the stand. Studzy fell to his knees. John found he had leaped from the dugout and onto the sideline, illegally out onto the pitch in fact, pumping his arms and now hugging Hanley. Delirious and John heard his own voice wailing, 'Yes, Studzyboy. You legend.'

Louisburgh were instantly deflated: an inquest between keeper and the full-back, players with their fingers laced together and flat atop their heads.

'Game over,' John said. 'Four points in it, fuckin. Game over.'

'Game over,' John said again to nobody, everybody, sinking back into the dugout. 'It's done.'

And as soon as the whistle for full time came, John was only elated. All earlier sourness had dissipated, all earlier despair and envy felt foreign, felt fictitious even. He bounded onto the pitch and arrowed for Studzy and Tony: cuddling both. Grinning, then laughing. The screeches from the crowd. The applause. John saw Mac yell right into Rooney's face before lifting Rooney off the ground. Grass sliced up by stud and the smell of earth. Red faces, wet and gleaming teeth. Studzy was speaking into DJ's ear and DJ's arm was roped tightly around Studzy's neck and now even tighter as they both giggled. John was on his own at this stage, smiling and slapping the back of whoever was nearby. He glanced over at the stand and spotted his father and mother, beside one another, and he waved excitedly and then spotted other parents – Rooney's aul pair, Studzy's dad, Tony's entire family complete with grandparents – and he waved at them, and while continuing to search his arm was cuffed: it was Rooney, and John embraced him, saying,

'Unreal, man, unreal,' and the sweat knotted Rooney's long hair so it was like seaweed strewn on a beach. In that moment, in the scramble and excitement, John honestly forgot that he hadn't played a second of football.

The celebrations continued in the dressing room. A brief pause while Barrett praised the turnaround, the attitude, and he mentioned something about Lavelle's that was soon drowned out by a pounding of the wall. Jokes were flying around: collecting laughs even if lame and didn't land and Luton Airport, even if East Midlands Airport. Studzy detailed the backheel and chipped pass into DJ and John shook his head at the crucial beats as if he had not watched it in real time only ten minutes previous. Ultan was being informed the first round was on him tonight and Ultan making a gravelly sound that must be laughter. Mac was arm in arm with DJ. Winning was like being tipsy and not overtly drunk yet: same cheery instincts, same notion that everyone liked you enormously, actually. The fog of under-arm spray. Gel being squirted into the cove of a rounded hand and the tiny mirror by the sink – the shard of glass, really – being tussled for half jokingly. Another mention of Lavelle's and Mac was saying he'd catch everyone down there later and he was out the gap with his gearbag slung over his shoulder.

To the boys, John asked, 'Story with Lavelle's? Is there a meal?'

A snort from Studzy. 'A meal? No.' The *no* elongated, monotone, complete with another piggy snort, and Studzy ruffled John's hair. 'Innocent boy.' They were all standing up, leaving together. The dressing room had emptied out: Ultan alone, sweeping and humming to himself.

Studzy grinned. 'We're going lushing with the team, bud.'

Saturday, 25th July

On account of the panel being granted the week off, this morning's training was especially brutal. Running first – gruelling endurance runs where everyone had to hurry to a cone by a set number of seconds otherwise collective punishment and John noted at this stage the nonappearance of the netted sack of balls and what this ominously indicated – followed by a myriad of strengthening and core exercises with John holding the plank position for a minute, a minute and twenty, another forty seconds – a voice overhead asking, 'What's forty seconds? Think about it, what's it to you?' – and the feeling of small cogs being manipulated somewhere dark and gooey in John's stomach and how this had some miraculous benefit for the abdominal muscles he supposedly possessed. Throughout, Barrett had been dour, taciturn, stationed on the margins, and only at the close of the session – when fellas were on hunkers or collapsed on their backs and rubbing their wan faces – did he step forward, proceeded to address the team. Afterwards, while staggering towards the car park, John wheezed to the boys, 'Fuck,' and they all steadfastly agreed.

And then Tony said wistfully, 'At least it was a good night.'

To be fair, it had been.

Initially, the entire panel had drank in the car park behind Lavelle's and John was frightened and anxious and quiet and then after three cans, he discovered he was talking to men he didn't know how to talk to. There had been group renditions of rebel ballads and John wasn't great on the lyrics but that didn't seem to be an issue. Later, they decamped to someone's house – John was fairly positive it was DJ's, a bungalow with a van plonked outside. Mac had given an emotional speech about the team and about his three little girls and then about his wife as John necked a teacup of gin – Mac's wife was sick apparently – and the world became fuzzy and smudged. Midnight arrived. More singing. Whiskey sloshed in the teacup. The fittest men John had ever known were blowing cigarette smoke into the night sky. John puked into a hedge at the end of the garden as Tony petted his back – the tempo of which increased and decreased according to whether heaves from John's mouth or dry retches – and Tony repeatedly informed John he was sound. Steam from the chalk-coloured puke wafted up into John's face and he looked back at Tony, warbling, 'I don't think I am sound.'

John awoke the next morning with a vomit stain friable on the leg of his jeans and a mild headache which must have been a hangover: his first ever.

A chunk of the panel had gone at it once more on the Sunday. Someone had sent a text to Studzy who then reached out to the boys. John had said he couldn't, cited work though he was off. In the end, it was Studzy alone who had ventured down to the pub and he had phoned John later in the week to explain in detail why the rollover had been fundamentally better than the previous night and John had missed out and should honestly regret it. 'Next time you can't not go, Tits. You have to celebrate proper as a team.' The phone sniffed and then went, 'Them the rules.'

At home today there was nothing for John to do, and there was nothing much to do tonight as drinking was off limits – a ban had been formally installed by Barrett – and so John went over to Studzy's house to do nothing as a group. It was John, Tony and Studzy in the cramped play-room as Rooney had replied, 'Karen :(' to Tony's invitation. The sofa was hard black leather with a daggered tear in one cushion that had been there for as long as John had been coming to visit Studzy. They played FIFA: a cup first with Man United that ended in an argument over a red card and then they created a World Cup tournament for a run with Ireland on Legendary difficulty. It was then this morning's training was mentioned. How tough, who did the worst, and then about Barrett's grouchiness. 'Ah, man,' Studzy was saying, 'I know what he was thick about.'

'What?' John said and he crossed the ball poorly. An aggrieved tsk of displeasure from Tony, and John continued, 'What happened?'

'A crowd went boozing during the week,' Studzy said. 'DJ and a few other heads at some hoolie.' Studzy glanced at John and then back to the TV. 'But it's not like there's a game this weekend.'

'Rules are rules though,' Tony said. 'And you yourself said that DJ is bad for the lush.'

'But look at DJ today?' Studzy said. 'He was the only one healthy at the end there when everyone else was dying.'

'I don't like how Barrett's so rigid about the tactics,' John said, and Ireland conceded from a ball chipped over the top. Tony dropped the controller in frustration and then picked it up again, saying, 'That's your fault, Tits. Why did you bring out the keeper?'

'He was going through one-on-one,' John retorted. 'What else could I do?'

'But you always do it though,' Tony said. 'Every game you bring him out for no reason. And it's not funny. I don't know why you're laughing.'

Leaning forward, Studzy equalised straight from tip – a long-range strike with Robbie Keane – and then Studzy settled back and said to John as if there'd been no interruption, 'What you mean, *rigid*?'

'Just. You know. The tactics are all defensive. Let them have the ball and you stand back there. Where's the fun?'

'It's not about fun, bud,' Studzy said.

'You reckon he'd drop DJ?' Tony asked after a while.

'Not a hope,' Studzy said. 'He's our best player.'

'Truth,' John said, and Tony went, 'I think it'll be you and DJ as full-forwards next game, Studz. Hanley dropped.'

'And you centre-forward, is it?' Studzy nudged into John.

'I hope so,' Tony replied, unbothered by John's hissing. 'You reckon Rooney will start?'

'Probably.' Studzy shrugged. 'He did good when he came on.'

John quietly agreed and Studzy said, 'And Tits. You could start as well.'

Tony nodded. 'Absolutely.'

John quietly agreed with this sentiment, too.

The game and John's unneededness had struck him intermittently throughout the week. Why he hadn't been picked, why he hadn't been first sub, why he hadn't been second or third or fourth sub, why he hadn't entered the pitch legally at all: none of it made sense unless John was not good enough, a badly player. John ruminated about quitting the team, but he could never send the text, and certainly not buzz up Barrett and offer his resignation, and vaguely broaching the notion with the boys proved impossible during a midweek spin. But last night, while prepping for training – taking out the socks from the drawer, sniffing the jersey inside the gearbag to check whether usable – John had come to a resolution of sorts, and it was a simple one: he would make the team. John promised himself this and said it aloud: 'I will start the next match.' It was not necessarily a goal aspired to in terms of a personal dream, an inwardly nourishing pursuit, but rather because John felt he should be on the team because others were on it ahead of him. Perhaps this wasn't the normal ideology of the motivated – this was vengeful, villainous territory – but it was what John saw when he opened his heart. Now that he'd been informed he wasn't good enough, John was going to prove he was better than everyone else.

In FIFA, they reached the quarter-final and lost three–two and there was tension because Tony had snapped at John to stop hogging the ball, before they eventually shook hands, restarted, went again for glory and Ireland lost this time in the semi-final to Germany. It was by now half seven and they had been playing for six hours. The room reeked of BO. There were two plates littered with the crumbs belonging to oven pizzas and a dollop of red sauce on one plate. The spicy mizzle of Doritos from Studzy's gob. Stunned, the boys watched the German players celebrating before the menu appeared, and then Tony asked, 'Any chance of a lift home, Studz?'

Tony had called shotgun, so John was in the back of the Peugeot and warned about putting his feet up. The sky seemed contrary, a leaden grey blotted here and there by white. 'State of this weather, honestly,' Tony said. 'It's July, like.' The car soon tore by the church and then Sweeney's, and John wondered why Tony was being dropped first. As if reading his mind, Studzy groaned. 'I completely forgot about you, Tits. I'll drop you on the way back, alright?'

It was an odd mistake, but nothing major and John replied, 'Yeah, cool.'

Climbing from the car, Tony said he'd see them tomorrow or Monday or Tuesday or something, yeah?

Then it was just John and Studzy returning towards the Island. 'You have no plans now, is it?' Studzy asked, and John caught sight of Studzy's quizzical gaze in the rearview mirror and answered, 'Nah. Spits.' Because of the short length of the trip home, John hadn't bothered to switch into the front.

'So you're not meeting anyone?'

Again, John caught Studzy's eyes in the mirror and, yawning, shook his head.

'Sound, sound,' Studzy said.

They were across the bridge and nearing Sweeney's when the car veered abruptly up onto the kerb. A thud. A loud honk from somewhere behind and then this noise flew by. 'Jesus,' John said, rousing in the back. 'What happened?'

'Sorry, bud,' Studzy said. 'I remembered the aul one wanted something from the shop. I just remembered, like.' Studzy wiggled the gearstick to double-check it was in neutral, wiggled it again. 'Could I borrow your phone, actually? I have zero credit and I need to ring her to find out what it is she wants. I forgot that, too.'

John labelled Studzy a dope, handed his phone over with the caution that he only had a bit of credit left himself.

'I'll be two secs,' Studzy said. 'I'll buzz her real quick out here.'

'No worries,' John muttered and once alone in the car, he slumped down and tipped his head against the window. He wasn't tired: or he was tired, but the tiredness arose from the sheer boredom of his life rather than true exhaustion. He wondered about how he might pass the rest of the evening. Maybe he'd finish *Final Fantasy X*? Or hunt online for some movie to download? Both possibilities depressed him, made him feel like a loser. Both thoughts made the evening stretch out further and further. This was his summer, this was the extent of it, and would his life morph in college, would it be ripped up anew, or was it this wheel rutting the ground forever and ever amen? It started to spit rain. A plink against the roof of the car, another. John sighed. He gazed out at faint blue eyes and then through them to Studzy, who was scampering towards the car. 'Cheers for that, Tits,' Studzy said, and the phone was lobbed back at John. 'The mother, like. Yapping on.'

The car was alive, a testy rev of the engine, and John said, 'Are you not going into the shop?'

'Man. Listen to this.' Studzy shook his head rapidly as if incredulous, as if preposterous. 'She told me she didn't need anything. After all that.'

'Oh right,' John said, unnerved, and then, 'Gas.'

They were by the Clinic Bar, the Pharmacy, then Connaughton's.

'So, how's everything with your one at work?' Studzy asked.

John shrugged. 'Yeah, fine. It's casual, I told you.'

What was the point of being truthful about her now?

Down the glass, teary drops zigzagged, and how that was once upon a time a vital race. John thought: why does summer always feel like it belongs to someone else?

'Her name is Amber, isn't it?'

'It is.'

'I say it'd probably be in as Amber Work in your contacts?'

'What?' John lifted his head.

Through the gap between the front seats, John saw the profile of a grinning Studzy. 'In your phone,' Studzy was saying, 'you probably have her in as Amber Work. Wouldn't you?'

They drove past the entrance to his estate and John heard himself ask in a small and terrified voice, 'What are you after doing to me?'

'No malice.' The same broad sharky grin and Studzy said, 'We're all going to hang out.'

She had given Studzy rough directions on the phone: Dugort and up the road that jutted behind the shingled beach, third house and too far if you see a derelict square of houses. 'What did you say to her?' John asked with the heel of both hands shoved into his eyes. 'And what did she say to you?' Studzy told him to relax. Studzy said, with his tongue protruding, 'She knew who I was, Tits.' The beach, the sea extending from a single silvered line to the entire horizon. John said, 'I think this is a bad idea,' and Studzy replied, 'Why you getting so upset?' Then grass along the centre of a humpy road and approaching her gate. The quaint whitewashed house, her banger at a hasty angle. Fuchsia glossy from the rainfall and overhanging a Ford Fiesta that hadn't been present on John's only other visit. Was this for real? What was Studzy hoping for? John said, 'I hate you, man. I hate you so much,' and Studzy was laughing. Amber was at the door: she had a ponytail and she was in a grey hoodie John had seen before and her expression impenetrable.

'Honestly,' John said to his best friend, 'I hate you.'

She led them through to the rear of the house and there was a step before you entered down into a conservatory. The blinds were pulled on one side and the other side faced onto green. A TV was on a chestnut table with newspaper beneath it, and the globed screen showed MTV2 and rock. The cleansed pong of sprayed air freshener, the particles of it still perceptible in the air, and it could not wholly disguise the tingle of weed in the room. There was a rattan armchair – which Amber sat sideways in with legs propped up, swaddling herself in a woollen blanket – and a couch from presumably the same set, which the boys squeezed onto and from where John now noted the mass of mushy dead leaves overhead: this loamy brown atop the slanted glass and should he mention it for something to say – fair bit of leaves up there, FYI – and what was going on here, honestly? Amber said, 'You guys really had nothing better to do?' and Studzy answered for both with a smile: 'No, we didn't, like.' By the foot of her armchair was a seashell ashtray, a bottle of Diet Coke with the label torn, and a small tin atop which a packet of her particular cigarettes rested.

Amber started to flick through the music channels and said, 'You played well the last day, Enda. In your match. Congratulations.' Each word pronounced as if it were heavy.

'Oh, thanks,' Studzy said. 'Thanks, Amber.' Studzy glanced at John and John continued to look straight ahead with his legs crushed together. 'Yeah,' Studzy went on, 'it was a class win for the team. And happy enough with my own performance, alright. I got two points. And I did set up the winning goal. So. I'm happy.' Amber turned her head towards Studzy, smiling but without teeth, a bemused look maybe, and then back to the TV, and Studzy said, 'Poor fella beside me here didn't get a run out though.'

'Yeah, pity for poor John,' she remarked coolly, and still the channels blinked by. 'Who're you playing next round?'

'Well. It hasn't been drawn yet but we should know this week sometime.' Studzy sniffed and John saw Studzy pinch at his crotch, his dick, once, twice. 'If we win the next game, we'll be in the quarters of the Championship.'

A moment and Studzy clarified for no one: 'If we win the quarters then we'll be in the semis.'

'Is that how it works, Enda?' Amber asked lightly and somehow Studzy didn't taste the sarcasm on her words. Studzy replied earnestly, 'Yeah, no, semi-finals is always after the quarters in the football. Four teams left and then the final follows that. You know, two teams.'

Studzy punched John on the arm. 'Isn't that right, kid?'

John assured Studzy it was.

'In the club's whole existence, the senior team has never got as far as the semi-finals in Championship,' Studzy said, and his right leg was shaking against John's. 'So, be historic if we managed it this year. Be serious.'

Studzy said, 'It be. Snerious.'

'Snerious,' Studzy said, and he frowned at John and said it again, 'Snerious, like.'

John knew he should repeat this in the voice, or at the very least offer a chuckle, but he chose not to do either.

'What does *snerious* mean?' Amber asked, and creases on her forehead like a stick dragged over sand.

'Ah. Just. It's,' Studzy stammered. 'It's a funny word, I guess. You can say serious in a funny way.'

Amber laughed, kind of. Biting his lip, Studzy took out his phone and proceeded to study its screen. Amber kept thumbing the remote and she sucked on the corner of her finger as if it were gashed and bleeding and at one point, she tucked a thin wire of hair behind her ear: just like that. It was a terrible mistake, coming up here, and everyone else must be realising this. To see Amber was nice, obviously, and he did feel worse re the four texts in his inbox, but this was wrong. Incorrect, like spotting a teacher out shopping. Incorrect, like his mother and father. What was Studzy hoping for, and could it really be that? Music played, becoming unjumbled and recognisable for at most thirty seconds, and then onto the next channel. John had

been holding in his stomach the entire time he had been in
the room, in her house. He noticed again the newspaper
underneath the TV and why was that there? He thought
too of the lack of photographs in her hallway: no picture
of the mother who was sick in the head, no gilded portrait
of Amber as a baby, as a girl in a communion frock, as a
now. The foreignness of someone else's home and
how Studzy's house smelled of browned mince and could
Studzy smell that, too? John peeked over at his friend
and Studzy was hunched up and slipping his phone back
into his pocket and Studzy turned, winked at John, whispered something that John couldn't catch. Then Studzy
said gleefully aloud, 'How's everything going with this
lummox, Amber?'

'You tell me, Enda,' she replied far too quickly and
inclined her head. 'He's not talking to me anymore.'

'What?' Studzy said and he gaped at John – for help,
guidance – and then Studzy emitted a high-pitched squawk
when neither help nor guidance arrived.

All eyes in the room were presently directed towards
John, who stared even harder at the TV.

'You see? He doesn't like me anymore,' Amber said. 'He
has stopped replying to my texts. Acts as if I don't exist in
work.' Everything being said sweetly: these mounting,
succinct phrases that cut and stabbed and made John seem
very callous but were so removed from his point of view
and context. 'I must have done something awful to him,
and I'd love to know what.' She let a moment go by, an

eternity it felt like, and then Amber said, 'Did he mention anything about it to you, Enda?'

Studzy said, 'Well.'

Studzy said, 'Just, am.'

'It's not like that at all, Amber,' John spoke up finally. 'I wasn't ignoring you. It's just my phone was broken and then I had no credit.' He swallowed, had to. 'And we've been training nonstop all week' – John faced Studzy, who gradually nodded in agreement – 'and in fairness work was ridiculously swamped—'

She interrupted: 'Did Enda not use your phone today?'

John opened his mouth wide and then went, 'I got it fixed yesterday.'

'And you bought credit, too?' she asked. The sugariness of her voice. This little inverted pyramid of a smile. Her face not distinctly displeased or angry. Not good: any of this.

John was red, his cheeks mottling or genuinely on fire. The memory of being interrogated by his mother about certain pop-up ads on the family computer when he was eleven and guilty of googling risqué terms like 'boob' and 'playboy boobs'. 'Phone credit too as well, yeah. It was a deal. Fix your phone and you get credit.' He glanced over at Amber. 'But it was my idea to ring you today. Wasn't it, Studzy? To come over here and see you.' John looked at Studzy and pleaded directly to him, 'It was my idea, wasn't it, Studzy?'

In front of a girl with the opportunity to brilliantly destroy someone you know: John wasn't sure he'd be able to withstand such temptation.

But Studzy did.

Studzy said, 'That is true. The credit and phone thing. Plus he did say to buzz you.'

'And his phone was broken all week?' Amber smiled.

'All week,' Studzy said, 'swear on my mother.'

'Tragic liars. The pair of you.' Amber shook her head and a sullen puff of air from her nose before she drooped down and pawed and then picked up the tin and her cigarettes. 'Anyway, I don't give a shit.' She swung her legs to the floor: the blanket was still bundled around them. The tin and cigarettes were nestled on her lap, and she began to fuss with her ponytail, tightening the band or rewinding it, a gigantic mystery to John either way. 'Do you smoke, Enda? I know *he* doesn't.'

The deranged notion within John to proclaim, actually, I love smoking, and it was successfully stifled.

'Yeah, I do,' Studzy said, and hesitated. 'You mean, like. As in weed?' Amber nodded and Studzy said, 'Oh. I do. Hundred per cent.'

'Great,' she said. 'Let's go for a stroll, so.'

From her gate they took a right and ended up at The Strand Hotel and two sandy football pitches and then, eventually, by the shingle beach. There was a stone wall and they stalled here: the capping of the wall was smooth and wide enough for Amber to raise herself up onto it and sit cross-legged. The boys stood before her. It was an altogether mild evening, though because John hadn't really spoken since the conservatory, he now shivered and said, 'Cold, isn't it?'

Then John literally said, 'Brrr.'

With an arched brow, Studzy remarked, 'It's not that cold?'

Amber removed the tin box from the pocket of her hoodie, clicked it open. Inside was a lighter and green Rizlas and other material and John looked off to the beach.

Plausible deniability, John thought.

John hadn't been at this beach in years. Driven by it, yeah, sure, but walked it, smelled it: years and years. He used to come here as a kid with his dad. A rockpool was someplace and that was where he'd guddle baby crabs from. His father would locate the crabs for John: shift the seaweed, indicate where a clawed creature currently scuttled, with the knees of his jeans becoming increasingly caked in greens and sludgy black.

This was a happy memory, surely.

'Watch senso, Amber,' Studzy said then. 'He's probably thinking of poetry or something like that. Amber, watch.'

Studzy had begun to deploy her name a lot.

Amber was finalising the joint – her fingers scrunching the paper which was now being sealed by the flat of her tongue – and she looked up while grabbing for the lighter. 'What're you looking at, John?'

John answered nothing and then went, 'Only I used to go fishing here ages ago. There's like a clump of rocks.' His hand twirled in a circle as he said this, which apparently symbolised rocks. 'Fished there, so we did.'

The clank of lighter, an ice blue spark then a flame. Lit, the joint was being drawn by Amber with her eyes closed and no mascara today. She exhaled, her face wreathed in smoke. A warm sour tang expelled into the air. 'Yeah?' Amber said and drew again. 'What could you fish for around here?'

The joint was passed to Studzy, and he didn't cough and gag as much as John had hoped.

'Crabs,' John said. 'You used to find them under the stones and stuff. Small ones, obviously.'

'Crabs?' Studzy snapped. 'Man. You have crabs, like.' Studzy laughed emphatically at his own punchline, and he elbowed John, and could he be whacked already? Was that possible? 'Crab boy over here, Amber. What you reckon?'

Amber smiled annoyingly at John and merely commented, 'Did you catch them with your dad?'

John tried to ignore her.

Then John said, 'No, actually, it wasn't with my dad,' and Amber maintained the same annoying smile.

Studzy pulled from the joint again, labelled the weed as top stuff. 'Quality,' Studzy said, with eyes flickering and his mouth an O. Studzy asked Amber where she had sourced it and frowned as she answered. 'Must get onto them now, myself,' Studzy said, and he moved to pass the joint back to Amber when John spoke up: 'What about me?'

They both looked at him and John was a little astounded himself.

'Sham,' Studzy said, 'you want a pull?' Studzy leant the joint towards John and John took it: alright, at arm's length as if it might explode, but John took it nonetheless. Carefully, John brought the joint to his parted lips, his hand only marginally unsteady.

He sucked it back.

Felt clouds, fluffy white clouds, and held them inside his lungs as they swelled.

A whistle of approval from Studzy.

The end of the joint burned brighter, momentarily. A ring of gold, apricot, then reverting to brown as John unstuck the joint from his mouth.

'Fuck,' John then announced, and he was less successful re the coughing and gagging. 'Jesus Christ.'

John coughed some more, and a hand removed the joint from his.

John was also obliged to spit. A slight head-rush like you had clocked your skull against the underside of a table. 'I'm sound now,' John said and then had to bend and spit again.

Studzy slapped his upper back, harder and harder. 'Good lad,' Studzy was saying, 'get it down you, Tits.'

'Tits?' Amber repeated. 'John. Is that your nickname? Really? You let them call you Tits?' Tilting his head, John peered up at her and nodded sheepishly. She bit her lower lip and looked from one boy to the other. 'Ah, John. Come on.' An inscrutable laugh and she looked away and held the joint in the V of her fingers. 'You guys love your traumatic nicknames. I can guess where Tits comes from, but what about Studzy? Where did they pull that one out of?'

Studzy asked what she meant, and Amber rolled her eyes. 'Like where does the nickname come from? Your name is Enda, isn't it? Your second name is McNamara?'

'Well. Me?' Studzy said, plainly confused. 'It came from me.' Studzy shrugged, shrugged at John. 'I thought it be a cool nickname. Studzy. It is a cool nickname.'

Amber squinted at Studzy. 'So you called yourself Studzy for no reason?'

'No,' Studzy corrected her, 'not for nothing.' Studzy's head moved side to side. 'Because it sounded cool.'

Amber covered her mouth with her hand as Studzy asked, 'What's so hilarious, like?'

The talk between them fell much easier after this. Prompted, Amber told Studzy about her forthcoming holidays – sorry, trip – and shaking his head as if in utter disbelief, Studzy said he'd love to do something like that, wow. The joint was like a game of pass the parcel – you had only got rid of the yoke when it was propped once more between your thumb and palpating index finger. Was it now a fun and good time? John wouldn't go that far, but he no longer wished to disappear completely. Why had she ruined things? A handful of walkers waded by and grave suffocating fear they might inform the guards and then forgotten once they turned behind The Strand Hotel and the rasp of their rain jackets receded. John had not missed her during the week, but now he realised he had, actually. Amber's absence had made his week worse. The sound of the sea constant – the tide tumbling forward and then peeling back out in a whisper – and he could not distinguish what was the sea from what was the sky: this singular deep dark blue. A cottony taste on his tongue, in the crevices of his rear teeth. A dry mouth. His legs would not really move, he couldn't shuffle from foot to foot, but that was alright: where else did John want to be? Amber now and again brought the sleeve of her hoodie up over her knuckles and now and again the sleeve slipped back down. Perhaps she believed John about the phone, the credit. This thought growing larger and larger in his mind as from the corner of his eye he watched her watching Studzy perform his impression of his manager at the petrol station.

When the joint was finished, they tossed it blindly – a scattering of embers, russet full stops, then gone – and while her phone bloomed, Amber said she probably had the makings of another one if they fancied it, and Studzy immediately accepted this proposal: 'Shit, yeah. Let's do it.'

'Fine,' she said, and she was more interested in the phone than the boys. 'But let me call my dad back.' She hopped from the wall and landed unsteadily, and Studzy offered his forearm.

Amber smirked. 'Alright, Enda. Relax.'

And as soon as Amber had walked clear of them, John pushed Studzy. 'Relax, Enda. Will you relax, Enda.'

'Shut up,' Studzy said, smiling. 'She's done me there, like.' Studzy lowered his voice: 'It's going well though, isn't it?' He stepped that bit closer. 'She's fierce sound. Amber.'

'She is, yeah.' John nodded and then winced. 'You think she believed me about the broken phone?'

'Ah, yeah,' Studzy said. 'And sure, what difference if she didn't? It's going good. Trust me. The pair of us are in here. Genuinely. *In.*' Saliva between Studzy's teeth and the suction sound of this: then he spat it out and went, 'You only need to say it to her.'

What was Studzy thinking, what was Studzy hoping for, and it was the answer John knew all along, and still John replied, 'What you mean?'

'You know what I mean, bud. We talked about it.' Studzy leaned in even closer to John, teeth showing wetly. 'We're in here. She likes you. You told her about me. And she's gamey, isn't she? Loose.' The hot smell of his friend's breath. The crusty wax that flashed on Studzy's fringe as he bumped his shoulder with John's. 'You say it to her, Tits. Suss it out. I'll go for a piss, right, and you ask her straight? Don't look so scared. Trust me.' Studzy checked over his shoulder and it was as if there was something in his mouth, a hardboiled sweet, a lozenge, before he said to John, 'And, bud, I'll go second. I don't mind that at all.'

'You're not wanting we, but like, then with her?' John couldn't comprehend his own stuttering question, but Studzy evidently could: Studzy's expression altered into one of offence – a tightening of his features as if blanched, this shrunken bitter mouth that now said, harshly, 'What are you saying? We agreed on this. We talked about it. Sharing her.' A finger pointed up at John and Studzy possessed a new underbite. 'Don't be backing out on me now. That's not fair. That's not on. There's malice in that.'

'Say it to her about me, John,' Studzy said.

Studzy said, 'Don't be scab, man. Be a good bud.'

John was clicking aimlessly through his phone when Amber returned. 'Watch slow coach,' Studzy said, and Amber made a dismissive face at this remark and went towards the wall but didn't clamber up it this time. Instead, she sat half on and half off, and the little tin container was to her left and opened.

Studzy peered at John. 'Actually, Amber. I have to go toilet.'

'Alright?' Amber replied. Her hands were busy – a thin scroll of paper, a filter being constructed, and the tin box was closed – and then she looked at Studzy. 'Do you want us to wait for you, is it?'

'Would you mind?' Studzy nodded. 'Thanks.'

John's arm was tugged, tugged harder, and then Studzy added, 'I'll be back in a sec.'

There were no streetlights up here and John watched Studzy cross the road and stomp cautiously through the overgrown grass: the glare from Studzy's outstretched phone bleaching the green to a cumwhite tint and then Studzy rounded something darker and John could see him no more. They were alone. Hands in his pockets, John pressed his arse against the wall and then inched nearer her. How to dredge up such a proposition and why did she have to wreck everything and had that validated Studzy's claim to her: for if it was wrecked irrevocably between him and Amber, shouldn't Studzy be allowed to try, feel, touch and hop on? Did John fear Studzy or love Studzy the most? Amber was wearing Converse and the laces were undone on the hanging foot. She had put her hood up so he couldn't see her whole face, only the tip of her nose, and was John a despicable person or an excessively kind and generous friend? He managed to say at last, 'Of course that fella needs the toilet.'

With her thumb, she was flattening bitty material along the paper. 'Why is that?' she said eventually.

'Ever since I've known Studzy,' John said, 'he's had the shittest bladder. The worst ever. Believe me. He uses the bathroom, so much.' John laughed here and Amber said nothing but cocked her head to indicate she was listening, had listened. John coughed, went on, 'It was funny what you said about his nickname. Studzy. I never thought of it like that. It's very funny.' She let out an agreeable hum and John's right hand was squeezing a wad of skin through his pocket, and he said, 'He's an absolute fool, Studzy, but he's a nice guy as well, isn't he? Now that you met him. I told you he's nothing like his older brother. I think Studzy's a good, good lad. He's a legend, isn't he? What do you think of him, Amber?' John cleared his throat. 'Do you think Studzy's nice?'

Whatever fiddly work she was doing stopped at once. 'Do you want me to get with him or something, John?'

The truth, and obviously John couldn't respond to it truthfully. He could only set his face to startled, then to mystified, then to angelically innocent as he said, 'What? Amber, no. Like, what?'

She didn't let up. She wasn't duped. 'Is that why you came up here today after ignoring me all week? That I'd shift your little friend?' Everything said evenly but the rolling paper was ruined by her clenched fist. 'Is that what you'd like me to do, John?'

'Well, I—'

'Is that what you want?' she asked.

'No. I only thought,' John said, and Amber started to shake her head and he instantly changed tack and exclaimed, 'Amber. You've the wrong idea completely. We came up to see you.'

'Don't lie to me,' she spoke over him. 'Is that what you want? You want me to shift your friend? Ride him, is it? Or all three of us together. Is that it? Did the two of you come up here with that idea in your dumb fuckin heads?'

It was the first verbal spike of anger and her hand suddenly gripped John's wrist, pulled it towards her, and Amber said, 'I'll do it, John. But I want to hear you say it.' Her body was trembling, he could see that, feel it, and she was twisting the sleeve of his jumper and it kind of hurt. Her eyes set on him, her face furious. 'Say it to me, go on,' Amber said to John. 'Ask me.'

John started and Amber told him to speak up.

'I don't want you to kiss him,' John admitted to her, and his heart was pounding. 'Or do anything with him. No, I'd absolutely hate that, Amber.' How hopeless and weak this sounded to his own ears, and John said, 'I'd hate that more than anything in the world.'

'Please,' John again, and she stiffened, allowed time to crawl by before she let go of him.

He was feeling empty, devoid, like no stomach, like no gut and organs, cruelly empty inside, and Amber was away from the wall, the tin container in her hand and then once more safely inside the front pouch of her hoodie. She took out her phone, peeked at it, and her eyes seemed shiny. 'This was never meant to be hard, John,' she said, and she laughed but with a shudder as if a cold, cold night. 'It was meant to be easy. It wasn't even meant to be a thing.' The look she gave John then – as if he was a nasty bully – and it was wrong: John did not see himself like that. It was an inaccurate summation. She had got it all wrong of course.

'We not smoking?' Studzy shouted over then. He had re-emerged from the grass, was stamping towards them, pace quickening.

'We're not,' Amber said, and the phone was a flashlight and directed at her feet, the unpaved road ahead. 'I've changed my mind. I have work tomorrow.'

'No way,' Studzy whinged, and John caught Studzy's bewildered glance and John looked away. 'Well,' Studzy continued, 'if you can't smoke, how about we go for a quick cruise, Amber? In my car.' Studzy retrieved his keys from his pocket, and they tinkled solidly in his paw. 'The night's young enough, like.'

'It is,' Amber said, and she began to walk, 'but I'm old, Enda.'

Studzy called after her, once, twice, and then, grudgingly, the boys started to follow.

Studzy tried to convince Amber a couple more times on the hike back, and at her door began to mention food and Hurley's chipper – 'The munchies,' Studzy joked, and he glared at John to laugh along – but there was no give. A goodbye, and the door was shut, and John registered the clunk of a deadbolt lock, and soon the boys were driving through Dugort and onto the Glon and finally Studzy talked: 'What happened, Tits?'

John said he didn't know what had happened, and an even terser silence flowered and into it, John now suggested that Amber might have pulled a whitey and that this was the root cause of her dramatic exit.

'A whitey?' Studzy turned from the road to leer at John. 'Are you an innocent boy?' John didn't respond to this accusation. Over a verge and a van materialised in front of them. The van was not exactly bombing it along but not slow either, and yet Studzy beeped at it, edged over to check whether possible to overtake, and John found he was clutching the grooved bar below the door handle. Under his breath, Studzy muttered obscenities, and John wasn't convinced they were entirely directed at the vehicle in front, and then Studzy said, 'Did you mention it to her? About me.'

The van turned left and Studzy shifted the gear from four to five, flew on.

'I didn't, bud,' John said. 'Like, I couldn't. I tried to bring it up. I tried, twice. Three times, actually. But she was dead silent and kind of spacey. So, you know, that's why I'm thinking, was she too stoned?' Both his hands were touching his chest. 'You get me?'

It wasn't the most elegant and coherent of lies but Studzy didn't bite.

'Fucksake,' Studzy hissed after a moment. 'That's probably why she wanted to go home. She got bored of you because you didn't say it.'

John agreed.

On a stretch, faster.

Studzy scratched at his neck. 'It's probably for the best anyway. She's not unreal or anything.' Studzy tsked. 'I'm happy to leave it. We'll leave it. I'm not interested in her.'

John nodded.

'Handy for the summer and that. Good for you' – a hand lifted from the wheel at this – 'and I'm not saying unbelievably bad, Tits. But she's not amazing. Still, good for you.' The crossroads after the Glon and now they booted down the main road towards the Sound. 'As a soft tap, she's handy. And she's definitely feeked loads and stuff like that. You can tell she's dirty. I can tell. So fair play to you, Tits.'

'Yeah.'

'And she's a bit weird,' Studzy said. 'Strange personality. A fuckin weirdo, to be honest. Like that was awful weird at the end there, wasn't it? Running off.'

'True,' John said. 'Yeah, truth.'

They were at Brett's Florist when the indicator ticked, and the car pulled in. John's estate was a five-minute walk away, a two-minute drive, and Studzy said, 'I'll leave you off here, Tits. Petrol. You know yourself.'

John nodded, undid his belt. A small compact light flicked on when John pushed the passenger door and now Studzy asked behind him: 'Did you ride her yet?'

'No,' John said, half out of the vehicle.

'Well,' Studzy said, 'you should ride her, man.'

John hesitated and then said, 'Yeah, no, I should.'

'You better,' Studzy said. 'Be an absolute waste of time otherwise.'

After a couple of steps, there came a beep, and John swung around to acknowledge it with a salute. And for a time, he watched as the Peugeot's tail lights burned through the blue of summernight.

Wednesday, 29th July

John thumbed a lift to Keel because his father was at a business thing in Dublin and his mother wasn't doing three round trips in a single day, and, presently, he began the short trek up the town for The Island Head. The sea was stretched behind him and then it vanished as he turned a corner. Overhead, gulls, shrieking as if they had dropped their wallets. The smell of sea salt and further along, exhaust fumes and then the scald of lumpy tar as roadworks and the texture of air suddenly different, too. He was feeling nervous. Apprehensive. He wasn't supposed to be working today and had been phoned up yesterday evening at seven then at half seven and, when he finally answered, two minutes past eight: it was Martina and his name was squawked twice before John responded. A change of plan and now a funeral reception was being held in the restaurant. They were already understaffed due to a tour group for breakfast and dinner. And would John please pitch in? Please please. Sprawled on his bed, John had asked who else would be working and agreed when he heard the names.

The car park in the hotel was jammed, and when John strode through the foyer he saw there were bodies three deep before the bar and he felt his jaw clench.

Nervous, apprehensive, but also now fearing the prospect of work itself.

He clocked in, changed, and the loud whir of the hoover and John checked from behind the partition to see who it was: Amber.

There were four on for the lunch: John, Zibby, Samantha and Amber. John couldn't exactly prove anything, but Amber had been meant to be doing the morning shift on Monday with him and yet Zibby was there in her place when John arrived. A coincidence, John had told himself, while not totally believing himself.

'John,' Amber announced crisply. 'You're finally here.' She started to haul the hoover through the restaurant. Her hair was in the usual clip combo at the back with wispy strings framing her forehead. She said, 'Do the bread right away, okay?'

'Yeah, perfect,' John said to her, 'no problem.'

John said, 'Thanks, Amber.'

The entire restaurant was set for lunch – bright white cloths, napkins like birthday party hats. He was halfway through depositing a bread roll on each side plate – conscious to use the tongs because Ethan was lurking around and twice in the past Ethan had berated John re hygiene – when Amber approached. A stack of menus clinched under her arm, the cooked smell of printed paper.

John continued dishing out the rolls, waited, bit his tongue and waited some more, and once she had reached his table, John remarked, really casually, 'Some amount of people for a lunch, isn't it, Amber? And only the four of us to cover it. It's mad.' Without looking at him, she agreed, 'Sure is,' and placed a menu between two settings and her voice was neutral as if John were a stranger. Or worse: a customer.

'Only the four of us?' John said, and her back was to him, and still he risked it and in a higher voice added, 'But I suppose, at least Teamo Supremo is on. At least we're here. Teamo Supremo, kay kay.'

Amber let out a hmm sound.

Nothing more.

He watched as she licked her thumb and moved on to the next table and he said then, slightly less casually, 'It's nuts though, isn't it, Amber?' He waved the tongs. 'Only four of us for this entire lunch.'

Amber answered, 'I heard you the first time.'

In the kitchen, John clasped a tray with both hands as it was loaded with plates of melon and spring rolls drizzled with chilli sauce. This was Amber's great idea: John would bring out the laden tray and someone more proficient would remove the dishes and John wasn't offended by this decision, no, he actively nodded and verbally concurred as Amber explained sternly that he should be able to carry out more than two plates by now. John smiled as he carried the tray into the restaurant and threaded by the bustling tables, smiled wider at Amber as she fetched the plates from him and then, frowning, John scurried back towards the kitchen with the tray flat at his side.

The mains were delivered out in the same way. The desserts. The choreography becoming more and more polished as they went along. It was manic, strenuous, and no space to ruminate about anything beyond what he was tasked with except, at one point, when Amber was returning to the kitchen with a single plate as John was shuffling out with his cumbersome tray. She held the door and looked at him, then past, and John had to continue on, was unable to hunch and meet her blue-grey-green eyes and ask, softly but pointedly, 'What the fuck, Amber? Will you please talk to me like normal?'

Time slipped away, and when John glanced at his phone it was almost four o'clock.

Ten minutes later and it was five on the dot.

By then John was collecting dishes scuffed with ice cream in the emptied restaurant. His feet were throbbing: this sensation of a clamp around the middle of each foot. Tiredness like a bulky waxed jacket over his shoulders. In the scrolled mirror behind the cash register, he noticed his forehead, glimmering, and from behind the cash register he could also notice Amber. She must have been sifting through the receipts, clarifying what had been paid on each table. Intense concentration anyhow: her lips twisted and up on one side and the indentations at the brow and John's name was being said.

'What, sorry?' John said, turning around to Ethan.

Ethan had his arms crossed high on his chest and creases had formed on the upper shoulders of his suit jacket. Ethan said, 'What time are you off?'

'Oh,' John said. 'Half five. Martina said that was sound. Cause I have training.'

Ethan clucked his tongue, scanned the restaurant, and hitched up his sleeve to peer at his watch. Theatrical, all of it. 'Zibby's gone into the bar, so you won't be leaving till this place is clean. Right?' No space for reply or argument as Ethan added tonelessly, 'Good man,' and then Ethan stepped towards the cash register.

Her name was said, and she looked up.

In the scrolled mirror, her head and her neck and the hairclip – a leopard-print design today – and in the background Ethan rubbing his mouth, or was it his chin, and regardless, John had to look away.

John picked up another plate and marched towards the kitchen.

His animosity towards Ethan had not increased since John had learned what he learned about Amber. He thought Ethan was a dickhead, absolutely, but he had thought Ethan was a dickhead since the initial interview for the job. Plus, Ethan was a creep: people had whispered this to John from the beginning.

So why didn't John hate Ethan like he so hated a side of Amber?

Well, because it was Amber's fault. It was Amber's fault entirely, conclusively. She was guilty and that was why

John was being so generous by being willing to talk to her and why she was so incorrect to not talk to him.

After clearing the plates and glasses, John and Samantha subsequently laid out the settings for tonight and Amber was notably absent. While they cleaned up, she lingered by reception with a blue ledger. Ostensibly to check off reservations and print menus – that's what she'd told them earlier – but John sensed the real reason. In fact, John would venture as far as to say he knew the reason. Samantha complained bitterly of course, and John stayed silent, loyal, and only once or twice agreed that it was completely unprofessional conduct by Amber. And when the restaurant was finally reset at quarter past six, Amber collected her handbag and left without a word. No farewell. No brisk wave. You couldn't exactly say she had stormed off with a filthy vindictive look fired in John's direction, but that was what John was going to tell himself had transpired.

Outside, he watched her car blow right at the exit, which he knew with a clench in his chest wasn't Amber's normal route home, but what could John do now?

Other than text her.

'Thx for saying bye'

Then text her once more for effect while in the car with his mother, zooming towards the pitch and training: 'I thought we could talk properly today??? But no?? Really mature by you.... Well done Amber well done.'

That final full stop, John felt, was particularly formidable.

* * *

The customary half-pace lap around the pitch and there was no Studzy amongst the pack. John had commented on this omission twice to Tony and Rooney and now as they stretched, he brought it up again with a hand over his mouth: 'Did Studzy say to you he wasn't coming to training or what?'

One knee planted, John had his right leg extended and the clench along the hamstrings that made the leg feel impossibly heavy, unusable, before a shout and John swapped from right to left and this ponderous feeling disappeared. Mac was leading the stretching. The prickling scent of nettles, bramble, as they were near the woods. The sun behind them and swathes of the pitch were freckled silver and gold.

Tony grabbed for the toe of his boot, rounding his back, and whispered, 'He hasn't been onto me anyways.'

John peeked over at Rooney, mouthed, You?

A sidelong glance from Rooney. 'I don't have his number.'

John's face wrinkled. 'What?'

Loudly, Mac commanded, 'Into a lunge, for the hips.'

Bodies shifted and reassembled, and hands were raised above heads on one side. Short, controlled puffs of air, a dim grinding sensation in John's hips, and then on the count of ten, everyone switched over and the hand aloft on the opposite side and it was like a dance.

Tony whispered, 'He's probably still working, Tits. What's the big deal?'

'Nothing,' John said, and he covered his mouth once more: 'He didn't text back earlier and it's not like him.'

And John couldn't drop it and he said again to Rooney, 'Do you actually not have Studzy's number?'

Mac shouted for the three young bucks to stop fuckin chatting, and then Barrett motioned for everyone to tromp their way over to him in the middle of the pitch, and John jogged beside Rooney and went, 'Like, really, man? You don't have Studzy's phone number?'

Rooney looked at him. 'Why would I have his number, John?'

Halfway through the second drill of the evening – kick passes with hard yards to cover in between cones, and John had accomplished two out of his five kicks with his left foot and surely this feat was noticed – there was a dust cloud in the car park. Then the slam of a door. Studzy emerged, jamming a hand into the sleeve of a flapping zip-up and he bounded first to Barrett before sprinting towards the group and John found he was not altogether happy to see Studzy, but worried.

Studzy fist-bumped Tony and Tony asked, 'Where were you, bud?'

His tongue sticking out and wriggling momentarily, Studzy answered, 'I was getting pussy, kid.'

Stifled giggles at this.

Fuckin Studzy, John thought adoringly, and Studzy went, 'Nah. I had to work overtime.' Studzy ground his heel into the grass. 'Barrett bullin at me then, like? As if I wanted to work late?'

Sympathetic nods and crinkled faces at this from the boys and John held out a fist but Studzy probably, likely didn't notice this gesture because Barrett was beginning to state what they'd be at next.

At the end of the session, as bibs were being stripped off, Barrett told everyone to head into the dressing room for a word. Inside, there was much sniffling, rustling as if crisp packets were being munched unseen, and the overwhelming rich stink of fresh exertion. John was beside Hanley and Studzy on the bench, and John was conscious that his thigh should not touch Hanley's. Water was chucked around, and John swiftly drank so he could hand it along to Studzy. John watched Studzy lift the bottle unnecessarily high and a long stream into his mouth and John wanted to say, 'Me and you, best buds for life. And women can head off, genuinely.' But of course John didn't and instead he positioned an elbow into his friend's ribs: 'Bad form today, Studz. Being late and that.' In response, Studzy eyed him and wiped his mouth, and John repeated himself as if the joke had landed successfully, beautifully, as if Heathrow Airport: 'Bad form, bud. Being late.' Next to Studzy, Rooney gestured for the water and Studzy passed it on after first squirting some onto his filthy knees, his boots, then the concrete floor.

Ultan said, 'Quiet, now. Shush,' and Barrett walked into the middle of the room, hands in the pockets of his club-branded gilet. 'I have news,' Barrett began.

Barrett then said, 'Away to Claremorris.' Barrett took an emphatic step back as if he had started a little fire. 'Next round of the Championship. The draw has been made.'

A collective intake of breath and John found his head was bobbing back and forth of its own accord and his mouth a tiny circle.

'A provisional date, as well,' Barrett went on and a hand was removed from a pocket, the right hand. 'Obviously' – Barrett bowed a touch at this, and then continued – 'dependent on how Mayo fare in the All-Ireland. But, from what we've been told. Myself and Ultan. It will be a quick turnaround on the club scene.' Gentle clucks of tongue between sentences. 'Provisionally. We'll be running out on the weekend of the fifteenth of August.'

Spontaneous discussions broke out.

Hanley remarked, 'Tough draw that. Claremorris? Tough outfit,' and Studzy tilted forward and said, 'Definitely, man. And away, too, like?' and Studzy's eye wide at this declaration. John was nodding along, agreeing with moody emissions of air despite not having a notion whether Claremorris were a tough senior side or not, and then John felt puzzled by something or other and what was it and a date echoed. The fifteenth, the fifteenth of August. A feeling like an unreachable itch between his shoulder blades as he tried to figure out why this date seemed relevant, why it bugged, why it resounded, and John realised with a start.

The wedding.

The sister's wedding.

John brushed his hands through his hair and seized a clump of it, managed to say breathlessly, 'My sister's wedding.' Studzy and Hanley stared at him with confusion and Hanley said, 'What's your sister's wedding?' And John looked from Hanley to the centre of the room and bleated, 'Is it the Saturday or the Sunday, Anthony?'

Mortifyingly: this hushed the entire dressing room.

Barrett turned to face him. 'What'd you say, Masterson?'

'Just,' John said, and he swallowed. Had to swallow again, actually. 'My sister is getting married on the Saturday. The fifteenth. So, I'm wondering if it's on the Saturday or the Sunday? The match.'

Barrett eventually nodded. 'We'll make note of that. We can request the Sunday. No need to panic.' Barrett looked towards Ultan, who was already scribbling on a piece of paper. 'And you'll be able to make the Sunday, you will, Masterson?' John answered solemnly that he would, yeah, for sure, Anthony, thank you very very much, and Barrett said, 'Right.' In a louder voice, Barrett then addressed the room, 'Anyone else attending his sister's wedding, hah?' Small jeers at this, sniggering, and Eoghan Moloney put up his hand and greater volume. Coleman the keeper uttered something, howls from his corner, and then Studzy raised his hand – John didn't turn to see Studzy's hilarious and truly funny gesture in all its glory but caught the motion in his peripheral vision. The room was laughing and John reminded himself it was with him and not at him and that realistically they were not invited to the wedding and John produced a noise from his mouth similar to an agreeable, good-sport cackle. John thought: team.

In the car, his mother flipped up the visor with its backlit mirror and asked, 'How did it go?'

'Grand, yeah,' John answered and shoved the gearbag between his feet. Crusty dirt like two handprints on the side of one leg, a khaki stain on his shorts. He was in a Mayo jersey. His cheeks were still warm and his fringe was glued to his forehead: he could feel it and also occasionally see the thready ends of this fringe over his left eye like the silhouettes of tree branches on a sunny day. 'It was only training.'

The car was reversing. 'A lovely evening to be out and about though,' Yvonne said, and John replied, 'Yeah. It was nice.'

'And did you score a goal?'

John frowned. 'It was training, Mam.'

Then John adjusted his legs, contorted the left to allow more room for the bag, and said with a tut, 'I did make a good block though.'

'Why am I not surprised?' she said, and John made an aggrieved face but happily and then in a lowered voice, his mother said: 'Well. For your information, I have spent the last half-hour talking to your sister. About Saturday and this meal with the Kilbanes.'

John bent down and unzipped his gearbag. 'How is Kay?'

'She's stressed. The poor thing.' His mother pinched at the skin under her chin. 'Denis's sister is after causing an issue. She might not attend the dinner after all.'

'Shit,' John said absently, and his hand was rummaging through the gearbag: there was the white shirt and he felt the velvet buttons of the waistcoat and then he found his slacks. He pulled them half out of the bag, flipped them till he located the pockets and the weight inside one. 'That's bad form,' John said, and he dug out his phone.

'An understatement, John. Kay is very upset by it. Isn't she a right bitch, that Kilbane girl? To do that.' Yvonne was shaking her head. 'So you better be on your best behaviour Saturday, you hear me?'

'Obviously, Mammy,' John said. He unlocked the phone and the screen declared he had a message. 'I'm always on my best behaviour.'

'Oh, yeah. The perfect son,' his mother said, laughing lightly. 'We'll be leaving for Mulranny early. Your sister wants to make a day of it.'

A text message and the text message was from Amber Work.

He sat up.

His mother was talking and talking at him, and the text read: 'If you are serious meet me in Alices now'

His mother said, 'Are you listening to me?' and in reply John said, 'Which?'

His mother let out a sigh. They were through the Glon. The turn for home was about five minutes away, less even. His grip tightened on the mobile. 'I'm saying, John, we will be leaving at four o'clock sharp on Saturday. Your father will be collecting us then, alright?'

'Yeah. Grand.' The message had been sent over an hour ago. But surely she'd know about training and the definition of *now* would have some leeway, be open to interpretation, though how would she know about training and it would be an additional ten-minute walk from his house to Alice's at the very least and that be without a shower and the cut of him currently and then John blurted: 'In the one car with Dad?'

'Yes,' Yvonne said. 'That's what your sister wants, so that's what we will be doing.'

He looked over at her, aghast, and then he faced forward again. He couldn't deal with this, too. No. One disaster at a time. They were almost at the Sound, practically at the estate. There was Brett's Florist. His mind was racing. More than an hour previous she had composed and sent this message, so he was technically an hour late, and if John was serious, he'd be there by now: and he was serious. John was serious when it came to Amber and he presently possessed very few options. John felt his mouth fall open, felt his tongue stir and wet his bottom lip, and then he asked, 'Can you drop me at Alice's?'

'Alice's. The pub?' She looked across at him. 'Why would I do that?'

'I can't explain,' he said. 'But I have to get to Alice's right now, Mam. Like, I really have to.'

John said, 'Please, Mam. It's important.'

Nearing the entrance to the estate and there was no click-click of the indicator. No noticeable dip of speed. A deep breath and John thanked his mother and her face had changed, her lips a minus sign that meant trouble. Yvonne said, 'You're making a nuisance of yourself, John.'

By Sweeney's Supermarket, over the bridge, and there was the stone façade of Alice's and John had the door open before the car had even stopped and his thumb was texting: 'Where r u?'

The lower windows of Alice's were all lit and it rendered the surrounding area – the wide car park, the bank of scrubby grass that sloped to rocks and the sea – darker than it should be at such an hour and it was like encountering headlights while walking late, and thus, a little blinded, John sidled around the righthand side of the building, picturing the paved smoking area at the back and could that function as a murky rendezvous point, and then he was ducking down by windows and praying that the numerous heads inside, drinking and eating, did not notice the flushed buck scurrying past in a Mayo jersey. His boots were tapping on path, and he stumbled as they crunched onto gravel. His laces were undone. His legs felt girly and some-how more naked for being in white shorts that showcased a healthy chunk of thigh. Now he was at the rear of the hotel. There were a couple of people by the emergency exit doors, smoke grey and climbing, and he skirted around to the furthest picnic table, crouching, and his boots now inaudible as he was onto grass, untrimmed dewy grass, and he hunkered by a chubby oil tank. No message received and John sent another one: 'In smoking area. Where r u???'

He was trembling and then the phone was, too.

The phone said: 'On way'

Only now did John wonder about what he would say, what Amber might say, and what would she like to hear. Only now did John think to interrogate what being a serious guy meant in regard to the enormity of being ashamed of someone while also perversely liking them a godly amount. To explain his perception of her as inferior to him and sort of soiled like a snotty tissue but also that she was the one person on earth he truly liked – honest, it felt like that a whole bunch of the time – and was that even explainable without making someone weep and or furious? What did he want from her? He didn't wish for purity, John reminded himself of that, but equally: it would be a good bit handier if her history was blank and then him with a capital J. What he wanted was to see her privately, be around her, have sex with her, yes, and not for anyone to judge and comment. Them: only. Only them. Was that evil? Was that unfair? His dignity was as valuable as hers, wasn't it?

Could you be serious and duplicitous? Lie to her face but seriously, but in a serious kind of way with tons of true mountainous emotion concealed behind the fabrication. He peeked over the oil tank, couldn't see her and then he could.

Slotting the phone into the band of his shorts, John stood and said her name.

She stiffened immediately, cocked her head in his direction.

Trepidation like a jabbed shot to the kidneys as she approached, like no homework done. She was in tight jeans and a black sleeveless vest top thing that was tucked into the jeans and around her arm, the handbag with its strap like chainmail and how many mornings throughout this summer had John, upon seeing that handbag atop the humped pile of hoodies and jackets, felt better, felt happier, had felt that perhaps this particular morning won't be horrendous and worthless, that perhaps this particular day might be good and worthwhile?

That was serious, surely.

That meant something serious.

'Hey,' Amber said. She was before him, arms folded, and then she tottered, nearly lost her balance, footing – she was wearing sandals with wedges – and had to press a hand to the oil tanker.

'You alright?' John said, but he didn't dare move and assist.

She nodded, but kept her head down, wouldn't look up, and what to say and how to start and then her hand reached out and plucked at the end of his jersey. 'The green and red,' she said to him, and there was a slight tremor in her voice.

'I wore it especially,' John said, and she laughed. What a perfect sound, he thought. To entice her to laugh, perfect, and she had to look up because he had stepped forward and they closed into one another and kissed.

A peck at first. Cautious as if both learning and the supple feel of her mouth on his and the squelch of sap breaking as they pecked again and god.

Another and another, closed mouths, slow and noisy, and her fingers were flat on his chest and then tugging down the collar of his jersey and the angles between them being revised.

Much too soon she pulled away, and when John opened his eyes, one hand was stuck to the hurlhead of her hip and the other limp and cowardly. Amber looked off to the side, her mouth moving still. He was stunned, and maybe she was too, and John didn't unclasp his hand for he didn't want to do that. The smell of smoke and booze, a waft of her perfume amongst it: cut flowers, candles. The yellowed windows behind caught the stray frizz along the central parting of her hair – it was let down this evening, hiding her ears and earrings – and the light caught too the curve of her arms and shoulders and her snappable collarbones and the dangling necklace he only noticed as it dangled where he always noticed and it all spilled out then.

'I don't know why you won't talk to me, Amber. Or I do, but I'm sorry. I'm not trying to mess you around and make you feel bad. I don't want to fuck things up. The opposite, actually.' Her spit likely still in his mouth as all this was being said and he swilled, drank, continued, 'Look, the phone incident was a hundred per cent bad form by me,

I should have texted. And the Studzy thing was a mistake. A misunderstanding. And Studzy's a massive fool in the first place. Like, don't mind him. Genuinely.' She shivered at this mention, or was she only anticipating something crucial and unlocking and as of yet unforthcoming, and John barrelled on: 'But we can go back to the agreement between us, can't we? Why not do that again? Fun and casual, that was the plan. Your plan, to be fair. And I love seeing you. Hanging with you, I love that, too. And this. This is the best, it's my favourite' – his free hand flapping between them, indicating the kissing as a concept, as an essential fact, and the aspiration to ride her and accomplish that carnal act embedded in this romantic spillage, yes – 'and you know, we need to go check on the tree, don't we? Our tree. Is it still growing, like?' He smiled at this, thought it might just land, and there was a sudden development at this remark: she removed the hand pinned to her hip and spoke firmly: 'Will you stop talking now?'

She was saying, 'Why do you have to talk so much?'

John started talking again in a bid to wholeheartedly agree with her and she raised a curt hand to his face and wobbled by him before stalling a foot or so from the rocks.

'Amber,' John called out dolefully, and she said, 'John. Stop. Talking.'

'Sorry,' he said. 'Sorry, I will.'

After a long silence, he heard her exhale and the sound of her handbag clipping open. Then a noise like something furry in a bush and he still resisted the urge to speak and plead. Now Amber held a cigarette between her fingers and her head was inclined and the same hand horned with the cigarette was braced against her forehead: the heel of it moving in a slow precise circle. 'I have a headache,' she said.

'Shit, sorry,' he said. 'Do you want me to run inside for some water? I could check for a Panadol even.'

'Dressed like that?'

'Yeah?' he said. 'I'll get it for you? No hassle.'

She looked at him and the indentations between her brow. 'You're alright.'

Across the gently bumping water, lights were melting like oil layered atop a puddle. It was cold, colder, or perhaps John just felt any chilly increment more thoroughly because he was in a pair of Gaelic football shorts.

'It's gotten too complicated,' Amber said then, and exhaled a knot of smoke. 'Us. Way too complicated.'

'No, it hasn't, Amber,' John said, and she glanced back at him, and he frowned. 'Okay, yeah. Maybe it has. But it doesn't have to be complicated. It can be easy again.'

'Well, I wanted it to be easy,' she said. 'Let me finish. I wanted to draw, like, a line between us. I was the one who brought that up, remember? But. For fucksake. Let me finish, John.' A pause, longer, and then: 'I thought it could be casual and now I know it can't be. I was wrong. There's too much feeling. Way, way too much. It was fun but it's impossible now. It's gone stupid. Completely stupid.' Another pull from the cigarette. 'And the Studzy thing, like what the fuck, John? Like what the actual fuck? Who

263

do you think you are?' Her voice spiked then dropped and the heel of her hand met her forehead once more and she began to laugh but to herself. Private low laughter. Uninviting. Scary. John winced reflexively. 'Whatever,' Amber said, 'I'm drunk. I don't want to be saying this to you. I don't want to be having this conversation right now.'

'I know, same,' John said softly. 'I'm not drunk, but I get you, where you're coming from. I don't enjoy talking like this either. To you.' Sentences were ricocheting through his mind and to pick one out and present it: onerous, exhausting, and what if what he said was the entire wrong sentiment? A tightrope and one slip and splatter. Driving the car and one swerve and crash, inferno, smouldering wreck. He took a deep, deep breath and he decided to tell a truth: 'You are the only good thing I have this summer, Amber. Honestly. The only good thing.'

She turned around and she looked saddened, the bushy eyebrows somehow sadder than normal, and to this unhappy face, John said, 'We can go back to the agreement, can't we? Why not, like?' His voice dry all of a sudden as he repeated, 'Why not?'

She answered, 'I don't know, John. I really don't know. I want it to be fair and I don't think—'

She shook her head and faced the sea again. 'I can't believe you're in a Mayo jersey right now.'

A moment, another, and then John said, 'I just love my county, Amber.'

He heard a snort of air, observed this reproaching wag of head, and John thought: Heathrow Airport.

She drew and drew on the cigarette and flecks of ash lost in the breeze and finally John said, 'Can we not at least try, Amber?' He had been thinking about the next part for so long, formulating it in his mouth, that when he said it aloud now, it was almost a surprise to him: 'I have a free house next Saturday. And you could come over?'

The cigarette was flicked into the rocks.

John said, 'What you think, Amber?'

With both hands, she wiped down the front of her jeans, wiped there again more carefully. She turned around and seemed to be studying him, watching his face: what portrait could she perceive that he couldn't? Amber said then, 'Fine,' and it didn't feel altogether like a victory to John even though his groin started to buzz and vibrate. It felt more like a loss: for her, for him, for both sides, and yet he did not rescind the invitation.

Then his groin was also ringing, and John realised why.

He seized his mobile and peered at its screen and he said, 'I have to answer this.'

He plugged a finger into his ear, stomped past the oil tank, and murmured to the phone, 'What's up?'

'John,' the phone said, 'I can see you.'

Startled, he looked towards the smoking area before recalling the existence of the car park.

The phone sighed. 'Get into the car. I'll drive you both home.'

Amber was staring at him, and John covered the phone and explained, 'My mam. And. She's.' He stopped. 'Do you want a lift?'

In the confines of the car, the smell of booze and fags was much more pronounced. However, his mother made no comment, merely introduced herself to Amber with not a single jokey reference to the previous phone call and now approaching the church in the Sound, his mother lifted her eyes to the rearview mirror and enquired, 'Are you going to your house or ours, love?'

Since Amber had slipped into the backseat, her gaze had been directed squarely out the window, staring out while gnawing on her bottom lip, and now John woke her, 'Amber,' and she looked forward. 'Oh, sorry,' she said. 'Mine if that's alright, Yvonne?'

'Of course,' Yvonne said. 'And where is that exactly?'

For the rest of the journey, it was as if everyone was holding their breath until they neared The Strand Hotel, the beach, and then his mother asked, 'Is it this turn here?'

'No,' John answered. 'The next one, Mam.' He leaned forward till the seatbelt snagged against his chest. 'There, on your right.'

A glance from his mother, and John tried to ignore it.

There were no cars in her driveway tonight. No lights on in the windows. The shaggy hedges were dark but silky-seeming: bitter liquorice, sort of like that. There was a profusion of thank yous as she climbed out, and John opened his mouth once to say, 'Seeya.' They watched her struggle for a time with the front door before lugging it open, and his mother remarked, 'I've met her now,' and with a grimace, John replied, 'You have.'

'A lovely girl,' Yvonne commented, and John didn't agree or disagree, and instead asked, coldly, could they head home now. Please.

Saturday, 1st August

He heard his sister's voice all the way from the car park – she was thanking someone, effusively, and then laughing, effusively – and he shared a look with his mother as they climbed up the dozen or so steps to the entrance of the hotel. There Kay was waiting and when John saw her – arms crossed with clenched fists and glancing over her shoulder as the automatic doors shunted aside with a baleful expression as if the doors were being particularly rude – John knew for certain: his sister was petrified. It was another thing about families: that he could intuit this, read it. Alongside the persistence of being a family member, perhaps that was its other innate privilege: you could observe a person nakedly, see clean through them when they were lying for love and attention and whatever else. And John sympathised with Kay. John felt bad for his sister: if he'd been tasked with exhibiting this Masterson foursome to an audience, he'd be scared, too.

Kay greeted Peter and Yvonne and then Kay said to her brother, 'How are you, John?'

Kay was in a black dress with a chunky brown belt complete with a silver buckle. A Jesus cross necklace and on her fingers, only the engagement ring: a pink and purpley rock bordered by sparkles.

Solemnly, John replied, 'Hello, sister.'

The hotel had recently been refurbished and had since acquired four golden stars: his father had mentioned this accomplishment twice, as if he had a stake in it. Tall windows. Crumbly-to-touch walls. Presently a sandstone path steered the Mastersons to the side of the hotel, where they stood under a length of striped awning. It was a fine summer's day: his father had also said this a couple of times on the drive over. The Kilbanes were sitting around a wicker table with a shiny glass surface and John put on a smile. He was introduced to them one by one: the parents, Gerry and Eileen, whose appearance reminded John of novelty salt and pepper shakers – both persons stout and rounded, no necks basically, and he could picture them slotting together, one arm over and one arm under the other – and Denis's two brothers and John began a fresh wave upon each introduction from Kay. Denis emerged, greeted everyone by name except John, who he feinted to thump in the stomach. Then Denis's father asked what everyone was having, and Peter replied no no no no, and both men badgered inside towards the bar, arguing in a delighted manner.

'Well,' Yvonne said, and she smiled and looked from Kay to the remaining Kilbanes and then to John, 'this is lovely, isn't it?'

John agreed. They all made a sound to show they agreed.

Then Yvonne mentioned the glorious weather and they agreed about that, too.

The drive over hadn't been as stressful or excruciating as John had imagined. Actually: John had enjoyed it once he heard the putter of the engine, once they were belted and moving. He sat in the front because his mother wanted to enjoy a cigarette while she was still allowed and they had all conversed agreeably – about the weather and the hotel, yes, but then, about what not to bring up at the dinner table in a comedic fashion with the real important stuff not to divulge remaining unsaid. It had felt nice. To hear them talk, to talk with them. Half an hour and in the end, he'd sort of wished the drive was longer.

The drinks were soon brought out and, gripping his arm, Peter told John he hadn't been sure what he fancied, and so John trudged inside himself to get a drink – sending a text to Amber while up against the bar counter: 'Hope work is sound 2day x' – and when John returned, he found himself being ushered to a chair between Denis's brothers because Kay had announced that John was sports mad.

A flatscreen television was mounted to the wall and the brothers were watching it.

Placing his fizzing Rock Shandy – Championship – alongside their pints of Guinness, John saw they were watching golf.

The brothers were both in polo shirts. One of the brothers was balding: countable hairs and these hairs were gelled and spiked which genuinely made John feel a bit weepy.

John couldn't work out whether they were older or younger than Denis. John had also completely misplaced their names.

The TV mentioned the new leader for the day, Tiger Woods – the sole golf reference that John recognised beyond the fact that a ball should roll into a small hole in the ground – and John cleared his throat. 'He's unbelievable, isn't he? Tiger Woods. Some golfer, when you think about it.'

The brothers looked at him and concurred and during the flashing ad break, the non-balding brother commented, 'I hear you're quite the footballer.'

It took a second for John to realise this was directed at him. 'Oh, yeah. I play football, alright.'

'Well,' the balding brother said, 'Denis informs us you are excellent.'

'I don't know about that.' John let out a scrawny laugh. 'But, yeah, I'm playing with the Island seniors' – with his chin he gestured over his shoulder and maybe that was towards the Island – 'so. Yeah. Seniors.'

'Fair play,' the non-balding brother said.

'We have Championship soon, against Claremorris,' John said. 'That's the focus, you know?' Both brothers faced him once more, and John had to vigorously itch the back of his neck. 'Championship.'

The non-balding brother declared, 'Fair play.'

At training this morning there had been zero drills, no ball work in any competitive sense, no sweat. It was all about the system: a sluggish breakdown of Barrett's prescribed game plan. John had watched from the periphery, John had masqueraded as a literal cone for ten minutes, and only at the end, the last quarter of an hour at most, was John deployed as a defender to actively learn where he should shuffle when the opposing team had possession. Hands cuffed behind his back, Tony had loitered beside John for most of the training, but worryingly, alarmingly, Rooney had been near ever-present as a defender during these phantom scenarios. Studzy, meanwhile, had been one of the two full-forwards for the entirety of the session: there was no suggestion that Studzy was anything but a starter now, no disputing of Studzy's certainty.

A very long hour passed and then a waiter escorted them through to the restaurant – candles lit in ornate threes, vast lilac curtains that were creased like the flimsy wrapping paper crinkled around runners – and Denis pulled out a chair for his own mother and then Yvonne. It was a round table. One space conspicuously empty and only now did the waiter retrieve the cutlery, the wine glass.

A vibration and John checked his phone.

Amber Work: 'Thanks x enjoy your saturday night'

He bit his lip and then sent back: 'At a family meal... So I won't hahah. Hope work ok? x'

They had been in steady contact since Wednesday – every day, John dutifully sent a text message containing at least one practical and replyable question, as he knew he would until at least the free house – but the exchanges had felt stilted. Hard to explain why, hard to pinpoint: because her demeanour in work yesterday hadn't been impolite or abrasive, because John did want to be light and chirpy with her but found it somehow difficult to be light and chirpy. This impasse was troubling in one sense to John, but in another sense, it was fine as long as next weekend happened. Next weekend had to happen and then things would settle, probably. Anger, resentment would be resolved: likely. He believed this, sort of.

'lol .. Enjoy the meal x' the phone said, and then his mother pinched his arm. 'Put it away.'

Across from John was a carafe of water with mint leaves swirling inside and for the duration of the meal, his attention was concentrated on watching this green dance and only snapping out of this mindless daze when he was eating or when asked a direct question – about the Leaving Cert, the forthcoming results – and each answer exhausted John, despite his best efforts. Another bottle of wine. A Rock Shandy was delivered from one of the brothers. A discussion about money and then funerals. Kay was quiet throughout the meal, blandly smiling at everything said. Kay was drinking water.

Before the dessert, Peter proposed a toast, and every glass was held aloft. Then Kay whispered and Denis rose and proposed a further toast to the generosity of Peter and Yvonne. Then Denis's father stood up and spoke about family and the great fortune of new members and a reference to his daughter being unfortunately ill tonight and Kay's jaw tightening at this mention.

After dessert, after a tussle over payment, Denis blinked at Kay, then at his brothers, and suggested a nightcap.

They left the hotel and headed to a pub down the road and from its urinal, there was an unfettered view of the coast and a luminous sea that was mirrored so perfectly above that above was simply the sea now, too. The mountains on the other side were like bad teeth and braces soon, but when you focused on the water, purely, there was this sensation of peering at eternity.

Neverendingness.

No lines no shape, just pale astonishing light.

And when John returned from the jacks, he was inspired to notify the table of this wondrous scene – 'A class view from the men's toilet, if you want to look' – and only Peter seemed to hear him. Peter replied: 'Must go check it out, son.'

The drinking continued.

Later, John looked down and the table had vanished: it was a disarray of empty glasses now, scuffed pints, sticky cider bottles with peeling gold flaked labels. The brothers and Denis were sitting at the bar counter, and someone else had joined them. Some other man. Peter was talking to Eileen and Gerry. His blazer was hanging from the chair, the top two buttons on his salmon shirt undone but not the sleeves. On a cushioned bench against the wall, John was next to his mother. Yvonne had switched to vodka – a wedge of lemon in her bubbling glass – and there was an expression close to amusement frozen on her face. John was feeling sleepy, bored. His phone told him it was nearly half past ten and then Kay slid in beside Yvonne with a sequined purse clamped under her arm.

'Almost over, thank god,' Kay said in a sort of whisper to Yvonne. 'I couldn't believe it when Denis said to come down to this hole. I almost killed him. And now one of the cousins has magically appeared.' Kay shook her head, set the purse on her lap.

'Not to worry,' Yvonne said, and she was staring straight ahead. 'We'll round them up after this one.'

Kay nodded, fidgeted with her necklace, and without looking at him, she said, 'How are you getting on, John?'

'Grand, yeah.' John sat up. 'It was nice to meet the Kilbanes, Kay.' He peeked at his mother and John insisted, 'They are very nice. The Kilbanes.'

'Thank you.' His sister laughed darkly. 'And yes, they are nice. They are good to me.'

His sister added, 'Except for one of them. The smelly rotten—'

'Stop it,' his mother said, and John was giggling.

Kay grinned thinly at Yvonne, and went, 'Oh. I won't say any more.' Kay showed her face around the room, smiling, then returned it to John and the face was no longer smiling. 'So what do you think about Westport?'

Yvonne immediately said, 'Kay.'

'Westport?' John said to his sister. 'What's Westport?'

Kay looked from Yvonne to John and back again: 'Don't tell me you haven't told him, Mam?'

Yvonne said, 'This isn't the time, Kay, I'm serious,' and John said, 'What about Westport?'

Something like a smirk on Kay's lips and she turned away from him, picked at the hem of her dress. A churning in John's stomach – bad news, death, a girl fancying someone not you – and his mother told him, 'We'll talk about this another time. Don't mind your sister.'

'No,' John said, 'tell me now. What's Westport?'

Yvonne glared at Kay and then spoke in a low voice, 'I need a place of my own, John. And so I'm looking at renting in Westport. That's it.' His mother took a drink. 'It's not far from the Island. And you'll be in Galway anyway.'

'But why Westport?' John asked.

'It's a nice quirky town, isn't it?' his mother began, and John interrupted, 'No, I mean why do you need to rent in Westport? You have a house.'

'Look what you've started,' Yvonne said to Kay.

Kay muttered something under her breath, and then Kay said, 'Calm down, John,' and John said, 'No, I don't get this. What the fuck?'

'Listen,' Yvonne said, 'your father needs somewhere to live. And so do I. End of story.'

Laughing, Kay butted in: 'We're all very diplomatic and modern, you see.'

'Kay, stop it right now,' Yvonne said, and Yvonne placed her glass within the shell of another on the table. 'At the moment,' Yvonne went on, 'I'm only looking at a few options. Westport being one of them.' Her eyebrows rose. 'That's all, John. Okay? We'll talk about it later.'

'Dad lives in Gaga's.' John looked from his mother to his sister. 'Dad's happy in Gaga's, isn't he? He loves the trees and shit out there.'

'He can't stay there forever,' his mother said, and his arm was being touched, held. 'He has been good enough to stay there till now, but his brothers have claims on that land. It will have to be sold.' Yvonne sighed. 'Let's talk about this another time, alright?'

'Sold?' He was loud.

'John,' Kay said, 'relax.'

'I don't get this. That's Gaga's house.' His voice was brittle. He didn't like the noise of it, but it was beyond his control. The grip on his arm tighter, tightening, and he squeaked, 'Leave it as it is, why don't ye?'

Yvonne said, 'I wish it was that simple —'

'It is that simple.' He shook his head, and his father was staring over with concern bunching his features. 'And what does that have to do with you moving to Westport? It doesn't make sense. You're not making sense, Mam.'

'John, not here, alright,' Yvonne said, and he jerked his arm free, and Yvonne pleaded once more, 'Just not here. For your sister.'

Someone was then calling Kay's name: it was the balding brother. He was still calling it. A horse bark, intensified.

The balding brother held up a tray of five tiny glasses, he was displaying this tray like it was a prize on a game show. The glasses were black and possessed a creamy head that was mushrooming over the lip of each. Kay acknowledged him, Kay did her laugh – how swiftly she could switch from sombre to fluffy and enlarged – and cried, 'You're gas, Cillian.'

Yvonne's name was also called by the balding brother. 'One for you, Yvonne.'

At this, Denis spun round, his mouth curled up on one side. Denis waved.

Yvonne said, 'Very good.'

Neither woman made shapes to stand, and eventually the balding brother got the hint, gave a thumbs up, and John watched as he hoisted himself back up onto the stool, wiggling for a moment as if there was a specific hook on his arse that was supposed to be reattached. The four men proceeded to down the little shots and who was gifted the spare: John couldn't tell.

He would never have guessed Cillian as the bald brother's name.

He would never have guessed his parents could live anywhere else but where they lived. The home house. He couldn't fix this. A stark truth. It affected him and he had no say. There were situations out of his control, things he couldn't mend and plaster and rewire. People: he couldn't fix.

Under her breath, Kay said, 'Denis is pissed anyways.'

'Alright,' Yvonne said to her, 'let's go. They've had enough.'

A flushed Peter was presently standing over them. 'Everything alright?' he asked, and John could feel his gaze, and Yvonne answered, 'Everything's fine, Peter. But we're going now.' She started to check behind her, searching for a handbag, found it. 'Where's your keys?' Yvonne said to Kay and then to Peter, 'We'll wrangle up these fellas. It's time for home.'

Farewells occurred outside the pub and then they had to redo them after waddling back to the hotel. Breaths visible at this stage. John shook hands with everybody except Eileen, who he bent and gave a kiss and the smell of Sudocrem from her cheek. The balding brother named Cillian said to John, 'We'll get you onto the field next time, Johnny boy.' John had no clue what this was referring to but replied, 'Absolutely.' It was late. Kay yawned into the crook of her arm. Logistics were being hammered out: Gerry and Eileen will be dropped home along with the brothers and if someone goes on a lap then Denis can hop in on that lift and Kay would return for Mam and Dad and Kay yawned again and amid this scrambled planning, Peter said, 'You're tired, Kay.'

Brightly, Peter said, 'Sure why doesn't John drive us home?' He turned to his son. 'You can drive us, can't you?'

'It's grand, Dad,' Kay said, 'I'm fine to come back,' and Peter said to her, 'No, your brother can drive us. Save the hassle.'

Yvonne said, 'Peter.'

'He's well able to, Yvonne.' His father looked at her, and his gestures were clumsy. 'A lot better in recent weeks, I'm telling you. A lot, lot better.' He nodded towards John. 'Aren't you, John? And it's only over the road.'

Arms folded, his mother said, 'I'm not saying a word.'

'Well, if you're against it and.' His father stopped himself and glanced at Kay and then in a new voice agreed, 'No, you're right, Yvonne. We'll just wait for Kay. Is that alright with you, love?'

Then the Kilbanes announced they'd be the ones to stall around for the second lift. Allow Kay to drop the Mastersons home first. And both John's parents venomously rejected this deal. Someone mentioned taxis and this was dismissed as a waste of money. A demure argument was soon occurring under the cool fluorescent rays of the streetlights. Voices as if from deep inside a cave. It was a circle of people who John was expected to love, glue himself to, and to fix the current predicament, John said, 'I'll drive. I can drive us home.'

Key twisted right and the car started as it was supposed to: the first major victory. A garbled whine and louder, louder again when John's foot accidentally pressed on the right pedal. His father was instructing him to stay calm. His father was in the back but propped between the seats and the stink of stout cloudy on his breath. John checked his rearview mirror, then the wing mirror to his right and the other after that and he thought he should inspect the rear-view mirror once more just in case. His mother was rigid beside him. 'You know what to do next, John,' Peter said. 'Take it handy, okay?'

John did, alright.

He knew and he told himself he knew.

With his thumb, John clicked in the handbrake's nubby button and then pushed the lever all the way down and that felt like a huge milestone. Wow. He had to take a second, another, before he seized the gearstick and lugged it into the faraway slot marked R. He lowered his right foot and carefully, incrementally, released his useless left. He waited for the biting point, anticipated it while holding his breath, and then he felt it, rumbling. A live animal. He was hunched over the wheel. His knuckles were translucent. You can do this, John told himself, fuck fuck fuck you can do this, and he applied more pressure with the right foot. The car was slowly, slowly rolling backwards and then the wheels were turning ever so slightly. 'That's it,' his father said in an excited whisper. 'You see the exit there?'

John nodded, and he eased the stick into the notch marked 1.

The car was inching forward, and his mother's hand reached out for the dashboard as they jostled onto the main road. Into second gear and presently thrusted up into third. Ahead, the road was straight. Third into fourth. The little red arrow hitting the dizzying highs of fifty kilometres in a designated eighty zone and John tapped the brake to remind himself it was there, that it worked. Then he exhaled and it felt as if he had emerged from a deep icy plunge.

'Brilliant driving,' his father said, and he slumped into the backseat.

John was a driver.

The driver.

It wasn't a tricky route home. The road was linear enough and dead quiet at this late hour, with only a single dodgy hairpin bend before the bridge outside Tonragee causing some concern: his father roused himself in the back as the bend approached, guided and then praised as the car wound itself along. They passed The Way Inn – ruby bulbs drooping over the entrance, cars in a line out front – and then they were turning off the main road, turning off from the road for home, and he had to instruct himself to do so.

They chugged up the hill to Gaga's and John brought the car to a shuddering halt by the unused front door. His father went, 'Well done, son. And there's plenty of room for you to reverse behind. You see that?'

His hands still set on the wheel, John replied, 'Thanks, Dad.'

'It was a great evening. Wasn't it?' Peter said. 'It was, I thought. Nice people, the Kilbanes. Nice conversations. I think Kay enjoyed herself. No, yeah, definitely.' His father was rummaging in the inner pocket of his blazer. 'Well. Goodnight, folks.' The seatbelt had already been unbuckled, and now the door was opened. 'You'll be alright to drive home, won't you, John?'

John nodded and then felt a hand cupping his shoulder.

'Goodnight, Yvonne,' Peter said. 'Lovely to see you.'

'Goodnight, Peter,' his mother said, and a strained closed-mouth smile.

'I'll catch you both soon again, I'm sure,' Peter said. He was outside the car and his right hand was holding the door open. The air was cold and fresh. The trees behind the house: whispering, gossiping. 'A fabulous evening now. It was fantastic to see everybody. It really was. To have us all together. Yeah, yeah. It's a fine hotel, too.' A long pause here. A delay like a scratched disc. The door swung back a little further, his father's fingers drumming against the casing on the inside. 'That's it, so.'

The car door was shut with a final bang.

In the rearview mirror, John watched his father step from the car. He watched Peter stamp his right foot for a moment before walking towards the backdoor, waving as he did. A sensor light pinged to life. A lurid yellow hue, shafts of it every which way, and there was his father directly beneath it: a shirt collar askew and flattened under the weight of his blazer, grimacing against the light, and Peter was not presently unlocking the backdoor, he wasn't heading inside. Why? Had he forgotten something? His wallet or spare key or? And then John understood. His father was waiting for the car to reverse. He was waiting to make sure they got out, safe and sound.

* * *

At home, they pulled the curtains and padded into the kitchen. John stooped against the counter as his mother offered her commentary about the night. The key for his father's car was in his pocket and when she had finished her review, he fished it out and asked her what he should do with it? 'Oh,' Yvonne said, leering suspiciously at the dangling key as if it was purring and abandoned. 'Just leave it there on the table. He'll probably be over in the morning to collect the car.' She considered John and then went, 'Or you might drop it over yourself, if he doesn't come?'

'Yeah,' John managed. 'Grand, yeah.'

He said he was going to head to bed, and he gave her a kiss on the cheek. 'Love you,' John said to his mother, and she replied, 'I love you, too.' She followed him to the hall-way, and when John placed one foot onto the stairs she said, 'Your understanding would really help me, John. About Westport. I've had enough battles with your sister, I don't need you to hate me as well. It's hard enough as it is.' His hand on the banister and one foot onto the next step. 'You hear me? I'm not superwoman.' He could sense her eyes pinned on him. He had heard the catch in her throat when she had last spoken. His hand gripped the banister now. He was steady. He took another step up the stairs.

Saturday, 8th August

All week he had been waiting for it, craving it, imagining doing it, and today was abruptly here, and he wished it was yesterday again. The shout up the stairs, the guttural pop of the car engine igniting, the knowledge that the free house was attained and his: all this precipitated consternation and not excitement. Stress rather than any consequential peace. You want something so awfully that when it arrives you fear it: a natural reaction, surely. Normal. A normal person, he was one totally. John lay in his bed for a while longer, staring at the ceiling, feeling his tongue swab fitfully at his dried lower lip. Amber was finished at twelve, so he shouldn't expect her before one. Half one was the earliest she'd be over, he reckoned. Two o'clock was probably the most realistic. Three, even. He had plenty of time and John did not want this spacious time. For it to happen right this instant – she'd step from the sliding wardrobe, nude, partially nude, he wasn't at all picky, and there'd be no requirement for speaking and negotiating, nor seducing flattery – or for it to be accomplished already and John was basking in its glow, he was slyly informing the lads, he was satisfied that he had not done anything incorrect: both preferable to further anticipation. Yes, to see her now, to kiss and pinch and poke and undress her: that be for the best, that be goodly enough. And with just these brief thoughts, his head swam and he could feel the teeny circuits of his body spark to life, his fingers and toes jittery, his cock wiggling a tad. He reached for his phone and he texted: 'Hey x still on to come over 2day?'

The reply dinged a minute later.

Short and sweet.

'Yeah'

Breakfast – Weetabix and its fibre, key – and then in the bathroom, John prepared himself: he shaved his upper lip and chin and patiently trimmed his semicircle of dark pubes before scrutinising the entirety of his naked self and how revolting he was from the hips up: lumpy and unsmooth and his cuppable tits which he presently cupped to more urgently loathe and he'd give up a lot to feel one day comfortable topless.

A whole lot.

He despised his body, and his face, and his hair, and he was starting to recall that he disliked his own personality a fair amount too, and so John spun away, yanked the cord for hot water.

It was lunchtime, half twelve, and he wasn't at all peckish: or perhaps more, he couldn't stomach eating.

He guessed she would have knocked off work at this stage and maybe she was currently on the way over here – what was it, a twenty-minute drive? – or perhaps Amber was showering at home or preening herself after the shower in front of a small oval mirror with perspiration beads and was she naked.

Rainbow-coloured blots and UFOs in the corners of his eyes as John shook his head to unclamp himself from such debilitating thoughts.

By now John was actively conversing with himself: 'Relax, man. It's fine, chill out.' He told himself: 'Man, honestly, you have this.' Studzy was still weird with John – blunt replies if any replies at all – so John texted Tony about training tonight and whether Tony needed a lift later. Then he texted Tony about Man United. Then about any subject that was conclusively not female or her.

John was pacing the hallway while his thumb responded.

He went upstairs and re-counted the johnnies stashed in his desk.

When two o'clock neared, John thought to text Amber – 'Your still coming yeah? haha' – but reminded himself that the fewer texts the better. Less equals more. Act smooth and cruel. His belly, however, was not complying with this prescribed smoothness, his belly was flipping itself over and over and over. It wasn't that John suddenly thought this was an unwise idea – no, a free house and someone creeping over was the best idea imaginable – it was rather that he felt sure he was a bad player in this idea: that he might be the one to spoil something magical, that he would undo it somehow.

He peeked out the living-room window: the hedges twitched, the birds were shouting at one another, but there was no sign of her.

John returned to the kitchen. He placed his mobile on the counter and found a strategic vantage point by the dining table where he could survey both the phone and the front door. He said to himself, 'It's going to be sound, genuinely. It's no biggie. Chill.' He awaited the text that would inform him of her being here and could he step outside, he awaited the piercing ring of the doorbell that would announce her arrival. He stared at the phone and now the door and repeated this sequence. He said aloud, 'Hey, Amber. How're you?' He said aloud, 'You look good, Amber. You always look good to me. I don't say that enough because I sometimes don't believe it myself, but it's truth. You're pretty, and I'm glad you're here and I kind of love you and I can't ever forgive you for being dirty and a bike and I'm sorry.' Two became half two and now it was quarter to three and in the end, there were no incoming texts, no shattering bell that carried through to the kitchen. Instead, Amber rapped hard against the frosted window on the front door.

Once, twice.

For a second, John was freaked, and he held his breath like home alone and monitoring for ghosts and or psycho killer intruders. Through the frosted glass, he watched her diminished silhouette shuffle, turn, and only when she thumped the glass again with a muffled 'Hello,' did John stride forward, swallowing something rigid and hard in his throat as he did.

She was peering over her shoulder as he opened the door and then she swung around, and he was shocked.

Speechless that she was present on his front step.

It was like he had expected someone else.

She was in a woollen jumper with sleeves that covered her hands, or sleeves she tugged down to cover her hands. Skinny jeans. Her eyes were ringed darkly, she had make-upped, and over her head, he could see no one in the estate and make out no particularly shitty car plonked on the kerb, and then she made herself taller to catch his gaze, and John said, 'Howdy.'

Amber half smiled. 'Hi, John.'

He stumbled back to allow her inside.

And once she was in the hallway, the why of Amber being here dawned on John all over again. The previous dread and puzzlement replaced instantly by choking horn-iness: this disorienting sensation as if half-cut and home early and parents calling him into the sitting room for a chat. John feared his elbow might topple the coat rack, that his body might inadvertently bang into the table crammed with photographs, that he might say something inappropri-ate and mood-torpedoing like, say, 'Amber, where did you park exactly?'

'At the back of the estate.' She glanced at him. 'Is that alright? Or is it too close for you?'

'No. That's perfect,' he said, and even John wasn't obtuse

enough to miss the sarcasm. 'I thought it might be hard to park. That's all. I was going to help.'

'Right,' Amber said, flatly. Her arms were hugging themselves and she started to search in the different corners of the hallway. 'It's a nice house,' she said after a moment, and John replied, 'Thanks.'

Then quicker, he added, 'It's my parents' house, like. But thanks.'

A joke, a middling to decent one considering the cagey circumstances he felt, but there was no reaction from her.

She sauntered further down the hallway, and then stopped. 'Oh shit. Are these the famous elves?' Her index finger neared but did not quite touch the painting. It showed a gang of elves in front of a mushroom house: some of the elves were farming, hoes and shovels in their puny hands, and some were simply flying around with insect wings. There was also a clothes line. A cow. His mother had finished it recently, showed it to John while it was still propped on the easel. A thin brush in her hand. Paint scrubbed thickly on the shield thing. 'What do you think?' his mother had asked without looking from the painting, and John had answered with effort that it was class, yeah, well done, and now Amber spoke: 'It's not that bad. The elves are funny. And their wings. Wait, are they wings?' – she looked at John and he shrugged – 'They look really cool anyway.'

John said nothing to this and then he went, 'Do you want a drink or something?'

'Sure,' she said, and her hand dropped to her side.

In the kitchen, he poured her a glass of water and asked after work this morning, and when he handed her the glass, she was talking about some issue with the freezer in the kitchen and a fruit salad and this irritating tour leader. Her skinny jeans were the colour of diluted denim, blue that was barely blue, like they had been left out in the rain. Her legs were crossed at the ankles. 'So, yeah. Typical,' Amber said in apparent conclusion, and John was not sure what to say next and just went, 'Yeah. Definitely.' She lifted the glass to her mouth. Her jumper was unfortunately baggy, he strongly felt, and her lips were especially glossy and wet today – from lip gloss or lipstick or her own little tongue? John commented, 'Sounds like a tough morning,' and she widened her eyes in agreement while she sipped. A thought seized John: he had kissed her and those lips. Then another followed this one: he had seen her half naked and sprawled. And a further starker thought careened along after that: those lips had been wrapped around his very own personal penis at one point in time.

John discreetly pinched at his privates as she placed her glass onto the counter. Then Amber cocked her head. 'You've had sex before, haven't you, John?'

A beat, and John answered, 'Yeah. Shit. I have, yeah.'

'Right. More than once?'

'What? Yeah, course,' he said, laughing kind of. Presently also kind of snorting. 'I have done it a fair few times, as a matter of fact.' Fair few times i.e. four separate bouts of penetrative sex. 'I don't keep count, Amber. And you know, I had a girlfriend a while ago?' He raised his right arm at her as if this should answer every single question she might have.

'Oh, I didn't know you had a girlfriend.' She smirked. 'You never told me that.'

'Well,' he said, and his face felt craggy, 'you never asked.'

'Fair.' She was looking at him and then not. 'Good to know you're not a virgin. I wasn't fully sure.'

At this, John bristled. 'I never asked if you had any boyfriends.'

'You didn't.'

'And,' he said. 'Did you?'

'One or two, John. Do you want to know their names and what we did together?'

'No.' He was glaring at the tiled floor. Suddenly furious: why? She was teasing him, teasing him about her superiority and prowess. As if she was better when the truth was: he was better than her. Much, much better. 'No, I obviously don't, Amber.' He looked up and played his sharpest retort: 'Do you want to know my ex's name?'

She smiled at him. 'No, I'm all good.'

She said, 'You get so worked up, John,' and he replied, 'When people are annoying me on purpose I do.'

'Aw. Do I annoy you?'

He moved his head. 'Not always.'

She was before him: when had she stepped forward? 'You're very annoying sometimes, too.'

'Am I, yeah?' he managed.

'You know you are,' she said and then Amber asked with cheeks flecked with red, 'Where's your room?'

Yesterday evening while still in his work clothes, John had sat before the family desktop and downloaded twelve specially picked songs for this encounter. It had taken the guts of two hours, much careful listening and evaluating, and now he sought to surreptitiously click alive this charged playlist on his MP3 player – the playlist was innocently entitled 'A' – and provoke the mood further. He had left her at the doorway and with his back to her, he now hastily thumbed the play button on the blocky device, explaining, 'One sec.'

He scrolled in a circle till the arrowed repeat symbol appeared and he thumbed that.

Plucked guitar string, hazy and lonesome somehow, and he whirred the volume lower.

He could hear her moving behind him, not speaking or commenting on his room but he could hear her move and then for sure he heard an unzipping sound, but he didn't peek. Something stopped him. A force. He could feel the arid mechanics of his throat as he swallowed. He could feel his lips reshape to an o as he exhaled.

The song began to play in earnest.

The Dire Straits sang about a lovestruck Romeo.

He heard her say, 'John?'

He turned from the MP3 player and his mouth fell open. There she was in a black bra and these lavender knickers that snapped about two inches down her thigh. Her face was undaunted. Her belly a little sucked in – he could tell from experience – and one of her feet was arched like ballet: red varnish on each toe and a tattoo he'd never seen before on her right ankle and he couldn't make out what this tattoo depicted because he had to take in the top half all over again. Boobs, her dainty shoulders, face and lips and neck and then returning to the boobs and then down to the cotton knickers. His mouth was still wide open, but he couldn't be expected to close it. Was there anything more sublime than this? Unthinkingly, he marched forward, and his hands were out and once they grabbed at skin – the area below the clasp of her bra, a clamminess atop the flesh he now grubbed and moved – he leaned in, and they kissed. Loudly, furiously, and one hand was palming her right tit, and presently squishing it. Kissing and kissing. Then his thumb was scratching at the cup of the bra, fumbling with the lacy material before eventually scooping the cup down. He opened his eyes then to see what he wanted to see: her nipple, not quite erect, a shy pink as if chapped. Eyes closed again, he found he was hunched and his mouth was gorging on this nipple. It was his first time undertaking such a brazen manoeuvre – the primal urge had arisen with Seóna, or at least the notion that John should have a go on Seóna's tit by his indisputable human right, but it had been unclear to John in the crazed moment whether an acceptable thing – and now it was as if he was sucking on the valve of an inflatable pool lounger but it was so much better, obviously, because hot and thrilling, because an unequivocally real person. She grasped one side of his head like a mother might, combed her hand through his hair, and his lips were still stuck to the nipple when her voice asked, 'Will we go to the bed?'

He stopped at once, rose and his tongue was writhing against the hard wall of her front teeth and then wrestling in her gob proper. He steered her towards the bed, with his thumb flicking her nipple and his other hand kneading her left arse cheek.

Ambidextrous.

The bump of the mattress against his leg and he removed his mouth from hers, flopped onto the bed.

He could not conceal his happiness.

Outside no longer existed.

Nothing was happening in the world but what was happening in this room.

The music had switched to the next song and the song after that one in fact: the pretty voice of Marvin Gaye. Amber mounted the bed with her knees before straddling him. One of his hands was crudely grappling with her arse, the fingertips of the other was feeling the fuzz on her lower back. Every sense fixated on her body and the instant. Her hair fell over him, and it was like being beneath a tree, it was like their woods on that afternoon together, and her hair soon became entwined in their kissing: in his mouth, between his teeth. Her hair became tangled up with their moving and stroking, their unbuckling, unhooking, undoing.

They had adapted to the carpet as the bedframe was being melodramatic. Totally naked, she was on all fours in front of his chestnut library and the ratty spines of his childhood books. Totally naked apart from his top, he was on his knees and holding onto the dough above her arse and how it splendidly gave under the pressure of his touch: fingers dabbed onto cake frosting, like that. Previously, he had been on top of her with stiff forearms and a clenched arse as if a core exercise, and he was breathing into her neck, onto the wires of her hair, and for a brief but nicer time they were forehead to forehead, and then they switched to her being lodged atop him – he watched in reverent awe and fascination as she bounced on his dick, his hands hovering above her hips as if physical contact might crack this astonishing illusion while her own hands covered her boobs – and now he was behind Amber and fucking her in that particular position, though just not at this exact instance as his cock had popped out. John mumbled an apology of sorts, though he hoped she might not have noticed, and he gripped his dick, pressing it towards the general area, but no give. He didn't think it was prudent to ask for directions, so he adjusted his height and tried again, and he was very incorrect on this occasion because a hand flashed above her shoulders. Then this same hand reached between the two legs and took his cock like one might take a Fanta bottle from a petrol station fridge, and guided it inside her as if simple and easy and not utterly hazardous. She let out a low sound and he could see her face, this expression as if momentarily sore and tender, and he swung his hips back and then forward, and her eyes were shut. The carpet was itching his knees. Small sheeny squares on her back: from sweat, and he'd lap up each glistening square with his tongue, honestly. Curtains drawn. She had insisted on a condom, and it was wrinkled and greasy as he steadily jutted his hips. Dolly Parton and Kenny Rogers were duetting in the background. The other thing: there were no pubes today. No inverted triangle of pubebrownness. Only stray zincky stubble and he had not made a comment about this. John knew not to bring it up: her business and none of his. He wouldn't bring it up.

'Fuck,' Amber said now, and she canted her head as if reading his bookshelf.

He could smell them both: sour, vinegary, yet appetising: he'd lick that smell up, too. He let out a grunt as he felt he should. As he felt Amber deserved. He said dissonantly, 'Yeah yeah.' It was a glorious spectacle to observe birdseye, the fucking. A privilege to see his cock inside of her and then not, to see the dimples appearing on her back now and again, and how he could squeeze her beautiful tit if he just leaned forward slightly and this turned out to be an idiotic impulse as his cock slid out once again.

A sigh from her, and John apologised, and Amber said it was fine fine, and quickly put him back in.

Her head was down low, and he could see the nape of her neck, and her fingers were halved on the carpeted floor: knuckles solely visible. And he was speeding up the tempo of his thrusts. He was suddenly pumping like hell. She made noises. He went faster and faster. Ten seconds of this, twenty, forty seconds. The sound of a ballistically happy dog wagging his tail atop a couch, and John was wrecked. It was like sprints, like circuits and ten-second rest between, and he was grateful when he felt her hand grab his wrist and heard her request that he slow down. He obliged. He heaved in and out and his chest was clanking. Was that experience tremendous for her or wholly tiring? Amber asked him then, 'Are you close?'

Baffled, breathless, he replied, 'To what?'

'To finishing?' Her voice haggard. Distracted almost. 'Like. Come.'

He wasn't close at all, but should he be?

Was it weird that he didn't wish to spill?

He'd had a precautionary wank this morning. Normal.

'Yeah, I am,' he lied and tried to compose his breathing. 'So close.'

'Good,' she said. 'Come. Please, come for me.'

'I will, I'm almost there.' He was moving inside her, but his dick was nowhere near close to tingling with a sudden surge of spunk, and it presumably would be bad form to whip his cock out and dart himself over her bum wouldn't it, disrespectful, and she encouraged him again, and in the deepest voice, John groaned, 'I'm about to burst.' And with a hipshake, he pretended to thoroughly ejaculate right that second.

'Oh no,' he cried.

In the bathroom, he swaddled the condom in toilet paper, flushed it, and swiftly masturbated into the same frothy toilet bowl while remembering what had just occurred in the other room. Then he drank some water from the tap, splashed some onto his face in an attempt to dim its colouring, and when he returned, she was under his duvet: blotchy-faced too as if nettle-stung and only her shoulders and up were visible as she studied her phone, and with a scowl, puffed her fringe from her eyes. Seeing him, Amber asked for a loan of a T-shirt, and he tossed one at her after first locating his boxers from the clothes strewn on the floor. She sat forward to shrug the T-shirt on and John didn't look away: it was his to see. Much too large for her, the T-shirt showed Bruce Springsteen jumping with a guitar and it only seemed posed and silly now that Amber was pointing it out as such. 'It suits you, though,' John remarked shyly, and she shook her head, but smiling. He slipped into the bed: his unfavoured lefthand side and only one pillow. She was back on her phone, and the screen cast a blue glow. The furthest curtain was flapping. The fragrance of sex was still in the air like the inside of his gearbag. The Dire Straits sang about Romeo and Juliet all over again. Looking straight up at the ceiling, John asked, 'What happened to your pubes?'

Amber frowned at him, phone flat to her chest.

'I mean you had them. That's all.' He added, 'I like it shaved, too.'

Amber asked, 'Are you a pervert, John Masterson?'

The answer to this was, realistically, yes, but John said, 'No. I'm only wondering.'

'Well. Thank you for wondering,' she said, and in the same mocking voice continued, 'You see, sometimes a lady likes to feel fresh down there and so—'

He interrupted, 'Stop, like. You know that's not what I meant.' The redness was returning to his face: he could feel it prickling. 'I was thinking was there a particular reason or something? Or style? I was only curious. And. Like.' He tasted the words in his mouth and then he went for it in a rush, 'Maybe the next time you could not shave?'

Immediate hysterics.

'Forget it, I was joking,' he growled, and her laughter spiking as she said, 'Oh my god, you are a pervert.'

A couple of minutes passed. Her laughter eventually ebbed away.

It was around four and training was at seven.

John was becoming conscious of this impending deadline and he was formulating means to potentially boot her politely from the house when Amber remarked, 'Leaving Cert results are out soon.'

He looked over and she was on her side away from him. 'Yeah. What is it? Next week. Next Wednesday.' He said for no reason then, 'Fuckin, shite enough.'

'Are you nervous?'

He considered this question for a moment before replying, 'Nah. Not really.' He blinked. 'I haven't thought about it much, to be honest. I want to get in and go to college, but like, what is college about? I'm not sure. Like, what difference will it make to me? How will it change my life?' His hand was out and above the covers. 'I know you go there to learn. Education. Degree. All that. But. What else, you know? Why should I be excited or nervous? I feel like I'm doing it because I'm meant to.'

Quickly, John said, 'Maybe that's dumb.'

'No. I get what you mean,' she said, and she flipped over. Her two hands were cosied in prayer below her cheek and a brilliant if intrusive thought ripened in John's mind: I had sex with you. 'I had a great time when I was there. You'll have fun, that's the truth. I probably had too much fun. And maybe that was my own problem. But I also never got what I was supposed to be doing? Or why I was learning this stuff? Kind of like you said, what good will this do me? I probably just picked the wrong course, I should have been doing something else, but it is a lot to take in. The experience and the total freedom.' She paused. 'It's daunting, I guess. It can be really daunting. You can lose yourself. You can easily lose control of your life.' Amber laughed lightly at this last part as if she had uttered something foolish. 'You can really get lost if you're not careful, is what I mean.'

Surprised, John only said, 'You went to college?'

'Yeah. In Cork.' Three subtraction signs emerged on her forehead. 'Why do you look so shocked?'

'I didn't think you did.'

'Why not?'

'I'm not sure,' he told her. 'I just didn't think you went to college.'

'Rude,' was all she said to this, and she turned away and onto her side.

'Sorry,' John said to the back of her head.

The back of her head stirred. 'Sorry for what exactly, John?'

'Just,' he said, 'I'm sorry for saying that about you and college.' This elicited nothing much, and so John went on, 'There was no malice, Amber. Obviously, you could go to college. I wasn't implying you couldn't attend.'

The back of her head shook. 'For your information, John, I did well in the Leaving Cert, and I got into college, no problem. So, yeah' – she twisted her neck and she glared at him for a second – 'I went to college, alright? I went and now you know.'

'I didn't mean anything by it,' he said, and Amber snapped, 'Yeah sure.'

John returned his gaze to the curtains, the ceiling. He rubbed his face. 'I say stupid stuff, Amber. I don't mean to. I'm sorry. I know I'm annoying. I do try my best not to be so annoying.'

No response to this, and no response to his next lengthy apology either. He stared over. There wasn't a blue glow seeping from her phone and did that make her refusal to speak better or worse? Her hair was scooped over one shoulder. And the white tag of the T-shirt was poking out, and John dared himself and reaching, tucked it back under the collar before he started to knead her neck, her shoulder. Thumb and palm. She didn't slap his hand away and John said in a lowered voice, 'What was the course you were doing in Cork?'

'Accountancy. For some fucked up reason I thought I was destined to be a hotshot accountant.' An exasperated sigh as she said, 'God love me. I only lasted a year. Completely lost interest, or maybe I just wasn't smart enough.' He heard her swallow and his hand had somehow meandered from shoulders to her chest and presently to the right of her chest. 'I dropped out before the summer exams. I knew I was going to fail, so I thought what was the point in sitting them? Save myself the embarrassment.'

'Shit,' John said, and it was hard to concentrate what with his adventurous hand. 'That's really tough.'

'Yeah. It was.'

John said brainlessly, 'Cork is awful far away.'

'It is, and maybe that was on purpose.'

'Right,' he said, confused. 'And are you ever going to go back to Cork? Or, like, college?'

From inside the T-shirt, she picked up his hand and separated it from her boob and said, 'I thought I was going to head straight back. Reapply for the following September. I thought I might do arts. Maybe focus on Spanish. I liked Spanish, I was alright at it in school. No, I was good at it. Anyway, that was the plan. I was saving up to afford it, that's how I started in the hotel, but, I don't know. I never did reapply for whatever reason. I still haven't.'

'You're heading off now anyways,' John mumbled, and clearing his throat, went on, 'Probably works out better for you not to be stuck in college. Like, for your travelling.'

After a while, she answered, 'Yeah. Suppose it does.'

'I actually have arts down on my CAO.' His hand was on her neck but no longer massaging and he tried to sound compellingly cheerful. 'So maybe I'll do Spanish in your honour. Though I didn't study Spanish for the Leaving, so you might have to be my private tutor.' He let out a nervous chuckle. 'Teamo Supremo will live on.'

'Nice,' she said absently, and then: 'Why did you put down arts?'

'I suppose, because,' he said, 'you can do loads of stuff after it? Good options after you graduate. Teaching, for one.' He explained his point further, 'Or like work in a bank, or an office. Or, I don't know, be a journalist?'

A squeak of scepticism as she said, 'Do you want to do those things?'

'Maybe,' he said. 'Teaching could be for me, like. It's what people do, isn't it?'

'Is that what you base your life decisions on? What people do?'

'Yeah,' he said. 'Doesn't everyone generally?'

'I sincerely hope not, John,' she said. 'Tell me, how are you so certain there will be a next time?'

'What do you mean?'

'Earlier you mentioned there being a next time between us when you were acting like a perv.' She flicked at his hand

and turned over to face him. 'And I want to know how you're so confident there will be?'

'Well,' he said, 'I hope there is a next time?' Her eyebrows were raised, and it took a moment before John could think to say, 'And, the agreement.' He grinned at her in what he hoped was in a disarming fashion. 'Like, our deal. That means we have to meet up.'

'*Our deal*,' she mimicked. 'Is that deal not done now, John?'

'No,' he said. 'Why would it be?'

A bemused, cynical look on Amber's face. 'Oh, did you not get what you wanted today?'

'Of course not,' he told her and then corrected, 'Or I did, but not with any malice.'

A puff of air from her nostrils and she shook her head and what was happening and why was he losing, and John went, 'And I thought there'd be a next time. Because.'

John: 'Because.'

'Because what?' Her voice was steeled for an argument.

He should tread carefully. He should speak carefully.

For Amber was presenting him with an out, a conclusion, and didn't John believe today was a goodbye in a way? Shouldn't he accept her gift of an easy farewell? Wouldn't it solve everything? Perhaps some harsh words would follow, maybe some sobbing, maybe some pouty gazes into the middle distance as she bustled into her car and drove off with a squeal of tyre, but it would be over, and it would be clean, and he would have gathered everything he desired from it: sex but also deep deep deep affection. It made perfect sense to say: You're right, there probably won't be another time. To proclaim: You're right, our agreement is dead. Yet he refrained. He absolutely did not want this to be a full stop. He feared a goodbye: feared losing this, her, them. Never being able to talk to her like this. Never being able to see her like this. He did not want her to be the one to decide to end that.

John said, 'Because I was hoping you'd come to the wedding with me?'

Amber recoiled. 'What wedding?'

'My sister's.' John had not expected to say this. 'My sister's wedding, I thought you might come with me or something?'

'Are you serious?' she asked, and she leaned further away. It was a fantastic question, one that probably required teasing out, much inner reflection, and instead John replied at once that he was, yeah. Hundred and ten per cent serious, Amber.

Her face was changed, taken aback but equally suspicious. Like she had been nipped at by a friendly dog. She sat up in the bed, looked at him and then to the side and in a neutral, cold voice asked for the date. He told her and then hurriedly clarified, 'Not the ceremony itself, but it be the afters. If you're up for it.' The same expression on her face – stunned, perplexed – as she said she'd have to think about it. She was out of the bed by now and tugging down the T-shirt as she crouched to sort through the clothes on the floor. Picking, choosing. 'Yeah, maybe, I don't know,' she said, flustered, and when she had gathered her bundle of clothing in the crook of an arm, Amber met his eyes and asked: 'Can I use your bathroom?'

He walked her to the car, stayed to wave her off, and then returned to his room. On the edge of the bed, he stared at his phone. It had been a hard-earned three points, an invaluable sum, and yet he somehow didn't feel like telling anyone. He didn't feel like pricking anybody with his success and indirectly reminding them of their own failure, nor did he feel like dropping unsubtle hints and revelling in the slow circuit of comprehension of his glory. He didn't feel like informing anyone about what had transpired today, apart from one contact in his phone. John texted: 'I know you are not talkin to me but I had sex with Amber... I thought you should know'

His mobile started to vibrate in his hand and the name that appeared on the screen was $tudzy.

Wednesday, 12th August

John knew he wasn't getting the maximum six hundred points out of six hundred points in the Leaving Cert, and that was fine. He had already decided he didn't want that. Honestly: no need and zero interest. He required three hundred and fifty points to be certain that he had some sort of spot in university, a guarantee he'd be down in Galway come September and partaking in one of the courses he had numbered on his CAO form, and so that was wholly what he desired. And it was an amount that had seemed pedestrian when he'd considered it last night, more than graspable, but an amount which now seemed, as he waded through the giddy shrieks and commotion on the stone steps of his school, as he encountered a winking Rooney inside, quite a steep and intimidating number.

Accompanied by his mother, John was presently ambling along a hushed corridor towards the principal's office and the results, and with each step, it was becoming evident to John that he had done terribly in his Leaving Cert.

It had been a shitshow, he was realising.

The secretary waved at them, gestured to the chairs set against the wall, and as John sat, a further flurry of disquieting prospects seized him: what if he had to repeat the whole Leaving Cert and what if he had done worse than Studzy and what if his entire existence was chained around the hotel and the Island, like Amber? He slumped forward, through his trackies he thumbed at the gummy cable of muscle above the face of his left knee. He was a failure. A pitiful substitute with the number twenty-four forever crumbling on his back like a fresco on a damp Roman wall. There was a tang of lemony disinfectant in the air. Every so often the speedy sound of a printer or copier printing or copying like a deck of cards being shuffled. His future was warped, everything was wrong, and then John's pocket rumbled.

Amber Work had sent a message at half seven this morning though he'd only glimpsed it when he woke at nine – 'Best of luck 2day x' – and this was another text from the same contact.

It read: 'Any update?'

Without replying, he silenced the phone and put it away. He exhaled loudly, deliberately, three, four times, seeking to rid himself of the jam-packed sensation in his chest and lungs, this accumulation of throbbing nerves, and he felt a gentle pressure on his elbow and so John flipped over his hand to allow his mother to hold it.

Then the principal's door bumped open, and John immediately stood.

Back in the empty corridor, John tore the envelope and extracted the sheet containing his results, his piece of fabled governmental paper, and he began to calculate as Yvonne pointedly looked aside. Beside History and English there was an A2, and there was a B2 by Art and there was a D2 for French and John declared in an uneven whisper, 'Four hundred and seventy, I think. I'm pretty sure. I got four hundred and seventy points.'

'John,' Yvonne said, and she covered her mouth.

They hugged before Yvonne took the sheet from him and started to tally it up for herself.

John couldn't believe it. He could not believe it. Suddenly trotting atop wads of cloud rather than the squeaky linoleum floor: it felt like that. His hand roved through his fringe, his hair, and he was smiling, hugely, dumbly. What was his first choice on the CAO again? It didn't matter now, actually: fuck it, he was heading to college and that was it and he was lighter. He was floating, he was floating away.

He retrieved his phone and texted Amber: '470 . Maddness......'

Soon his phone said, 'OMG'

Soon his phone said, 'WELL DONE'

Soon his phone said, 'You never told me you were a genius kk', and at this stage John had returned to the front entrance of the school. It was bustling. Voices and laughter. John was beside Rooney and Rooney was asking what did he get? John informed his friend, and received a hearty congratulations before John fired the same question back.

'Four hundred,' Rooney said with a goofy smile. 'And Karen got five hundred and ten. Can you believe that?'

John congratulated him, congratulated him about Karen, too, and John knew it wasn't a competition of course.

'We are buzzing,' Rooney said then, and he whispered conspiratorially to John, 'The party house is on for definite, Tits.'

'Yeah,' John said. 'The house.'

'It'll be savage,' Rooney said, and he tilted from John while shaking his head. 'I can't wait. Galway. College. It's going to be so much better than here.'

John wagged his head enthusiastically, John wanted to believe what Rooney was saying, and then John remembered Tony as if pinched on the underside of his arm, and he went, 'Did you hear from Tony yet, actually?'

'No,' Rooney said, and his voice changed. Dulled. 'Shit, yeah. No, I haven't. I say he got on fine though? Got the points?'

John was in the middle of concurring when he heard his name excitedly called.

He swung round and he was hugging Orlagh Landey, then he was hugging a little less warmly Audrey Irwin before Audrey went over to say hello to Yvonne, who stood alone from the other spectating parents. Orlagh was telling a story about how her hands shook so much when she was given the envelope that she almost dropped it and can you imagine: a definitively unfunny story and yet John was giggling along, for laughter was currently contagious. John's phone was vibrating constantly by now: cousins, Kay and then Denis, and a slew of texts had arrived from the work crew – Hughie Denton first, Zibby, Samantha – and John smiled harder, and he thought: Amber. 'Isn't it insane though?' Orlagh said. 'We're finished.' John and Rooney agreed. It was mental. Orlagh had got four hundred and twenty-five points. Audrey had got five hundred and sixty including an A1 in art which was classic. So, not counting Karen as different schools, John had, so far, done better than two out of three of his peers. Pretty impressive, though obviously: not a competition. Orlagh asked, 'What's your plan for later?'

There was training tonight, there was Championship in less than five days, but a special dispensation had been granted to the boys. A message from Ultan that the club was proud of them, that they had been given permission to enjoy themselves. Ultan had said: 'BUT GO EASY . ULTAN .'

John and Rooney looked at one another and then John said, 'Drinking. Not sure after that. But. Yeah. Drinking.'

More heads arrived in then – Brendan Hare followed by Niamh Regan and John thought for the first time in a long time about Seóna and what was it she wanted to do again and was it nursing? – and Yvonne was suddenly gesturing at John, motioning John over with a phone to her ear.

'Okay, he's here now,' Yvonne said to the phone. John expected an aunt on the line, or the croaky tremor of an older relative, but it was his father: 'Johnny. I'm thrilled for you.'

'Hi, Dad.' Instinctively John was slinking from the crowd.

Because of the noise and not for any other reason.

'Are you delighted with yourself?' the phone asked, and then the phone answered, 'You must be delighted.'

'I'm very proud of you,' the phone went on, and John could hear something closing, shutting, and then the phone let out a gasp. 'Very proud.'

'My man,' the phone said.

'Thanks, Dad,' John said, and he held the phone tighter to his ear. He was in a corner. A narrow glass window before him. 'No, it's good. I'm happy with it. Thanks. I'm really happy.'

'You should be,' the phone said, 'and I'm sorry I can't get in for the lunch, but your mother has some money from me for tonight. You enjoy yourself. And I'll catch you tomorrow.'

'Thanks a million, Dad,' John said. 'Yeah, I'll see you tomorrow. Definitely. I'll come over, or something.' From the window, a view of the football pitch and people filing up the slickened steps. Gloomy overhead but it wasn't drizzling any longer. And you'd take that. You'd make do with that. John turned around and he said into the phone, 'I love you, Dad.'

'I love you too,' the phone replied, and John saw his mother in the same position as earlier, alone and smiling placidly at everyone and no one.

*   *   *

They left after this, John just had time to slap Brendan Hare on the head, and they popped home to change before they were on their way again to the lunch in Westport. Yvonne was listing the extended family members who were pleased for John and then the Dutch ladies who were pleased, and he was nodding along in the passenger seat, blandly promising to ring everybody later. His phone had cooled, and he sent Amber a text accusing her of informing the whole hotel. She replied: 'Whats wrong with that? Everyone is excited for you x'. When they neared Westport, Yvonne asked, 'And how did Tony get on?'

Tony had always been Yvonne's favourite. Tony always made sure to stick his head into the sitting room when he was visiting.

'Not sure he's got his results,' John answered.

'It's past noon,' Yvonne said. 'He must have them by now.'

'Yeah, well. He hasn't got on to me yet?' John had texted Tony twice already. Rang Tony and it had beeped to his clipped voicemail.

'He wants medicine, isn't it?' she asked and John said yeah, in Dublin, and his mother clucked her tongue before she stated, simply, 'I hope he gets it.' Then his mother's shoulder tipped towards John's side of the car: 'And what about the buck himself? Our Enda.'

John hadn't checked in on Studzy this morning, hadn't sent a best-of-luck message or a subsequent how-did-you-do text or anything like that. In John's head, he was doing Studzy a favour. John was being merciful. But Studzy had texted while John was changing at home: 'I heard you did unreal Tits!! LEGEND'. It was a kind message, and originally John had been going to respond with: 'Thanks bud! see u later?' But then he'd amended and wrote instead: 'Thanks bud! how u get on???'

In reply, Studzy merely sent a cryptic ';)' and then a moment later another text arrived from Studzy: 'Bottles bought. U owe me money'

Now John said to his mother, 'I think Studzy got on fine. Like, he wasn't the best student, Mam? It wasn't exactly his thing.'

Yvonne let out a laugh. 'I can imagine.' She peered knowingly across. 'Maud did tell me he was a bit of a terror. But he's a nice lad, Enda. He's been good to you. He means well.'

To a large extent, John felt he agreed with this sentiment.

John said, 'Yeah. No. He does mean well, alright.'

Kay was already at the table, and she had a balloon that said in sparkly letters GRADUATION – 'All they had in the shop,' Kay explained – and a card that depicted a cartoon hedgehog graduating in a cap with golden tassels – 'I thought this one was just cute,' Kay explained. John thanked his sister before Yvonne asked a waiter to take their photo: three of them standing with John clasping the balloon and afterwards, while looking at the small screen on the camera, John noted that you could see the waiter's slackened face in the mirror behind the Mastersons. Sitting, they talked about the exam results for five, ten minutes – Kay had lots of questions and John didn't possess that many answers and it reached the point where John gruffly passed the sheet with his formatted results to his sister so she could figure it out – and once conversation had drifted towards more fertile ground in the wedding – how close it was now, how near – John said he had to use the toilet and he slunk out to the front of the café, onto the busy street. There, John tried Tony again on the blower.

Still it beeped to voicemail.

He texted Tony: 'I hope everything sound?'

He texted Tony: 'Studzy bought bottles FYI'

And when John was about to wander back inside, his phone rang and who else would it be: Tony said, 'Howya.'

His voice was low and husky, maybe defeated, and unconsciously matching this volume and mood, John murmured, 'Are you okay, bud?'

'Yeah. Sorry. Hold on,' Tony said, and there was the sound of hasty movement, Tony's voice tiny and saying something tinier, and John was presently thinking up tactics to help diffuse his friend's failure, to compensate for Tony's loss and colossal personal embarrassment. Because surely Tony had lost, Tony hadn't got the points for his first choice and hence this reticence. On the phone line there was a sudden whoosh of air and Tony's voice was louder: 'Well, Tits. Sorry about that. I'm out with the fam.'

'That's fine, bud,' John said. A sympathetic exhale and then John probed once more, 'Did it go alright, Tone? With the results.'

'Oh yeah. I should have texted you back earlier, but. Yeah, all good. Very good, actually.' John could hear his friend smiling: a sticky squelch as teeth were unveiled. 'I did it, John. Five ninety points. And with my HPAT score, well, I definitely got medicine in Trinity.' Tony started laughing. 'Ah, I'm still buzzing, man. I did it.'

'Tits,' Tony said. 'Are you still there?'

John replied, 'Yeah.' John said, louder, 'That's great news, Jesus. Huge congrats.' Did these words of praise ring hollow? John hoped not but they felt hollow, weightless to him as they left his mouth. John thought stupidly, strikingly: it should be me, it shouldn't be him but me. John thought: I should be going, I should be best. The sensation that Tony had confiscated this dream, stolen this grand achievement from John.

Tony began to apologise for his silence, began to explain what happened – Tony hadn't slept last night and he'd snuck into the school first thing this morning expecting the worst, and was in a kind of daze afterwards – and John hummed along, purred, 'No worries,' when appropriate, and Tony presently swerved course and said: 'But, John, Studzy text me there about your results. That's serious, Tits. You buzzing?'

'I am, yeah,' John said and then he went, 'It's not a competition though, Tony.'

'I know?' Tony said.

'I'm just saying,' John said, and he found he had walked a good bit down the street. 'You sounded like you were comparing us there and it's not a competition? But look, forget it.' His thumb was in his mouth, the nail between his teeth but not quite biting, rather gnawing. 'I'll miss you in Galway now, Tony.' The sun was poking through above: a glare on windscreens, shopfronts. John was happy for his friend, but something was blocking him from fully expressing this. Jealousy? Not exactly when his mind slowed to consider. No. Loneliness was closer. Hatefulness was even closer than that again. He hated that Tony was leaving him, he hated that Tony did best. 'It's meant to be a class place for college, Galway. The student life there is meant to be unbelievable. So, you won't get to experience that. But, Dublin is probably good craic, too?' John paused. 'I haven't heard much about college in Dublin, but I'm sure it's alright.'

'Yeah. Hopefully it is. It'll be strange being on my own up there.'

'True,' John told Tony. 'It probably will be strange. But at least none of us be around annoying you.'

'No,' Tony said and this ripple of laughter. 'I'll see you loads though? I'll definitely be visiting. Have to stay over at this party house. Rooney's bigging it up, like.'

'Yeah, maybe,' John said, and he looked up to where the sun had been a moment before: cloud now, a burnished grey. 'I suppose it depends on space in the house, if you can stay over.' His voice was authoritative. 'Probably be events on and stuff so the house might be full. Or we could be busy, so you mightn't be able to stay just when it suits you, Tony.' John scoffed nasally. 'You've made your choice, bud? Can't come crawling back to us, like.'

Silence on the other end of the phone and into it, John said, 'Nah. I'm only messing.' John waited and then said, 'I'm genuinely happy for you.'

Eventually Tony said, 'Thanks, John.'

The rest of the lunch zoomed by. No explicit mention of the touristy town they were currently eating in. No further word about relocation plans that were in all likelihood decided. As their plates were being cleared, John brought up Tony, illuminated his mother on his results, and Yvonne said she was thrilled for him. John shared this zeal, John said, 'No, it's brilliant. Tony worked really, really hard.'

Kay yawned and enquired which one was Tony again?

From beneath John's elbow, the slender neck of a brown bottle protruded with its distinct golden cap, like a worrisome signet ring. John's lips were wet and the faint whiskers above his lips were wet, too. He was in a sloping field by a stream and its tinkling music like daintily struck wind chimes. Colloquially this field was known as The Swamp and a pack of boys had gathered here this afternoon, twenty in all. The class of o-nine. His friends, his dearest pals, plus a fistful of unlikeable dicks. They had been out here for a can and the first sup of Buckfast and now John took his second nick of tonic wine. It was sweet with a syrupy tang that invited John to announce with a connoisseur diction, 'A very, very fine bottle.'

Studzy agreed. Studzy lifted his own bottle skyward, seemingly to review its grooved heel. 'It is some beverage, lads.'

'The best going,' Tony said. Tony was standing opposite John: John had winked at him earlier and received a curt thumbs up in return.

'You know you can tell by the lid if it's a good bottle or not?' Studzy addressed the circle of boys. Rooney caught John's eye as Studzy unscrewed the bottle's cap in methodical stages. 'You hear that?' Studzy tightened the golden cap and then repeated the opening, ear cocked towards the bottle's neck. 'There. That little click is proof that you have a stellar bottle.' The bottle was transferred from one hand to the other and a clunk as glass met Studzy's bulky watch. 'The bad ones don't make that noise.' Studzy sniffed. 'That's a fact.'

John was nodding along seriously; everyone was nodding along except Rooney.

Then Frank Kiely cried that Studzy was talking pony and Studzy held this aggrieved pissy face towards Frank for a second and then the air-hockey slot of Studzy's affronted mouth curled and Studzy burst into giggles: so everyone else did, too.

John was in a shirt – light blue with see-through buttons, sleeves hiked to the three-quarters position on his arm as he had read online that women horned for *visible wrists* – while Studzy was decked out in a short-sleeve chequered shirt with an inexplicable hood. Tony was in a white polo and this new puka shell necklace. A shirt collar spilled out from under Rooney's slimtight jumper, a paisley pattern on the shirt. Or a shitey hippie pattern, as Studzy had exclaimed. Every boy in the field wore some cut of denim jean as every boy was hoping to be inside a sweaty and frenetic nightclub later.

The plan for tonight had been concocted by Studzy. Lush in this spot till eightish and then hitch a lift to Castlebar and line up dead early for Clowns and get in when it was empty, when it was conceivably easier to gain entrance, and bum around till the club was crammed. John had Hughie Denton's provisional driving licence in his arse pocket. Studzy had inspected the ID by holding it first against the sun and then holding it up to John's face, sucking his teeth as his eyes toggled between Hughie's picture and John's loathsome mug, before returning it to John with the verdict: 'It'll probably work.'

There was now about half remaining in the bottle, and John jiggled it. The line of the dark liquid sloshed and roiled, and John re-estimated: less than half. There was a whiff of burning from cigarettes and rollies, the scratch of lighters. Amber had texted an hour previous – 'Where you going tonight? x' – and John only realised right at this instant and he replied with his tongue pressed above his lip: 'Clowns . hopefully xx pray 4 me hahah wbu kkk???' He took another slug. Another after that as he listened to Rooney and Tony discuss the strengths and gaping holes of the Claremorris side – all chatter orbited Championship – and then John's phone vibrated: 'Working split so nowhere x'

John already knew Amber was rostered for this evening: he had checked the rota on Monday morning and noted this fact. John had also noted, from the crusty Tipp-Ex layers and the near unintelligible scrawls, that Amber was not supposed to be on a split shift today. Originally, she'd had this Wednesday off but she had swapped with Samantha so that Amber wouldn't have to work on Saturday the fifteenth of August.

John had felt a shudder of disquiet when he'd discovered this adjustment.

He didn't like it.

He didn't like how she hadn't mentioned it to him. He didn't like the idea of her explaining to someone why she needed that specific evening off. He didn't like the image of her tagging along with him to a family wedding and what family might say, think, reckon.

Now Rooney asked John, 'Who you texting?'

'No one,' John answered. Then: 'My mam.'

A squirt left in the bottle, and this dropped into John's gut with a sizzle. John shook the bottle to confirm it was empty, John proceeded to upend the bottle completely to doubly confirm it was empty. I'm finished, John thought. 'Finished,' John said to no one in particular, and then John barked Studzy's name.

From across the field, Studzy gazed over and John yelled at his confuddled face, 'I'm finished, bud.'

John repeated his upside-down bottle stunt.

'I'm behind,' Studzy howled, and he hoisted up his own bottle, gulped and gulped. A snaking dribble of mulberry ran down his chin before Studzy dragged it away with the back of his hand. Studzy said to John, 'Let's rob some cans.'

At six, Rooney had to leave to meet Karen and her mates, and there was a salvo of abuse distributed in his direction. Raising his middle finger, Rooney shouted he'd catch them all later in the club. Others started to become restless after this first exit. Boys began to order taxis. Solicit parents for lifts. John suggested to Studzy they should do the same, but Studzy winked. 'Don't mind it, Tits. I'll sort us.'

A while later and it was only Tony, John and Studzy in the field with their legs dangling over the stream. They had seven cans between them: a mismatch of cider and Dutch Gold and four of them were currently swimming in the brown water in an attempt to render them frosty and cool. Music from Studzy's phone, dance mostly, and it was crap, and still John commented regularly: 'Good tune, that one.'

The music switched to a rap song.

John drank his lager and remarked, 'Good tune, that one.'

Studzy nodded at this and as if Studzy had only figured it out, only counted them up there and then, Studzy proclaimed, 'The three bucks left.' He raised his can and John and Tony knocked their tinnies towards it. 'And listen,' Studzy said, with a finger cutting through the air, 'fair fucks again on the results, lads. Two of ye. You deserve it.'

'The doctor here,' John piped in, smiling at the stream. 'Unbelievable.'

'Truth,' Studzy said. 'Some fuckin job, Tony.'

'Thanks, lads,' Tony went. His face was rouge around the cheeks, his face went red when he drank. 'You'll both have to come up to Dublin.'

'Kid. You won't be able to get rid of me,' Studzy said, and they laughed for a time. The brown water glistened in obscure patterns and then it didn't and then it did again and John looked up from it as Tony said to Studzy, 'What you get today, man? Tell us.' Tony clapped Studzy on the back and gawked across at John. 'He has to tell us, doesn't he, Tits?'

John went, 'Mr Secret here.'

A terrible joke, but wait, actually: it was hilarious and Heathrow.

'I'm not Mr Secret,' Studzy said with a pout.

'You are, bud.' John grinned and rocked Studzy via the shoulders. 'You love a secret.'

Tony said to Studzy, 'If you don't want to say, it's fine. We're only codding—'

Studzy interjected, 'No, I'll tell you. I'm not Mr Secret.' Studzy kind of moved his upper body but he didn't exactly go forward or back and then Studzy said while staring intently at the stream, 'Two hundred and seventy points.'

'Sham,' John said and it took him only a short second or two or three to locate the words for the next part: 'Well done, Studz. That's really good.'

'Yeah, well.' Studzy was smiling. 'Not nearly as much as you two brainboxes, but for me, it's loads, like.' Studzy still looked at the stream, but his head was at an acute angle now as if investigating a coin somewhere in the water. 'I bet you didn't expect that much anyways.'

'No, we did,' John said, and he changed his face: set it to frowning and thus cordial and understanding. 'I knew you put in the hours.' Tony was nodding along, and John thought to reach across to shake Studzy's hand and Studzy peered down at John's paw before eventually clasping it. 'Huge congrats,' John said.

'Will you get into your course with that?' Tony asked and then Tony's voice trailed off as he went, 'What was it you were going for again, Studz, sorry?'

John answered for Studzy, 'Science. He applied for the fish science.'

Studzy took a slurp of his can and drips fell onto the front of his shirt, but he didn't seem to notice. 'I don't know if I will have enough points, to be honest. Probably impossible for NUIG, but I have Marine Science down for the IT in Galway and I might get that. But be close.' Studzy shrugged. 'It's usually three hundred points needed, or a bit above. So. Tight enough.'

'Imagine though,' John said, and he was beaming at Studzy. 'Us in Galway? The carnage.'

'Yeah,' Studzy said, and he shrugged again, 'we'll see.'

'You could always get rechecks done on your results, Studzy?' Tony said after a moment. 'Be worth a shout if you are that close.'

'Maybe,' Studzy said. 'Yeah, I might do.'

'Fuckin, can you imagine,' John said then and John did not have anything else to say. John picked at the grass around him, felt his jaw shift from side to side. They finished their cans and cracked three new ones and from the corner of his eye, John spied Tony lumbering to his feet. 'Piss,' Tony explained almost ruefully, and before he could stomp off, Studzy had seized his wrist: 'Here, Tone. Would you mind ringing your aul one for a lift into town?'

Tony muttered under his breath.

'Thanks, bud,' Studzy said, and he let go.

John sniggered and watched over his shoulder as Tony's lanky frame dipped behind sunny gorse, and Studzy said then, 'I say you both thought I was going to fail the Leaving Cert, didn't you?'

John turned to Studzy and Studzy spoke over John's breathless incredulity: 'No, I say you all thought I'd be lucky to get basket-weaving or whatever. The lowest possible outcome. That I'd do the worst ever. You're probably fierce surprised, aren't you?'

John laughed awkwardly – it was a gag, right? – and Studzy hunched his shoulders and went, 'I wouldn't blame you if you did, man. Honestly, I wouldn't.'

'Nah,' John replied, still half laughing. 'I had faith in

you.' And because this was presumably a giant skit, John felt he should quip, 'Mr Scholar, like.'

Studzy grinned at this but no laughter from him. Studzy said, 'Mr Stupid, more like.'

'Enda,' John said, and his mouth was askew. 'You're not stupid. And, like.' John's voice was higher. 'What did Tony say there? About the rechecks if you need them.' Studzy glanced at John and John continued, his voice higher again, 'You could easily make up the points and get the course in the IT? Or maybe even NUIG?'

John said, 'Easily, bud.'

'I don't know,' Studzy said, and he rubbed his chin into the bicep of his right arm. 'I just don't know.'

'Don't know about what?'

'I don't know if I'm bothered.'

'With the rechecks?' John said, and Studzy replied, 'No, not just that.' Studzy tutted and then said, 'But am I bothered with leaving here?' His arm jerked and droplets of cider. 'I don't know, the petrol station offered me full-time hours there last week. And the football is going well for me. I might be better off sticking around this place, even if I somehow got a course.'

'Oh yeah?' John said.

'And it's a lot of money. College. Accommodation and the fees. Books, you know?' Studzy looked at John. 'Between us, I'm not sure the parents can afford it. It's serious bean. A serious, fuckin, investment or whatever you might call it.' His tongue was making a clicking noise. 'It's a shit ton of money when you think about it.'

John hadn't realised college cost money, truthfully. Or no, he had of course – textbooks, pens, deposit and rent – but he'd never suspected it couldn't be afforded. That it might cause an issue. A predicament for someone. That was news to him. That was new. John turned to the stream, the water that glimmered prettily now and again, and he could only repeat himself, 'Oh yeah?'

'Let's be real, Tits. What benefit would I get out of college? What good would it do me?' A snorted chuckle from Studzy and John sensed his friend's sidelong stare, but John could not face it suddenly, nor cackle along as if one huge funny joke. The music had stopped from Studzy's phone: when exactly, John wasn't sure, but the stream's sounds were more pronounced. Had been for a while. This trickling, that softened plopping. 'It'd be a total waste of money on me. Wouldn't it, John?' Studzy said. 'Even if I somehow got in, be a total waste. A shit investment.'

'That's not true,' John said, and he was trying to keep his breathing to a minimum.

'It is,' Studzy said to John, 'and you know it. Be a waste of everyone's time.'

Studzy reached for his phone and John flinched at this movement. John should disagree with the previous statement, obviously, clearly, but the longer he left it to reply, to articulate his disagreement and confidently announce how Studzy was well able for college, the harder it became. John should be a good friend, and a good friend would say this. But, John told himself now, a better friend, a true bestest friend, would just not say anything at all. Let Studzy arrive at his own decision, be settled with his own convictions. Different folks, different strokes. The playlist started again. Sniffing, Studzy leaned forward and spat into the stream: a glop of fizzing phlegm, and John watched this be swept along by the brown water. You can position yourself anywhere in a relationship if you allow the other to want and want, to be desperate, to be clawing at your heels. You can tell yourself a whole lot of things about another person and believe them, if you can manage to prop them beneath you like a rung on a ladder. This was knowledge John was learning. John did not speak, the music played, and soon Tony appeared in John's peripheral, rushing back towards them. To Studzy, John said, 'Watch,' and they both craned their necks. Tony was indicating somewhere behind him with his thumb. Tony possessed a scowl as he said, 'My mother's waiting. Hurry on.'

A thunderous downpour as they peeled into Castlebar and jumping from the lift, the boys sprinted towards an alleyway with arms clenched above their heads. Sheltered from the rain, they shared the remaining can of Dutch Gold. An occasional comment, an occasional belch, but it was mostly contented silence. When they'd finished, they placed the can delicately in a corner as if a small gift for a wandering stranger and then they squinted up at the sky and it was John who said, 'Will we chance it?'

Studzy nodded with a stern expression, but Tony requested could they stall a minute longer. Using the vague, murky reflection of a nearby window, Tony combed upward his fringe, spiked it that inch higher, and then, while exhaling, Tony ironed out his polo shirt with flattened palms.

Tony faced the boys. 'I look alright, yeah?'

Instantly, Tony was informed he looked unbelievable, John and Studzy both told him he looked sharp, and then Studzy posed the same question and a similar chorus resounded: you look class, Studz. And the hood? The hood on the shirt is practical as well as stylish. Then it was John's turn to ask: 'I'm sound too, yeah? The shirt, my hair.'

John added, 'And I don't look fat, do I?'

The boys gawped at him before Studzy wrapped his arm around John's neck. 'What you on about fat? You're a beast.'

'You're looking strong, Tits,' Tony said, and he flexed his arm.

Studzy said, 'You're a tank, bud. A tank.'

John smiled from beneath Studzy's tightening grip. John said, 'Thanks, boys. Thank you.'

These were his friends.

They were in the queue. A parallel row of steel barriers had been set up: clanking and wobbling as bodies weaved around them. It was busier than John had expected for not even ten o'clock. Studzy was beside John. Tony was ahead and now Tony peeked back at them. This was another of Studzy's ideas. 'Three's a crowd,' Studzy had explained and John thought: it is, yeah. A pair of bouncers were at the entrance. Black jackets with luminous bands like soccer captains. They were letting most through without checking ID: a lift of chin after a brief stoppage and you were bouncing up the twinkling stairs. John whispered Hughie's date of birth to himself – fifteenth of February, nineteen eighty-nine, fifteenth of – and Studzy said to him: 'It will be grand.'

The queue moved and a trio of girls staggered up the stairs.

Studzy said, 'We'll be grand.'

Tony was next.

John watched Tony nod at the bouncers before they had even clocked his presence. Then Tony was speaking but one of the bouncers put out a hand – Tony wasn't getting in, a relief to John as John could wield the hero card and accompany the poor loser drunkard Tony home – and then the same fella shot a thumbs up to someone unseen.

The hand was dropped.

Tony was past the bouncers and climbing the stairs.

Four lads were next – heads skinned at the side and IDs were thoroughly checked and John tried not to notice this scrupulous investigation – and then it was John and Studzy. Without being asked, Studzy presented his Age Card to the leftmost bouncer and the other bouncer gestured at John with grubbing fingers like money.

'Hi,' John said, and he transferred over the provisional licence.

The bouncer looked at the document, glanced at John and then back to the pink paper, and from the side of his mouth, the bouncer asked, 'What's your name, boss?'

John answered, 'The fifteenth of Febru—'

Then John corrected himself, 'I mean, sorry. Hughie. My name is Hughie Denton. Sorry.'

The bouncer tutted.

The bouncer said, 'Your hair, Hughie. It's gone a different colour.'

John opened his mouth to counter with some plausible argument – for instance, that his type of hair was the exact type of hair that darkens when rained upon as it was just that type of strawy hair, you know? – and nothing arrived out. Studzy had been waved through and he waited before the stairs. Bleak failure, the end of John's night, the end of John's life in fact, until the bouncer sighed. 'Go on, you chancer.'

'Thanks a million,' John immediately squawked.

John had got in.

He was in and at the top of the bright stairway and ecstatic to pay a tenner to a disgruntled woman. The notion to tip this woman even flashed as his hand was stamped with a gurning clown. Studzy was shoving John in a friendly manner and John was giggling uncontrollably. Banging through the double doors, they found Tony biting his nails and Tony's eyes were wide when he saw them. They hugged one another, the three boys. John scanned all around him, John sucked it down. Strobe lights slicing through fog. There were steps that descended into what must be the dancefloor. Cubbies at random in the walls. Poles at random, too. A bar occupying the width of the entire righthand side. A surprising number of shelves. This was a nightclub, this was his existence beginning now.

'Fuck my ass,' Studzy said in a hoarse voice. 'This will be snerious.'

Studzy then said shots repeatedly like a stammer. The three of them were soon flopped over a sparkling bar counter and tipping small glasses of liquid into their mouths. It was like brine, it was like toppling beneath a wave.

Smacking his lips, John said, 'Unreal.'

Then they were upstairs – this magical place had another floor – and Tony was buying three pints. Liquid already spilling from the glass and more slopped onto the floor once they cheered. Music was booming, a thud in John's chest, this trill in his ears, and John had to yell so that Studzy could hear him say, 'Good tune, that one.'

Suddenly everybody was there.

Everybody John wanted to see in the whole world was inside the club.

John was hugging, John was bumping against people. He was chatting to Orlagh for a time, and then Rooney and Karen appeared: Rooney was clutching Karen's hand as he shouldered open the door and John zipped over instantly. 'You made it,' Rooney said with a huge smile. 'He made it,' Rooney said to Karen and Karen said, 'Hey, John.' And then John was with Orlagh and Studzy at the smaller bar upstairs. More shots were bought by Studzy: tequila sloshing down the hatch and the taste was fire, blue flames scorching John's throat, and for a sustained period after this drink, John had to stand stock-still at the bar, avoiding eye contact, otherwise John knew he would puke. He was sure he'd spew up his lunch and guts and maybe even his heart.

But he managed to endure.

After two gruelling minutes, John managed to show a pleasant face to Studzy and the far more concerned Orlagh, mumbling, 'Love tequila.'

John then turned to order two pints and when he spun to ask Orlagh what she was drinking, her and Studzy were pressed against the wall. The pints were handed over and John stood watching his friends smooch while sipping from one and then John decided he should probably wander off.

He prowled through the downstairs, squirming by groups, and Studzy's pint was mostly on the ground. Hypnotic lights. A song receded and another took its place and John discovered he knew this song. He sang along as he circled the dancefloor. Then he stopped and astutely poured Studzy's pint into his own and left the empty glass on a shelf. John thought: aha. Shiny foreheads. The reek of vodka and Red Bull. Perfume and sweat. He was in the thick of it. He lifted a fist in time with the music. He was searching for familiar faces. Where had they disappeared to and had they evacuated to somewhere special without him and should John vomit into a sink?

A hand gripped his collar then, hauled him backwards, and John was sprawled in a leather booth.

He was next to Karen and on his left side, John was being harangued by Rooney: his principal subject being Galway and the house, the house, the house. Rooney motioned at the teeming dancefloor. 'We will be gone from these crappy spots soon enough, Tits. Finally. We can go to proper clubs, you know? Gigs. Live bands. Concerts. Performances.' Rooney licked his lips and grabbed at his drink: a glass of Coke that was definitely not totally Coke. His mouth missed the straw and then found it. 'Me and you will have such a buzz down there.'

There was a disco ball spinning from the ceiling and John was nodding at this as he replied, 'Be good to be somewhere different, alright. New things.'

'Man. Exactly that. Exactly.' Rooney carefully put down the drink and then stretched across John's lap to take hold of Karen's hand. 'We went to suss the house last week. It's a lovely gaff. Lovely windows. A fireplace, a chimney. A huge kitchen table. Then it has the four bedrooms.' Rooney spoke to Karen: 'Doesn't it, babe?'

'It's very nice,' Karen informed John, and Karen extracted her hand from Rooney's.

'You heard it there, bud,' Rooney said. 'It will be class to get away from here, Tits. Fuckin, university. A new city.

New people to meet. New girls for you.' Rooney stopped himself here, his eyelids twitched but did not fully close, and Rooney said, 'Unless you're still with that one from the hotel?'

'Nah,' John said automatically. 'I'm not.'

'Oh. You're all finished with her?'

'Yeah, well,' John said, 'we were never a big thing. And I'll be gone soon, won't I?'

'True, man.' Rooney tried to nod sombrely. Soberly. 'You're better off single down there, for sure.' Rooney reclined, his arms draped over the back of the booth, and then Rooney sprang forward to the edge of the seat. 'And I know you mightn't consider this yet, but to get away from certain heads from around here be good, too. Do us both good. Honestly. The likes of Aaron English, Frank Kiely. And, no malice' – Rooney showed his hands at John as if stick-up – 'but fuckin the likes of, fuckin, Studzy, too. No malice.'

'Well,' John said and he kind of chuckled, 'Studzy could end up in Galway.'

'Let's not play that one again.' Rooney leaned in towards John. 'We squished that.'

'No, I'm telling you the truth, Rooney. Studzy did well.' John slanted his head. 'He got two seventy.' At this Rooney snorted and threw his hands up and John went on nonetheless, 'You can laugh but he's not far off from NUIG with that, and not at all far from the science in the IT. And with the rechecks? Like, he could get another ten or twenty points from rechecks. It's very possible he gets in.'

John grimaced. 'I'm just saying, Rooney. No need to laugh.'

'Fuckin hell.' Rooney was shaking his head. His eyes were glassy, unfocused, even as he stared directly at John. 'We can't get rid of him, can we? He's like shit in your shoe.' John made a sound bordering laughter and Rooney continued, 'And of course he could only barely get into the IT. The fuckin dopey idiot.'

John looked across at Rooney. 'That's not nice.'

'Nice?' Rooney made a face. 'That guy is an absolute dickhead. You've no idea what a dickhead he is. No idea. He doesn't deserve nice.' Rooney pointed at his chest. 'Also. Am I wrong? Did you apply for anything in the IT?' John shrugged and Rooney lifted the finger from his chest and stabbed it towards John. 'Don't be a hypocrite, man. You know it's the truth.'

'Anyways, I don't give a shite,' Rooney said. 'If Studzy gets in, well then, I hope he enjoys Galway for the week he's there before he flunks out. The dumb fuck.' Rooney's mouth was beady. 'I won't see him anymore. I don't have to interact with him.' Rooney snarled, 'May he rot. The dirty cunt.'

'Don't say that,' John said after a deep breath.

'Why? Why shouldn't I?'

'Because it's nasty. It's bad form. You should take that back. Everything you said there. Take all that back now.'

With pursed lips, Rooney grabbed for his drink, and this exaggerated sup before Rooney said to John, 'No, I won't take it back.'

Without another word, John rose and barged by Karen.

John was on the stairs marching up and there was a girl crying at the bottom and mirrors all along the bare wall – funky-shaped shards of mirror – and the lights were brighter in the stairwell. Or just switched on. He could see himself. A shirt with the top two buttons undone and his hair frizzy and bloodshot blue eyes that belonged to his father. He tried to calm himself. Make sense of the exchange. Make sense of his own heated reaction to the exchange. John was drunk: that was a fact. Words and actions become unreliable when drunk: another universal unquestionable fact. You're pissed and Rooney is definitely pissed, he told himself. Rooney probably meant nothing that bad by what he said, plus Studzy was an unrepentant dick to Rooney sometimes, and honestly a word like *dirty* can have a lot of different connotations considering context and if John assumed the very worst, the very mean, the very base, was it, more or less, on him and his own buried, unspoken beliefs? John put his head against the mirror, breathed in and breathed out till his surroundings stopped shaking, and then he took out his phone. It was half eleven and he knew he couldn't text Studzy, so he texted Tony: 'Where u?'

Then he looked at Amber's most recent message – 'I hope good kk' – and the one before that: 'How's it going? x'

There was the slamming of a door from below and John

rapidly pocketed the phone and resumed jogging up the stairs.

The upstairs was rammed. On the dancefloor, bodies wound together, twisting, and how boys couldn't dance but jump and jump into others. John tunnelled his way to the opposite side of the room. He leaned against the wall and felt its dampness and his eyelids were heavy and his phone buzzed.

Tony: 'Clowns. You?'

John replied, 'But where exactly?????'

He was watching the dancefloor while awaiting Tony's next braindead text message, and his eyelids were heavier still, and John thought how it might be wise to have a quick nap here – conserve energy, refocus – and when he allowed his lids to close, he perceived gigantic shapes and strange orbs of light and the music pumping redly: each decisive note red. His body toppled forward suddenly and John opened his eyes. The dancefloor was as before: the dismal light, the spheres from garish beams which periodically revealed a face. What would John do if Amber was somewhere in that dancefloor, loose and free or indeed anticipating him? Chase after, hunt her down, or work incredibly hard to avoid and avoid her knowing he was nearby? The idea of seeing her with others: horrifying. The idea of him and her together and others seeing them and their reaction: equally horrifying. What would he do with Amber? The endlessly pertinent question: what was he to do with himself?

His phone vibrated then.

It was a minute to midnight. He had one new text message.

Tony: 'Smoking area. You?'

Friday, 14th August

Except he wasn't ignoring Amber, no no no, but it just so happened it was her idea to meet up today: a rarity, fair enough, but not explicitly incongruous. She had reached out and John had replied yesterday – admittedly late as he'd had to deal with his second ever hangover in the morning, as he had to work till half ten, as he had to complete a final secret boss in *Final Fantasy* – and she'd been the one who'd suggested a stroll before his training. She even had a venue in mind: the woods.

Their woods.

She offered to collect him, and John thought about it and then declined and asked his father for a lift – informing Peter that he was heading to the pitch early as they were going to puck a ball about. And once his father exited with a honk, John walked behind the dressing room to where the smaller goals for the kids lay disassembled and wedged his gearbag between these rods. Then he vaulted over the furthest cement wall and hiked up a bank of soft ground and yellowed grass, arrowing towards the formal entrance to the woods.

John was early – she'd said five and it was half four – and he paced the car park.

It was quiet: two parked cars.

From time to time, John emitted something aloud that had been meant to stay firmly within the conflict playing out in his head.

Then at five, the Citroën pulled in with a cough and ratata of pebbles. 'Hey,' John said, and Amber waved as she climbed out. She was in black leggings, a flimsy cardigan, and a top with stripes across it. John was in olive combat pants, a white T-shirt that declared he hearted New York. She locked the car – she had to use the actual key and not a beeper and she double-checked it was secure by jerking the handle – and he was nearly beside her at this point and right away John veered off script: 'It's good to see you.'

She smiled at him obliquely. Dangerously. 'It's nice to see you, too, genius. Congratulations again.'

'Oh, yeah,' John said, and he had forgotten about all that. The Leaving, his entire future. 'Thanks.' He exhaled theatrically. 'I was lucky, really. Fluked a couple. Fuckin, A2 in Accounting, can you believe that?'

'No luck,' she said to him. 'Give yourself some credit.'

With a grin, John said, 'Alright. Credit, credit,' and he was contemplating straying further and further off script as he admired her eyes and the general zone of her face, when Amber said with an arched brow, 'Will we go for that walk, so?'

The official woodland walk was a three-kilometre loop, and they encountered a jogger and a woman with dogs and then no one as Amber asked about what was happening next with him. John knew, at a certain stage, he would have to wrestle hold of the conversation but not yet. Before they neared their tree, he would grab control of proceedings but not quite yet. Though no longer technically in the wider world, it was still summer in the woods. A brilliant emerald roof, rich green foliage, but there was a notable accumulation of debris on the margins of the footpath: crisp leaves mostly, though some were mulching. Head lowered, she walked with her arms folded and her keys in a fist under the opposite arm and now and again the jingle jangle of the keys. 'I'll know Monday what exact course I got and that, but I'll be in Galway, for definite. In September, like,' John said, and Amber told him it was super exciting. A period of silence as they went one by one over a small stone bridge – the water below long drained out, pure muck now and rutted as if horses had stampeded through it – and John kicked at some leaves as he tromped across and thought: dusty old leaves.

Then John thought: was that a poetic and clever thing to say aloud?

'Dusty old leaves,' John intoned gravely and did a parody version of his previous kick.

Amber turned around. 'What?'

'The leaves,' John said, and he indicated with a tilted head the leaves spilled along the ground. 'They're gone old. And kind of dusty.'

She looked down sceptically. 'Yeah.' Amber glanced at him. 'Summer is almost over, I guess? It went so fast.'

'Yeah, it's intense, isn't it? It was only June there, and now.' John puffed his cheeks. 'Crazy, like.' She nodded slowly at him and then John said, quicker, 'Oh, fuck. You'll be off soon too, won't you? Your trip. When're you flying again?'

'Yeah, that,' Amber said and there was an incline in the path ahead of them and now they were cresting it and John wondered was that the extent of her answer, and he was about to change the subject when Amber said, 'I meant to tell you. That has been delayed.'

'Your trip?' John said. 'Why?'

The three subtraction signs etched on her brow: John could see them, faintly. 'My friend can't go till the new year. Something has come up. And I don't want to do it on my own, the travelling. So I'm going to wait till then. It suits me better, really. I can save that bit more. And leave for a way, way longer time. Like, really stretch it out.' A head-shake and Amber admitted, 'It's frustrating and it's not ideal right this instant, but it might work out for the best. Long term and stuff.'

Why wasn't he shocked, why wasn't he surprised, why were his expectations set so low?

John said, 'That makes sense, to be fair.'

'The hotel gets so much quieter during the winter season. You wouldn't believe it. It dies. Usually, it's one person on and you might have, I don't know, four guests? Max. And that's a busy morning. So. Like. It's.'

John finished Amber's sentence: 'Soft money.'

Amber looked at him. 'Yeah, exactly.'

'It is frustrating.' Amber sighed. 'But it makes sense to wait. It will be worth it in the end.'

John agreed. He bucked his shoulders and said, 'Whenever you go, it will be class, Amber.'

She nodded at him and then she strode ahead.

There was a downed tree a little off from the path, and she clambered atop it and now so did John. It was windy enough for leaves to shiver and the sky glimpsed through the diamonds and squares overhead was blue. He put his hands between his thighs. John could not swing his legs while atop the trunk, but Amber could if she wished. The sound of whispering and small unimportant things snapping in half. Amber was engaged with her phone and then not and she refolded her arms: her phone, he only noticed, was being carried inside her cardigan pocket, the bulk of it prominent. An opportunity presented itself and he should use it, but John chose not to, and after a while, Amber spoke: 'A busy weekend ahead for you.'

'You said it. Hectic with Championship Sunday and obviously, the wedding, too.' In a screechy voice he had never heard before, John went, 'I'm a busy bee, Amber.'

She kind of laughed. 'Have your family arrived for the wedding?'

'Most have. I'm skipping this dinner drinks thing tonight with the training, but like, my aunts and stuff are up for that. And the cousins and shit arrive in the morning.' John was nodding along as if agreeing with someone unseen who was very smart and eloquent. 'Should be an alright day. Hopefully no rain for the wedding.' A beat and then: 'And the match, too, now that I think of it.'

She looked at him as if awaiting more and John's hands were being crushed by his thighs and then Amber brought up what John was meant to bring up: 'Do you have any details about Saturday? Like, what time do you want me to come at? I know it's casual. An afters' – monotone when she said this and then her normal voice again – 'but just a rough timeline so I can be ready and dropped over? Wait, no' – she tugged at his arm – 'should I drink at this? Are you drinking?'

'Oh, I'm not, because of the game. But if you want to, you can?' John said. 'And time? Yeah. What time is good to arrive at?' John repeated this dreamily, once, twice, and then added, 'I'm not sure, to be honest.' Amber cut in: 'It be after dinner anyway? Do you know what time you will be sitting down for the dinner? Your sister will probably have this all planned out, John. You could ask her. I don't want to show up early and intrude or anything.'

'Yeah, no,' he said, 'I could ask my sister.' He looked at Amber. 'I'll text her and check, will I? Yeah. I'll do that. Hold on.'

Quietly, Amber said, 'Whatever suits.'

Phone in hand, John clicked through its contacts till he located: Kay. He began typing and he was astonished as the characters began to materialise on the screen. It read: 'If I bring someone to the afters of wedding what time should they arrive at? Thx'

It was sufficient. It fulfilled its intention. John stared at the message, thumb floating over the send button, and then he clicked the blinking cursor back to the start and added: 'Hello sister'

John then added a smoothing template he had deployed previously when aiming to gently coerce: 'Hope this is sound but'

He added an apology to the end: 'Sorry 4 late notice'

Finally he amended the initial chunk of text: 'If I bring my girlfriend Amber to the afters of wedding what time should she arrive at? Thx'

He stared at this version of the message and then John deleted it, word by word, character by character.

'You text her?' Amber asked then. She was rubbing her hands together and John watched this for a moment, a soft swishing sound like a rubber against copybook page, and instead of answering her question, he went, 'Are you cold?' She smiled at this and let the back of her hand onto his cheek. A sensation like fingers spidering along your neck, a sensation like a nibbled earlobe, and John took a sharp breath at the contact. 'You are,' he answered himself, and she let out a bashful laugh, blamed her shitty circulation, but did not remove the hand, and John found he was adjusting his jaw so he could kiss it: kiss this hand as if he were seeking to suck a splinter from the skin. She said his name and he gazed up at her but did not stop and his lips venturing lower and lower to her wrist, her arm, and his mouth wider as he kissed the flesh slowly, deeply. A noise like a dog drinking from a bowl. She was still. She did not stop him. A whimper from her mouth, maybe. His right hand reached and touched her knee, now her closest thigh and he wrinkled the leggings. The fuzz of her forearm in his mouth and wetly matted thereafter and he kept his eyes locked on hers. 'John,' she said tentatively, and then more definite, 'John,' and she wrenched his face towards her own.

They kissed.

And John's right hand endeavoured to paw at that space between her thighs. Through the starchy nylon, he felt what he wanted to feel and then he felt it give somewhat under his pressure: under the circular motion of his two fingers, index and middle. Still kissing, he felt her lips crack into a smile, and he kissed this smile. He heard her whisper with discernible amusement, 'Not here.'

A final peck and she leaned away, and he righted himself. An erection, of course, and he discreetly paved his forearm over his prick, humped his back: now who could tell? He muttered, 'Sorry about that.'

She laughed again. Louder. 'It's alright. But maybe not so public a place next time? The path is literally right there.'

John managed to chuckle at this but wasn't that the crux of it. Wasn't that their ferocious predicament.

He said, 'Yeah, sorry.'

'Stop apologising, it's fine,' she said, and she was looking ahead when she asked, 'Your sister has hardly replied?'

'Oh,' John said, 'I don't know.'

Amber smirked. 'Do you want to check, maybe?'

'Yeah, I will.' He took out the phone, unlocked it, and he did have one new message – had he sent the text by mistake? – and John clicked, and it was from Studzy. He didn't read it, rather he flipped the phone over and slotted it back into his pocket. He said, 'Nothing yet.'

'Right.' Amber frowned but not in a legitimately sorrowful manner: more playful, jokey, with pouted lips. 'You could ring her later and let me know? Not ideal with how stressed she's probably going to be though.' Blue was still glimpseable overhead. The trees still green and a frailer green when pierced by whatever bit of sun. She turned to John then and so John turned to her. 'Do you think you could just ring her now to find out? Get it out of the way. I don't want you to be wrecking her head later.'

She asked him, 'Is that alright, do you think?' and John said, 'That makes perfect sense. Yeah, let's do that.' And his hand did reach once again for his pocket but this time it merely held the phone before leaving it exactly where it was. 'Actually, Amber,' John announced. 'There's been a bit of a mix-up. With what I said about the afters.'

She eyed him and her face transitioned from an arrangement of placid nothingness to puzzlement.

'You see. Well.' He hesitated, he laced his hands together and then unlaced them and tried again. Arduous to make the words appear, to get them out: they were glued to his throat. He was afraid. 'The thing is.' The ball levitating in the air as you tussle on the six-yard line and you should fist the ball clear or leap and catch it clean, but you can't do nothing, otherwise they will score, and you will lose: John knew the situation was like that. 'The thing is I actually can't invite anyone to the afters. There was some confusion and I thought I could, but it turns out I can't. Or I don't think I can.' He stopped and then he blinked painfully and said, 'No, you can't come, Amber. I'm really sorry. But you can't come tomorrow anymore.'

Her face was no longer puzzled.

'I am sorry. Genuinely. And like.' He licked his lips. He wanted to be tactful. 'Probably be awful weird both of us going anyways. We work in the hotel and then we are suddenly there together. It'd probably be really uncomfortable for us both. Can you picture reception seeing us? Imagine. They'd be so annoying, like.' He let out a half-laugh at the last statement, but she didn't acknowledge the hilarity in kind. It seemed to John that she had not even recognised his abrupt disclosure – the flutter and closing of her eyelids, he could see this, but he could not make out flushing anger or disappointment or crinkling sorrow and tears – and John resolved to just keep speaking rather than grapple with any incriminating silence. The knife had been drawn: swing, swing away. 'I didn't think it was a huge deal. I know I asked you, and I'm sorry about that, but I assumed you wouldn't be able to get off work. It was such short notice. Or that you would want to go in the first place? And like, you didn't want work to know about us?

Anyway it's not important. No need to be upset over missing it. You're not missing out on anything, really.' He waved his hands in a gesture of: he didn't know what. John explained, 'It's not a big deal at all, when you think about it, Amber?'

He heard her inhaling and then she hopped from the trunk. A step, another, and without facing him, Amber spoke in a steady tenor: 'It's your sister's wedding, John. How is that not a big deal?'

'I mean that it's literally not that important.' John shrugged. 'It's not essential for me and you, is what I'm saying. Like, we don't have to go? It doesn't affect us. I have to, yeah' – both hands out and opened as if imploring a ref for a foul – 'but I don't want to go myself. My family are nuts. It's all fucked up with Mam and Dad and we have to pretend it's not. Pretend it's fine.' He shook his head. 'It is a pretty crap situation I'm in, as a matter of fact, Amber. It's going to be awkward as fuck for me.'

Her back was to him still, and he pleaded to it, 'You're better off not going. It will be a nightmare.'

He said, 'Amber. Say something.'

He said, 'It's shite for me, too, so I don't think this silent treatment is completely fair. Or if you're mad at me. I don't think that's totally fair either.'

She swung around, and her eyes seemed irritated. Itched. Reddish, anyhow. 'What are you on about fair? You asked me to go to this wedding and now you're uninviting me the day before and you're on about fair? I got a dress, I booked a hairdresser, and you're on about fair?' The words freighted with fury, outrage, but not surprise, and her voice was climbing: 'How can you say that to me with a straight face? Like what's your problem? Do you think I'm that worthless?' Her questions were piling up and at some point, he'd surely be allowed a right to reply and maybe it was now. John tried to interrupt, and Amber snapped, 'No. We are not doing that.'

She exhaled. 'I knew you'd take it back. I just knew it, that's the worst thing about this. I knew you'd say' – here followed a poor imitation of John's voice, a bully version of his voice – '*oh sorry, Amber, you can't come*. I knew it. Even when you asked me, I knew it. And still, look at me. Look at what happens.'

It felt as if his facial features were being tugged down by little hooks and ropes and John managed to say, 'That's not true, Amber.'

Suddenly she was laughing, and he winced. 'How is that not true? You just did it, John. You just did it right now. Do you just say these things, or do you actually believe them?' Her eyes were big and evil as she turned towards him, her front teeth were biting at her bottom lip so that the lip was no longer pink and fleshy but pale and white. 'It's more mortifying for me that I care. It's pathetic. I don't know why I care so much? Why do I keep setting myself up for you?' She looked away and he was down from the tree, and she said, 'Like, this is who you are? It's you all over. This is how you think of me. Of course you'd take it back. Of course. Why do I do this to myself?' She was talking as if he wasn't in her vicinity. She was talking like how John talked to himself. 'I knew you'd do this. I knew it. This is you and why do I allow you to make me into a fool?' A pause, a long one, and then she said, sharp, 'I have to go.'

Amber took a step forward. Sharper again: 'Yeah, I'm going.'

He said, 'Wait, please,' and in reply, Amber said, 'Leave me alone, John.' She faced him: her eyes were wet, her lips clenched shut. 'I'm not doing this again. We'll stop here.' Her voice did not break but it was on the border, he felt. It was on the brink. 'I don't hate you. In fact, I'm happy I met you, I am happy we hung out. It was fun, but it's finished. Alright? It's over now.'

He didn't race after her, he didn't yell her name with a scattering of new excuses, he didn't try to convince or bargain. No, he simply slumped back against the tree trunk and watched her figure walk away and once she'd disappeared from view, he turned his face up and watched the trees being frisked by the wind while his mouth released tiny noises, like he had mistakenly handled something boiling hot.

John said to himself, 'Come on, come on.'

He pinched the bridge of his nose, and he said, 'It's alright. It's fine. You're fine.'

A figure was coming along the trail, and so John hastily lifted himself from the trunk, staggered right, wiping his nose with the back of his hand as he trod on. He said to himself, 'You had to do it. You had to. And she'll be at spits, and you'll be doing loads away from here. You'll be gone and she'll be at nothing. Man, she's dirty, like. That fucker Ethan and stuff, and then others. Imagine, man? She's no good. You couldn't bring her to the wedding. No, man. No. You couldn't.' He walked on and on, not quite an aimless wander but a following of the established pathway until John found the gap and bumbling past this, their tree. It was nowhere near as readable as he'd recalled but using his palms, he did find the strange grooves and scars: dulled brown etchings amid the brittle greyish bark. He retrieved his set of keys and, placing out a steadying hand, he began to hack.

Soon, sweating.

Tongue between his bared teeth.

After a time, he stepped back from the tree. He dabbed at his forehead, his mouth. The white underarms of his T-shirt were now darkened to a spoiled pewter tint. His face was deformed by feeling. His mouth was whimpering to itself. The key's bitting was silted with grime and bark. He ran his fingertips over the markings, old and new, and his fingertips became sticky. Another step back, another again while he promised himself: 'It's sound, man. It's for the best. You're sound.'

John walked off then, and the trunk read after him:

JOHN

4

AMBER

He didn't scramble back over the wall on his return to the pitch. Instead, he went the long way round via the main road and by then his eyes had copped on. It had only gone half six but there were already a couple of bodies out on the pitch. He collected his gearbag without even a hint of subterfuge and changed. None of his own buds here yet: John had met Studzy for food yesterday, had exchanged texts with Tony, but he had not spoken to Rooney, nor had he made any effort to and vice versa. John began to half-heartedly jog across the pitch, touching his heels. Something had been demolished within him, a load-bearing structure had crumpled, and the worthy and smart reasons why this had to be were currently leaking their rich substance. He wanted to stop thinking. He needed to. He proceeded to stretch. Barrett and Ultan were in discussion, heads almost touching, and then both men turned to observe him and John looked away. Quickly, he began another stretch – on all fours, arching his spine – and Tony and Studzy were wandering over to him by then.

A fist-bump to Tony, and Studzy avoided the proffered fist but tickled John's neck and said, 'Did you not get my text?'

Rooney was a couple of steps behind these two.

'No,' John said, 'I don't think I got any text.' Frowning, John read the sky for a moment as if the text might be flapping up there, and then said, 'Did you send me one?'

'Obviously,' Studzy said and made a face at Tony and Tony leaned towards John and whispered terribly, 'Did you hear about Seamus Fallon?'

John shook his head and Tony exclaimed, 'Oh, Tits.'

Rooney sidled nearer the boys as Studzy recounted the events: at training on Wednesday, Seamus Fallon had pulled up on the first run and thereafter could not jog without pain and agony, never mind sprint. 'He was at the physio today, and I hear no good,' Studzy told them. 'It's the same thigh that's always at him and it's goosed. Like, hanging off.'

'Sham alive,' John said with true feeling.

Rooney asked was that a hundred per cent fact and without looking at him, Studzy replied, 'That's what I heard. And Fallon's not here tonight, is he?' Still not looking directly at Rooney as he said this last part.

John said, 'Fuck me,' and Tony concurred with John: 'A huge loss.'

Studzy went, 'It screws us up badly, alright. But.' Studzy rolled a nearby ball backwards with his studs and scooped it up into his hands. 'There's a vacancy in the starting fifteen now, isn't there?' Studzy eyed the posts and stuttered forward and John watched the ball curl over the bar.

At different points throughout training, Barrett reminded them about Sunday and Championship, the challenge of Claremorris, as if anyone could forget. Barrett said,

'Sunday. The heads are right, the mind is right, bodies are then right,' and John understood what this meant absolutely. There was no explicit mention of Seamus Fallon beyond a single slithering line: they'll wait and check on certain players. Wait and check and see.

To end, two squares were laid out with orange and green discs. The setup: three dribbling attackers versus three tackling defenders. In a fluorescent bib, John was put with Rooney and Tom Cafferkey, and they watched the first teams go at it.

It was intense, it was physical.

The attackers had maintained possession for less than a minute – whether this was good or atrocious, John did not know yet – and now John's team was up.

They were pitched against Studzy, Eoghan Moloney and Raymond Cooney. Presently the ten-to-fifteen-second window when the attackers could dribble around unharried, solo, hop, gather a feel for the space and then a signal from Ultan and the bibs bounded into the square, all at once. John zoomed towards Eoghan Moloney and Moloney sidestepped John's first flick of wrist and then shrugged John off with an arm before manoeuvring away with a hop. John chased after. Hard turns in the turf as Moloney twisted right then left. Eyes on Moloney's back. The memory of tag in the yard, tip the can in the estate below a rose-gold sky. The grass was heavy, John's thighs were burning already as they propelled him up from the heavy grass, and Moloney was forced to veer to the right otherwise out of bounds, and John was on him. Shoulders colliding, and Moloney cradled the ball and John put a hand across for it and then pulled it back so no foul, and Moloney modified his body to solo the ball and when he did, John pounced. The white ball bounced free. A belated shoulder from Moloney which John handled with grace, dignity, and a murmured insult and spinning around, John rushed to help the nearby Tom Cafferkey with Raymond Cooney: both facing Cooney with their arms spread, ferrying him towards the corner like a spooked sheep, and eventually Cooney was forced over the sideline.

It went on like this.

The aggression was rising. There were clumsy tackles as people grew tired, clattering tackles from pure frustration. Faces were ruddy, red and pink. Mouths had new under-bites that huffed like vents. Hobbling to his feet, Studzy accused the bibs of constant fouling, and Rooney told Studzy to shut his moaning and John pushed Cooney as Cooney was not wearing a fluorescent bib. It was competitive, it was a competition: this was all inevitable, John felt. It seemed to be the point: actually.

There was a jersey to win.

Then John's team were back in the square and they were the attackers. John picked up a ball and advanced across the length of the square, soloing, left and right foot. Another solo and then Ultan signalled, and the non-bibs were in the square. Cooney went towards him, and John used his hop to shift the ball from one side of his body to the other, moving away all the while. Words being shouted from along the periphery: unintelligible but the bouncy rhythm encouraging. John soloed. Tom Cafferkey had been dispossessed already – the shitbag – but Rooney still grasped the ball: John could see Studzy yanking at Rooney's jersey. Moloney was rushing towards John now, and unthinkingly, John dropped a shoulder as if heading to the right before decisively strutting in the opposite direction. Moloney was deceived, Moloney lurched at nothing, and John was past him. The square seemed to be smaller and smaller. The sound of rushed, shortened breathing. His thigh muscles on fire like he was being pursued up and up a flight of stairs. John hopped the ball and trotted on and soloed and he could make out Cooney coming towards him and the shouting and where should John go next and then a force ploughed into the small of John's back and he was sent spiralling over the sideline.

A whistle was blown, and John was flat on the ground.

He felt his fingernails rake through the soil.

He knew who had done it. John just knew.

He rose to his feet and spat, 'You're a fuckin fucker.'

Moloney looked at him with amused disdain as if John was a tourist cuddling a map. Moloney said, 'Will you simmer down, young buck,' and John stomped towards Moloney and then pointed: 'You prick.' The whistle was blown again, Cooney put a hand on his arm and John shook it free whereupon John was nearly tossed sideways, but was held up then by the very same hands that had tossed him in the first place: Moloney had John's collar bunched in two fists, and John swung from left to right, and John reached across and grabbed some part of Moloney. A chunk of jersey and additionally John's left hand grappled with a section of Moloney's neck and now more of Moloney's jawline and face. They were tottering, small roundabout footsteps. Others were piling in, not so much attempting to cleave them apart as pushing one another. A scramble of bodies with the two of them at its core. It felt good to John to be angry, to express his anger. It was refreshing despite the high possibility of a daddying, a professional head-kicking. To unleash his frustration and hurt: felt nourishing and good. Moloney pressed a fist to John's chin and jabbed it up deliberately – not quite a punch, but forceful – and as if he truly desired an answer, Moloney asked, 'Who's the prick?'

By now an almighty scrummage – the entire panel was involved, and unrelated pushing matches breaking out between the bibs and non-bibs and was that Rooney and Studzy squaring up? – and in the middle of it, Mac was robustly clawing John and Moloney's arms apart like dead electrical wires being whisked from the socket, and they were no longer clamped together: John and Moloney. They were separated and Mac was saying stuff. Mac was saying stuff to both of them while herding Moloney along. John was being called a little cunt by Moloney, and John retorted sublimely, 'No, you are.' The collar of John's jersey had been split in half. Schoolyard scraps and torn shirt pockets: a memory of. Appeals for calm. The whistle.

Specks of spit like diamonds. Moloney was saying, 'You hear me, yeah?' and this was presumably for John's attention, but John's attention was drawn to the escalating situation between Studzy and Rooney, and John saw Rooney shove Studzy again and they were chest to chest, foreheads kissing, and then John discovered he had tackled Rooney to the ground. 'Don't you touch him,' John blurted, and Rooney was stunned and then Rooney was furious. The two of them became a ball amid the caked legs and leather boots until hands breached them apart, and when the contact to John's upper lip had occurred, and whether it might have been just an unintentional flailing arm, impossible for anyone to know. Like slipping on muck, there was impact and suddenly John was somewhere different and felt his body different: suddenly John was being held as his gob filled with coins, which, by the time they were emitted from his mouth, had miraculously melted to liquid.

Then John was on one knee as blood continued to drip.

Crimson splattered onto the bib but more of it was beaded to the grass.

The mob had disbanded.

It was over as swiftly as it had happened.

Tony had a placating arm around Rooney, who was wagging his head.

On his haunches beside John, Studzy was gaping at the trickling blood and when John caught his eye, Studzy stated, 'Man,' with a toothy grin, and John asked, 'Why did I do that?'

Five minutes later, Barrett called everyone into the centre of the pitch. Barrett did not condemn or give out. Barrett merely told them that these things happen, but that they also stay put. Whatever it was, whatever had started it, was over now. Barrett said to the group, 'No more. You understand?' In front of the panel, handshakes were duly performed: John and Moloney, Studzy and Rooney, Tom Cafferkey and DJ – John had no clue what that one was about – and finally John and Rooney, and neither looked at the other as they briefly held hands.

Studzy dropped him home and John was glad when he saw the blank front windows and remembered that they were all out.

In the bathroom upstairs, he winced at his appearance. His upper lip was a mess: plump and plum-coloured and also it resembled a plum that had a bite taken from it. He widened his mouth, cocked his chin and with his index finger, he dubiously poked at the two fleshy chunks at the bow of his lip. It stung. He touched there again, and it stung once more, and still John had to prod it one final time. He sighed. He pressed his finger to the lip for one final, *final* time.

In his room, he lay on the bed and covered his face with his hands and began to think and maybe because he was still delirious from the fight, still reeling off its adrenaline, or maybe because he was simply sad and lonely, he reached and unlocked his phone and texted Amber: 'After destroying my lip ... so I wouldn't have been able to kiss at the wedding ha xx maybe for the best you not comin haha'

An hour passed and there was no response.

Even after his shower, even after dealing with his mother and his hysterical aunts downstairs, even after he sent a clarifying text – 'That was a stupid joke. Im sorry' – there was no response from the contact labelled Amber Work.

Saturday, 15th August

Awoken by a door. Footfall. And the creak of the stairs and how in the bottomless black he still knew it was the penultimate step that creaked. Claws of soft white from under the doorframe and he rolled away from this light. Two voices were whispering at the top of the stairs, now they were remonstrating and not whispering, and then his mother's voice as she hissed for them to be quiet. When he checked his phone with the one eye still shut, the screen informed John it was half seven. A gurgle and then a toneless thrumming from downstairs, which was the shower. His sister was getting married today: this fact loud in his mind, all of a sudden. Married, his sister, Kay was going to be married: wild, improbable, and then a not so outlandish notion. A two-litre bottle of water was by his bed: he glugged it till he had to punch his chest to swallow. Was he happy and excited for today, for Kay? Sincerely, with no malice, John did not believe he was either.

In the kitchen, a fry: he could smell it from the stairs. Coarse, smoky, and his nose wrinkled with disgust. It was his aunt at the hob, and she asked what did he want? A declining hand to John's mouth as it was unfeasible to enunciate this early in the morning. Championship and so he had his Weetabix, plus strawberry yoghurt for healthy bacteria, and then, in the end, only three blackened sausages as they were going spare, plus a rasher with spittle on its charred fat. Conversation flew over John's head as he ate. The house phone, ringing and ringing. Now his mother declared his full name: John Martin Masterson. He glanced up. She was in her dressing gown, but on her face makeup – lips retraced redly and eyelashes that reminded him of ink blotted on the tip of a malfunctioning pen – and Yvonne cupped his face, moved it this way and then that. 'Your sister might butcher you is the only problem,' Yvonne said, and John pouted like kiss-kiss and his mother laughed, let go of him.

His sister didn't kill him, but the look she gave was fairly chilling as John sought to explain the how – an accident at training, fundamentally not his fault – and then John thought to unfurl the chunk of lip as if physical proof was required for total absolution and Kay turned from him at this stage. 'He just better not ruin the photos,' Kay said to Yvonne. 'I'm serious, Mam.'

Makeup and hair were being conducted in the living room.

Feet drumming up and down the stairs.

At half ten, a text message arrived from Tony: 'Hope today is class'

John replied, 'Thanks bud'

Tony had phoned John last night and John had pretended not to hear the phone rumbling on his desk. Tony had sent a text that read: 'Tits you must talk to Rooney. He is upset as well. Please man'

John had ignored this text.

At eleven, his dad arrived: John heard multiple beeps in succession and who else would do that, who else would find that funny? From the landing, he saw Yvonne braced against the front door, she was still in her dressing gown and John waited a moment, listened for a moment, before stamping down the stairs. Yvonne announced: 'Here he is now.' She smiled at John, she brushed the shoulders of his suit jacket. 'My handsome man,' she said, and in a more formal tone, Yvonne spoke out the door: 'I'll leave you to it, Peter.'

Leaning against the passenger side of a sleek black Merc, his father saluted this remark. He was in a navy suit, and a tulip shrouded in gauze was pinned to his lapel. When he saw John and the lip, Peter shook his head. 'Your mother's after informing me. What are you like?'

Ignoring this completely, John did a lap of the car. Ribbons were tied to the wing mirrors, pink and white, and his father craned his neck to look at the car in full now, too. Peter asked, 'What you reckon?'

John said it was cool yeah and he timidly kicked a wheel once, three times, because wasn't that an action you undertake when scrutinising cars, and then John glared at the sky and commented, 'No rain, anyways. Hopefully there will be a bit of sun.' His father nodded severely, rattled off a forecast he had read in the newspaper and the promised high teens, and then they talked more about the rented Merc, they talked about the match tomorrow, they talked about the Mercedes-Benz brand of automobile in general, and they talked about the weather once again. Hands in pockets, John slumped beside his father, staring at the home house, its busy windows, the ghostly shapes occasionally discernible, and they lapsed into silence until John felt a hand squeeze his shoulder: the gold band still snug below the faintest corkscrews of hair. His father said, 'It's going to be a great day, son.'

The pressure on his shoulder was firmer for a second, and John agreed, 'Yeah. One hundred per cent, Dad.'

There were hydrangeas tied with lace from every other pew, and an arrangement of hydrangeas and pink roses and shaggy ferns were atop the altar and they walked towards this, arm in arm: John and his mother. It was half an hour before the ceremony. The tut of heels on tiles, the bright click of polished dress shoes. Seated, John waved over at Denis's family, trying to recall names and connections, and he felt a pinch on his arm and Yvonne said to John in a tiny lilting voice, 'Look who it is.' It took a second before John realised: the sister. The troublesome sister. She was here and slotted beside her father, her face uptilted and the mauve-coloured booklet twisted into a cone by her hands. Still smiling across, his mother said, 'There you are. Family always wins out in the end.'

Yvonne wore a slanted hat with feathery wires that she kept almost touching and a mint dress which she now had to smooth down as Denis approached. 'Darling,' Yvonne said to Denis, and she kissed him on both cheeks.

John shook Denis's hand. John stood again and shook the two brothers' hands. Denis's face was pale and newly shorn and the same tulip as John's father pinned to his chest. The smell of incense. Burning candles that shifted so you could tell when the church doors were nudged open. People talking, this spiky inconsistent din. People hunched across pews to talk, and the periodic explosion of laughter. John was rising to his feet to shake more hands, to peck Denis's mother on her powdery cheek, to be formally introduced to the sister who offered her fingertips. Denis's brothers' names were written in the booklet: Cillian Kilbane, the best man, and the other brother named Donal and John would never have guessed Donal either. Sunlight was streaming through the stained-glass windows, coloured spikes of sun, and a pleasant heat on one side of John's face, and shadows extending, like the slender arms of a clock. There was ample space in the church and when John peeked again it was practically full.

Then everyone rose.

A solid hush. Music began to play in plinks, an unhurried melody. Necks strained and John was on his tippy-toes and he didn't expect to feel anything profound, sentimental, as his sister carefully walked with Peter. He did not expect to feel his face twitch as if resisting a sneeze, he did not expect to feel his eyes water as she walked slowly and carefully by. His sister: endless drives together in the backseat, Christmases, her number the second ever number he had keyed into his mobile, a look shared and he knew what she was thinking. His sister. Good or bad: perhaps there was no such distinction in memories. Her hair was down, a veil clipped to the back of it, and her dress was white, obviously, and it trailed after her as if snagged along the way. Kay looked beautiful and why wouldn't she. His father was beaming beside her, pride swelling his face. Peter grasped Denis's hand and pumped it vigorously, Peter kissed Kay on the cheek, and John arranged his legs so his father could slide past: a pat of John's arm and Yvonne held her face out for Peter to peck it.

And they were married.

The kiss. Shouts and cheering like a wicked goal. Kay's and Denis's hands laced together and upright in the air. The marble tiles were golden from the sun as they walked out to further applause. John's mouth wide and open, John was clapping madly. Following Denis and Kay out of the church were his mother and father, their arms roped together, and it was easy, John thought in that radiant moment, to believe in reconciliation. To believe that people could be fixed to your desire. It was very easy. But he would not believe. A hand touched his back then, and John slipped into the dazzling aisle.

Outside the church, he gave his sister a hug. He told his sister she looked great, honestly, and then he said with a minor stutter, 'And, to be fair, so do you, Denis.' The response from both: JFK Airport, genuinely. On the steps, a milling crowd, and pleasantries sweeping across it and John was shaking more hands. He was embracing aunts. He was explaining to cousins about what had happened to his lip. John felt light and buoyant. Happy, yes: incredibly happy. The sun overhead, and the blue in fainter ripples around it. Suit jackets were folded on arms. Booklets being improvised as fans. Presently, photographs were being taken and John was beckoned over for the bride's family photo. Assembled like a squad, all five Mastersons for Denis was snared in it now. Face inclined at his prudently chosen angle, John showed his teeth for the camera, his tongue pressed against the scaly roof of his mouth, and the little pop of saliva on his gums as he held and held this delighted pose. Held it till.

Flash.

At The Island Head, a musty red carpet was laid out before the sliding doors, and inside was a table with a bucket of sweaty beer and a collection of glass flutes with fizzing liquid. Behind this table was Hughie Denton: Hughie winked at John, then Hughie touched his own lip quizzically. No one was working in the restaurant, the lights were off – too early for dinner, too late for breakfast – and still John glanced through the doors sporadically, still John stood at a certain distance to these doors, as if someone might peer out, as if someone might leap from the darkness. The gap subtly increasing between the knot of a tie and the restraining collar. Peter and Yvonne were still beside one another, circling the room. A text arrived from Studzy: 'Enjoy 2day bud!!! tell kay I was thinking of her ;) She knows WHY ;)'

John giggled, held the phone close to his chest as he replied, 'CHEEKY FUCKER . haha thx man... Let me know how the meeting goes ?'

And Studzy's reply landed as the wedding party was being ushered towards the rear of the hotel: ';) .... Will do bud'

The hall was laid out with twelve round tables draped in white cloth and a smaller cream cloth atop this with roses embossed on it, and a straighter table was set up on the stage – the arrangement of flowers from the altar at its feet – and bodies were two deep around the plywood bar in the corner and its shutters just rolled up. Zibby and Samantha were blocking the double doors to a small patio, Martina in a blazer was shuffling people towards the tables, and John pretended not to notice them as he was marshalled along: John only nodded over once settled in his assigned seat at Table Number Two. Drinks: wine, stout, pints of bright lager as if internally lit by a bulb. There were a couple of kids running excitedly between the tables and each joyful squeak from their mouths a distinct arrow of noise. His mother and father were seated on the top table, and they waved down.

Samantha was overseeing Table Number Two and John smiled up at her as he gave his order and Samantha thanked him with a musical inflexion, and when she came around again – scanning for drained water jugs, pouring wine over shoulders – John made sure he was visibly enthralled in a conversation about the pitiful state of Man United's summer signings.

Then everyone up, stamping the parquet floor as husband and wife entered.

For starters, John picked the vol-au-vent – unbelievable – and went beef for main and the speeches were beginning just as his plate, lapping with a shallow pond of gravy, was being collected. The balding brother rapped the microphone's head, and a static noise then a puff of air. 'Excuse me, folks,' Cillian said, and his upper body was swaying. 'Excuse me.'

Denis's father's speech was short and sweet about Kay, and as if to compensate for this, Peter's speech was extensive. Stuff about Kay as a little girl, as a teenager who loved her dancing, as a wonderfully kind-hearted woman and his glasses were removed at this descriptor so as to drag a finger under his eyelid and two small red definitions on the bridge of his nose. Further stuff about Kay's college degree, London. Stuff, inexplicable, about John. Stuff about Denis and himself spending many hours together grooming the jungle lands of Polranny and how Peter knew then that Denis must love his daughter. 'Otherwise, why would he spend so much time with me?' Cue huge laughter, fists bouncing against table. John noticed how often his father employed the word *We*. We are so proud. We love you so much. John noticed how his mother stiffened up at the beginning of the speech, he noticed how she smiled very hard throughout it.

The best man was incoherent. Knock Airport: that bad.

Microphone tapping back and forth against his bottom lip, Denis read from three separate pages without looking up once: but it was a good speech. It was genuine. It was impossible not to smile and fill in every pause with applause or cheers or eventually hoist a glass high during Denis's toast for his stunning new, am. Wife.

Desserts were served, teas and coffees zoomed around the room. John unbuttoned the sleeves of his shirt, hiked them up. It was hotter. Tables began to thin out, tables began to be dismantled and John watched Zibby lug one towards the back of the hall and John was reading a message from Studzy – 'Meeting boring. Bus is leaving at 12 2morrow' – when he sensed a presence to his right: it was Samantha crouched by his chair with a blue pen behind her ear and this ambiguous grin across her face. 'Tell me,' Samantha said, and the grin was suddenly malevolent, 'when is she arriving?'

John pulled a face: sunken brows and a double chin to demonstrate his totally real and true bafflement. He put his phone away in stages and said, 'Well, hello to you, Samantha,' and Samantha flicked her eyes towards the ceiling. 'Fine. Hey, John. Now tell me. When is she coming?'

Samantha whispered her name then: Amber.

John was cornered. It was like someone scary and older asking to borrow his phone for a sec, and he could only mumble, 'What you mean?'

An eye-roll from Samantha. 'I get it. You're a mysterious guy. Whatever. But' – her voice changing all at once, softening, lowering in volume – 'I know the situation.' She bumped her shoulder into John's leg. 'I had to swap shifts with her, didn't I? So, tell me.'

A band was setting up on the stage.

He saw his sister and Denis winding through the tables.

Another bump into his leg and John looked back down at Samantha. 'Later on, yeah. I think a bit later on, she'll be here.' A hand touched his fringe, the same hand scooped up his fringe, and John said, 'I think not till after nine. Between us, now. But yeah, no, after nine and probably closer to ten, when I think about it. Amber will be here then.'

'No way,' Samantha said. 'I thought I'd catch her before finishing.' Samantha frowned at the table and then at John: 'Why is she coming so late?'

An answer might be too generous a term for what was next emitted: 'Just, like, you know, that's the time she'll be here like.'

'Annoying.' Samantha adjusted her arm and a small round watch slid into view. 'I can't imagine you two will take photos?' John tsked, said he couldn't promise they'd do that, no, and then John added: 'Ha.' Samantha stood up, touching his arm for a second. 'Look, I won't say anything. But you won't be able to hide it now? Every member of staff in this hotel will be informed by midnight. I can guarantee you that.'

John laughed at this. 'True. They'll know everything.'

A final look, and Samantha took a plate from the table, gathered another atop of that, and she was gone. The oozing sensation in his stomach that John had done something bold, said something very bold, remained however.

The band began to play: enthusiastic at least.

Half nine and John was sure he saw Samantha by the entrance to the hall, peering over at the dancefloor, and he felt guilty, and then his father grabbed John's arm and said, 'Isn't it fantastic?' And it was. John was up at the bar and between Denis and the two brothers: they were tipping tumblers of amber into their mouths and John cheered with his 7UP. It was ten o'clock, eleven, and midnight. The idea flowered to text her – 'Weird being in the hotel when not working haha', or 'Samantha is a weirdo', or 'I miss you kk' – but he resisted it. John knew he could no longer do that. It was half one in the morning. People in each other's arms. Ties had disappeared. His mother was with her sisters. His father was sitting on his own, arms crossed and smiling, and John sat beside him for a while. It was hotter and hotter. It was two o'clock and John was out on the rear patio, hunting for fresh air. He walked to the paved edge and inhaled, allowed the air to spread itself till his throat constricted, and then John finally exhaled. There was a group of three opposite him. Cigarette smoke crisp against the earthy and moistened smell of the night. Light burning from a heated lamp, a bronze glaze over the shrubs and hedges and the lawn that fell away into blue. He'd probably head home soon. He should. Rest and recover for the match tomorrow: no, false. Today. Rest and recovery for the Championship match that was today. He was thinking of this, planning his discreet exit, when he turned round and clocked the woman sitting atop a picnic bench. In partial darkness, the woman was wearing a puffy white dress and glittery white heels that rested on the seat. With a hitch in his voice, John said, 'Sister?'

Kay cocked her head and then smiled. 'Brother.'

'Why you out here?' He stepped nearer, cautious as if encountering a wounded animal. 'You okay?'

'It's roasting in there.' The rustle of her dress as she lifted her shoulders. 'I needed a break.'

'Right. Same, actually,' he said, and he hesitated before climbing up beside her on the bench. It was quiet for a time between them, and the cool air became steadily colder, less and less appetising, and then Kay asked, 'You don't smoke, do you, John?' He shook his head and Kay grumbled, 'I should have guessed.'

After a moment his sister sighed. 'What a day.'

'Yeah. It was class.'

'It was long,' his sister said. 'And it's still going. But it's nice, I suppose.' Her fingers were splayed out in front of her, then the digits straightened and the new ring conspicuous as spurting blood. 'It's nice to see everyone. To have the whole family together.'

'It is,' John said, 'and Kay, honestly. It was an unreal day. Savage. I'm really happy for you and Denis and stuff.'

She made no comment to this but inclined her head. Kay then asked, 'Do you think Mam and Dad had fun?'

'Oh,' he said, and he thought about it. They'd been smiling for sure, they were often playfully batting away what someone said to them, they were often side by side, and did all that amount to fun? 'Ah, yeah. Like. I'm sure they're having a ball.'

She made a sound. An unconvinced sound.

Then she told him, 'They aren't bad parents, John.'

'No,' he agreed, 'they're not the worst.'

'They are good people. And they are very good to us. Well.' She paused. 'To me at least. Too good sometimes. The show they put on today.' She let out another sigh before she went on, 'It's stupid, I know it is, and selfish, but it made today nicer for me. Easier, I don't know. More special. I do love them both. I worry about them both.' Unhurriedly, she reached for a pint glass on the table, clear liquid, water probably as no sniffable acidic stench, and she took a gulp from it and then said while replacing the glass by her side, 'At least you'll be free from the madness soon in Galway. Lucky you.'

'Yeah,' he said, 'I will, I guess. I'm excited for that. College.'

'You don't sound excited,' she said. 'It will be good for you, John. You'll have the best time. I loved college. Loved it. And it's so handy you have a house sorted already.'

John went, 'Actually, I'm not so sure about that.'

'Right. Dad told me—'

John interrupted, 'I only just decided I'm not living in that house no more. I don't get on with the people who'll be there, so I think better if I stayed somewhere else.' It was the first time he had voiced this aloud, and yet John understood this was what his intention had been for a long while. 'I'll have to start looking for a new spot. Once the offers come in Monday, I'll start looking. Probably be a right pain, but, like, I think be much better for me, personally, if I didn't live with them? As a person, I'd be better.' All this brand new information to John and equally not at all. 'Different strokes, different folks kind of deal, you know? With the fellas in the house.'

A sidelong glance from Kay. 'Okay. You'll find somewhere. It might be tough, but you will eventually.' She suggested then, 'Living with new people might be better craic anyways.'

'Yeah, maybe,' John said.

'And what about your girlfriend? Is she making the cut for Galway?' John faced Kay in surprise and Kay cackled: 'Did you think Mam would not tell me?'

'Nothing's fuckin sacred in this family,' John said. 'And Mam should know better than anyone else why that's a bad thing.' Kay cackled once again: her head rocked back and into the night a throaty laugh and John couldn't help himself but join in. The group on the patio looked over, and Kay shouted hellos at them, and it was John who revived what had, by conversational laws, been allowed to wither: 'I don't have a girlfriend. Just, FYI. That, sort of, ended recently.'

'I'm sorry to hear that,' Kay said, and she yawned into a fist and quipped, 'Well, you'll meet loads of new girls in—'

John spoke over her: 'She was cool. The girl. My girlfriend, if you want to call her that. She was nice and cool and kind. I did really like her, to be honest. But, she works up here and stuff, and it didn't make sense going forward.' His hands were moving, making shapes between his legs, and his sister commented, 'Oh right,' and John's face felt to him small and tightened as he continued: 'There was other stuff, too. Stuff she done that wasn't particularly great. Pretty bad, actually. To put that out there as well. But I think she's really cool. I hope there's no bad feelings between us. I hope we're sound. Yeah, I still really, really like her. I do.' While nodding along to all this with a slightly bewildered expression, Kay took another drink and a click within John's brain and he gestured at the pint glass of water and said, 'Are you pregnant?'

A smirk and Kay answered, 'No, John. I just don't drink anymore.' She shrugged and the white dress whispered beneath her. 'It didn't suit me. I did silly things. We both decided, Denis and I, that it didn't suit me.' She smiled at John, but it was laboured, and it felt like John had stumbled into something grave and secret, it felt like he should say something against this disclosure, amend it, cancel it out, or challenge it and make it more palpable. Kay was the one to speak: 'To tell you the whole truth, I was pregnant. Dad knew. Not sure Mam did.' A second and then, 'Well, Mam never let on she did, but she probably knew. But I can tell by your face that you sure as shit didn't know' – John smiled gingerly at this because he was meant to – 'but I was pregnant. That was why the move from London originally happened. Why it all happened so fast. Why I left the job and came home.' A deep breath. Dispassionate words fell out next: 'But I'm not now. No, I'm not pregnant.' A laugh followed that was forced. 'It might not seem it, John. At this exact moment, when you and your friends are heading off, but life is very small. Life is tiny.' The group on the patio were stumbling inside: a yell and Kay flapped a hand in their direction without looking. 'Not in a bad way, exactly,' Kay said then as if correcting an error, 'but it is small. And if you can get some happiness, whatever that may be, wherever, then. Brilliant. You should latch on to it. If you can find a bit of happiness, you're doing better than most. Well, I think so anyway. I'm happy with Denis, and I hope that I'll be happier here soon enough. I want to be happy here and I want Mam and Dad to be happy, too.' She shook her head, all of a sudden. 'Right, that's enough.' Laughing to herself, Kay climbed down from the bench, and then she was before John, wiping her dress, fixing a strap. 'I'm starting to sound like a religion teacher.' She slapped her cheeks and once more John laughed because he was supposed to. 'I better go find my husband.' She eyed John for a second. 'You alright?'

John said yeah, just tired, and then his sister asked, 'Will we go back in?'

Sunday, 16th August

His head was tilted against the tinted window of the bus and currently this pleasant rattling against his temple. He was content to watch the parade of cars and trucks zipping by in the opposite direction, content to watch the slash of tyre through grimy pools of water and the landscape of north Mayo as it tumbled up and down and was eaten by animals. Also, John was content not to talk to anyone despite being nestled next to Tony. Around him, afloat above him, there was no conversation or jokes. The general mood on board was pensive and stiff. The mood was exam season and the paper handed out but not yet flipped. The mood was, at its root, fearful: the fear of losing today, the fear of not being in the starting fifteen. Rooney was a couple of rows down from John with small white head-phones, and neither had acknowledged the other. Studzy was behind John and Tony and when Studzy leaned forward, both of their seats rocked. John's lip was still noticeably swelt and he rolled his tongue under it and felt the scar like a gully. The sedating purr of the bus's engine as they approached Claremorris, and presently a squeak from Tony's Lucozade Sport bottle and then a loud sloshing noise as the same bottle was being shaken in John's face and John opened his eyes to say, wearily, 'No, I'm alright, bud.'

Seamus Fallon was at the front of the bus: the decisive leg, that royally goosed thigh, propped across the aisle.

Now the bus trundled through the town of Claremorris before swinging onto a narrower road. A blue and white flag flapped from the garden of a house. A large bear in a blue jersey was bound to a streetlamp: the teddy's fur was drenched, its head slumped as if in public humiliation. Then an entrance set back from the neighbouring houses and the bus turning into it. Floodlights. The canted roof of a stand now visible. Tony elbowed John. 'I think we're here, Tits.'

From his gearbag, John plucked socks, shorts, a United jersey, gloves, and then finally extracted his pair of World Cups: the boots had been scrubbed this morning and additionally John had scraped his fingernail along the edge of each stud till gleaming silver. He placed everything beside him on the bench and unzipped his tracksuit top. The dressing room was hectic and Ultan sidled through the congested space, asking each player individually, 'Gloves?' The flush of toilet, and the sink did not hiss afterwards. Barrett issued questions to the room and then answered them himself: 'Is our preparation complete? It is, yes. Do we know the game plan and how best to effect it on Claremorris? We do indeed.'

Out on the pitch for the warm-up and balls being knocked around and John received a pass and hopped the ball and the upward splatter of weak brown and then he punted it on.

The rain was falling in short, slanted lines.

The grass: glossy and beaded like a dog's soaked coat.

Rooney was jumping up and down, knees to his chest, and Tony was beside him, pawing the ground and then his toes. Studzy held a ball and soloed it, changed direction, and soloed again. Stuttering about aimlessly but with purpose writ on his face, John swung back and forth his elbows until someone spoke to him: 'Yesterday went well, Masterson?'

'Yeah. It was brilliant,' John said, startled, and it was Barrett. Barrett was talking to him. 'It was very good. Thanks, Anthony.'

Barrett seemed to be scanning for something tiny and nimble hurtling across the pitch as he said next, 'And there was no fighting, I hope?'

This was a wry joke. A hardboiled joke.

Wasn't it?

John gave a half-laugh anyway. 'No fights. I'm off them now.'

'Right.' Barrett met John's eyes for a moment, and he asked, 'You're feeling fit today?'

Obviously, John thought and then it struck him and he answered, 'I am, yeah.' John was nodding. 'Feeling very very fit.'

A slap on John's shoulder, and Barrett was bellowing for someone else's attention, Mac's attention, and when John looked round, Tony's neck was markedly swivelled in his direction, Tony's chin was elevated.

In answer, John offered an indifferent headshake, as if nothing substantial nor interesting had transpired.

And was that a lie?

No, it was not, and yet what was churning inside John's stomach? Why did he feel unprepared and why did he feel judged and why did a chill spread through his body?

Returned to the dressing room and the back of John's head was tipped against the plaster wall. His gloves were still on, his gloves were flat atop thighs that glowed a splotchy pink on the inside like a rash. The damp of his socks, his fringe a single black spike. Across from John, Tony was wiping his chin over and over. Who was starting. Rubbish on the floor – banana skins, crumpled plastic bottles – and chunks of muck and grass now being added to it as boots were picked clean. The sickly warmth of drenched bodies. Rooney was pissing and he did wash his hands afterwards. Now Seamus Fallon wobbled into the room, and then appeared Barrett, who slammed the door after him.

'Listen up,' Barrett said. 'I have some news. Seamus has had to drop out of today's squad. Unfortunately.' Fallon was pinching his Adam's apple, and those nearest were reaching across to console him: groping the unproblematic left thigh. Barrett continued: 'It's a shame for Seamus, and it's a shame for us as a team as well. But look. It's why we have the panel. To cope with these knocks. Alright?'

Barrett said, 'The team.'

The first surprise was Rooney named at full-back and John was trying to gauge whether Mac had tweaked something during the warm-up, or had been axed entirely, when the second surprise came about: it proceeded the declaration of right half-back, it was the tersely stated, John Masterson.

His name, yes, and for a moment, John didn't recognise it. John Masterson.

He could not recognise it as his own.

John Masterson.

It didn't register: you want something and then you get it.

A jersey was then pitched his way, and John almost caught it. The number seven on the back. The silky feel of the jersey's sleeves. The fresh prickling smell of laundry. Barrett was still yammering on, but John could no longer hear what was being said. Numb, disoriented, dizzy nearly, and then a weight on his chest, as if being squished by stone, and he took a breath. Not overwhelming triumph resounding through his body, but dread. John's name had been said and he was starting: slowly processing this information, making sense of it. This was what he was good at, this was what he had going for him this summer. Wasn't it? Another deep breath and facing the wall, John hoisted the jersey over his head and had one arm through its sleeve when he had to pull it completely off again so he could first remove his soaked Man United top. Full costume on, John only now copped who else was starting by who else presently wore a jersey. DJ, Hanley, Cooney, and yes, Rooney, and there was Studzy, and Mac had number eight on his back: Mac was in midfield. Studzy winked at John and John's stomach felt like it was comprised solely of viscid puke and water, a mixture that was steadily spinning. Tony was given a jersey and on the back was displayed the number twenty-one. Gearbag between his boots, John stowed away the wet United top, folding it atop his track-suit pants, and then he thought to confirm that his mobile phone was switched to silent and reached inside his pants. He thumbed the phone alive to check the sound was off and instead saw he had one new message.

He opened it, gloved hand guarding the screen.

'best of luck kk'

As he read it again, John felt a breath, cold and long, escape from his mouth.

And then Mac shouted across at him, and John threw the phone into the gearbag.

Standing: everyone.

The dressing room even more cramped.

Small geeing comments being muttered at random. Bleats of positivity. Muffled clapping due to the padded gloves. The scrape of studs as fellas shuffled about, and then John was crouched, rooting inside the gearbag until he clutched his phone and John was reading that message one final time.

Then Barrett was talking, Barrett was pointing at an indi-vidual and then someone else. Subject matter: controlled aggression and no lip to the ref. Subject matter: snappy passes into the forwards. A finger towards John and then Rooney as Barrett told them to keep it basic at the back. Now Barrett ordered the team to squeeze in closer. An arm was tucked around John's neck, another, and so John tucked his arm around DJ and Hanley. 'Tell me this,' Barrett said. 'Do you boys want to win today?'

John answered, 'Yes.'

Piled into the corridor and the team was being led out by Mac and the rain heavier: silver arrows overlaying the green as John peeked beyond a humpy shoulder and now the rain was atop John's head, down his neck.

The ripple of applause like spooked birds ascending.

The stand was packed. His father somewhere out there, his mother, too. Perhaps his sister and brother-in-law. The whole family. All here to watch him. And her and her father: possibly. Unlikely, incredibly unlikely as he was pretty sure she was on a split shift today, extremely unlikely, but maybe.

Claremorris were already out.

The referee at the centre of the pitch, studying his watch.

Two cones and a rapid handpassing exercise between the fifteen starting players, and the ball was greasy. The ball was soon stained. Studzy said to John, 'Get stuck in, Tits,' and a fist was lifted to John's face. The substitutes wandered over to the dugout and among them, John observed Tony carrying the first-aid box with his mouth suckered up to a full stop. Now John was squatting for the team photograph and of course, not smiling. He glowered, he held his breath, sucked in his gut, and glowered. Above the stand, a cloud marbled with sunlight. Water bottles were handed around and John was seized then by a desire to hear what his dad might have to say. What advice his father might impart right at this instance. Or actually: John would just love to hear his dad say, 'You're well able, son.' To hear that would be enough: never mind believe in it. Balls being gathered up, wrangled into a mesh bag by Ultan, and Mac was calling everyone towards him. A huddle. The honeyed smell of crowded men. Arms wrapped tightly around each other. Nervousness apparent in the sulky expressions, the shaky knees. Boots, shiny. Wet faces, red cheeks and cool damp breath, glittering. The emphatic whites of Mac's eyes at certain junctures, the rain delicate on his lashes. 'I believe in every lad here. I believe in this team. So let's go out here today and hammer these bastards.' A defiant roar at this, a moment when John lost himself completely, the individual dissolved, and he was solely the right half-back for the Island senior football team, his identity that alone, and then they all dispersed: each player drifting out towards their own patch on the pitch, the grand arrangement of fifteen across the field, and to the righthand side of the forty-five line, facing the car park and the steaming muddle of cars, there was John Masterson. The grass oozing when trodden by his boots. Rain dripping from the nearby dugout and running too from the roof of the stand. With his wrist, John dashed at his nose and then pointlessly spat on his gloves and rubbed them together. Nerves swelling, nerves to be expected, but terror less so, and John sought to hide both from his face: a veil spread over it, covering what he felt. The jersey was sticking to him, sealing itself to his body, and he pinched it from his stomach. Presently his man was scuttling towards him. Similar build. Similar age. They clasped hands and then side by side, they jostled. Shoulders and elbows connecting. In the centre of the pitch, the referee with the ball under his arm and he was checking his watch once more. The whistle was around his neck. From the crowd, mysterious shouting and jeering. The referee seemingly satisfied with his watch, and now shifting the ball from the crook of his arm. The four midfielders were banging into one another. The assembled and feverish crowd, louder. The referee held the ball in both hands, the whistle was in his mouth. After today: his summer might be over, or his summer might go on. The shriek of the whistle. The ball was thrown up,

the ball hanging in the air.

Acknowledgements

Thank you to Ciara for her love, warmth and belief: this book is for you, kid. Thank you to Sally Rooney for being the best reader of my writing and a wonderful friend besides that. Thank you to Joe Joyce for helping me through every little bump in the road: a true comrade. Thank you to my agent Angelique Tran Van Sang for believing in this novel, and for her kindness outside of the work. Thank you to Colin Barrett for reading an early draft and telling me to send it on. Thank you to Tom Morris for his generous perspective and generous humour. Thank you to Niall MacMonagle for his enthusiasm and excellent notes. Thank you to Ferdia Lennon and Nicolas Padamsee: long live Catch Up. Thank you to Rebecca Ivory for the voice notes. Thank you to Clara Kumagai, Nicole Flattery and Oisín Fagan. Thank you to Michael Magee and Rebecca Watson for helping to trim the first chapter into shape.

Thank you to three legends of the game for guidance on GAA drills: Beano Conlon, Ruairí O'Donnellan and James Keane. Thank you to Ruth Storan for the fashion tips. Thank you to Brian Gaffney for always encouraging. Thank you to Evan Jones. Thank you to Ronnie Conlon.

Thank you to Dave O Carroll for his infectious positivity. Thank you to my bestest buds in the BBB.

I'm immensely grateful for the financial support I received from the Arts Council of Ireland, and I would also like to thank the Arts Council and the University of Galway for appointing me in the role of Writer in Residence during the editing of this novel. Thank you to John Kenny and I'd also like to acknowledge the true kindness of Sarah Bannan.

Thank you to Kishani Widyaratna for trusting in this novel and for her insightful editorial notes. I feel privileged to be working with Kish and the entire 4th Estate team. Thank you to Patrick Hargadon and Patricia McVeigh for their amazing work in publicity. Thank you to Matt Clacher for his enthusiasm and support. Thank you to Tayiba Sulaiman for finding my emails funny. Thank you to Eve Hutchings for her tremendous work as project manager.

Thank you to the Meaghers for all their generosity and fun. Thank you to the family: aunts, uncles, cousins and grandparents here and beyond. Thank you to Kathy and Johnny. Thank you to Mam and Dad for their bottomless love and support. Finally, thank you to Daithí, Jack, Charlie and Lily: illumination, one and all.